THE FIRETEAM

THE FIRETEAM

MIKE VAN HORN

THE FIRETEAM

Published in the United States of America

ISBN: 978-1-7339293-5-6

Cover by Lauren Reneau

Bridge image from pixabay.com
Thompson submachine gun image from Shutterstock

A fireteam is a small military unit of infantry...and is the primary unit upon which infantry organization is based in the British Army, Royal Air Force Regiment, Royal Marines, United States Army, United States Marine Corps, United States Air Force Security Forces, Canadian Forces, and Australian Army. Fireteams generally consist of four or fewer soldiers and are usually grouped by two or three teams into a squad or section.

—Military Wiki

CHAPTER ONE

Cole Jelcik turned his left hand so the palm faced upward. He glanced at the watch face poking out from the sleeve of his jacket.

1:58 p.m.

Cole insisted the other two members of the Fireteam wear their watches in a similar manner, with the face on the underside of the wrist. His younger brother, Tanner, had once asked why.

"Because you can see the time without taking your hand off the forestock of your rifle when you're pointing it at something...or someone."

Tanner had nodded, grinned, and loosened his watchband.

That was one of the many things Cole liked—no, loved—about Tanner. You didn't have to tell him something twice. If he saw the logic in someone's position, especially Cole's, he generally came around to adopting it as his own.

Cole looked up from his watch and turned to see Tanner in the back seat. He was adjusting the cable that led from the Midland X-Talker walkie-talkie on his belt to the headset above. They purchased the units at a Cabela's the previous year and were satisfied with their performance. The headsets featured vibration sensing throat microphones that were several generations removed from current military gear but served their purpose just fine.

"Remember, code names. Got it, George?"

Tanner smiled and gave him a thumbs-up. "Got it, Ike."

Tanner completed the adjustment to the walkie-talkie then zipped his jacket, hiding the wire and assuring it wouldn't swing free and catch on his rifle.

Cole turned to the driver, Dominic Santo. "Got it, Audie?"

Another smile, another thumbs-up. "Yeah Ike."

1

Unlike the Jelcik brothers, who had hulking upper bodies, Santo was slight. He stood 5'7" and weighed barely 150 pounds. This made him six inches and roughly 80 pounds smaller than Tanner, whose brother Cole was even larger.

The trio had used random code names for every robbery. But it was not until they'd gained notoriety that they'd settled on their current versions. Press reports took note of an armed robbery team that used military precision and brandished World War Two weapons.

After the team made off with $44,000 from a Lincoln Savings Bank branch in Des Moines, Iowa eighteen months earlier, an FBI spokesman was quoted as saying "The suspects were very precise, they had a plan and executed it. The threat of violence was real. They moved in an almost military manner...like a squad or fireteam."

Cole read the quote the following day on the Des Moines Register website, a smile forming on his face.

The Fireteam was born.

Cole came up with the code names. He'd learned, again through press reports, that the jackets they wore were considered "Eisenhower style." He had no idea what that meant, having purchased them from Dickies, a major supplier of workwear in the United States.

It turned out that General Dwight D. Eisenhower made the waist length olive drab jacket popular during World War Two. He was Supreme Commander of the Allied Forces in the European theater of operations. His steady hand guided the Allies to victory over Nazi Germany. Eisenhower was in overall command of the D-Day operation in Normandy and remained in charge through the eventual victory in Europe.

Eisenhower was much admired as a leader. He would go on to be elected president of the United States in 1952 and serve two terms.

And his nickname was Ike.

Peering over Cole's shoulder and reading the same article, Tanner cracked, "Ike, huh? Sounds like a good name for a boss."

Cole became Ike in their radio traffic and, just as important, in their conversations in front of witnesses inside the banks they robbed.

The permanent names for Tanner and Santo soon followed. Cole did some research on the war and settled on George, after General George Patton, for his brother. Both Patton and Tanner were hard chargers. Cole noted that both men needed to be reined in on occasion.

Through further research Cole learned about Audie Murphy. Murphy earned every military combat award for valor available from the U.S. Army, including the Medal of Honor. He survived the war and became an actor in Hollywood. He appeared in a number of Westerns and war movies and actually played himself in the successful film *To Hell and Back*.

Murphy was resourceful, courageous, and reliable in a fight.

And Audie Murphy was just 5'5" tall.

Cole assigned the name "Audie" to Dom Santo.

Now they were sitting in a stolen Hyundai Santa Fe Sport Utility Vehicle in an Olive Garden parking lot in Racine, Wisconsin. It was the last Wednesday of March, and it had dawned sunny and cool. The restaurant was on the north side of Durand Avenue, a four lane east-west artery that ran through the city's commercial district. They were parked at the rear of the property. Cole insisted they park as far away from the dumpster as possible, lest an employee taking out trash get too good a look at them.

From the front the Santa Fe appeared normal. That is, just as bland and anonymous as any other midsized SUV. The rear window, however, was missing. In its place hung a piece of clear plastic that had been carefully sized and cut to fit any Kia or Hyundai SUV that had the misfortune of having its rear window smashed out. The sizing of the plastic was carried out in the workshop area of their business back in Columbus, Ohio.

The team also had similar pieces of plastic cut to fit the rear windows of sedans from the same two Korean car

3

manufacturers. When traveling to do a bank job they made sure to bring a selection of pre-cut pieces. This allowed for quick installation.

The plastic installation was necessary because the technique used for stealing the vehicles they used in heists involved first getting past the rear window. Santo had perfected the method, first learning of it from other inmates during the 26 months he had served in Lebanon Correctional Institution—or LCI—in southern Ohio.

Dom Santo was a car thief. Well, now he was a bank robber. But in his heart he was a car thief. It was in his DNA. He took a job during his senior year of high school doing valet parking at a downtown Columbus restaurant. After a few weeks of driving cars—many of them high-end luxury models—from the front door to the nearby parking lot, Santo had an idea.

He went online and purchased a key copying kit for $129. It consisted of a hollow cylinder that the user filled with an accompanying compound. A key could be inserted in one end and, when removed, a perfect impression remained. When taken to the right hardware store, one that didn't ask many questions, a working copy could be made.

Dom stole his first car the week of his 18th birthday. It was a jet black 1975 Chevy Corvette Stingray. He'd had his eye on it for weeks. The owner, a slick-looking asshole that didn't tip, was a regular at the restaurant. Santo had no way of getting the man's address from the Department of Motor Vehicles, so the plate number did him no good. But he had befriended one of the waitresses inside the establishment and got the driver's name from her.

He found four listings online of matching names in the Columbus area and began his search. The second address he scouted paid off. There sat the Corvette under outside covered parking. It was at an apartment complex in the city's north end, just off Morse Road.

The next time the man—Dom thought of him as "Jackass One"—slid up to the restaurant, dumb-looking hot blonde in

4

tow, Dom surreptitiously made an impression of the key before returning it to the valet manager at the stand out front.

Dom sweated bullets at an Ace Hardware when getting the key copied. He was pleasantly surprised that the clerk at the key-cutting machine seemed to have absolutely no interest in the reason for the replacement request. Dom, in turn, did not offer one.

Dom's birthday fell on a Thursday. It had been a shitty day at school, as most seemed to be. There was an assembly in the auditorium and many of the soon-to-be graduating seniors were lauded for their academic and athletic performances. There were references made to the colleges they would attend. Dom, who had no prospects other than continuing as a worker bee at the restaurant, sat and silently fumed.

Two days later, on Saturday night, Dom watched with a smile on his face and a predatory look in his eye as the Corvette pulled in front of the valet stand. Jackass One was with the same blonde. Ninety minutes later the couple appeared back at the stand. Dom made sure to busy himself talking to another patron so a different valet handled the retrieval of the Corvette from the lot. He didn't want to be remembered by the owner in the sequence of what would happen.

Dom got off work an hour before midnight. He drove his beater Toyota straight to the apartment complex and parked on a side street. He moved cautiously to the covered lot with the copied key in hand. He was somewhat surprised to find that the key worked perfectly. He slid into the Stingray and turned the ignition while trying to quickly familiarize himself with the instruments and layout of accessories.

The car had a manual transmission. Being a valet, Dom had experience with this. Still, he handled the Corvette awkwardly while navigating out of the lot. He turned his head nervously, expecting the owner to appear.

Ten minutes later he was on a two-lane road north of Columbus doing 120 miles per hour with the speakers blaring "Enter Sandman" by Metallica.

Dom realized he had no plan. As this understanding set in he decelerated and steered the Corvette back toward the apartment. He parked on the street, a block away from his Toyota. Easing the door of the Stingray closed he had an inspiration. He reached back in and reinserted the key into the ignition. Before closing the door he made sure it was unlocked.

Smiling, he made his way back to his Toyota. The Corvette would almost certainly disappear by morning. He would be without blame—in his head anyway—and Jackass One would lose his ride.

A niggling thought struck him as he started the Toyota. The episode had been energizing, but he realized he had no plan. Subsequent events over the next few years showed that this was a problem he never really solved on his own.

He had always needed a mentor, someone to help him effectively employ his skills.

Dom looked back at Cole and watched the man prep his weapons. Their eyes met.

Cole winked.

CHAPTER TWO

The men had driven to the area earlier in the day from Columbus. It took over seven hours riding in the lumbering truck that would also serve, if all went as planned, as their getaway vehicle.

They checked in at a low cost hotel, a Travelodge, on the north side of Racine then summoned a cab rather than an Uber. They could pay cash for a cab. Cole had a strict rule against using credit cards on these "work trips." There was to be no paper trail.

They left their cells at home for the same reason. Otherwise the FBI would be able to show they were in the area at the time of a robbery by accessing geo data on the phones.

All three men dressed as though they were catching a flight —sensible pants or jeans with comfortable hooded sweatshirts. They were, in fact, headed for Milwaukee's Mitchell International Airport. It was located 25 miles north of Racine, a short distance from downtown Milwaukee. Lake Michigan lies barely a mile to its east.

Cole, Tanner, and Dominic each carried backpacks. They looked like any other travelers. But the backpacks contained no clothes, no snacks, no electronics.

Unless you counted the USB cables in Dom's pack.

From roughly 2011 to 2022 Kia and Hyundai neglected to build engine immobilizers into their models. These devices helped determine if the key being used matched the ignition. A thief could quickly tear the casing off the steering column of the vehicle. This exposed a plug. A USB cable—the "A" version of the cable—could then be fitted over the plug. Turning the plug with the inserted cable would start the car. An engine immobilizer would have prevented this because it would detect that a paired key was not being utilized.

7

Dom first learned of this while serving his prison sentence in Lebanon. Another incarcerated car thief by the name of Grover—Dom couldn't remember his first name—described the process to him.

Ironically they were on a work detail at the time in the institution's prison industries plant. They were running a stamping machine.

Making license plates.

Dom remembered shaking his head. He had taken elaborate measures to steal many of his cars. It had led to his capture and prosecution. When he was released from Lebanon Correctional he surfed the net, seeing dozens of TikTok ripoff videos made by inner city amateurs. They were loosely identified as "Kia Boyz."

The typical video showed mask-wearing thieves dangerously joy riding and crashing the stolen vehicles. This craze had peaked in 2022 when the two Korean vehicle manufacturers accounted for roughly 40 percent of vehicle thefts in the United States. In Cleveland, two hours north of the Fireteam's Columbus base of operations, the figure was 57 percent.

The window, so to speak, was now closing. Both Kia and Hyundai were scrambling to provide software updates and even steering wheel locks to their customers. Lawsuits were filed everywhere. But there were still thousands of vulnerable cars and SUVs out there.

There was no better place to find them than an airport parking lot.

They asked to be dropped off directly in front of the terminal. It was a few minutes past 9 p.m. There were few outbound flights at this time of day.

Cole paid the cabbie and led the way through the automatic doors.

"OK guys, let's find the baggage claim."

That was easy. The terminal wasn't exceptionally large and was easy to navigate. The airport was named after Milwaukee native Billy Mitchell, a World War One pilot who was considered the father of the United States Air Force. But compared to Chicago's O'Hare, the last airport the team had made use of before a robbery, it was on the small side.

They knew from studying online schedules that a United flight was due in from San Francisco any minute. Cole glanced at the display screens as they walked through the terminal and saw that the flight was on time.

They followed the signs to baggage claim. There were six carousels. Cole checked the monitors and saw that the baggage from the San Francisco flight would appear on number two. The men found seats nearby. They made small talk while waiting.

Dom: "Pizza tonight?"

Tanner: "Pizza and beer."

Dom: "Some local stuff? PBR?"

Tanner: "Giddy up!"

Cole: "We'll split a six-pack. Just two beers each."

That ended the discussion.

Ten minutes later Cole saw a man moving down the corridor that led from the concourse gates. Cole had assumed that the first squirter from the United plane would be exactly like the first one from every commercial flight. That is, usually a man, carrying an upscale travel bag, and fooling with his phone. He would be wearing at least one piece of expensive apparel. He would be in a hurry. He would not bother looking at the baggage claim area—unless it was with a mirthful, self-satisfied expression since he would not have checked any luggage—and he would rush through the terminal and pass through the front door at a speed normally reserved for a doctor responding to an emergency.

This man did not disappoint. He checked every box. He hurried past Cole and his team without a glance. Cole watched him exit the terminal and, ever so slightly, shook his head. The man was the type who unbuckled his seatbelt the moment the plane touched the tarmac. He would be the first to stand when the aircraft came to a stop, and he undoubtedly would have pushed his way to the front of the aisle, passing all passengers

9

seated in front of him so he could be first off the plane. It was fifty-fifty, Cole theorized, that the man engaged in a phone conversation while standing in the aisle.

Cole fought an urge to follow the man and beat him senseless.

"You want to kick his ass, don't you?"

Cole turned to see Tanner grinning at him. He grinned back. The brothers' faces mirroring each other.

"How did you know?"

"Two reasons." Tanner held up a pair of fingers. "One, *I* wanted to kick his ass too, the prick...and two, while you were looking at him your eyebrows lowered and one corner of your mouth pulled back. Don't forget that we've had a few wrestling matches get out of hand over the years. I've seen that look on your face up close and personal."

Cole's grin widened and he reached his hand toward Tanner. The men bumped fists.

Dom sat across from them, noting the family resemblance. Same features, same dark eyes and jet-black hair. He shook his head and let out a sigh that drew their attention. "Fucking brothers."

All three were smiling as more people streamed in from the concourse area and found their way to carousel number two. A buzzer sounded signifying that luggage was on the way. The carousel began to move. Cole stood.

"Let's go to work."

This final stage of the odyssey that was modern air travel was relatively subdued, nothing like the gauntlet of check in/bag drop/security that signaled the beginning of a trip. That was a cattle call. Here, at the end, all of a traveler's anxiety had drained away.

They ambled toward the crowd, stopping a couple feet behind a group of a half dozen people who were intently watching the bags float past. Occasionally a passenger bent over to check a tag on a suitcase, sometimes lifting it off the track, sometimes allowing it to continue on. Cole nonchalantly watched as a few people secured their bags and drifted toward the exit. He nodded at Tanner and Dom and all three moved in the same direction. With their backpacks they appeared to be three anonymous travelers trying to find their way home.

They walked out the sliding doors. Cole led the way to the shuttle pick up area. The team preferred to harvest their vehicles from surface lots. Cole knew there was much better security, in the form of cameras and personnel, in the parking garages. They shuffled to a shuttle that bore the markings *SAVER PARKING—'A' LOT.*

Cole took a seat in the back. Tanner sat on the left side near the luggage rack. Dom selected a spot across from him. This configuration was by design. Cole wanted the team to have eyes on all sides of the shuttle. Once they entered the Saver lot they would have a better chance of spotting a target vehicle.

The shuttle reached its capacity and the driver, a dark-skinned man of indeterminate age, took his seat behind the wheel and pulled the folding door shut.

"Next stop, Saver lot! Locations please." He eased the vehicle away from the curb. His voice had a lilting, accented quality. Cole thought he might've been Haitian.

A few passengers called out the row numbers and letters, having committed them to memory. Others fumbled through purses and wallets until they found the receipts they'd received when they parked in the lot at the beginning of their journey.

After four locations were called out there was a lull. Cole called "E-7" in a bored voice.

He had committed the layout of the Saver lot to his memory several days earlier. As the other locations were being called out Cole mentally plotted them to the map in his head and selected a spot as far away from the other riders as possible. He'd then settled back until they reached the lot.

Cole then took note of the other passengers. On the rear seat next to him was an Asian couple in their twenties. They were immersed in their phones, texting rapidly. A large bearded man sat next to Tanner on the left side. This was the shortest seat due to the luggage rack. Dom was on the right, squeezed between two well-dressed women in their thirties—

one white, one African American—and a family of four that featured two boys.

The parents looked exhausted, the boys ornery. The older boy appeared to be about ten. He wore a Green Bay Packers jersey. The boy next to him was an inch or two shorter and wore a sweatshirt, still bearing a price tag, that showed a likeness of the Golden Gate Bridge.

The older boy felt Cole's eyes and gave him a challenging look. Cole smiled easily, pointed to the jersey, and said "Go Pack Go!"

The impertinent expression vanished and a smile appeared. The boy started to say something but his brother spouted "Go Bears!" Instantly the jersey wearer punched the smaller boy in the chest. Golden Gate Boy squealed and counterpunched.

Both exasperated parents grabbed a son as the other occupants of the bus looked on. Most had smiles on their faces. While attention was diverted to the fight, Dom, just three feet away, looked at Cole and mouthed *"Fucking brothers."* Both Cole and Tanner stifled laughs.

The shuttle slowed and turned into the Saver lot. Several heads turned in the direction of the lot, three with purpose. As the automatic arm of the gate rose and the shuttle pulled forward all three members of the team began their scans.

Tanner and Dom were targeting vehicles from the two Korean companies. Cole was doing this as well but his scan also had a second objective. He was looking for surveillance.

Cole had a sixth sense. He saw things that others missed. It worked when reading people and it worked when reading situations. Tanner had been around him his entire life and had come to take it in stride. Dom had experienced it now for over two years. He was still a little unnerved by it.

A year earlier they had pulled the plug on plans to steal a vehicle from a surface lot at Lambert International in St. Louis. Cole sniffed out a police presence as they cruised the lot. They had the confused driver return them to the terminal. They still did the robbery the following day after going to their backup plan, stealing a Kia from a Walmart parking lot.

12

They found out later that St. Louis police had nabbed a pair of would-be car thieves at the airport later that same week. By that time the Fireteam had successfully pulled off their bank job and were back in Columbus.

If Dom ever had doubts about hitching his wagon to Cole's star they no longer existed.

The driver navigated to the first drop off. The large man next to Tanner rose and reached for a suitcase on the luggage rack. The vehicle came to a halt and the driver turned toward the rack. He saw with chagrin that he had been beaten to the punch by his passenger but his expression brightened when the man held out a few dollar bills and said "Thanks, partner."

By this time Cole, Tanner, and Dom had all situated their backpacks on their laps. They unzipped the packs a few inches while continuing to scan the rows of parked vehicles. The shuttle made two more stops. The professionally dressed women seated next to Dom left at the first, the Asian couple on the rear seat beside Cole at the second.

This left just the robbery team and the family. The shuttle was nearing the far end of the lot and the section Cole had selected. The driver stopped and Cole and his men stood. Each handed the driver a couple bucks as they stepped down. Cole was last in line. He glanced at the family. The driver would be dropping them off in another row on his way back to the entrance.

Both boys stared up at him, expressionless. Cole smiled and winked before passing through the door.

As the shuttle moved away all three men reached into their backpacks and withdrew gloves. They were tight fitting nylon gloves. The palms and fingers had a coating of rubber that allowed flexibility while assuring no fingerprints would be left behind. They then retrieved walkie-talkies from the bags and turned them on. The sweatshirts of all three men had kangaroo pockets. The walkie-talkies went inside the pockets. They slung the backpacks over their shoulders.

Cole spoke quietly. "See anything?"

13

Tanner responded first. "Pretty sure I saw a Forte on my side two sections back."

Dom added, "I saw some SUVs on my side, a row over. Could be Hyundais." He hesitated before asking, "How about you? Are we clear?"

Both Dom and Tanner knew that if Cole had been alerted by any hint of cops their shopping trip would be scrubbed. The fact that Cole allowed them to leave the shuttle was a good sign.

"I want to walk to the end of the lot to be sure, but I think we're OK. You guys head back to the cars you spotted and let me know over the walkie-talkie if you have a winner. Remember, eleven and twenty-two." The Midland X-Talkers offered 36 different channels. Cole always selected a primary as well as a backup in case of problems.

Each man walked away in a different direction. They looked exactly like what they were, a car theft team looking for targets. They carried bags loaded with gear and moved amongst the rows of vehicles swiveling their heads. Tanner, in particular, always felt self-conscious during this phase. He once brought it up to Cole and the older man eased his mind.

"Think about it...every person in the lot is carrying gear and looking at cars. Everyone in an airport lot looks like a car thief."

Tanner thought for two seconds before responding, "Good point."

Cole reached the end of the lot without seeing any indication of a stakeout. They had robbed 17 banks in the last two and a half years yet he still had no indication the FBI was getting close to catching them. He'd come to believe that the near miss in St. Louis had nothing to do with the Fireteam's activities. Ironically, it was local police trying to get a handle on the Kia/Hyundai problem. It served to keep Cole on his toes. An operation designed to catch small time criminal joy riders could end up snaring Cole's team of major players.

Cole removed the walkie-talkie from his sweatshirt pocket. He spoke a short message, "Ike is all clear." He was grateful for the gloves as the temperature seemed to have dipped under forty degrees. All three men wore an extra layer or two under their sweatshirts. They would be fine as long as they kept moving and wrapped up the job quickly.

Dom's voice came through his speaker. "Audie has a positive."

Cole walked briskly toward Dom's area. Though there was not as much security in the Saver lot as inside the covered garage Cole knew there were cameras that would be recording them. No sense making any moves that might prematurely draw the attention of anyone monitoring the video feed. Cole knew that once they began to work on the car they would be vulnerable to discovery.

Cole caught sight of Dom near a grey Hyundai Santa Fe with Wisconsin plates. The trio preferred SUVs like the Santa Fe or Tucson from Hyundai. The Kia Sportage or Sorento would also be excellent. The rear cargo area of these vehicles were perfect places to transport their weapons to the objective and, of course, the stolen money on the way out.

Tanner arrived seconds after Cole and checked out the Santa Fe. "Outstanding! I have a match that is damn near perfect!"

The men's backpacks carried three specific sets of items. Tanner's was filled with nearly twenty license plates. All were stolen from Kias and Hyundais. Only a few were Ohio plates. All three men kept an eye out for these vehicles in the Columbus area. They were particularly interested in out of state plates. The lots near John Glenn International Airport on the east side of Columbus were excellent hunting grounds.

Their usual procedure was to have Dom go in alone—he seemed to draw little attention—and make off with a plate. If the vehicle came from a state that required two plates Dom would try for the one in front. They also had terrific results in the many hospital lots around the greater Columbus area as well as The Ohio State University.

The team had several dozen plates in their collection. They were always handled with gloved hands. They wrote the model and color of the victimized vehicle on the back of each plate with a permanent marker. Before each robbery Tanner selected a dozen or so representative model/color combinations and packed them in his backpack. He cut pieces of cardboard to fit between the plates so there would be no sound of metal on metal to draw the attention of anyone within earshot.

Cole made sure all three of them went through the stack before a bank job. He wanted three sets of eyes on the choices that made the trip. They wanted to make sure they had something that was a close match for the models they expected to see on the job. The first time they set up the backpack before a robbery Dom flipped through a half dozen plates and shook his head.

"I probably *made* half the damn things in Lebanon."

Cole's backpack was stuffed with four windshield-sized pieces of clear plastic. One size fit the rear window of SUVs while the other size was big enough to cover openings of cars like the Kia Forte and K5 or the Hyundai Elantra or Sonata. In a pinch they would settle for a sedan but they preferred a sport utility. Cole's bag also contained a commercial stapler that shot heavy gauge staples into the interior of the stolen vehicle to hold the plastic in place. If they tore a piece of plastic during the install Cole would have a backup, whether they were working on a car or an SUV.

Dom's bag, in addition to several USB cables, held a selection of screwdrivers, a utility knife, needle-nose pliers, a 6-inch long nail punch, a heavy wooden mallet, and a bathtub mat that was covered with suction cups on one side. The metallic items were wrapped in washcloths held in place with rubber bands, again, to mask the sound of clanking metal.

Cole and Tanner fanned out. Each moved three or four spaces away from the Santa Fe. They scanned the lot for several seconds. Dom took up a position at the rear of the vehicle and sat his backpack on the ground. He knelt and tilted the opening toward the nearest overhead light and began to quickly fish out items, stashing them in his pockets.

Cole, satisfied, turned toward Dom and hissed, *"Do It!*

Dom rose with the bath mat in his hands. He had cut a small hole in its center back in Columbus. He slapped the suction cup side on the center of the Santa Fe's rear window. He had pushed the handle of the mallet into the right rear pocket of his jeans. He withdrew it now as well as the nail punch from his sweatshirt pocket.

Both Jelcik brothers moved toward the vehicle. They watched Dom, in one practiced motion, place the nail punch in the mat's opening and swing the mallet viciously. They heard the glass shatter but in the dim light and with the mat in the way could not see the extent of the damage. Dom swung the mallet a second time and a large portion of the window exploded into rock salt sized chunks.

Dom used the mallet to create an opening large enough to scramble through then climbed onto the bumper and dove in headfirst. He left the mallet on the ground.

Cole grabbed Dom's bag and pushed it through. Tanner quickly retrieved the mallet and broke out the remainder of the glass. The brothers then tossed their own backpacks into the rear compartment before moving to the front doors, one on either side. They saw that Dom had already stripped the cowling from the steering column and was fitting the USB cable onto the exposed plug.

Dom turned the ignition and the Hyundai started. He pumped a fist and hit the lock button. The brothers scrambled in, Cole in the front passenger seat, Tanner in back.

"How about that shit!?" Dom nearly shouted.

"Shut up dammit!" Cole was looking for signs of danger. All three men were breathing hard.

From the rear Tanner interjected "Any parking ticket up there? Any parking ticket?" He was referring to the ticket the owner would've gotten from the automatic dispenser upon entering the lot.

"Get goin' Dom. I'll look for it." Cole was checking the dash after opening the glove box and center console. "Nothing. Get a card ready Tanner."

They approached the exit and pulled up to the booth. A sleepy-eyed man in his sixties held out his hand for the expected ticket.

"Uh sorry, misplaced the damn ticket." Dom said it with what he hoped was an embarrassed look.

The man sighed. "Got to charge you the maximum daily rate before I can let you oot then." His pronunciation of "out" identified him as having Canadian roots. "Let me see what the plate reader says."

He punched some keys and leaned forward to view a computer screen. "Gonna be thirty-two dollars."

Tanner reached forward from the back seat and handed Dom a Visa prepaid debit card. It was part of a large stash the team maintained in Columbus. If tracked, this one would show that it had been purchased at a Target store in Indianapolis. Dom handed over the card and waited for it to be processed.

Six minutes later they were in a dark parking lot three miles from the airport. Cole and Tanner quickly cleaned up the broken glass before stapling in the replacement plastic. Dom removed both plates from the Santa Fe and attached an Illinois plate to the rear. It was stolen from the front of a silver Santa Fe months earlier. It was possible that the owner never noticed. As long as they avoided close scrutiny they should be fine.

Fourteen minutes after leaving the airport they were on Wisconsin Route 32 South, heading for their hotel.

CHAPTER THREE

The night of the Milwaukee airport car theft, some four hundred miles to the southeast, a group of men sat around a fire in Dayton, Ohio. The flow of conversation was easy, interspersed with laughter every few minutes. Glow from the fire reflected off their smiling faces and the whiskey glasses that sat beside them.

"Well I have to say I didn't see that coming. The University of Kentucky?" This from the owner of the house, Mike McClary. Mike was a tall, sturdy-framed man in his early sixties. He and his wife Marge owned the house on Oak Street in Dayton's historic South Park neighborhood. They had settled in Dayton from their native New York after a several year odyssey as Mike chased his dream of becoming a major league baseball player. It hadn't quite happened. Along the way the McClarys had lived in enough residences in minor league towns to last them several lifetimes. They had made the Oak Street house their forever home.

Sitting to Mike's right was Mark Garcia, a close friend and retired Dayton firefighter. "Took me by surprise...I was sure he'd pick one of the academies. Really thought it would be the Air Force Academy. I like Colorado. Megan grew up there." He tipped his head toward the house where the four wives were gathered in the kitchen. "Would've enjoyed visiting Colorado Springs for a few home games."

Paul Hull sat to McClary's left. He was a retired Air Force Combat Controller. Paul had been an enlisted man in the service and had earned a number of combat awards before being medically retired after a serious leg injury sustained in a parachute jump. Paul was nearing his fifty-first birthday and had recovered more or less completely from his physical injuries. He still had the demons of combat in his head and dealt with them nearly every day.

19

Paul spoke, "Aww. The Air Force has plenty of officers. Henry should give football his best shot. Kentucky's in the Southeastern Conference. There's no better training ground for future NFL players. Besides, we all know the enlisted personnel run the show in the military, right Woody?"

Gatewood "Woody" Dowdell was the fourth man in the group. He was the lone African American. It was Gatewood that had requested this get together. He had also been a Combat Controller and, like Paul, had sustained a serious injury in the service of his country. In Gatewood's case it had resulted in the loss of his right leg below the knee after an improvised explosive device detonated under his vehicle in Iraq in 2016. He now wore a prosthetic leg. He was no longer in Air Force Special Operations but was still on active duty as the senior enlisted man in charge of security at nearby Wright-Patterson Air Force Base.

"Damn Straight, Sticks. The Dowdell family has given more than their fair share in the service of the good ol' U.S. of A."

Gatewood referred to Paul as "Sticks" after Paul's habit of printing the *L's* in his last name in such a way that they angled downward and resembled hockey sticks. The fact that Paul had the same last name as a family of National Hockey League royalty—no relation—also contributed to the nickname. Dowdell hung the handle on Paul when he was an instructor to Hull's class as they grinded their way through the "Pipeline." This was the intense two-year program that created the warriors the Air Force contributed to United States Special Operations.

Gatewood and his wife Roberta had three children. Vida was the oldest. She had breezed through West Point and was currently piloting Army V-280 Valor tilt-rotor aircraft. William, the middle child, was a recent graduate of the Air Force Academy. He was being groomed to fly fighters and was currently wrapping up a stint at AFIT, the Air Force Institute of Technology at Wright-Patterson. His parents were enjoying having him close by. He would be leaving for flight school in the next few months. The youngest Dowdell, Henry, was the subject of this evening's gathering.

Henry was a highly recruited wide receiver. He played his high school football at Wayne High School in Huber Heights, a Dayton suburb. His football ability caught the eye of dozens of schools. The fact that he scored 1540 on the SAT was a bonus.

Henry had received full scholarship offers from half a dozen Big Ten institutions, virtually every mid-major school in the Midwest, and all three Service Academies. He had also been on the radar of the University of Alabama. His father hailed from the Yellowhammer State and worshipped Crimson Tide football. Alabama eventually extended a tentative offer that was contingent on another recruit—one they rated higher than Henry—backing out of his commitment.

When Henry cautiously approached Gatewood to say he had taken Alabama off his short list he feared the reaction. Gatewood surprised him.

"Hell with them! Go someplace else and beat their ass!"

Henry would get his chance. Kentucky was also in the SEC and regularly scheduled the Crimson Tide. Earlier that day Henry had informed Gatewood and Roberta of his final decision. He would announce it the following day in conjunction with a release by the social media arm of UK's athletic department. Gatewood sent a group text to Mike, Mark, and Paul. He wanted to tell them in person. It was late March and winter was reluctant to bow out to the more moderate temperatures of spring. Mike suggested the four couples meet at his house and enjoy a cozy fire.

"I wanted to tell you three in person. You've always supported Henry and I thought you deserved it." Gatewood looked at each of his friends in turn.

McClary raised his glass. "A toast."

The others reached for their tumblers and held them up as well.

Mike hesitated for two beats as he considered his words. He opened his mouth to begin the toast but was interrupted by Garcia.

"Go Wildcats!"

The men laughed.

"Thanks Mark, couldn't have said it better myself." Mike sipped his bourbon and the other men followed suit. Mike turned to Gatewood. "If you don't mind me asking, how did Henry do with this NIL thing?"

NIL was the Name, Image, Likeness policy now in place that allowed NCAA athletes to be financially compensated while competing for their chosen college or university.

Gatewood puffed his cheeks and slowly breathed out a sigh. "Well, let me put it this way, they're paying Henry more money to catch footballs than you made in your first three years in the minors combined."

He turned toward Mark and then Paul as he continued. "He'll make more than a rookie firefighter in Ohio and more than Paul and I made as Combat Controllers, at least until we made it to E-6 or E-7." Gatewood was referring to enlisted ranks.

The fire crackled. Gatewood turned his eyes to it and seemed to stare at events from another place and time.

The firepit was an oversized square. It was in the center of the McClarys' small back yard. Mike and Marge had paved the entire yard, an area roughly 40 feet wide and 50 feet deep, and built permanent bench seating around three sides.

The eyes of the three other men were also drawn to the fire. After nearly a full minute Mike spoke. "Henry has his priorities in line, you shouldn't worry about him when it comes to money."

The subject of money and the entitled attitudes of some young people had come up in their discussions before. They had all seen stories of college students who had extravagant expectations of possible employers. When these presumed salaries and benefits didn't appear it generated disappointment and often anger.

Paul added, "I'm not worried about Henry. I've seen how his sister and brother turned out...and his momma and daddy aren't half bad themselves."

22

Gatewood beamed at Paul. There was a mutual respect between the men that went back to their time as Combat Controllers. Woody was a legend in the Air Force Special Operations community. Both he and Paul had ascended to its most elite unit, the 24th Special Tactics Squadron, and carved out reputations as top performers.

"Kind words, Sticks. Just for that I'm gonna pour you another two fingers of Mr. McClary's bourbon." Gatewood rose and reached for Paul's tumbler.

Paul held it out. "Sounds good. Two glasses is my limit. After that we'll have to get going. Lauren has to be at the lab early tomorrow."

Garcia stood and reached for Mike's glass. "I'll give Woody a hand. I can do one more before we need to get going too. Better check on the wives while I'm up, make sure we're clear to hang another half hour."

As Gatewood and Mark moved off toward the house Mike reached for another piece of firewood. Warmer temperatures were on the way but this evening it was just a few degrees above freezing. He turned to Paul.

"I've been meaning to talk to you about something."

Paul thought he might know what it was. The previous summer he and Lauren were put in a dangerous, nearly unwinnable position. They, and their extended families, were threatened by a killer. The McClarys—as well as Gatewood—had assisted them in ways Paul would have a hard time repaying. They hadn't discussed how it was resolved since that day in August. Paul settled in to see what Mike had to say about it.

He was surprised. Mike brought up a completely different subject.

"Do you remember a conversation we had a year or so ago about a small distillery in Kentucky?"

Paul's face showed puzzlement. "Uhh, a conversation with you about a distillery? You'll have to be more specific, Mike. You *do* remember what you do for a living, right?"

McClary smiled. He and Marge owned Jasper Spirits Consulting. They filled a niche between their clients—distilleries and wineries—and bars, retailers, and state liquor agencies. The couple ran the business from their Oak Street home.

"Good point. This was something we discussed back before the uhh," he searched for the right word, "*trouble* you and Lauren ran into last August." He continued. "It probably didn't stick with you because we talked about it in passing."

As Paul waited, he searched his memory but nothing came to him.

Mike leaned forward and smiled. "Peepaw Bourbon."

Paul tried without success to stifle a laugh. It came back to him.

"You're talking about the guy down there in some holler that wanted to give that name to his bourbon?"

Mike nodded. "Yes, his name is Owen Johnson. Owen Bishop Johnson to be exact. He grew up in a little unincorporated burg called Sawyer, Kentucky before going on to make a ton of money in real estate. He's from a close family and decided to use a big chunk of his money to make his grandfather's bourbon recipe famous."

Paul thought back. He and Mike talked about this briefly sometime the previous winter. He had forgotten about it almost immediately.

Mike continued. "He got to the point where the bourbon was nearly ready to market and reached out to Marge and I to help develop a plan. But there was an argument over the name. He wanted to name it after his grandpa, whose name was Tutor Bishop."

"Oh yeah, and there is already a Bishop Bourbon on the market, right?

Mike nodded again. "Right. So he started looking at other possibilities. Some of his people wanted him to put his name on it but Obie—that's short for his first two initials—wouldn't have it. The recipe wasn't his, it was his maternal grandfather's."

"I remember. His *Peepaw.*" Paul grinned. He thought back to one of his deployments to Afghanistan when he had been attached to the 75th Ranger Regiment, specifically the Regimental Reconnaissance Company. There were a couple country boys from Tennessee in the unit that loved to talk about their families, including their meemaws and peepaws. The two Rangers took a ribbing from the rest of the unit.

"Yeah, terrible name for a bourbon, just terrible. It would have absolutely no chance of selling in ninety percent of the country. But Obie couldn't be persuaded to change it. Not until you got involved."

Paul suddenly remembered that he'd made some offhanded remarks about using the grandfather's other name.

Mike saw the realization on Paul's face. "That's right, you said 'Why not use Peepaw's first name, Tutor? You could put it in bottles that look like books, it would be popular in college towns.'"

"Oh yeah, *I have a session tonight with the Tutor,* like that." It was all coming back to Paul now.

"Well, big guy, guess what new spirit is about to be released?"

Paul was incredulous. "You've *got* to be kidding me?!?"

"Nope, Tutor's Bourbon is about to hit the market. And Obie wants to meet you. He wants you to come down to Sawyer. And not only that, he wants you to come on board with us and help with the rollout."

Paul was speechless. The McClarys had approached him more than once about coming to work for them. He hadn't been ready to commit. After separating from the military he had concentrated on healing his leg. He exercised for hours each day, working out in his basement gym and going on long bike rides. His mind was occupied with books and podcasts and by visiting historic sites. The perilous situation that he and Lauren had found themselves in the previous year was closely tied to one of Paul's interests, the Wright brothers.

"Why me? I don't know anything about the bourbon business."

Mike leaned in. "Obie doesn't care about that. After I passed on your idea he asked about you. He's about people.

I told him you were a Combat Controller. Obie was in Army Intelligence before he hit it big with his real estate business. And I also told him you weren't a ne'er-do-well...at least not a *complete* ne'er-do-well." Mike tried to keep his expression serious but failed.

"Wow Mike, I don't know. I'd have to think about it...and I'd have to talk to Lauren."

Mike's face changed. It assumed a guilty look.

"Well, actually, I've discussed this with Lauren and she's completely on board."

Lauren had urged Paul to start a second career for the last two years. He hadn't been ready to commit. He hadn't really found anything that seized his interest, not that he'd been looking that hard.

Paul nodded slowly. "Well, I can't say that surprises me."

The back door to the house swung open and Gatewood and Mark emerged. Each of them carried two bourbon glasses.

Paul turned to them then looked back at Mike. "But I don't even know if this Tutor's stuff is any good." He reached up to accept a tumbler from Gatewood.

A wide grin spread across Mike McClary's face.

"You tell me. It's what we're drinking tonight."

Paul stared at the tumbler and the golden liquid inside. The fire crackled in the background, its flames reflecting off the glass.

Hmmm.

CHAPTER FOUR

Cole pulled back the slide of his backup weapon. It was an M1911A1 .45 caliber pistol. He let it spring back, loading a round into the chamber. The weapon was a reproduction, not an original, but looked exactly like the iconic firearm used for decades by the United States military. Both Cole and Tanner wore the pistols in belt holsters on their right side, partially covered by their jackets. He did a quick check of the Olive Garden lot to confirm there were no watchers before twisting his muscular upper body in the front seat and sliding the pistol into his holster. He turned his wrist and again checked the time: 2:03 p.m.

Cole did not choose exact times for the robberies. He generally selected a window. There was an ebb and flow of customer traffic with most banks. His goal was to hit the front door when there were as few customers inside as possible so he and Tanner could quickly establish control of the situation.

Cole usually chose mid-afternoon to initiate a robbery. It allowed for any lunchtime rush of customer traffic to subside. It also helped them avoid significant traffic issues during the getaway. Their targets were typically in smaller cities but even they generated late afternoon road congestion. There wasn't a specific *Go Time*. It was more by feel. Yet that didn't stop him from nervously checking his watch.

Tanner spoke. "Carbine is good."

Cole saw that his brother was holding his primary weapon, a semi-automatic M1 Carbine. It too was a reproduction of a World War Two weapon used by United States military units. It was just under thirty-six inches long and its magazine held fifteen .30 caliber rounds.

Tanner kept the rifle low, below the level of the window. His right hand slid to his backup weapon in the holster on his hip. It held the same style pistol that his brother carried. Tanner's eyes were trained on the parking lot. His head moved from side to side.

Cole could see that his brother was beginning to amp up. To a point this was good. Cole didn't want his team to get complacent. They had pulled off enough of these jobs that this was a concern. On the other hand he knew that Tanner tended to go from zero to sixty just a bit quicker than he would prefer. Giving Tanner a code name based on George Patton, considered by many to be the most aggressive military figure in U.S. history, seemed appropriate. He decided to try to slow Tanner's roll a bit.

"Easy with that thing, George. Remember, It's for scarin', not for shootin'. Although that pop gun of yours won't do the trick as well as mine." Cole smiled and patted his own primary weapon.

It was another modern copy, not an M1 Carbine, but a "Tommy Gun." Originally developed in 1918 by United States Army Brigadier General John T. Thompson to help end the stalemate of trench warfare in World War One, the Thompson's many variants gained fame during the Prohibition era. The original model was capable of fully automatic fire.

Cole's version—he had stolen it so he thought of it as his— was a semi-automatic model. That is, when the trigger was pulled one bullet was fired. The reproduction, manufactured by Kahr Arms in their Worcester, Massachusetts, factory, would not perform like a machine gun.

Still, it scared the hell out of people.

The Tommy Gun was used during Prohibition by both the good guys—police and the FBI—and the bad guys. This included organized crime. It was utilized during World War Two to great effect by the Marine Corps in the Pacific theater against the Japanese and the Army in Europe in the struggle with Nazi Germany.

The weapon picked up several nicknames including the Chicago Typewriter and the trench sweeper. It played a role in countless war movies and black-and-white gangster films. It was sometimes shown with a 50 or 100 round cylindrical magazine. Cole's version had a 30-round stick magazine that protruded from the bottom of the weapon. It fired the same .45 caliber round used in the brothers' pistols.

Tanner grinned. "Yeah, I can't argue with that. Nuthin' like a Tommy Gun to get a bank employee's attention."

Cole nodded and smiled. "Did the trick for Johnny Dillinger back in the day."

The Olive Garden was on the north side of Durand Avenue. The Wells Fargo branch sat barely one hundred yards to the south across the roadway. The team had a clear view of the bank from a spot through a decorative line of trees that fronted the Olive Garden property. Dom was watching the building through binoculars as the Jelciks prepped their weapons.

The men had performed a communications check on the Midland X-Talkers and throat microphones before leaving the hotel. Each of them wore an earpiece inside one ear to hear transmissions. Dom's walkie-talkie was in the cup holder. A Uniden digital police scanner sat on the Santa Fe's console between he and Cole. It was tuned to the frequency used by the Racine Police Department. It was a portable unit that looked similar in many ways to the team's walkie-talkies, but its technology was significantly more advanced. The $700 price tag reflected this. The team had honed in on the proper police channel the previous night after returning from the airport.

They had been in the Olive Garden lot for fifteen minutes. Cole tried to minimize the time they were exposed to passersby. This stage of the operation would not last much longer. They would either go soon or they would find a new vantage point.

They'd slept late at the Travelodge in Racine before finding a nearby pancake house. They spent an hour there in a corner booth going over the plan while loading up on carbohydrates and caffeine. They paid with cash—they always paid with cash—and returned to the hotel.

Cole had requested late checkout so they were able to take their time assembling their gear. They used the restroom. They situated their equipment. They spent fifteen minutes going over the room to make sure they left no trace of anything that might lead the authorities to their identities. All three men slipped on their work gloves before leaving the room.

They left in two vehicles. Dom drove the Santa Fe with Cole in the front passenger seat. Tanner followed in the truck staying tight on their rear. Cole stressed this. He didn't want another vehicle—particularly a police vehicle—to slip in behind the Santa Fe and get a good look at the plastic that covered the rear window opening.

They reached the stash area and positioned the truck. It was the lifeline they would use in the getaway. They removed their weapons from the storage area of the truck. This freed up room for their backpacks. They piled these in and closed the storage unit.

After the transfer they assumed their positions in the Santa Fe. Dom drove, trying to blend into traffic while at the same time making an effort to avoid red lights. It took seven minutes to reach their jumping-off point at the Olive Garden.

"Not much traffic at the bank. No walk-in customers are inside right now as far as I can tell." Dom turned his head a fraction of an inch to his left and brought the bank's drive-thru into view with the binoculars. It was on the east side of the building and was completely visible from their vantage point. "Looks like it's definitely a down period for them...maybe one car in the drive-thru or ATM machine every ten minutes or so."

"Let's have a look." Cole reached for the binoculars.

The drive-thru area was a point of interest for Cole. Some banks now set up remote versions that were situated some distance from the building and made use of video screens and pneumatic tubes to facilitate transactions. This style represented a slightly lower risk to the team since drivers did not have a direct view into the bank. The Wells Fargo had a standard drive up window. Any customer paying attention— not screwing around on their cellphone—would be able to look through the teller's window and potentially view the robbery. A call to 911 would inevitably follow.

Cole glassed the building to confirm Dom's assessment. Periodic chatter emanated from the scanner. Cole judged it to be inconsequential. They had been monitoring the scanner all morning and had heard few "ten-codes" used. These were the cryptic shorthand numerical codes that law enforcement used to identify specific situations. One such code, "10-4," had long ago become commonplace in the civilian world. It appeared to Cole that much of the Racine PD's radio traffic was in plain speech. This had become more customary after the terrorist attacks on September 11, 2001.

Ten-codes were not uniform across the country. As a matter of routine Cole had his team memorize specific codes used in the jurisdiction of each robbery. For the Racine job he took special pains to make sure they recognized five in particular; Ten-23, Arrived at Scene; Ten-31, Crime in Progress; Ten-35, Major Crime Alert; 10-37, Investigate Suspicious Vehicle; and 10-40, Silent Run, No Lights or Sirens.

Dom would be in the Santa Fe when the Jelciks were inside the bank. If he heard one of these codes it probably meant that a bank employee had somehow triggered a silent alarm or someone outside the bank had reported suspicious activity. It was his responsibility to immediately alert the brothers over the walkie-talkies.

As Cole removed the binoculars from his eyes he pushed down a niggling thought. Many large American city police departments had begun to encrypt their radio transmissions. Chicago, 75 miles to their south, was an example. Cole knew it was just a matter of time before this precaution was taken by the smaller cities where the Fireteam generally operated. He hadn't mentioned this to Tanner or Santo, but he knew that, like the closing window of easy thefts of Kias and Hyundais, their current methods were becoming obsolete.

"Dom's right. Get your masks ready. Watches on timer mode. Game time, boys."

The men had thin navy blue microfiber ski masks rolled up on top of their heads. They looked like watch caps. The elder Jelcik brother had instructed the team to wait until the last possible moment before pulling them down so as to not draw unwanted attention.

Both Cole and Tanner had a large carabiner attached to the belt loop on the left rear area of their jeans. Fourteen-inch heavy duty Carhartt tool bags—two for each man—hung from them. They were constructed of tough Duramax material. The bags folded nicely when empty, allowing the men to sit on them while inside the SUV. The flexible handles of the Carhartts slid easily inside the carabiners.

The four lanes of Durand were split by a median strip approximately fifty feet wide. A standard two-lane road, Elwood Drive, ran north and south on the east side of the Olive Garden property. Once crossing Durand, Elwood continued south and bordered the Wells Fargo lot.

The bank was situated inside a cluster of businesses that formed a commercial lot. The west side of this commercial lot was bracketed by a road even larger than Durand. This was South Green Bay Avenue, a six-lane road that had a median splitting its northbound lanes from those running south. South Green Bay was their escape route after the robbery.

To initiate the job the team had to first cross Durand, continue past the Wells Fargo property, then curl into the lot and park directly in front of the bank's main entrance. This approach allowed the team to keep the bank in view from the second they left the restaurant parking lot. They would be able to see any last second walk-in or drive-thru customers.

Dom pulled the Santa Fe through the Olive Garden lot, turned onto Elwood, and came to a stop at Durand. The men looked to their left in unison to check oncoming westbound traffic. After two cars passed Dom pulled forward and braked in the median as more vehicles approached from the right. Seeing a break in the traffic Cole remarked, "After the red van. Masks down when we get across." The tone was businesslike.

The Jelcik brothers used both hands to pull their masks in place the moment the Santa Fe cleared Durand. Dom tugged his down with his right hand while keeping his left on the wheel. All three pairs of eyes took in the bank building as they drew even with it on their right. There were no vehicles at the drive-thru or ATM lane. A woman was visible through the teller window. She appeared to be speaking to someone out of sight. She was smiling.

Cole thought, *That'll change.*

Dom buttonhooked the Santa Fe into the bank lot and accelerated slightly as he angled toward the main entrance. Just before the SUV drew even with the double doors Cole shouted, "Start watches!"

All three men pushed buttons on their watches. Three high-pitched chirps sounded nearly simultaneously. Cole and Tanner jerked open their doors before the Santa Fe came to a halt.

They were committed. There was no turning back.

CHAPTER FIVE

Dom watched as the Jelciks exited the vehicle and strode confidently toward the bank's entrance. He did not feel the cool air that entered the interior of the Santa Fe. His eyes stayed on the brothers.

Just look at those damn guys...like a couple of Starship Troopers...all geared up...no fear...couple of natural-born heroes.

It didn't occur to Dom that Cole and Tanner would be facing unarmed civilians that posed them virtually zero physical threat.

As planned, Cole reached the front door first. He pulled it open and stepped aside as his brother pushed past and reached for the second door. Tanner jerked it open and Cole burst through with the Tommy Gun up.

The service counter was directly in front of him, about forty feet ahead. The drive-thru window was on the far side of the counter. Corridors ran off to the left and the right. They would be a challenge. In planning Cole had stressed that Tanner had to immediately get eyes on the offices that ran down both sides of the left corridor. The right corridor housed the vault as well as a set of restrooms.

Cole quickly closed on the counter. He sensed Tanner dashing off to the left with his M-1 raised to his shoulder. To this point the Jelciks had not uttered a sound.

The movement caught the attention of the tellers behind the counter. There were two of them, both women. One was a pretty young redhead, the other a dishwater blonde in her thirties. The redhead looked up from what she was doing and caught Cole's movement when he was only fifteen feet from her. She went rigid. The blonde sensed her coworker's unusual state and turned. She looked first to the redhead then followed the woman's gaze to take in the sight of the large masked man moving toward them with a weapon. The blonde opened her mouth to scream.

Cole recognized this and quickly swung the Tommy Gun toward her with his right hand while raising his left index finger to his lips.

"Quiet!"

He said it in a commanding voice, but at a conversational level. It would not have been loud enough to alert anyone in the offices. Both women froze.

"Hands up where I can see them!"

Both women complied immediately.

"If I even *think* one of you tries to trip an alarm I'll kill you both!" Cole believed the act of making a bank employee think their actions could get others killed was powerful. They might consider going for an alarm at personal risk, but they wouldn't endanger others. He watched the women and knew he was right. He smiled. *Good, decent people....perfect!*

"Come around to this side. Be quick!"

Cole herded the frightened women from behind the counter and made them lay on the floor near the right corridor. They were now out of sight from vehicles that might come to the window. The angle would also make them difficult to see from anyone outside of fifty feet of the front door. Dom would warn them if anyone approached that perimeter.

Cole glanced at the inside of his left wrist. Thirty-seven seconds. He spoke again, this time it was not directed to the tellers.

"Ike has taken down the counter." His throat microphone would have picked up and broadcast every word he'd uttered since coming through the door. He knew his partners could've pieced together his actions by paying attention. But he wanted to spell it out, make it crystal clear. His teammates were occupied with their own tasks. Especially Tanner.

Cole kept watch on the women while flashing a look to the office corridor. He waited for his brother.

Tanner followed Cole into the lobby for two steps then wheeled to the left. His carbine, fitted with a 15-round magazine, was ready. He carried two extra magazines in an inside pocket of his jacket. He had his index finger on the trigger. Cole had made him promise to keep the finger outside of the trigger guard but Tanner told himself that was an unnecessary precaution.

Got to be READY!

He moved with purpose down the corridor. He tried to quickly ascertain the layout. Santo had cased the bank several weeks earlier and had used the restroom. This is how they had pinpointed the location of the vault on the right side of the building. Santo could not risk walking down the left corridor without drawing suspicion so the team did not know the exact configuration of the second passageway.

Tanner quickly realized that the rooms on the left were set up as small meeting areas, no doubt used for conferences with clients. He could see three rooms on the left side of the hall and all were dark. He immediately turned his attention to the right side. There were three open doorways. The walls to the right of each door were glass, allowing the occupant to look out to the hallway. Tanner moved toward the first door, hugging the right side of the corridor to cut the angle of view of anyone inside.

An officious looking woman in her late fifties sat at a desk. She was peering at a desktop computer screen over half-rim reading glasses that attached to a chain around her neck. She had a frown on her face. Tanner stepped into the doorway.

Annoyed, the woman looked up. Her eyes grew wide and her mouth formed an O. There was a desk phone to the left of the keyboard and a cellphone to the right. The woman was paralyzed for just a second then quickly recovered. Instinctively she began to reach for the cell, thought better of it, and moved her hand to the underside of the desk.

"Unh-uh." Tanner took a quick step into the office and thrust the barrel of the carbine to within a foot of her face. The woman froze again. Tanner brought a finger to his lips and hissed, *"Make a noise and I kill you, and everyone else in this building!"*

He gestured for her to stand and moved aside so the doorway wasn't blocked.

"Out the door and into the lobby. Keep quiet. My partner is out there with a gun."

The woman moved clumsily to the door and looked to the lobby where Cole stood over the tellers. She looked back at Tanner as if seeking a way out of the situation then walked away tentatively.

Tanner turned toward the second office.

Herschel Knuckles sat at his desk and laconically punched computer keys. He spent some time each day after lunch catching up on sports news. Today he was scrolling through the *NBA.com* website looking for stories on his favorite team, the Milwaukee Bucks. Herschel also followed Brewers baseball and Packers football but basketball had always been his favorite. It had been since, he supposed, as a kid he had watched a distant cousin, Harvey Knuckles, dominate local hoops while attending Racine's St. Catherine's High School in the late seventies. Harvey had gone on to star at the University of Toledo before being drafted by the Los Angeles Lakers. He spent most of his pro career playing overseas.

Still, Harvey had been a pro and Herschel had idolized him. Wells Fargo allowed its managers some leeway in decorating their offices and Herschel's walls included a fair bit of sports memorabilia. There were two autographed pictures of African American basketball players featured in the center of the far wall where Herschel could easily see them. One featured NBA superstar Giannis Antetokounmpo of the Bucks. The other featured cousin Harvey.

Most every customer that entered his office knew about Giannis. Very few knew of Harvey. The photos had sparked several conversations with bank visitors over the years. Herschel was convinced that, in a small way, they had helped increase business. If not, well, he didn't care, he wasn't planning on taking them down.

Herschel had just clicked on a page that featured the arena giveaway nights at Bucks games. He saw that a competing bank was sponsoring a Giannis action figure at an upcoming game. He frowned. This was likely to steer more people seeking loans to the competitor. Herschel had numbers to hit and—

He sensed a form through the window to his right. Hershel quickly backed out of the NBA page and turned with a smile on his face.

Tanner took in the sight of a black man at a desk turning toward him. He saw a look of horror appear where a smile had just been. Before the man could react Tanner was on him.

"Hands where I can see them. Go for an alarm and everyone dies!"

The man was in his fifties and was undoubtedly the branch manager. His location further from the lobby indicated this, as well as the trappings of his office. Still, there was one more room to clear in the corridor and Tanner couldn't take a chance that there was another person to deal with. He kept his voice low and threatening.

"Get up! Don't make a goddammed peep. Walk down the hall to the next room."

The man stood and walked unsteadily to the door. Tanner followed him to the final room. Because of the building configuration the plan at this bank was to quietly and quickly gather all employees and patrons. The fact that there were no customers had been a plus. Tanner now needed to secure the last room. Cole had worked out the sequence. Once the person in the first office was sent out Tanner could use the occupant of the next one to lead him down the hall.

Tanner jabbed the barrel of the carbine in the manager's back. "Inside the last door. Say 'What's up' to anyone inside."

The man reacted without thinking, "But nobody's ins—"

"SHUT THE FUCK UP AND JUST DO IT!"

39

Tanner's forceful whisper was loud enough to be heard in the lobby. He had lost his cool a bit and was gratified to see that the last opening led to an unoccupied breakroom.

Tanner exhaled and tried to assume a more even tone. "OK, out to the lobby. Hustle!"

He then spoke for the benefit of his teammates through the throat microphone.

"George has cleared the corridor. Moving to lobby."

In the Santa Fe Dom heard Tanner's call. He looked at his watch and saw that less than two minutes had elapsed since he'd started it. He had been instructed by Cole to give a quick situation report from outside the bank once Tanner had secured the corridor.

"Audie is clear. Audie is clear."

That done, Dom continued to scan his surroundings. He had detected nothing but normal traffic and had heard no calls that raised concern from the police scanner.

Still, he was on edge. He had backed the SUV up to the bank to allow for a quick exit once the brothers returned. He was uncomfortable, feeling exposed sitting behind the wheel wearing a ski mask. He realized he also felt a hint of guilt for occupying a handicapped parking space. Dom smiled through his mask. He eased his grip on the .45 pistol between his legs and refocused on the traffic. He waited for the next call in his earpiece.

He knew that Cole would be working his magic next.

Cole watched Tanner march the manager into the lobby. He had all three women on the floor. The Thompson pointed in their direction with a hint of malice. He had already evaluated them. The tellers, he was sure, had not reached the level of responsibility to have full access to the vault. One look had told him this. The woman from the first office almost certainly did. She had a spark of defiance in her eyes but she tried to avoid looking directly at Cole as she approached him after leaving Tanner.

She was trying to hide something.

Cole was almost certain she had vault access. He also believed she would resist his team in every way possible. She would try to buy time, hoping the police would show. He could break her but it could get messy.

He focused on the face of the black man being frog-marched toward him by his brother.

Cole had a knack for reading people. It was more than that. It was a gift. It wasn't something he worked to develop. It was innate. He had always had it. Tanner had long since accepted it, even taken it for granted. Dom was amazed by it and still a bit confounded.

Tanner and the manager approached. Cole locked eyes with the man for two brief seconds and he was sure. He smiled.

"What's your name?"

The man answered softly. "Herschel Knuckles."

Behind the man Tanner smirked and let out a short mocking laugh.

Cole's eyes immediately flashed to those of his brother.

"Check the restrooms, George...*Now!*"

Tanner, rebuked, retracted his smile and hurried down the corridor. Cole looked back to Knuckles and said, "Cool name." Then, "OK Herschel we don't have much time...give me your wallet."

Knuckles was confused. "My...wallet?" *Why the hell would these guys break into a bank to steal a wallet?*

Now Cole shouted, "Give me your damn wallet...NOW!" He swung the Tommy Gun toward the man's chest.

Knuckles complied. He nodded his head several times as he pulled the wallet from his right rear pocket and handed it over. Cole flipped it open and quickly found the man's Wisconsin driver's license. He read from it in a clear voice.

"Hershel Robert Knuckles, 227 Bristol Place, Elmwood Park, Wisconsin."

He slid the license into a pocket of his Eisenhower jacket before handing the wallet back to Knuckles. He saw Tanner returning from the restrooms giving him a thumb's up.

"Alright Mr. Herschel Robert Knuckles of 227 Bristol Place in Elmwood Park, Wisconsin...you're going to get us into the vault. Right now. If you don't I will be coming to pay your family a visit." Cole could tell by the man's expression that he had a family.

Knuckles stood unmoving, staring at Cole. He began to sweat. He unintentionally opened his mouth an inch.

Cole smiled and nodded up and down as he said to Knuckles, "You believe me, don't you?"

The manager responded with his own nod, mirroring Cole. "I'll need to get the key out of my office."

Cole shot a look at Tanner. "Take him George. Fast. He reaches for an alarm, shoot him."

"Damn straight, Ike." Tanner grabbed the man's shoulder and pushed him back toward his office.

Bank vaults weren't all the same. In fact many of them weren't vaults at all but simply secure areas of the building that housed extra cash, documents, records, and other valuables. Older institutions and large main branches usually did have the style that featured the massive doors seen in movies or on TV. But many smaller banks and Savings and Loans got by with smaller areas that, though still secured with a host of high-tech features, looked much less imposing.

They were still called vaults.

The vault in the right hallway of the Wells Fargo was the size of a large walk-in closet. There were two steel doors at its entrance. The exterior door had a combination lock. It was already open. The internal door required a key. Hershel Knuckles provided that when Tanner prodded him back through the lobby from his office.

Cole looked at Knuckles and spoke slowly.

"Here's the deal Herschel. We know some of the cash bundles are booby-trapped. Might be dye packs, might be tear gas, might be explosive charges. Probably some combination of all of those. We have four bags here."

42

Cole glanced at Tanner who had backed toward the three women and was covering them with his carbine. He nodded and Tanner reached back and released his two Carhartt bags from the carabiner on his belt loop.

"You and I are going into the vault and we're splitting the money into all four bags. I'm relying on you to avoid putting the booby-trapped bills in the bags."

Herschel protested, "But I—"

"SHUT UP! You might know which ones are bad and you might not. I don't give a shit. You're going to do your best to keep from screwing us because if you don't I'll be paying you a little visit." He patted his jacket pocket where he'd stashed Knuckles's driver's license and allowed himself a menacing smile.

Knuckles was now perspiring freely. He nodded.

"We're going to go for the big bills first. Don't screw around with the ones unless I tell you to. Grab those two bags from my man George and let's go."

Knuckles complied then turned back to Cole.

"Open it!" Cole checked his watch and saw they were approaching three minutes and thirty seconds.

Gotta MOVE.

Knuckles held the bags in his left hand and inserted the key with his right. It shook slightly but he found the slot on his first try. The key turned and the steel door slid open smoothly when Cole reached past the manager and shoved it. Cole pushed the man inside as he spoke for his teammates' benefit.

"Ike entering vault."

There were shelves on both sides and more on the far wall. They were mostly empty but to Cole's practiced eye what was inside would be well worth their efforts. He saw stacks of banded cash, many in denominations of $20 and above.

"Open the bags...BE QUICK!"

As Knuckles unfolded Tanner's two bags Cole readied his own. Soon all four Carhartts were receiving bundles. Knuckles stopped from time to time and tossed a bundle to the floor.

Cole smiled at him. "Good man. Hope you guessed right."

43

Knuckles looked at him and seemed to project a bit of steel from his eyes.

Cole frowned and gestured with the Thompson.

"Back wall of the vault...NOW!"

The look of defiance vanished from Knuckles's eyes. He backed away with his hands at chest level, palms out.

"Don't shoot! *PLEASE!*"

Cole backed out and spoke for the throat mike. "George, get the women up and move them to the vault."

Tanner hesitated. He wanted to ask why. This hadn't been part of the plan. Long experience with his brother helped him overcome the urge.

"Roger Ike, on the way."

The Jelciks jointly shepherded the three female employees down the hall and into the vault. The brothers could almost smell their fear. The young redheaded woman was whimpering and was helped along by the other two. As they stepped into the vault the woman from the first office turned toward the Jelciks with a look of pure hatred in her eyes. The half-rimmed glasses still hung from her neck.

Cole smiled at her. "Nice doin' business with you, honey."

Tanner chuckled as his brother closed the vault door and turned the key.

"You crack me up, Ike."

CHAPTER SIX

Lauren Hull arrived early for work the day after the firepit get-together at the McClarys' house. She had to be at the Kettering Health building in downtown Troy at 5:30 a.m. Ordinarily she might have begged off accepting such an invitation on a weeknight. Mike and Marge's house was a thirty-minute drive from the Hulls' place outside of Troy. But Lauren knew that Mike was anxious to ask her husband to join the spirits consulting business. She correctly surmised that the hastily arranged celebration to announce Henry Dowdell's college choice would provide the opportunity.

Lauren had recently turned forty-six. This meant that she had now spent as many years out of the military as in it. She and Paul met in New Mexico. Lauren was working as a lab technician with the 377th Medical Group at Kirtland Air Force Base in Albuquerque. At the time she was somewhat disenchanted with her career choice. She was born and raised just seven miles from the base. The work was interesting, but she had joined the Air Force to see the world and, just maybe, meet her future husband. Fate brought that husband to her.

Paul was in New Mexico training to become a Combat Controller. He was running up a path on the Embudo Canyon Trailhead near the Sandia Mountains when he bumped into her. It was the prelude to a relationship that would last a lifetime. The couple had no children, but lacked nothing else of importance.

Lauren's twenty-three years of service included duty stations all over the globe, time in two combat zones, and multiple promotions. She ended her military career as a warrant officer, having started in the enlisted ranks. Along the way she acquired professional laboratory skills that allowed her to easily transition to the civilian world.

Lauren and Paul bought a house near Troy after a fair amount of deliberation. Wright-Patterson Air Force Base was located nearby outside of Dayton. The Veterans Administration medical facilities in the area were a significant consideration as Paul's leg injury required months of care and rehabilitation after he left the Air Force.

Lauren had been a Medical Laboratory Technician in the service. There was a shortage of qualified "Med Techs" in the region in the private sector. Housing prices were within their price range, especially as compared with a number of other areas they considered. And they had friends—Gatewood and Roberta Dowdell—nearby.

Once she and Paul had decided to settle in the area Lauren applied at several hospitals. She had three job offers within weeks. She chose the one from Kettering Health, a new facility in Troy. Once on staff she replicated her steady rise in the Air Force. She started as a Med Tech, rose to supervisor of the Blood Bank, and was now a department head in charge of the entire lab. This was in the space of just two years. Her extensive experience in the Air Force was the key factor in this rapid advancement.

Lauren led by example in the lab. She tackled the toughest procedures and cases in the department, only delegating tasks to subordinates when they had been sufficiently trained. She also worked more than her fair share of odd shifts and holidays. This had been a point of contention with Paul. He believed she wore herself down by staying late at the lab and by trading shifts with coworkers who wanted to attend a kid's ballgame or recital. Lauren thought these things were positive gestures that stimulated teamwork and enhanced the performance of the department.

They hadn't had fights over this—not really—but it was a sore subject in the Hull household. The only other aspect of their relationship that even hinted of discord had to do with their cat, Chappy. Lauren had lobbied to get a kitten for years and Paul had been lukewarm at best to the proposition. She finally caught him at a weak moment and, after agreeing to let him name the feline, got his approval. Paul named the little orange creature after one of his heroes, John Chapman, an Air Force Combat Controller who was killed in Afghanistan early in the Global War on Terror. Chapman's actions on a lonely mountaintop called Takur Ghar were exemplary and resulted in him being awarded a posthumous Medal of Honor.

Chappy the cat grew to the point that he was a few pounds over his ideal body weight. He tormented Paul with his penchant for chewing cellphone and computer charger cords and for perching on food contact surfaces in their kitchen. Truth be told, Lauren wasn't particularly enamored with these traits either but she loved Chappy nonetheless. They had done their best to cat-proof their house. Lauren believed her husband was warming to the cat.

So far on this Wednesday things were going smoothly in the lab. Lauren's phlebotomists were accomplishing the blood draws on schedule. These were typically done early in the morning in order to get the samples to the lab at the beginning of first shift. The patients didn't love it—often complaining of being stirred from a sound sleep to be jabbed with a needle—but it made the most sense for most hospitals that had in-house testing equipment.

Lauren took lunch at 10:45 so she could return to the lab and cover for those that went at more traditional times. She found the cafeteria nearly devoid of diners and walked to the order station. She eyed the board.

"Hello Mizzus, what can I get for you today?"

Lauren turned to see the cafeteria manager, Larry Jonas, approach the register. Jonas was a round man in his fifties. He had a shock of brown hair that was grey at the temples and a beard to match. Both his hair and his beard seemed to be eternally in need of a trim. He wore a hairnet more or less the entire time he worked the counter. His beard net invariably hung below his chin, completely ineffectual.

Lauren liked Larry. He was cheerful and provided an excellent selection of dishes in the cafeteria. She overlooked his token effort to cover the beard. She supposed that would change immediately if she ever spotted any fragment of it in her food. She also took no offense with his inclination to call the married women on staff "Mizzus." He referred to single women as "Miz." Lauren knew a number of women had complained about this, in particular those in their thirties and above that had never married.

"Oh hey there Larry, let me see." Lauren looked over the menu board. Her eyes hesitated briefly on a couple of Larry's tastier options before sliding to the "Healthy Fare" section. Her job responsibilities kept her behind a desk for much of the day. This, combined with her ever-changing hours had resulted in a few extra pounds. In the military she burned the calories easily. She tried to control her intake whenever possible.

"I have some of my lemon meringue pie today...you better get it while you can. It won't last through lunch rush." Larry's eyes seemed to sparkle.

Larry, you evil SOB! Lauren was glad he couldn't hear her thoughts.

"Thanks Larry, I'll just have a side salad and an order of cottage cheese. Oh, and a medium cup for the soda dispenser."

"Suit yourself." Larry's smile was still there but seemed to shine a bit less brightly. Larry loved to hear compliments about his food and his lemon meringue generated a good number of them.

Lauren paid and while Larry worked on the order she grabbed a paper cup and walked to the soda machine. She started with the ice, filling her cup nearly to the top. As she turned to the Diet Coke tab she saw a younger woman with short blonde hair approach the ice machine. The woman, who was an inch shorter than her, glanced at Lauren's cup and exclaimed, "Oooh, great! They have good ice here!"

The woman was a stranger but Lauren couldn't help herself.

"Yes! Nugget ice...the best!"

Both women laughed.

Lauren considered herself a bit of a snob when it came to ice. She and Paul had an under counter unit installed in their house. It made nugget style chewy ice very similar to the machine at the hospital. Lauren would go out of her way to patronize restaurants and convenience stores that carried the "right" type of ice and avoid those that didn't.

"Looks like I've found a fellow ice aficionado."

The woman responded, "Absolutely! This is great. I'm going to be a regular at this machine."

Lauren noted that the younger woman was dressed in business casual clothing, not the scrubs most hospital employees wear. She assumed the woman was visiting a patient.

"Planning to spend some time here?"

The woman nodded, "I sure hope so. I was just hired! I'm a radiology tech and I just interviewed. They offered me a job on the spot! I'm so happy and...and I'm gushing, sorry."

Lauren began to respond, "That's great! Tell me—"

She was interrupted by Larry at the counter. "Mizzus, your order's ready...Lauren?"

Lauren nodded to the man and held up a finger, "Be right there." She turned to the blonde.

"I'm having a quick lunch. Would you like to join me? Anything I can help you with? I work in the lab but I'd be happy to answer any questions about the hospital."

The woman's smile widened. "That would be great!" She held out a hand. "I'm Lacey Billingham."

Lauren planned to be back to her desk by 11:15. She was still sitting with Lacey at 11:35 when Paulette from the lab came into the now crowded cafeteria looking for her.

Despite spending more time than she'd planned Lauren barely finished her modest lunch. She and Lacey were engrossed in conversation. Lauren learned a great deal about the new hire. Lacey would graduate in six weeks from Ohio State in Columbus. Her degree fit a need at Kettering Health. The hospital had been trying to fill a slot left open by a retirement for several weeks. Lacey planned to pursue additional education and become certified with MRI equipment. She was engaged. Her fiancé, Matt Wells, held a four-year degree in Automotive Technology from the University of Northwest Ohio in Lima, which was located 50 miles north of Troy.

Matt accepted a job with a company in nearby Piqua and had started the previous week. The couple planned a late June wedding in their small hometown in northern Ohio. They were high school sweethearts that had stuck together despite taking different educational paths after high school. The pair had been in the area looking at rentals when Lacey heard about the job opening and scheduled the interview.

Lauren surprised herself by telling Lacey that Paul was considering a new job.

I can't believe I said that. I don't even know this girl.

They spoke excitedly for over a half hour. Anyone witnessing the conversation would have sworn that the attractive brunette and the pretty young blonde were perhaps an aunt meeting her niece for lunch.

"It's all happening so fast!" Lacey's blue eyes were wide. "I mean, new town, new job..."

Lauren cut in, "New husband." She smiled, "Well, soon, anyway."

Lacey returned the smile. "I'm sure about that part. Matt is the one. The rest of this...I just hope it works out."

"Well let me know how I can help. Call me anytime." The women exchanged phone numbers.

Lauren followed Paulette back to the lab. She was thinking that she might have just made a new friend, one that was half her age.

CHAPTER SEVEN

Dom Santo followed the events happening inside the Wells Fargo through his earpiece. The throat microphones that the team wore had transducers that fit against the neck below the larynx. They absorbed vibrations that emanated from the trachea and converted them to signals broadcast by radio frequency. Voices did not come across exactly as they did when using standard microphones—they were more mechanical—but the three men had practiced with them and they easily recognized each other's transmissions.

Technically known as laryngophones, throat mikes were originally developed during World War One by the British for use in open cockpit airplanes. Background noise is not picked up by throat mikes, making broadcasts in windy or noisy conditions more effective than with standard equipment.

This allowed Dom to hear not only Cole and Tanner's situational updates but everything they directed toward the bank staff. He could not hear responses from the employees. This was somewhat frustrating. During the critical stages of their robberies Dom found himself leaning forward slightly trying to pick up every detail that was happening inside the bank a few yards from his position in the getaway vehicle. His eyes narrowed as he followed the electronic narrative. He had to force himself to give the proper amount of awareness to the police scanner and the world beyond the windshield.

Dom noted that Cole sounded in charge. He was commanding, no nonsense. Tanner came across as more dangerous, slightly on edge. Dom could hear it in their somewhat robotic voices. He smiled.

Exactly what I expected.

Dom heard Cole speak to someone he called "Herschel," telling him to go for the big bills. He then heard the "Ike entering vault" call.

Dom checked the running display on his watch and noted that they were approaching the four-minute mark.

Not perfect, could be better...but not bad.

The vault call was his cue to open the rear liftgate door on the SUV. The brothers would be exiting the bank very soon and would toss their Carhartt bags directly into the rear compartment. They would also be carrying their weapons and, in practice runs—Cole had insisted on practicing every aspect of the jobs—the men found this allowed them to enter the vehicle without unnecessary delay. It was just too awkward for men as large as the Jelciks to maneuver two Carhartt bags—bags that hopefully would be full—and a long gun through a car door.

During one practice in the shop bay of their building back in Columbus Tanner had dropped his carbine onto the concrete floor. He had thrown open the door and flopped backward into the rear seat of the vehicle. Both bags were in his left hand. He tucked them into his lap. The carbine was in his right hand. Its stock contacted the door and as Tanner fell back its barrel caught on the rear section of the opening. Tanner's momentum caused him to lose his grip and the weapon clattered to the floor.

Cole had been outside the vehicle observing. He bent down to retrieve the carbine and became furious. Dom's first thought was that Cole was angry about damage to the weapon. But the M1 Carbine was a tough piece of equipment. It had been developed as a shorter alternative to the standard M1 Garand rifle issued to most American infantrymen in World War Two. The carbine accompanied many U.S. paratroopers when they jumped into battle.

No, Cole was infuriated about something else. Tanner's carbine had been fully loaded. Cole realized this when he picked it up. Though the chances of accidental discharge were remote—this wasn't a bad movie—it was not impossible. A gunshot could've killed or injured one of the men. At the very least it would have drawn attention from people outside their building.

Dom remembered Cole's rant. It was epic. One line in particular stood out. "Goddammit T, I oughta knock you ass over applecart."

Tanner had sheepishly looked up at his brother and muttered, "Bitch, bitch, bitch." Both Jelciks then burst into laughter.

Dom remembered thinking, *ass over applecart?*

After another full scan of his surroundings Dom opened his door and moved quickly to the rear of the Santa Fe. He popped the liftgate and pulled upward. The door rose to its full height. Dom quickly moved back behind the steering wheel, again feeling self-conscious about the mask. He gripped the wheel with both hands. He forced himself to resume his scan, to keep his head moving.

It was difficult. He fought the urge to keep his eyes locked on their escape route. The configuration of the bank building was such that it resembled a lower case 't' from above. The top of the 't—technically known as the ascender—faced north, pointing at Durand Avenue. The main entrance was on the west side, on what amounted to the left point of the crossbar.

Dom had backed the Santa Fe toward the building so the front of the vehicle faced west. Steady traffic flowed on Durand off to his right. In front of him beyond a parking lot was a day spa. Dom knew that a Verizon cellphone store was on the other side of the spa. South Green Bay Avenue was just beyond. A narrow service road ran behind the spa and Verizon building before connecting to the larger road. Dom saw sporadic traffic on the service road but nothing that seemed out of the ordinary.

Cole dropped the key to the vault door on the floor. It would be in plain view of anyone that entered the corridor. He didn't care if the employees locked inside were quickly rescued. In fact he preferred it. The longer they were inside, the greater chance of something odd happening.

That manager didn't look particularly fit...he has a heart attack in there, we're looking at felony murder.

53

Cole hadn't planned to detain the employees in the vault—the Fireteam had not done this in any of their previous robberies—but something he saw in Knuckles's eyes spurred him to take the precaution. They generally left bank staff and any customers on the floor when they departed a building. Cole knew that standard policy in most financial institutions after a robbery was to immediately lock all doors on the off chance that the perpetrators tried to return. Once the brothers exited they were free of any physical threat from the bank's occupants.

The brothers left the heavy outer vault door open and moved to the front entrance.

"Ike and George outbound."

After making the call Cole turned to Tanner. "Remember, bags in the left hand."

He was referring to the method he preferred for moving from the building entrance to the vehicle. Cole knew that roughly 75% of banks used an IBNS, or Intelligent Banknote Neutralization System. The usual version involved hollowing out a stack of banknotes and imbedding explosive dye packs. When triggered the permanent dye marked the money, making it difficult or impossible to use. There were a myriad of variations to the system. Booby-trapped stacks kept at a teller's workstation were stored next to a magnetic plate in safe mode. Once handed to a bank robber they were activated.

In most cases the banks employed radio transmitters located near the doors that triggered a timer in the pack. After ten seconds—sometimes longer—the explosive detonates. The pack is ruptured and the dye—usually a blood-colored version known as Disperse Red 9—covers anything nearby. Some of the bills are destroyed by the explosion. The dye coats any bills in proximity as well as the perpetrators of the crime. Often tear gas, specially developed glue, or other agents are added to the loaded stacks.

Cole anticipated this. His tactic of singling out a responsible employee and demanding their driver's license was meant to stifle an overt act by a teller or manager. In most of their robberies they weren't able to access the vault and settled for the cash in the teller drawers. The tellers typically knew which stacks were loaded. Getting the person's license and threatening their family was a powerful motivator. The *last* thing a teller would want to see outside the bank's door was a red cloud.

The Carharrt bags were an important part of Cole's planning. They were selected for several reasons. The Duravax material was tough and tended to contain the explosion. Cole researched the explosives used in the stacks, made some educated guesses, and tested homemade versions on several bags. He blew apart nearly a dozen styles before settling on the Carharrt version. The Duravax fiber also helped contain the heat that the explosives generated. It was generally over 400 degrees and was included as a feature of the device to make it difficult for the criminals to handle their booty.

Once settling on the specific bag, Cole began to modify. He coated the inside of each bag with four coats of liquid rubber. This was purchased in aerosol form from any of several home improvement stores. When the spray dried it left a thick flexible barrier. Multiple coats made the bags more or less airtight. Now in addition to containing an explosion the bag was able to keep any dye or tear gas seepage to a manageable level until the team was able to dispose of it.

Cole thought four bags in a robbery was the best number. Two folded bags fit easily on each carabiner. The flexible handles made them easy to manage. They also had a significant capacity and held an enormous amount of cash when full. But—and this is key—even when their take from a robbery resulted in a lesser number of bills, the stacks were always divided as evenly as possible between the four bags. In this way any detonation would only ruin the cash inside that particular bag.

Cole pushed open the inner door. Tanner moved through it to the outer one. Despite having complete trust in Dom's ability to warn them of danger over the X-Talkers both brothers instinctively swept the parking lot. Seeing the open

55

Santa Fe liftgate ten feet away Tanner pushed open the outer door. Cole brushed past and strode directly to the vehicle with the Tommy Gun in his right hand, the barrel pointed toward the ground. Cole swung his left arm, tossing the Carhartts into the rear compartment. He quickly engaged the safety on his weapon and laid it on top of the bags.

Cole moved aside and hissed as Tanner approached. *"Remember...the SAFETY!"*

Tanner gave his brother a look that was somewhere between indignant and outraged before answering.

"No shit!"

He tossed in his two bags before fumbling with the safety of the carbine and adding it to the compartment's contents. Tanner slammed the gate closed and the Jelciks quickly returned to their positions inside the Santa Fe.

Cole commanded, "Go! Masks up!" He pushed the stop button on his watch and glanced down—4:22.

Dom already had the vehicle in gear. He wheeled the Santa Fe left in the direction of the service road that ran behind the property and provided access to South Green Bay Avenue. As Dom turned onto this side street he saw a larger SUV, a metallic blue Chevy Tahoe, heading toward them. All three members of the team watched as a woman wearing bug-eyed sunglasses passed by on their left. She held a ridiculously oversized cellphone to her face and paid them no attention whatsoever.

Tanner turned in the backseat and tracked the vehicle.

"Turning into the ATM lane...we're good."

Before turning back his eyes fell on the Carhartt bags in the rear compartment. He imagined them exploding in his face. He winced and turned back to the front in time to see Dom wheel right and enter the traffic stream on South Green Bay.

It was barely 3.5 miles from the Wells Fargo to their vehicle transfer point. Half the drive was due north on South Green Bay. Dom drove in a measured style, trying to avoid red lights where idle eyes from nearby stopped vehicles might notice something out of the ordinary. All three men were perspiring

56

despite the coolness of the day. Periodic calls came over the police scanner. There were no ten codes that raised their concern. When they reached Washington Avenue Dom signaled and made a right. The second half of their drive was uneventful. They reached West Avenue. Dom slid into the left turn lane, swung the Santa Fe north again and there, on the right, was their destination.

Mound Cemetery.

The stolen SUV entered the grounds of the cemetery and followed narrow roads to a section near the rear of the property. There they found their getaway vehicle, nice and safe.

It was a Chevy Silverado 5500HD pickup truck, the Crew Cab version that had four doors and a second row of seating. It had been specially modified to act as a burial vault carrier. It was royal blue and white. A two-thousand-pound vault rested squarely in the center of the truck's flatbed.

Dom pulled up behind the truck and all three men jumped out. Cole moved to the rear step of the truck and sprung onto the bed. He gripped the concrete lid and strained to pull it open. Either he or Tanner assumed this role after robberies. Dom did not quite possess the upper body strength to open the lid on his own—although he was working on this in the gym.

Tanner and Dom began to pass gear up to Cole. All three men watched their surroundings as they did so. There was one car a few hundred yards from their location in the cemetery but no people close enough to threaten them.

After the money and weapons were inside the vault Cole eased it shut. He had modified the unit, adding a clasp-style lock on one side. He engaged the lock before jumping down.

Four minutes later they were on Route 31, heading south. There was an excellent view of Lake Michigan on their left.

The Fireteam was on its way home.

CHAPTER EIGHT

Paul awoke with Lauren the morning after the gathering at McClary's when her alarm sounded at 4:30 a.m. He had not slept well. He tried to clear his mind several times but invariably the offer to assist Mike and Marge with the Tutor's Bourbon project swam into his head.

Lauren made her way to the shower. Paul spent a few more seconds in bed before forcing himself to roll out.

Get up and make your bride some breakfast you lazy so and so.

Paul entered the kitchen and started the coffee maker. He gathered the items necessary to make omelets. The Hulls had the entire kitchen remodeled after settling in the area and buying the ranch-style house. It was now outfitted with an upscale refrigerator and stove. These went nicely with Lauren's ice machine. Paul turned toward the island in the center of the kitchen and stared into Chappy's green eyes.

The cat was once again in forbidden territory. They had tried squirt guns, fly swatters, even a device that delivered a small static electric charge. Nothing deterred Chappy from perching wherever he damn well pleased.

"Not wasting any time today, huh Chappy?"

The cat's eyes narrowed. In that moment Paul felt kinship with the field mice beyond the trees that bordered their property.

The Hulls lived on the oddly named Polecat Road a few miles northeast of Troy, a town of 25,000 or so. Troy was located on Interstate 75, a major north-south artery. The Hull house wasn't secluded, not exactly, but the meandering tree-lined nature of Polecat Road gave them a degree of privacy.

Paul turned back to the stove and worked on the omelets. Minutes later Lauren slipped into the kitchen. She made for the coffee and scratched Chappy's head as she passed.

59

"You know you're just encouraging him, right?" Paul leaned against the counter sipping from his own mug, a look of mock disgust on his face.

"Maybe we should use reverse psychology on him. You know, pick him up when he's on the floor and put him on the counter...scratch his head when he's up there?" Lauren observed Chappy, who was still on the island.

Paul nearly spit out his coffee. "Oh yeah, that plan can't miss. What do you suggest about the cord chewing, buy him his very own?"

Lauren considered. "Hmmm, the plan could have holes...let me think about it."

Paul finished preparing the omelets and brought the plates to the island. Lauren took a bite and asked, "Did you use cheese in these?"

"No, sorry. Next time I—"

Lauren interrupted, "No, that's great, I'm...trying to cut back."

Paul's coffee mug stopped halfway to his face. He looked at her for a beat. "You're serious?"

"Yes. I'm...well, I haven't had a chance to exercise lately, so..."

Paul nodded. "All those crazy hours. The extra shifts. I get it, but you look great."

"Thanks Paul. But still..." She took another bite of her omelet and chewed. "There's supposed to be a new schedule coming to our department next month. Maybe that will help."

Paul's eyes went to the ceiling and he muttered, "Hallelujah to a sensible schedule." He looked back at his wife, "You really do look great."

Lauren smiled.

Paul tried to add levity. "For someone pushing 50."

Lauren flipped the piece of omelet that was on her fork. It hit Paul in the center of his forehead and stuck. For a second neither of them reacted. Then both burst out laughing.

Paul spoke, "I just qualified for my second Purple Heart."

"You had that coming, Master Sergeant." She was referring to Paul's last rank in the service. Lauren reached across the island and peeled the omelet segment from above Paul's eyes. She turned to Chappy.

"Might as well start the new plan right now. She dropped it in front of the cat. Chappy eyed it for a second, sniffed, and tentatively took a bite.

Paul watched, "Oh yeah, this can't miss."

After finishing breakfast Paul cleaned up, rinsing the plates and utensils before putting them in the dishwasher. He put the frying pan in the sink and ran some water in it, adding a squirt of dishwashing detergent to help loosen the residue.

Lauren slipped on a heavy jacket and grabbed her purse. She retrieved the key fob to her Jeep Grand Cherokee from a basket on the counter. As she approached Paul for a quick kiss goodbye she had a thought. They hadn't really discussed Mike McClary's offer last night on the way home. Lauren drove since Paul had two bourbons. Her husband seemed lost in his thoughts so she kept the sparse conversation on Henry Dowdell's decision to attend the University of Kentucky.

"So, any thoughts on Mike's offer?

Paul sat down his mug and stepped to her. "Well, I have to say I'm curious, maybe even intrigued. I'm going to think about it today. Maybe a nice ride on my bike, that always helps. Might check out this Obie Johnson guy on the computer."

Lauren was thrilled. "You're actually *intrigued?* Oh wow, that's a first!" Ever since Paul's medical retirement she had hoped he would find something. She'd actually prayed for it.

Paul leaned in and brushed her lips. Lauren responded with a longer kiss before hugging him tightly and burying her head in his chest. She turned toward the door to the garage, a wide smile on her face.

Paul, slightly confused, turned to retrieve his mug for a refill. Chappy was looking at him like Paul was a zoo animal.

The omelet was gone.

Paul changed into workout clothes and made his way to the basement. He was careful to close the door so Chappy couldn't follow. The feline had a habit of getting himself tangled with Paul during exercises on the various pieces of workout equipment. This posed a danger to the cat. It also annoyed Paul to no end.

The gym took up half of the basement. A wooden wall with large windows separated it from the other half, which was unfinished. Paul had outfitted the gym with a range of equipment and accessories that allowed for full body workouts. He spent thirty minutes on various pieces, concentrating on flexibility. He toweled off and returned to the main floor, again watching for the cat before closing the door.

Paul changed into biking shorts. The high temperature today was expected to be in the fifty-degree range. He should be fine with shorts but thought he'd need a couple layers on his upper body. He selected a skintight long-sleeve shirt made of moisture wicking material then pulled on a high visibility neon green hooded sweatshirt.

Glancing at the clock on Lauren's nightstand Paul saw that it was not yet 7 a.m. The sun would be up in a half hour or so.

Just enough time to clean up the bike from my last ride... maybe a little lube on the chain.

Paul pulled his bike from the storage rack in the garage and mounted it on a freestanding pole designed for just this purpose. By the time he had completed his tasks the sun was beginning to peek over the farm fields to the east. Paul filled a water bottle and donned a helmet. Before setting off he grabbed a pair of gloves.

My legs will be fine but my fingers will be right up front in the wind.

He turned left out of the drive and pedaled down Polecat before reaching an intersection. He debated for a second—Paul had favorite routes in both directions—before opting for a right turn. This allowed him to intersect with a bike path a few minutes later. Once on the path he no longer had to constantly check for traffic. He let his mind wander.

The path was the Great Miami River Trail, Miami being the name of the county in which the Hulls resided. The bike path in this direction led to Piqua, a town similar in size to Troy about fifteen miles to the north. Paul settled into a rhythmic pace and let his mind drift.

The offer from the McClarys had piqued his interest. They hadn't talked money. Paul wasn't too concerned with this, not really. He knew that his friend would probably be more than fair when it came to compensation. It was more about the nuts and bolts of the job. What the hell would Paul actually *do* to earn the money? He didn't really know that much about bourbon and sure as hell didn't know anything about liaising with possible customers—people who knew more about the product and the process than he did.

Paul pondered these points as he rode. After a time he reached for his water bottle. He was surprised to find that it was nearly empty. He'd been drinking from it automatically for miles. He realized he'd not only reached Piqua but had completed several loops around the path that encircled the town.

Oh man, talk about spacing out.

His odometer showed he'd ridden 16.8 miles.

Time to head home.

Paul showered then dressed in jeans and a sweatshirt. He made another cup of coffee and padded down the hall to the converted office that had once been a third bedroom. It usually became tricky at this point. Chappy was determined to get into the office. The forest of phone charger and computer cords that hung from the desk were like, well, catnip to Chappy. Paul fended off the thoroughly frustrated feline with a sock-covered foot. He opened the door and quickly stepped in before pushing it shut. Coffee splashed over the rim of his mug and spotted his sweatshirt.

Damn cat!

Paul fired up both the desktop and his MacBook. He settled in and pulled up email on the desktop. Not much there. He sipped his coffee and turned to the laptop. Paul typed in "Owen Bishop Johnson" and settled back.

Paul was mildly surprised to see that Johnson had a Wikipedia page. Scanning it he saw that Obie was, in fact, a native of Sawyer, Kentucky, which was located in the eastern part of the state. He was actually born in a hospital in Somerset 40 miles to the northwest. Paul noted the date of birth and calculated that Johnson would now be in his mid-seventies. He attended a country high school before enrolling at Western Kentucky University two-plus hours due west in Bowling Green. The Wikipedia page actually said that this distance was "as the crow flies."

Paul smiled imagining the rural nature of central Kentucky. *I'll bet more than one crow has actually flown the route.*

Paul continued to read. Johnson was part of what was known as Hilltopper Army ROTC while at WKU. He graduated with honors with a degree in Business Administration and Management. Upon leaving school he accepted a commission in the Army. Johnson spent four years in Army Intelligence, rising to the rank of captain.

Hmmm, captain in four years, not bad. Some of those guys in Intelligence aren't nearly as sharp as they think they are. This guy? Hmmm.

After leaving the army Johnson went to work with a real estate firm in Nashville. Eight years on he had started his own company, Sawyer Johnson Properties, LLC. The company was now a major player in the Nashville area as well as resort areas throughout the continental United States. A few years ago the name of the company changed to Sawyer Johnson Holdings, LLC to more accurately reflect the fact that the parent company had branched out to other endeavors.

Such as bourbon.

Paul sipped. The coffee was nearing room temperature and he'd had his fill. He looked down at the stain on his shirt, again thinking, *damn cat.*

64

There were a few lines about a distillery being built near Johnson's hometown a couple years earlier but very few specifics. Paul finished the Wikipedia page before backing out and looking at other results. Johnson wasn't exactly secretive, but there were significantly fewer online stories about him than one might expect.

He's definitely more low profile than Donald Trump ever was.

The most interesting mention Paul found before ending his search had to do with a car.

But not just any car.

It seemed that Obie had finished second in the bidding for the green 1968 Ford Mustang GT Fastback that actor Steve McQueen had driven in the movie *Bullitt*. The high bid was $3.4 million. With commissions and other fees the total price was $3.74 million.

Paul chuckled. His father loved that movie. For some reason the movie's epic car chase through the hills of downtown San Francisco captivated him.

Well, the guy can't be all bad.

Paul locked his fingers behind his head and leaned back in his chair.

Maybe it is time to get a fresh start. A man can only read so many books to keep busy. It would certainly make Lauren happy.

He eyed the clock and saw that it was after 9 a.m. Technically it would be into business hours for the McClarys, but they worked from their house. Paul grabbed his iPhone. He selected Mike's name from his favorites and dialed, expecting his friend to pick up or his voicemail to kick in.

He got neither.

"Hello?" It was Marge's voice.

Paul brought the phone down from his ear and checked the screen, wondering if he dialed the wrong number. He hadn't.

"Uh, hi Marge. I was calling for Mike. Is he driving?" Paul thought the couple might be in a vehicle together.

"Oh, hi Paul! No, Mike is twenty feet up on a ladder. I wouldn't let him take his phone up because, well, you know Mike. He would answer calls from up there."

Paul heard a male voice in the background shout "Would not!"

He grinned, shaking his head.

"OK, I have to ask. What—"

Marge cut in. "Perry jumped from the electric line to the spouting on the corner of the house. We were cleaning up from last night's fire and we saw it happen. One of the long gutter nails came loose and the whole thing is pulling from the house. Mike's up there fixing it. I'm holding the ladder."

"And my phone!" The male voice again.

Paul slowly shook his head. Marge was formidable in many ways, but she was petite. If the ladder tipped with Mike near the top his wife would have very little chance of forestalling a disaster.

Perry was a possum that lived in the South Park neighborhood. He often appeared on the wires above the houses at night when the McClarys were enjoying a fire. Paul had actually given Perry his name one night several months earlier when the possum appeared and did his high wire act. The name stuck.

"Forget about Mike, how's Perry?"

Marge laughed, repeated Paul's question for Mike's benefit, and said "All good. He scrambled up to a shingle then jumped back onto the wire."

"Attaboy Perry. Listen, I won't keep you. I just wanted to say that I'm interested in helping with the Tutor's Bourbon thing. Let me know when we can get together and talk about the details."

Marge's voice rose, "Wonderful Paul, just WONDERFUL!"

In the background the male voice called out "What, WHAT?"

CHAPTER NINE

The morning after the Racine robbery the team assembled in the office of Klean Sooner, the commercial cleaning company that Cole and Tanner started six years earlier. It was in an 80-year-old two-story brick building just east of downtown Columbus. It had been home to a thriving neighborhood hardware store in a previous life. In the two decades since the store closed the building had fallen into disrepair. In the last few years, buildings of similar ilk had found new life as microbreweries or trendy urban loft apartments. This resurgence had thus far eluded the block anchored by the Klean Sooner building.

That was just fine with the Jelciks. The worn exterior of the structure combined with the less-than-glamorous business it housed made it stunningly forgettable to passersby. One would be hard pressed to design a better front business for a bank robbery crew.

The Jelciks were originally from Oklahoma. There were plenty of things about their childhood that they disliked—or even resented—but they loved the state itself.

Well they loved the nickname anyway. In 1889 thousands were drawn to Oklahoma Indian Territory in hopes of claiming quarter-mile tracts of land. Those who jumped the gun and crossed the border early to make claims were dubbed "Sooners." The word was adopted as the nickname for University of Oklahoma sports teams in 1908. The term Sooner came to represent the can-do attitude of Oklahomans.

This had always appealed to the brothers. Their upbringing made it imperative that they adopt the Sooner spirit.

The Jelciks were born and raised in Bartlesville, a city of 35,000 people in the northeast corner of the state. It was 50 miles due north of Tulsa. It was also as far away from the cultural centers of the country—Los Angeles to the west and

New York to the east—as one could get when it came not only to distance but to being trendy.

Their father, Tom "Turk" Jelcik, was a factory worker and amateur taxidermist. He was a barrel chested man who liked to think his nickname derived from his air of mystery. In fact it was because his thin legs—legs he passed on to his sons—combined with his oversized upper body to make him look like a turkey.

The boys' mother, Tammy, was a hard-working woman who was completely dedicated to her family. This was something that set her apart from her husband. She was a dishwater blonde who didn't eat enough and worried about everything—her boys, Turk's fidelity, the electric bill, and the tornadoes that rolled through their corner of Oklahoma on a regular basis. She was named after 1960s and '70s country music star Tammy Wynette whose biggest hit was "Stand By Your Man". Tammy Jelcik seemed to take the song's title as a directive on how to live her life.

As events unfolded her sons would use black humor to joke that Tammy should've adhered to another of Wynette's hits, "D-I-V-O-R-C-E."

The brothers came to the building at 9:45 a.m. Both wore cream-colored long-sleeved button-down Klean Sooner shirts. They rode together in Cole's pickup truck from the small house they rented on Bruck Street in the city's Hungarian Village neighborhood. The house was just ten minutes from Klean Sooner. They unlocked and entered the office. Tanner walked to the small TV in the corner, thought about turning it on, and decided against it. He went to the coffee maker, grabbed the pot, and walked down the hall to the restroom to fill it from the sink. Cole strode to one of the two large wooden desks and flopped down. He punched the playback button on the flashing answering machine and grabbed a notepad.

There were three messages. By the time the last one finished playing Tanner had the coffee going. Two minutes later they saw Dom walk past the front picture window and turn into the doorway. He wore the same cream-colored shirt as the Jelciks. His hands were full.

Tanner pulled it open and Dom entered.

"Greetings gents. I bring breakfast!" Dom walked to the second desk and sat down a rectangular box and a cardboard carrier with three large coffees. The cups and box all featured the logo of Buckeye Donuts.

Cole rose from his seat. "Donuts? Dammit Dom, don't you know this stuff is poison to physical specimens like us? Gimme!" He selected a maple long john and bit off nearly a third of it.

Tanner walked over and eyed the selection. He chose a round chocolate covered donut with the center hole stuffed with peanut butter.

Dom pulled the lid from his coffee and tore open a sugar packet. "That's their specialty, the original Buckeye donut."

Tanner snorted. "Buckeye Donut, Buckeye Laundromat, Buckeye Carwash... the word Buckeye's in front of half the businesses in this town. There's probably a goddammed Buckeye Massage Parlor."

"I just drove past it. Called for an appointment. They have an opening at noon."

Tanner eyed the smaller man. "Are you—"

Cole snickered.

Tanner turned to his brother then back to Dom. "Santo, you're a smartass."

The men spent twenty minutes reviewing the Racine job. The drive back to Ohio had been uneventful. They stopped once outside of Indianapolis at an upscale convenience store called Leo's for fuel and food. The Silverado burial vault truck held a whopping 65 gallons of diesel fuel and the team had plenty on board to make it home if they'd decided to keep moving. But Cole thought they were in no immediate danger and okayed Tanner's request for a pit stop. They used the restroom—alternating so someone was with the truck at all times—and bought roast chicken and energy drinks to get them through the final leg of the drive.

Once back in Columbus they entered Klean Sooner through the rear overhead door. They didn't touch the burial vault but spent several minutes cleaning up the cab. The men had taken off their Eisenhower jackets when they left the cemetery and slipped on pullovers and sweatshirts. They made sure the jackets were removed now as well as any food wrappers or travel jetsam that would be a tip-off about their trip.

After retrieving their cellphones from the office desks they locked up and headed home. The Jelciks to the Hungarian Village section due south of downtown and Santo to his apartment on High Street on the north side, a mile or so beyond The Ohio State University's campus. All three men were asleep before midnight and, with no time clocks to worry about punching, slept late before rendezvousing in the morning.

"Let me ask you a question." Dom topped off his coffee from the pot Tanner made and turned to Cole. "Why lock those people in the bank vault? Why not lay them out on the floor like you usually do?"

Cole nodded, "Fair question...I don't know. I just had a feeling about that Knuckles guy, the manager. He was cooperating. Tossing some stacks on the floor that might've been loaded. But something about the way he looked at me after topping off the bags...let's just say I didn't want to have to shoot him."

Dom smiled, "Or have Tanner shoot him."

The words had barely left his mouth and Dom knew it was a mistake.

Tanner reddened and jumped to his feet. "Shut your damn mouth Santo! I should kick your scrawny ass right here! Maybe take your share!"

"Sit the hell down!" Cole stood and put a hand to his brother's chest. "Ain't nobody takin' nobody's share." Cole guided Tanner back toward the desk he'd been sitting on before turning to Dom and wilting him with an angry glare.

70

Dom shrunk back. "Sorry guys. Just kidding. Bad joke... sorry." He looked from Cole to Tanner then back again. "I don't know why I even asked about the people in the vault. I trust both you guys. Tanner, you're a freakin' soldier on these jobs and Cole, you're...you're a damn walking lie detector. You say the man was hinky, he was hinky." He paused for a second then added, "Knuckles, what the hell kind of name is that anyway?"

Cole chuckled. Tanner didn't, but the corners of his mouth edged up in a smile.

Dom exhaled, thinking to himself, *You DUMBASS...when are you going to learn not to screw with Tanner? Tanner doesn't play.*

Cole and Tanner topped off their coffees as well. After locking the front door the trio trooped down the hallway, past the restroom, and into the converted work bay. The Silverado was in the center. It was flanked on each side by well-worn panel vans that prominently featured the Klean Sooner logo.

All three men carried keychains. A few of their regular clients entrusted them with keys necessary to access their buildings after hours. Each member of the Fireteam had a key to the burial vault on their keychain as well as an ignition key for the truck. Tanner climbed onto the bed of the Silverado and used his key to open the lock. He strained to lift the lid and peered inside.

Cole spoke, "No sign of dye, right? I didn't notice anything when we pulled in last night."

"No dye." Tanner sniffed. "No tear gas. Hot damn! Boys, I think we have four clean bags!" He reached into the vault and began to hand the Carhartts down to his partners.

Dom was excited. "Wanna guess the total take? We all throw in a hundred dollars? Closest to the total wins?"

Tanner jumped down. "I'm in. What was our biggest job? Two-fifty? Two-sixty?"

"Two-sixty-two-five." Cole was helping Dom arrange folding chairs around a small wooden table in the corner of the work

71

bay. Cleaning supplies and equipment were stacked nearby haphazardly. A weight bench and rack stacked with steel plates occupied much of the area. This corner of the building was not visible from any window.

Dom added, "That was a helluva day."

The team had pulled off eight robberies before the big hit in Clayton, Missouri, a suburb of St. Louis. All eight were accomplished with the same method. The office workers were herded to the lobby by Tanner while Cole took charge of the customers and tellers. The older brother would hone in on a teller and demand his or her driver's license. Money from the teller drawers was divided between their four bags.

In the Clayton job Cole noticed that the outer vault door was open. He called an audible, so to speak, and improvised. The result was glorious. They made off with over a quarter of a million dollars, most of which had just been delivered to the bank by a Brinks truck coming from a downtown St. Louis casino. After that, vaults became the team's primary goal. Racine was just the third time it had panned out.

Tanner joined his partners. Before sitting he pulled a can of Copenhagen snuff from a back pocket. He held it in his right hand configuring his grip just so and jerked his forearm up and down. The motion caused his middle finger to strike the can's hard top creating a series of slapping sounds. This "packed" the tobacco inside. Tanner opened the can, reached inside, and pushed a generous pinch between his lower cheek and gum.

He looked at Cole. "Dip?"

Cole held up a hand and Tanner flipped him the can.

Before abandoning his family Turk Jelcik taught his sons three things: how to hold a grudge, how to play poker, and how to dip tobacco.

Cole took a pinch and tossed the can back. Neither brother offered the can to Dom. They knew there was no point.

Dom crossed his arms and cocked his head. He eyed the four bags on the table. "I'll say $100,000. There can't be as many big bills in there as we took in Clayton. A hundred-K would still be a sweet take."

Tanner guessed next. "I'll say $121,233."

Dom laughed. "Can you be more specific?"

"Watch and learn, goombah, watch and learn." Tanner often used Italian-American slang when speaking to Dom, who maintained that his father's side of the family had roots in Sicily.

Both men turned to Cole. Dom prodded, "What's your guess boss-man?"

Cole reached for one of the Carhartts and hefted it. "I'll go with 110-K."

Each man took a bag and began to count. Cole added the totals using a calculator app on his cellphone. He then emptied the contents of the fourth bag onto the table and the trio counted it together. The final number was $111,250.

"Damn boss, you missed it by less than two grand. That is impressive." Dom gave Cole a mocking two-handed bow before pulling out his wallet and handing over a $100 bill.

Tanner's wallet was also out. He too fished out a $100 bill— the men always walked around with plenty of cash—and handed it to his brother.

Dom snickered, "Wow, you just came into two hundred dollars of cold, hard cash. What'll you do with all that money?" He raised a leg and let his work boot come to rest on the pile of bills on the table as if using a footstool.

All three men roared.

They flipped through every stack looking for hidden devices of any kind. The self-sealing paper bill straps were left on, making the money easier to organize. Every denomination from $1 to $100 was represented. After assuring that the currency showed no signs of dye Cole counted out three stacks, each consisting of bills that showed considerable use. All three stacks contained $2,750. He slid one to each of his partners. "Be smart, you know the rules. Don't do anything to attract attention."

Cole worried about another huge potential problem with the cash. In addition to loading the stacks with dye and explosives, financial institutions often "baited" some of them by recording the serial numbers. The bills could leave a trail that might be traced by law enforcement.

Closing his eyes Cole did a quick calculation. He separated another $4,000 from the stacks of larger bills and slid it toward Dom. "That's seed money for scouting the next job."

Dom accepted the cash then asked, "So the rest is going to the storage unit?"

Cole nodded. "The backpacks. Just like we agreed. I'll take it over this afternoon." He hesitated then looked each partner in the eye. "You trust me right?"

Dom nodded, "Absolutely."

Tanner grinned, "Well, I know you don't want me to kick your ass so, yeah, I think you'll do the right thing."

Cole gave his brother a look that said *in your dreams* then stood.

"Okay boys, time to get back to our day job. We have an ozone job in Dublin tomorrow so get one of the vans ready. Use number one for that. And it's month-end. That means the parking garage treatments start back up next week. Get number two outfitted for that so it'll be ready to go Monday."

Both Tanner and Dom groaned at the mention of the parking garages.

"Things were a thousand times more sanitary in the restrooms at LCI after bean soup day in the cafeteria. I hate the parking garage jobs."

Tanner was more concise, "The goddammed parking garage jobs suck."

CHAPTER TEN

It was a crisp day in Ohio. The cloudless blue sky provided a sapphire backdrop to downtown Columbus. The official first day of spring occurred ten days earlier but winter hung on, an unwelcome houseguest in the Buckeye state. Today would see temperatures above sixty degrees for the first time this calendar year.

Cole pulled his Ford F-150 out of the small parking lot at Klean Sooner. Three of the Carhartt bags sat on the floor of the passenger side. Each held $33,000. He drove south for a few blocks before coming to a red light at Broad Street. Cole flipped on his left turn signal and punched up channel 62, Outlaw Country, on SiriusXM radio.

Cole loved his truck. It was the King Ranch version. It had four-wheel drive and had a rear seat, full leather interior, and a number of luxury features. His brother owned the exact same truck, right down to the color, Rapid Red Metallic. There were half a dozen Ford dealers inside the I-270 beltway surrounding Columbus. The Jelciks contacted all six and started a bit of a bidding war when they made it known they would be buying two of the trucks. They ordered them together from a dealer on the north side of the city and even though they paid nearly $75,000 each, got a good deal.

The purchase was made through Klean Sooner as a business expense. Cream-colored custom decals were affixed to both sides of each F-150. Cole had removed them today from his truck before leaving the office. The storage unit was rented using a fake ID. He didn't want his business or his real name connected to it in any way.

Cole smiled remembering the first time Dom caught sight of the trucks. "How the hell are you gonna tell them apart?"

Tanner tipped his head and pointed to the rear windows.

Dom looked and shook his head. "For Christ's sake, you've *got* to be kidding me."

Tanner's truck sported a six-inch sticker of a Silverback Gorilla. When Dom turned to Cole's truck he knew what to expect...a Grizzly Bear sticker.

The brothers had a long-running debate over who would win in a fight, a Silverback Gorilla or a Grizzly Bear. Tanner was on Team Silverback; Cole, Team Grizz. Neither brother remembers exactly when the discussion began but both agreed that by high school it had spread to their football teammates. The sides were evenly split. Cole moved on to play at Southeastern Oklahoma State University and carried the debate with him. In the lone year that he attended the school the Gorilla-Grizzly argument threatened to split that team as well.

The summer before Cole's senior year at Bartlesville high school—Tanner would be a sophomore—they worked for a farmer, baling hay. They spent a good chunk of their earnings at a tattoo parlor downtown. Their body art was unveiled during the football team's first two-a-day practice. The incoming freshmen expected to see the Bartlesville Bruins logo, which resembled that of the UCLA Bruins in color and design. Players from the upper three classes, however, were not surprised by what they saw.

Cole's Grizzly was on his right rear shoulder, somewhat low on his enormous deltoid muscle. Tanner's Silverback was on his equally large left shoulder, slightly higher on the deltoid. Both creatures were in fighting positions, facing outward. Due to their difference in height, when the Jelciks stood next to each other the relative positions of the tattoos made them look like they were squaring off against each other.

Their teammates loved it. Turk was not pleased, believing both sons had pissed away an entire summer's wages. Tammy thought the artwork was wonderful. The tattoo shop went out of business the following year.

On the occasions that the men showed people the tattoos Cole always stood on the left—calling his brother his "right-hand man"—and he and Tanner would lean into each other.

Then, of course, flex.

Billy Joe Shaver's "Old Chunk of Coal" came up on Outlaw and Cole bounced his head to the twanging guitar flowing from the truck's speakers. He turned it up.

What a truck! What a day!

Cole made the turn onto Broad. He stopped a block later behind a Honda Civic and smiled. When researching trucks on the internet he found an article on the J.D. Power website that said the Ford F-150 was the most popular vehicle sold in his native Oklahoma. This did not surprise him. He'd spent nearly 25 years there. It only took an hour or so on the roads of the Sooner state to come to the same conclusion. The F-150 had a cowboy vibe, which was important in Oklahoma.

Cole remembered the article mentioned that the Honda Civic was Ohio's most popular vehicle.

Sounds about right. His smile broadened.

Eastbound now on Broad, Cole could see downtown Columbus in his rearview. The population of the city was pushing a million.

I reckon it's OVER a million on any Saturday Ohio State has a home game.

Most Americans thought of Buckeye football when Columbus was mentioned. But the city had an NHL hockey franchise and a champion professional soccer team. Cole had come to learn that it was a growing metropolitan area with good schools and a strong economic base. It had a reputation as a clean city.

Well, people that think that might want to come with us when we do the parking garages.

The F-150 approached Drexel and Cole made a right turn. The downtown area of Ohio's capital city floated out of his mirrors. Cole watched it go.

That's a big-city skyline...damn near, anyway.

He was on Drexel for less than a mile when it T'd into Main Street. He caught a red light and waited with his left blinker on. A song with an unhurried guitar background and melancholy vocals came up on the radio. Cole glanced at the display and saw that it was "T-Model Blues" by Lightnin' Hopkins. He turned it down.

Mood music. Good for playin' in the background.

The change in music caused him to mentally shift gears. He thought back to the early years in Oklahoma. The Jelciks lived in a wood-framed house on the outskirts of Bartlesville. It had been part of a farm at one time. The town grew to the point that it almost reached the property and the owner sold the land to developers. When the economy took a downturn in the 1970s the developer put his plans on hold—they never came to pass—and the land turned to scrub. The house was rented out for most of two decades until the last tenants, Turk and Tammy Jelcik, scraped together a down payment and bought the place.

Cole Thomas was born just before his parents made the purchase. Tanner Lynn came along two years later. Turk worked as a welder in a local factory and Tammy stayed home, trying to keep up with the boys. When Turk's hours were cut back at work he started an informal taxidermy business, mounting whitetail deer and the occasional trophy bass for friends in a shabby out-building behind the house.

Tammy took an hourly job cleaning offices at night to make ends meet. She often dragged the boys along. It was during this time that Turk's interest in being a family man waned. The boys didn't immediately realize it. Tammy did. Turk disappeared after dinner most nights, saying he had to meet a customer about a possible taxidermy job. There seemed to be fewer and fewer actual projects and significantly more meetings.

Tammy got the cleaning jobs through a man named Cyrus Borgia. He was a go-getter who owned a dry cleaning business and had no qualms about working around the clock. Borgia hired housewives to tidy up offices after hours. He paid them

78

fairly, keeping a small profit. In his own way Borgia was one of the first socially conscious employers in Oklahoma.

But Cole felt the sting of embarrassment every time he saw his mother wipe out an ash tray with a damp cloth after first dumping its contents in a waste basket. After smoking was banned in businesses his mother no longer had to perform this task. No matter, there were plenty of other aspects of the job that hinted of shame to a young boy.

The Jelcik sons noticed an uptick in arguments between their parents. They spent as much time away from home as possible, often getting in trouble. They threw rocks through windows, stole bicycles, and helped themselves to the contents of mailboxes, looking for anything of value.

The boys often dodged brushes with the law and may have gone over the edge if not for one thing: football.

Both boys were standout players, particularly on defense. They got by, initially at least, on brute strength. Their upper bodies were man-like at an early age. Youth coaches would put the brothers on the edge of the defensive line and turn them loose. They terrorized opposing quarterbacks and ball carriers.

They loved it.

They had to tone down their path to delinquency to keep playing football. Outwardly they did this. The boys, however, simply learned to backburner their predilection for breaking laws.

By Cole's senior year he was one of the top defensive players in the state. He dreamed of playing for the Oklahoma Sooners down in Norman. Division 1 major college recruiters looked at him as a "tweener." That is, his overdeveloped upper body and slender legs did not quite fit the physical requirements of either a defensive lineman or a linebacker. But Division 2 Southeast Oklahoma State University took a chance and offered a partial scholarship.

No one in Cole's entire family history had ever spent a day of their life in college. Tammy helped Cole wade through the admissions paperwork and loan applications and Cole showed up in Durant—a couple hundred miles south of Bartlesville—

on time. He more than held his own as a freshman on the football field as well as in the classroom. The strength program, though not on the level of the Ohio States of the world, was sophisticated enough to turn Cole into a player that could, in a couple years, be on the radar of NFL teams.

And then Tammy got sick.

It was pancreatic cancer, an evil bitch of an affliction. Cole returned home.

Turk left.

Cole realized he was doing nearly ten miles per hour over the speed limit. He had a vice grip on the steering wheel.

For Christ's sake! He glanced at the Carhartt bags on the passenger floor. *Nearly $100,000 in stolen cash and I'm speeding. DUMBASS!*

He braked gently and checked his mirrors. No cops. He was less than a mile from his destination.

Once Turk ran off, Cole and Tanner were left to care for Tammy. There was a smattering of help from extended family. Bills piled up. Tammy made it less than three months before passing.

The bank took the house. Turk never came back.

The Jelcik boys never forgave either of them.

Cole saw the storage facility ahead. He pulled into the drive and eased toward the security gate. A van was in front of him waiting for the gate to open. The usual procedure was to pull up to a keypad, punch in your code, and enter when the gate opened. It closed automatically. Because the van was in front of him Cole decided to wait for the gate to close completely rather than try to rush through. He didn't want to draw any undue attention.

As he waited Cole looked to the sky. He'd selected this storage unit because of its location. It was on the east side of the city, relatively close to John Glenn International Airport. It was to be a safe place to stash their "bolt bags," backpacks loaded with debit cards, fake IDs and other items that he and his team would grab before running from the law if it became necessary. It wasn't the team's only hidey-hole for stolen bills. Cole also rented a safe deposit box in a downtown bank.

From his position near the gate Cole could see a plane on final approach to the airport. He turned back to watch the van pull through the gate and sensed more movement overhead. Looking to the east he saw a formation of birds moving together in a choreographed manner. There appeared to be thousands of them. They flowed through the air as if they were one great liquid being. They formed a cloud that changed its shape, size, and direction every few seconds.

It was a murmuration. Cole knew this because Tanner was fascinated with the phenomena. Cole had checked it out online, telling Tanner "They're starlings. Scientists think they do it to confuse predators like hawks from attacking the group...happens mainly in the fall and winter, almost never after March."

Cole watched the swarm assume new shapes and move away. *I can see why Tanner likes those things.* Cole remembered it was nearly April. *That might be the last one we see all year. Have to remember to tell him.*

The gate closed behind the van and Cole eased the pickup to the keypad. A minute later he was inside the fence. The storage business consisted of a series of rectangular buildings with lime green steel overhead doors. He found the correct unit and angled the truck near the door to make it difficult for anyone to see what he took inside. Cole used a key to open the heavy-duty circular lock. He pulled up the door and nonchalantly checked his surroundings.

All good, nice.

Cole quickly opened the passenger door to the pickup. He snatched all three Carhartt bags, closed the door, and entered the unit. It was ten feet wide and thirty feet deep, one of the larger sizes the business offered. He tossed the Carhartts inside and pulled the overhead door shut. Cole had rigged the interior with battery-operated lights that operated by motion

81

detector. They snapped on revealing a seemingly random collection of boxes and freestanding shelves. The boxes displayed an unrelated collection of labels. The shelving was cluttered with miscellaneous items.

There were three folding lawn chairs leaning against one of the shelves. Cole grabbed one and opened it before situating it in an open spot near one of the lights. He then moved a stack of boxes and waded toward the rear corner of the unit. A black steel 55-gallon drum was there. Its top was open, exposing a hodgepodge of various lengths of angled steel. Cole examined the pieces for a few seconds before reaching in. He grabbed two of them and lifted. The entire collection of steel rose up revealing a false bottom.

Cole reached in and came up with three black nylon backpacks. He made his way back to the chair and slid the Carhartts toward it with his feet. He opened all the bags and began to transfer cash to the backpacks in equal amounts. He knew each nylon backpack already held $7,500 in Visa prepaid debit cards. By adding the cash to each one they would contain $40,500.

The modified drum was Cole's idea. Three months earlier Klean Sooner had been called in to do fire damage clean up in a factory near the Anheuser-Busch plant on the north side of the city. Cole supervised the work, which was done at night. He noticed a second shift factory employee operating welding equipment and had a brainstorm. He approached the man and waited for him to finish welding together two halves of a metal frame.

"TIG welding, huh? Is that the style you always use here?" Cole had picked up just enough lingo from Turk to make it look like he knew what he was talking about.

The man, apparently happy to answer someone that had an interest in his work, answered, "TIG, MIG, Stick...I can even do Plasma Arc." He smiled proudly.

Cole looked impressed and nodded. He put a thoughtful look on his face and rubbed his chin. "Y'know, I've been looking for someone to do a little project for my company.

Probably too small a job for someone like you...but I'd pay cash."

The man brightened and asked for details. Cole laid it out for him and waited.

"Hell, I could knock that out in fifteen minutes. You'd bring the materials, right. I mean, I couldn't give you anything from here." The man glanced around, aware that there was a company policy against this sort of thing.

"Oh absolutely. I'd bring the stuff in...would pay you a hundred bucks. We're finishing the cleanup tomorrow night. That work for you?"

The man eyed Cole. *A hundred bucks is a hundred bucks... but a hundred untaxed bucks that the old lady doesn't know about...*

His smile widened.

The next night Cole arrived with an empty steel drum in the van. It had held the brand of floor stripper Klean Sooner used to remove floor wax from high gloss floors. Cole pried the lid loose before loading the drum into the van. He stopped at a Home Depot and bought several six-foot sections of angled steel.

At the factory Cole dragged the drum to the welder's workstation. He didn't say as much to the welder, but he directed the man to make a container with a false bottom. He had him use the cutting torch to reduce the steel to a pile of pieces ranging in size from six inches to a foot in length. He then directed the lid's outer lip to be cut away. This done, Cole selected two of the smaller lengths of steel pieces and had them welded in upright positions on the top of the lid, a foot apart. Finally he had the worker attach four 2-inch sections of the angled steel to the inside of the drum. They were equally spaced along the inside circumference, twelve inches from the top rim.

Cole was pleased. He would eventually stack a few rows of bricks in the bottom of the drum. The lid would no longer catch on the top rim. It could be lowered—using the upright pieces of steel as handles—into the drum until it came to rest a foot below on the 2-inch pieces that acted as supporting brackets. The pile of cut steel went on top of the lid in such a way that the matching handles were camouflaged. With the right amount of weight at the bottom and a proper arrangement of angled pieces at the top it looked and felt like a full drum of scrap metal.

The entire center section was open, allowing for the Fireteam's loaded bolt bags.

After adding the cash to the backpacks Cole lowered them back into the drum. The bags were nearly full. Cole lifted the lid back onto the brackets then spent a minute arranging the steel on top to hide the handles.

He nodded, smiling to himself. *Amazing how much an old drum of scrap is worth these days.*

Cole folded the chair and returned it to its place with the others. He tucked the empty Carhartt bags under an arm and pulled up the door before ducking through. It rattled down on its tracks when he closed it. After reattaching the lock—and checking it three times—Cole was back in the truck. The F-150 cruised back to the entrance. Cole punched in the code and waited as the gate opened in a series of fits and jerks.

A fine day. A damn fine day.

He looked again to the sky and saw no trace of the starlings. Cole brought up Outlaw and heard the heavy blues-rock groove of the guitar on Johnny Cash's version of *The Devil's Right Hand*. The driving riff sounded unlike anything else Cash ever recorded. It was a song about a man with a gun that was unable to control destructive urges.

As Cole left the storage lot he thought of Tanner.

His expression changed, the smile fading just a bit.

CHAPTER ELEVEN

"It was definitely them?"

A feminine voice answered, "It was them."

"We're sure?"

"One hundred percent. We're sure. They had the jackets, the Tommy Gun, the comms...No doubt about it."

"Shit. Anybody get hurt? Any shots fired?"

"No and no."

"What was the take?"

"A little over a hundred ten thousand."

Tyson Foxx let out a low whistle. "Damn, they get into the vault?"

Special Agent Rita Kekich nodded. "They got into the vault."

They were walking quickly down a polished hall of the FBI Chicago field office west of downtown. It was a three building, 800,000-square foot complex.

Tyson, a youthful-looking 45-year-old with a runner's physique was struggling to tie his necktie as they walked. He was supposed to be on vacation and scrambled to the office when he got the call. "How is the video quality? I assume we got video?"

"We got video. I got a quick look but tech has it now."

Kekich was 32. A native of Colorado, she'd spent six years in the Honolulu field office. This was her first time on a major task force and Foxx had taken her under his wing. She was a former college golfer, which served her well in an environment that was still male-dominated despite the best efforts of decades of politicians. She was a redhead with freckles and looked a bit like the actress Amy Adams in *Trouble With The Curve*.

They reached the door to the conference room and Foxx paused to put the finishing touches on the tie. "Everybody here?"

"Everybody's here."

"You're starting to sound like a parrot, Kekich. Lighten up."

She stared at him for a beat.

"Your tie's crooked."

Kekich opened the door and they went in.

Bank robbery had been a priority of the FBI pretty much since its inception. In the 1930s criminals such as John Dillinger robbed scores of banks, capturing the attention of the public. In 1934 it became a federal crime to rob any national bank or state institution that was part of the Federal Reserve System. Jurisdiction was delegated to the FBI.

The Bureau utilized advancements in technology and investigative techniques to apprehend perpetrators and deter further robberies in every decade since. After the deadly attacks on American soil on September 11, 2001 the FBI shifted a significant part of its focus to combat terrorism. Still, the number of bank robberies in the United States fell from more than 7,000 per year in 2001 to fewer than 2,000 twenty years later.

A number of FBI agents looked at bank robbery as a personal affront. Tyson Foxx was one of them. He attended La Verne University, an NCAA Division III school in the San Gabriel Valley area east of Los Angeles where he ran cross country. After graduating he attended Stanford Law, earning a number of honors and attracting interest from many of the most successful firms on the West Coast.

Foxx spurned all of these offers and instead pursued a position with the FBI. Eager for new challenges, he happily accepted a posting in Springfield, Illinois after excelling at the Bureau's training program in Quantico, Virginia.

In Springfield he played a significant role in the investigation and arrest of Ali Saleh Kahlah al-Marri, who pled guilty in 2009 to providing material support to Al Qaeda.

Foxx was promoted and accepted a transfer to one of the largest field offices in the country, Atlanta. While there he continued to gain experience and earn accolades. He was part of three kidnapping cases—all successfully resolved—and was a key component of the Violent Gang Task Force. In addition, Foxx played a major role in an Atlanta-based investigation that revealed that hackers could steal data from cellphones that used public charging stations.

Foxx had done it all. Many in the Bureau believed he was on track for a senior position. He had worked in a smaller office and a large urban area, investigated a variety of crimes, and been part of task forces. He'd been successful in almost every endeavor. He now ran the Violent Crimes Task Force concentrating on bank robbery, having transferred to Chicago after receiving another promotion. His sights were now firmly focused on the Fireteam.

Foxx and Kekich entered the room. It was early Thursday, the day after the Racine robbery. Seven agents were already in the room. A few were sitting around the large conference table texting or talking on their phones. Two were at the corner coffee bar doctoring cups. A female agent stood in front of a large video monitor. She was pointing a device at the screen. Foxx glanced at it and saw it was divided into six segments. Two showed empty chairs, the other four were filled by faces in front of different backgrounds.

"Alright people, sorry for the delay. I was on the way to Wrigleyville with my wife...we just dropped the kids at school...had tickets to Cubs opening day. I guess the 'Fireteam' had other plans for me."

Foxx used a hint of sarcasm when he spoke the word. He was not particularly pleased that the Bureau had given this team of potentially violent bank robbers such a flattering nickname. The FBI had a long history of referring to offenders with made up names. The Bandaged Bandit, the Mummy Marauder, the Shoebox Suspect, these were all names assigned to perpetrators in the last few years. Some agents thought these catchy names generated publicity that helped in their capture.

87

Foxx didn't buy it, at least not in this case. Fireteam is a distinctly military term. Foxx thought it was a slap in the face to those who took part in combat for their country. But he wasn't consulted before the name was floated to the media so he'd decided to grin and bear it.

Everyone found seats. As they did, the two empty chairs on the screen were filled as well. Foxx surmised that the remote stragglers were listening to the audio feed coming from the room in Chicago through Bluetooth devices and scrambled to their stations when they heard his voice.

"First things first. Give me any and all reasons that the robbery in Racine *wasn't* done by the gang we've been targeting." Several sets of eyes looked at him blankly. A few in the room looked at legal pads on the table in front of them.

A voice tentatively spoke from the lower right corner of the video screen.

"Well, as I understand it, they herded the Wells Fargo employees into the vault and locked them in before leaving. I believe that's a different tactic than we've seen in the past, right?" This came from a detective in the Des Moines police department.

All eyes went to Foxx, as if waiting for him to give the statement—and the detective who uttered it—credence. It was at this point in meetings that subordinates could be chopped down at the knees.

That was not Foxx's way.

"People? Give me your thoughts. You've had some time for analysis while I was playing bus driver." He smiled and held his hands wide.

One of the coffee drinkers spoke. "Well sir, I just came from tech. They've completed the initial enhancement of the video. It's pretty clear. The point man has a Thompson. No doubt. A hundred percent. How many of *those* have we seen?"

A voice piped up across the table, "Exactly zero since what, the 1950s?"

The coffee drinker continued. "And the tail gunner had a carbine that matches the weapon in previous robberies to a T. The Eisenhower jackets are the same color. And the—"

"What about the bags?" This from a woman at the top center of the video screen. Foxx recognized her as a detective with the Terre Haute, Indiana PD.

"We got an excellent angle on the tail gunner's bags from one camera when he led the manager from his office. When it was frozen and our folks tweaked the resolution it was pretty clear that they were Carhartt tool bags. Either fourteen or sixteen inch. It all matches."

Rita Kekich tentatively added to the discussion. "Well, all of these details have been made available to the public in one way or another. Newspaper reports have talked about the weapons and the jackets—the World War Two aspects of the cases—and anyone can go on *fbi.gov* and watch video from a couple of the robberies. Theoretically the Racine robbery could be a copycat."

A senior agent in the rear looked doubtful, on the verge of condescending. Another piped up, "And this copycat team just *happened* to come up with the same old school weapons?"

Conversation broke out among the agents in the room. The faces on the video screen—all belonging to task force members who were police detectives from jurisdictions that were victimized by the robbery team—joined in, adding to the clamor.

Foxx allowed this to go on for a minute. He cocked his head and looked at Kekich, raising his eyebrows as if to say *you really got them going*. As the conversations began to spin down Foxx lifted his right hand and raised his index finger. Gradually the room quieted as the occupants and those watching remotely noticed.

"One question. We all know there is one thing the Fireteam does that definitely has *not* been released to the public. No copycat gang would know about it. So if it happened in Racine, it has to be our gang."

At least six voices spoke, nearly in unison.

"It happened."

CHAPTER TWELVE

On Friday morning, the second day after the Wells Fargo robbery in Racine, Foxx sat in the passenger seat of a government-owned dark blue Chevy Suburban. He was working on a laptop, piecing together a series of questions he would ask the bank's employees at the interviews they would soon be conducting. Every few minutes he would pick up his iPhone to make or answer a call.

Kekich drove. They decided the day before to meet at the FBI complex and depart from there. Their route to Racine was circuitous. They drove several miles west to the I-294 Beltway and followed it north for a half hour before linking up with I-94 for the remainder of the trip up through Wisconsin.

The more direct path would've taken them east into the city to the Kennedy Expressway—the 18-mile-long stretch of highway that cut through the heart of Chicago—where they would hop on the northbound lanes and make their way up I-94. This route would have taken them in the vicinity of Wrigley Field, the Chicago Cubs ballpark.

The Cubs would be hosting the San Francisco Giants later today in the second game of the season after winning in a rout the day before. Traffic in the area wouldn't be quite as bad today but it would still be daunting. The agents did not want to take a chance of being jammed up on their way to Racine. Wells Fargo had agreed to keep their Durand Avenue branch closed until the following Monday to allow the FBI and Racine detectives to thoroughly examine the site and interview employees. Foxx did not want to keep them waiting.

Kekich noticed that her boss was not his usual upbeat self this morning. He generally greeted her each morning with an "Aloha" as an homage to her years spent in the Honolulu field office. Today he seemed preoccupied. When she came to his eighth floor office to see if he was ready to leave he simply nodded at her before turning back to his view of the Chicago skyline.

"Okay, I can understand not getting a shaka sign from you today...but no 'Aloha?'" The shaka sign was the extended thumb and pinky finger hand gesture used by Hawaiians to say "Hang Loose." Natives also used it as a way of saying "things are great."

Foxx gave her a brief smile before gathering his computer and other materials. "Sorry. Aloha Agent Kekich." He remained lost in thought on the elevator.

Several makes and models of vehicles were available in the motor pool. Contrary to public perception the FBI wasn't limited to indistinctive sedans and Suburbans with tinted windows. But Foxx explained to Kekich that a Suburban with tinted windows is exactly what the witnesses would expect. So that's what they requisitioned.

There was finally a break of more than a few minutes in Foxx's work. They were passing Six Flags Great America Amusement Park on their right, more than halfway to Racine. Foxx looked out the window, pensive. He didn't seem to register the roller coaster tracks that towered in the middle distance. Kekich tried to bring him into the present.

"Really surprising the Giants fired their manager one game into the season. It was a bad loss, but there's what, 161 more games to go? Seems like a really short leash."

Foxx, a lifelong Giants fan, jerked his head toward her. "What?!? They fired their manager? Are you kidd—"

"April Fools!"

He saw her smile. "Okay Agent Kekich, just trying to get my attention?"

She began, "Well, you have to admit—"

He cut her off with a wave of his hand.

"Ahh, sorry Rita. It's this case. We've been on this task force for six months. This gang has been operating for two years—maybe longer—and we're just chasing our tail."

Kekich nodded. She knew Foxx was not used to failing. She kept silent in hopes that he would fill the void.

"This point man...the guy called Ike...he's a different cat. This driver's license thing...he seems to know exactly who to pull it on."

It was the driver's license tactic that Foxx was referring to at the meeting the previous morning. He had made the decision early on not to release this bit of information to the public. The last thing he wanted was a slam dunk technique for avoiding loaded and baited money stacks to be revealed to other potential bandits.

Kekich drove on as her superior continued.

"Maybe we release it on our website? Use the media and request public input?"

Kekich shook her head. "I don't see how that helps catch these guys."

They rode in silence for two minutes before either spoke again. It was Foxx.

"Gotta be another way to get at them."

They made it to the Wells Fargo a few minutes after 9:30. The initial interviews had been conducted by local police detectives at the bank on the day of the robbery. Foxx requested more extensive interviews so he could be present. The Racine police department offered the use of their facility but Foxx wanted to do it at the scene of the crime. This sometimes brought out memories that otherwise stayed hidden.

Kekich pulled the Suburban into the parking lot. Both she and Foxx took laptop bags into the building. Three members of the Racine PD and the four Wells Fargo employees were inside. After introductions were completed the entire group assembled in the largest conference room to the left of the lobby. Foxx explained that they would interview one employee at a time while the others waited in the larger room.

"If you don't mind, we would like everyone to stay until these individual interviews are completed so we can review the entire incident together."

There were nods all around.

"Let me say here at the beginning that we have absolutely no suspicions of any involvement by any employees of this company. This robbery team has been conducting similar thefts for some time."

The looks of concern on the faces of the employees seemed to ease.

"I know this could turn into a bit of a long day. We appreciate your cooperation and we've arranged for lunch to be brought in."

The manager, Herschel Knuckles, spoke. "That's okay Agent Foxx. The company is paying us for a full day today. Besides, this day at work can't be any worse than Wednesday, can it?" He turned to his fellow employees and they exchanged nervous smiles.

Foxx, Kekich, and two members of the Racine Police Department trooped down the hall to a second meeting room. It was smaller than the first so Foxx directed the others to their seats. He arranged the room in such a way that the interviewees would, hopefully, feel slightly less intimidated. The police officers—both detectives—took seats in the corner of the room. The FBI agents sat on one side of a small rectangular table. A chair for the witness was across the table.

They started with the redheaded teller. Her name was Whitney Hayes. Her hair was a slightly bolder shade of red than Kekich's. She admitted to being scared out of her mind at the sight of the two armed, masked men.

"I thought I was going to pee my pants." Her face reddened when she said this, matching her hair. She told the agents that she had already given the company her two-week notice. "My husband suggested it. He has a good job in construction and we'll get by until I find something else. He's really, umm, pissed about this. I don't know what he'd do if he ever got a chance to get at these guys."

The second teller was next. Ariah Leigh had light brown hair and hazel eyes. She was 34 and had worked at the branch office for seven years. She repeatedly mentioned that the bank stressed the fact that employees were to comply completely if a robbery occurred. "I'd like to think that I would've given them the dye pack money in my drawer if they had me empty it...but I don't know."

They took a break for pizza, sitting around the large conference table and talking informally before getting back to it.

The third witness was Lindsay Risha, 54, an assistant manager. She still appeared angry over the incident. "I've worked in banks since college and have never been involved in a robbery. These guys, these...*thugs*...I hope you put them away!"

They asked each witness for details. What kind of footwear did the men wear? What names did they use when speaking to each other? Did they communicate with the driver outside the building while in the bank?

Kekich asked if any hair was visible on the edges of the men's masks. If so, what color was it? Was it straight or curly? She asked if they could tell the robbers' eye color. In past robberies the suspects had taken care to hide their hair completely. This incident was no exception. Both Hayes and Leigh thought both men had brown eyes. This matched witness statements from previous robberies. Risha had another take.

"As far as I'm concerned their eyes were black...especially the asshole George that came in my office and pointed the gun at me."

Knuckles was the last to be interviewed. Before meeting with Foxx and the others he'd spent much of his time in the main conference room on his phone. He also struck up a conversation with the third police officer, a patrolwoman who had been first on the scene of the robbery. They talked sports until it was Knuckles's turn to be interviewed.

"I couldn't believe it when that man asked for my license. All I could see was the machine gun. He read off my address and said he would come for my family if I didn't help them. We are already trained to cooperate to avoid making the situation worse...to escalate things."

Foxx nodded. "Completely understandable. You did the right thing."

Then, shifting gears, Foxx asked, "What was your overall impression of the men?"

Knuckles blinked. "I don't understand." He was puzzled.

"Well, you've had experience dealing with people, reading body language. What is your general sense of the dynamic between the two men? Who would you say was in charge?"

Knuckles nodded. "Oh, the guy with the machine gun was in charge, no question. I had a basketball coach like him once... seemed to always know what I was thinking. My mother was that way too...could look at any of us kids and read our minds." Knuckles looked down. "I gotta admit, when he had me in that vault I thought about rushing him, you know, maybe catch him off balance. A stupid thought...could've gotten all of us killed. But that man looked right at me and his expression changed. It was like he was readin' my mind."

Foxx nodded. "That's when he locked you in the vault?"

"Yeah, we're damn lucky a customer came in a few minutes later and called you guys." He looked to the detectives in the corner, "Well, I guess she called *you* guys."

Foxx made some notes on his laptop before coming to the end of the interview. "Any further thoughts? Anything we forgot to ask?

Knuckles shook his head slowly. "Can't think of anything. The boss, he was a bad guy. You threaten a man's family, you should be put away. But that first guy, the one that came in my office and pushed me down the hallway with a rifle in my back? He's a real problem. He definitely needs to be in a cell."

Knuckles paused, "Or be put down."

Foxx nodded.

The FBI agents departed Racine just after 3 p.m. After the interviews they had the bank employees walk them through the building, reliving the robbery. When they got to the vault Foxx could see that a couple of the women held back.

"We're not going to ask you to go back in there."

Relief showed on their faces.

Foxx and Kekich spent their last hour in the bank in the large conference room reviewing the day with the Racine detectives and the patrolwoman. The Wells Fargo employees were excused. Three of them went to their work areas to finish the day. Hayes, the redhead, left the building.

Kekich was once again at the wheel. "Well what do you think Ali'i?" It was the word for noble or chief in Hawaiian.

"You picked up quite a vocabulary in the islands didn't you?"

"I probably know more Hawaiian words than anyone in Dove Creek, Colorado."

Foxx nodded. "My money would be on you, that's for sure." He turned back to the windshield before continuing. "Well, it's them, obviously. All the tactics fit their M.O. Right up to the point of locking them in the vault. That appears to be an improvisation by Ike."

"Agreed." Kekich signaled and passed a semi in the center lane. "Anything there to push us in a particular direction?"

Foxx was thoughtful. "I'm not sure anything we learned today was earth shattering." He paused for a second. "I've been thinking, we've been going at these guys in a pretty traditional manner. You know, 'follow the money.'"

Kekich waited.

Foxx continued. "We've tried to track the bills that were taken from the robberies. This team has been exceptional in avoiding bills with recorded serial numbers. Call it luck. Call it good planning with the driver's license angle. When they do get stuck with baited money the bills end up all over the Midwest. There's no definite geographic indicator to their origination."

Kekich knew all this. She said simply, "Yep."

"The team was stuck with dye packs what, three times?"

Kekich nodded and repeated, "Three times."

"All three times the packs exploded and the robbers tossed the bag immediately—nice touch, those bags...treated with

97

liquid rubber...four bags to minimize exposure. So they never get the dye on their person, they dump the bad bills, and they're smart with the rest of the cash. They steal cars from airports and dump them in cemeteries. There are never any prints in the cars. No one ever sees the vehicle exchange. We haven't been able to get at them in the normal ways. I'm thinking we need a new approach."

"Like what?"

"I'm still working it out, but I think we need to concentrate on what happens in and near the robbery locations *before* they're hit. They have to be casing these banks, scouting them. They almost certainly decide *not* to hit some banks—maybe *most* banks, for a reason. We need to expand our investigation around old robbery locations and see if anything catches our attention at other banks—banks they *didn't* rob."

"Look for anomalies?"

Foxx nodded, "Exactly."

Kekich saw the Six Flags coasters ahead to the left. "Sounds promising, definitely worth a shot. We'll get field agents back out to the areas, maybe involve local police. We dump the data into our computers...yeah, I like it."

As they drove on, Kekich commented on the witnesses. When she got to Risha she chuckled, "I definitely wouldn't want that assistant manager pissed at me. She was *still* mad. Lucky she didn't try to scratch George's eyes out."

Foxx nodded. "You got that right. Messing with George would be a...problem."

Kekich turned solemn thinking of the second robber. They both knew he had fired his weapon into the ceiling during a robbery the previous year in Peoria, Illinois. FBI behavioral analysts had looked at all the data on the suspects. They'd determined that George was violent, a danger. If he hadn't killed anyone in his life to this point it was probably just a matter of time.

They passed Six Flags and Foxx shifted gears, "That thing that the manager said, Knuckles, about having a coach that could tell what he was thinking. Ever have anyone in your life like that?"

Kekich nodded and smirked.

"Yeah, my older sister."

CHAPTER THIRTEEN

An online inquiry with MapQuest told Paul that the drive time between his house outside of Troy and the Tutor's Bourbon Distillery near Sawyer, Kentucky was four hours and nineteen minutes. For most of the drive this appeared accurate. Paul took I-75 from Troy south through Dayton. He reached Cincinnati 45 minutes later just as the sun broke the horizon to his left and crossed the Ohio River into the Bluegrass State, making good time. An hour and twenty minutes later he reached Lexington and stopped for gas and another cup of coffee.

It was Monday morning, less than a week since Mike McClary floated the idea of helping with the account. The Hulls and McClarys met again three days later—Saturday—to discuss it over dinner. This occurred at the Coldwater Café. It was situated in a former bank building in Tipp City, between Troy and Dayton. Mike and Marge laid out their expectations of the job, although they admitted they didn't know exactly what Owen Johnson had in mind. Paul repeated his doubts but finally agreed to meet with Johnson after Marge implored, "Just go check it out. If it's not for you, step away. It won't affect our friendship."

Paul exchanged emails with Johnson's administrative assistant, Charlie Hunter, and they agreed to meet this morning at 10 a.m. Hunter offered to put Paul up in a hotel in Somerset, Kentucky but Paul declined. He figured on leaving at 5 a.m., giving himself plenty of time.

The previous night Paul spent a half hour searching for podcasts to download for the drive down and back. By the time he was back on the road in Lexington he had listened to two episodes of the *Black Rifle Coffee Podcast* that featured interviews with special operators he'd served with. These were

101

bittersweet for Paul. Names of lost comrades were mentioned, but hilarious stories were also told.

After that he did a pod on SETI, the Search for Extraterrestrial Intelligence. Much of this episode involved terminology Paul did not quite understand. He felt he was coming into a room full of people having a serious discussion, which, in fact, he was. Much of the search was passive. That is, we on Earth are just listening for signals from aliens. Another aspect though was active, and involved intentionally sending signals into space to contact other beings. Those in favor of active search argued that we have been sending signals into space for decades with our radio and television broadcasts. Why not try to craft a message that is more representative of our world?

Paul had to admit he came down on the side of caution. *Why advertise the fact that we're here? Why draw the attention of aliens to us, clueing them in to our planet's natural resources? Don't we have enough to worry about already?*

Paul passed more billboards than he could count touting various Kentucky bourbons. He saw the first one advertising Tutor's a few minutes after returning to the highway from his stop for gas. He passed huge expanses of grass—not yet reaching the deep green shade that it would later in the spring —that were segmented by what seemed like miles of white wooden fencing... Kentucky horse farms. Here and there pairs of thoroughbreds played together like puppies from the same litter. Not quite two hours south of Lexington, Paul reached Mount Vernon. He followed his navigation system's directions and got on Kentucky Route 25, heading toward Somerset, a half hour distant. Exit signs no longer featured names like Lexington or Richmond. Instead Paul saw signs for Stab, Acorn, and Honeybee. He was on state two-lane highways now. He debated starting another podcast. His grey Ford Escape's GPS system showed he had just 33 miles to the distillery outside of Sawyer. The unit also showed a drive time of over an hour.

How can that be right? An accident up ahead?

As he drove Paul began to observe a phenomena he'd noticed years earlier. That is, the faster a vehicle was going when it passed him, the better the chance that it was a large pickup truck that got poor gas mileage. GMC Sierras, Dodge Ram 3500s, Ford F-650s, they all blew past Paul as he cruised along four miles per hour over the speed limit. Some of these monsters were adorned with construction company signage and outfitted with toolboxes inside their beds. Invariably the busy contractor had covered his dash with old paperwork and empty coffee cups. But more often the trucks were driven by someone who looked like they could be a neighbor down the street. The more box-like and blunt the front of the truck, the better chance of it riding the rear of the vehicle in front of it.

Occasionally the vehicle flashing past him would be a two-door beater with an aftermarket rear spoiler bolted to the trunk. The paint job was often in such bad shape that it reminded him of a spacecraft that had survived the intense heat of re-entry to Earth's atmosphere. Invariably the driver of this vehicle would be a white male between the ages of 16 and 25.

Those kids drive like they are in a Formula 1 race.

The next episode in his queue was from a podcast called *Hardball*. It was on baseball great Nolan Ryan. The episode notes showed that it was 43 minutes long. Paul shrugged and touched play.

At Somerset Paul crossed the Cumberland River and took US-27 south for 25 miles. At Parker's Lake his navigation system then directed him to take KY-3257 toward Sawyer. He was now traveling northeast which seemed to Paul to be a bit odd after coming south all this way. A couple miles on he was directed onto still another road, KY-896.

A phrase his grandparents used swam into Paul's head. *You can't get there from here.*

His progress slowed significantly. The road wound through tough, rocky hills and hollows—Paul knew the locals called them "hollers"—requiring him to slow to 25 miles per hour at times. He noticed that the compass display at various times showed he was pointed north, east, south, and west as he wound through the hills. He now understood why the final 33 miles would take over an hour.

Paul glanced at his watch, now concerned that he might be late for the appointment. *That certainly wouldn't make much of a first impression.* His military background left Paul somewhat of a fanatic when it came to being on time. He saw that he should still reach his destination a few minutes early.

The podcast wound down. Paul enjoyed listening to Nolan Ryan's unrushed, folksy responses to questions from the interviewer. The Hall of Famer's cadence seemed to go perfectly with Paul's current surroundings. He knew the man was from Texas, but somehow his laid back delivery fit the Kentucky hills just fine. The podcast ended when Paul was three miles from Sawyer. Five minutes later he saw a collection of buildings come into view.

Three signs caught his attention. The first said simply *SAWYER KENTUCKY, UNINCORPORATED.* The second was a small white sign displaying the words *POST OFFICE* with an arrow. Paul smiled, remembering that Sawyer claimed to have the smallest post office in the country.

The third sign was much larger and obviously newer. An artistic font spelled out *TUTOR'S BOURBON, 2 MILES AHEAD, 1000 TUTOR DRIVE, DISTILLERY TOURS AVAILABLE.* Bottles of bourbon shaped like upright books were pictured below the words.

Well, what do you know? Paul couldn't help grinning, seeing his offhanded remark to Mike McClary apparently become reality right in front of his eyes.

Paul slowed as he passed through the sprinkling of small wood-framed homes. Some were well tended, some less so. He pulled to the side of the road when he reached the post office. It was a red wooden structure, really just a shack. It was perhaps ten feet wide and a few feet deep. A single window covered with metal mesh was situated over a white wooden hand-lettered sign that read *U.S. POST OFFICE SAWYER, KY.* While puttering around online looking for information on Owen Johnson's business Paul discovered that having the smallest post office in America was Sawyer's claim to fame, or at least what passed for fame in a location as out of the way as this. The interior had just enough space for a few post office boxes, a chair, and a sorting table. Unfortunately for Sawyer the Ochopee Post Office in the Florida Everglades claimed to be slightly smaller. This led to ill feelings for some inhabitants near each office.

Paul brought his left hand to his face and covered a smile. *That must be the same attitude that led to the Hatfield-McCoy feud.*

In fact, the McCoys originated from an area of Kentucky just a few miles—and a dozen or so hollers—east of Sawyer. The Hatfields were from an area just east of that, beyond the West Virginia state line.

Paul eased back onto the road and, traveling almost due north now, followed the directions to Tutor Drive. The road was wider than the one that led into Sawyer. Its surface looked new. A mile into this final leg of the drive the road made a gentle curve to the right. Paul got his first view of Tutor's Distillery through the left side of his windshield. Several buildings were situated in a shallow valley. They were interspersed with copses of adult trees. A river flowed beyond the buildings, giving the entire scene a hint of charm.

Looks like a scene from a Christmas movie...pretty.

A large rectangular building stood out, not quite dominating the scene. Even from this distance—nearly a mile —Paul could see that it was constructed of wood. Tutor Drive took another bend and the scene disappeared just as quickly as it had come into view.

Paul approached the distillery property and followed the signs to visitor parking. He found a spot facing a wood and stone fronted building bearing a sign that said *WELCOME CENTER.* He got out of the Escape and stretched. It was a fine, clear morning. The temperature was already in the mid-sixties. It would climb a few more degrees by noon. Paul had checked the *Weather Channel* app on his phone before leaving and knew this part of Kentucky would be several degrees warmer today than his home up in Troy.

Paul pocketed his phone and opened the door to the back seat. He took a blue sport coat from its hanger and with a couple twists and shrugs pulled it on. He hadn't been sure how to dress for the occasion. Lauren suggested he look professional, but not *too* professional. He'd opted for forest green pants that fell somewhere between casual and dressy, a white long-sleeved dress shirt, and the blazer. No tie. He hated wearing dress shoes. Well, not hated, but certainly *disliked*. He'd opted for a pair of almost-brand-new Merrell trail shoes that he—and more importantly Lauren—thought went well with the pants.

If I get the idea that the people at Tutor's think the shoes look goofy I can say I expected to do a lot of walking at the distillery.

Paul checked his reflection in the rear window, the angle of the sun being just right. During his Combat Controller training in the Pipeline a wise instructor told him to always check a mirror before a formal meeting with a superior.

"Rule of thumb...don't show up in the Colonel's office with crud in your eyelashes or your zipper down."

That wise instructor just happened to be his buddy Gatewood.

Paul saw flecks of grey in his short black hair—nothing he could do about that—but his eyes were crudless. He turned his back to the Welcome Center and nonchalantly checked his zipper.

All good.

He locked up and strode to the building.

Wide glass exterior doors slid open revealing a vestibule area with a stone floor partially covered by a large floor mat that displayed the Tutor's Bourbon logo. Paul stepped through the vestibule and went through a second set of doors.

He found himself in an expansive lobby, 60 feet deep and 80 wide. A large, curving reception desk was at the rear, built into a dark oak wall that also featured the company logo, this one made of polished metal. The entire floor of the lobby consisted of tightly packed red bricks turned on their sides. A corridor ran off to the left. A wide opening on the right led to a gift shop. Paul saw a woman behind the desk and began to move toward her when he noticed a display of some sort to his left. He turned to look at it and did a double take. On top of an elevated base of the same bricks was a collection of copper kettles and spidery tubing.

It was a still.

Paul altered his path to approach the display. He saw a gold plaque affixed to its base. It read:

ORIGINAL STILL
One Of Two Original Stills Used On This Property By
"Peepaw" Tutor Bishop. Circa 1930.

Paul found himself reaching for his phone to take a picture. He thought better of it and turned to the desk. As he approached a smart looking middle-aged woman in a company shirt smiled.

"You must be Paul Hull." She stood and held out a hand. She had short dark hair and was about six inches shorter than Paul, putting her in the range of 5'6". She wore a grey sweater with the company logo above the left breast.

Paul smiled and nodded as he advanced to her and they shook hands over the desk.

"Hope you had a nice drive down. I'm Charlie Hunter."

Paul was still gripping her hand. *"You're* Charlie Hunter?" Before the last syllable escaped his lips Paul's face began to redden. Lauren had sometimes accused him of being a bit of a male chauvinist. Not in a malicious way, exactly. He was more protective of women than men. He was leery of putting female members of the military in units intended for ground combat for example. It wasn't that he doubted the ability of any woman that could meet the physical qualifications. He had completed multiple deployments to Iraq and, more often, Afghanistan. He'd fought enemies that had archaic, even violent, beliefs about the fairer sex. Paul didn't like to imagine what could happen to women in those situations.

Occasionally Paul's preconceptions led to awkward public moments, like the one he found himself in right now. He realized he was still holding Hunter's hand.

"Uh, sorry." He released her hand.

Hunter's nose crinkled as she smiled. "It's okay, I get that a lot. My given name's Charlene." Her voice had a light, sweet Kentucky twang. "Obie keeps telling me to sign my emails with 'Charlene,' or at least use it with 'Charlie' between my first and last name. I get in a hurry sometimes."

"So you prefer I call you..."

"Oh Charlie for sure. Believe you me, I'm not sure I even answer to Charlene half the time. Now, can I get you anything? Coffee? Do you need to visit the restroom?"

Paul shook his head. "No...thank you. I'm just fine."

Charlie nodded. "Well, Obie's on the phone with a supplier." She glanced at a clock mounted above the company logo on the wall behind the desk. "You're a few minutes early—Obie will like that, by the way—feel free to browse through our gift shop until he's off." She gestured to Paul's right. "Oh, and go ahead and take a picture of the still. Everybody does." She smiled again.

Paul decided the gift shop would be an excellent way to kill a few minutes. He and Lauren had done a couple bourbon distillery tours with the McClarys and he'd been impressed by the quality and selection of the gear.

"Good idea. I might just do some shopping."

Paul took a couple shots of the still and one of the plaque then walked into the store. He realized it was much larger than he originally assumed. A handful of customers were browsing.

An older couple—probably grandparents—were holding up shirts from the child's section, debating sizes.

This must have more square footage than my house! There were shelves filled with hats and t-shirts covering half the wall space. Floor displays contained racks of upscale shirts and sweaters. Freestanding oak and chrome shelves were sprinkled throughout, offering Christmas decorations, decanters, several styles of bourbon glasses, and bourbon-flavored treats. All were decorated with the Tutor's Bourbon design.

There were large windows on three walls. The one to his right faced the parking lot. The window on the far wall offered a view of other buildings on the property. To the left through a large stand of trees was a picturesque view of a river in the distance. Sunlight reflected off the moving water and glinted off a hint of metal somewhere in the trees.

Metal pipes of some kind?

His eyes were drawn to the far side of the shop near the checkout area. Hundreds of bottles of bourbon lined the wall. There appeared to be several sizes. The bottles, though, were all shaped like books. Paul smiled and made his way to the wall.

Most of the bottles were 750 milliliter or one liter sizes. There were smaller sizes all the way down to 50 milliliters. A tag below these small bottles said *INSTRUCTION MANUAL SIZE.* This made Paul chuckle. The largest size was three liters. It looked like an oversized book from a fairytale. He approached it and peeked at the price tag. He let out a low whistle then quickly looked up to make sure no one noticed.

Paul stepped back to take in the wall in its entirety. Most of the bottles were turned so their "spine" faced out. They covered the shelves exactly like books in a library or bookstore. On either end of a given size bottles were turned to show the label on the wider front side.

Hunh...must allow them to pack more bottles in a display space.

Paul stepped away from the bourbon wall and drifted though the merchandise displays. The color scheme of most items was medium grey and navy blue. This coincided with the labels on the bottles. He eyed a rack of handsome long-sleeved button-down shirts with the navy logo on the left breast. They were near matches of the sweater Charlie Hunter wore. He selected a large and held it up.

"I think that would look damn fine on you Paul, damn fine."

Paul turned to see a rancher-thin man in blue jeans and a grey denim work shirt with the Tutor's logo. He had a shock of white hair and smile lines around hazel eyes.

"Owen Johnson. Call me Obie."

He held out his hand.

CHAPTER FOURTEEN

Paul followed Obie out of the gift shop. He was gratified to see that the older man wore a pair of trail shoes not unlike his Merrells. Obie waved and smiled at Charlie, who was on the phone. He was leading Paul toward the corridor opposite the gift shop when he hesitated and veered toward the display featuring the old still.

"Well, this is how it all started, Paul. My Peepaw Bishop made moonshine—which is basically un-aged bourbon—with this here still during Prohibition...probably before, truth be told."

Paul smiled, "I was admiring it when I came in. Even took a couple pictures."

Johnson nodded, "Everybody does. You don't expect to see something like this in a fancy lobby. I heard tell of a farm equipment manufacturer up in Coldwater, Ohio that had an old manure spreader on display in their lobby. Had it painted gold. Really caught people's attention. That's where I got the idea."

Paul hadn't heard of the plant and said so.

"Well Paul, they've been out of business for years. Don't know what happened to the spreader. My wife—Martha—hopes I never find out. I have a tendency to buy things like that, give 'em a home. She says I have a...what's the word... *predilection* to collect oddball things like that." He chuckled.

Paul hadn't planned to bring it up but he already felt comfortable with Johnson and thought this was a good time to ask about Steve McQueen's Mustang.

"Is it true that you were in the running for the car from *Bullitt?*"

"Well—" Obie began to answer when the front door opened and a group of a dozen or so people entered the lobby. He tilted his head to the corridor and gestured for Paul to lead the way. Johnson joined him and they walked together.

"Like most things you read in the newspaper—or these days on the internet—there's a *hint* of truth to the story. That car went up for auction in January 2020 in Kissimmee, Florida right before COVID hit. We had a lot going on here and I didn't make it down. I lined up a proxy bidder and told him I'd go as high as three million—you see both my Peepaw and my Daddy loved that movie."

Paul listened intently, hardly noticing when Obie came to wooden double doors and pulled one side open before ushering him in. They entered and Johnson stopped just inside the door. Paul turned his back on the office interior and waited as the story continued.

"Well, the price hits three million and my contact is pushing me to go higher. Problem was, I had the call on a speaker phone right here in this office, and *Martha* was sitting five feet from me. We had just signed a note for ten million with a bank up in Lexington." He grinned, "Let's just say a higher bid just wasn't in the cards that day. The car went for 3.4 million...with commissions it was 3.74. I put my money to better use. Built the new rickhouse you'll see a bit later. The stories say I was the second highest bidder. Not true."

He considered a few seconds before smiling again, "But close." Then, "It's the damnedest thing Paul. Did you know that car was right up the road in a garage outside of Somerset, Kentucky for decades?"

Paul had read that the whereabouts of the car were unknown for some time before it turned up, but couldn't recall the specifics.

"A fella by the name of Bob Kiernan from Somerset bought that Mustang from an ad in the back of *Car and Driver* magazine in 1974 for $3,500. Drove it for a while. Got nervous I guess. Stored it away. If I'd found out about it while Peepaw or Daddy were alive I'd've showed up in Somerset with a blank check." Johnson looked reflective. "Still kick myself sometimes."

Obie blinked away the thoughtful expression and put back on his smile. "Well, come on Paul, let's get down to business." He gestured to a large desk. It was made of a slightly different wood than that on the outside of the building. Paul sat in one of two comfortable leather chairs in front of it while Obie settled into a swivel version behind it covered with the same leather.

"Let me first say, your reputation precedes you. A Purple Heart, *four* Bronze Stars, an Air Force Combat Controller... with the *Two-Four* no less."

Paul was impressed by the man's familiarity with his former unit. The 24th Special Tactics Squadron. It was the Air Force's "Tier One" unit. Operators from the Two-Four were assigned to the Navy's SEAL Team Six and the Army's Delta Force under the auspices of the United States Joint Special Operations Command, or JSOC.

It took two years to complete the "Pipeline," the physically intense and highly technical training required to become a Combat Controller, or CCT. Upon completion, the newly minted CCTs were assigned to an Air Force Tactical Squadron. If they were top performers there they *might* get a crack at joining the elite of the elite, the Two-Four.

Combat Controllers were experts at coordinating extremely complicated air-ground missions featuring large numbers of strike aircraft. They were assigned individually to components of SEAL or Delta operators and blended in seamlessly. They considered these their "customer units." They trained with them, fought with them, and sometimes died with them.

Paul's accomplishments as a CCT earned him a sterling reputation and an enormous amount of respect in the JSOC community, and, not that he cared, almost none in the private sector. Yet here was this businessman in the hills of Kentucky that seemed to have a fair grasp of his past.

That's when Paul remembered Obie had been in Army Intelligence.

"I just tried to carry my share of the weight."

Johnson looked him in the eye and paused. Finally he said, "Well, you certainly did that son, you certainly did that." He slapped the top of the desk with both hands signifying a change in topic.

"Now then, let's get down to brass tacks. The reason you're here is *I* want you on board with what we're doing with my peepaw's bourbon and *you* want to try to figure out what this is all about and where you might fit into it. That sound about right?"

"I guess so, Mr. Johnson."

The bourbon executive waggled a finger. "Please, Paul, it's Obie."

Paul nodded in agreement.

Johnson continued. "The McClarys have done some excellent work for us. Our bourbon is in state stores all across Kentucky and Tennessee. That's prime territory for this product. Jasper Spirits Consulting played a significant role in bringing that about. I respect the fact that you are friends with Mike and Marge. Anything you might do for Tutor's will be done with them as your employer. I would not contemplate trying to hire you as a direct employee of this distillery."

Paul let out a short sigh of relief. He thought there could be a small possibility of a job offer from Johnson. If that happened he would have politely declined and headed back to Ohio.

"The next step in our growth is to penetrate the markets in state stores in the Midwest. Tutor's is sold in specialty shops and privately owned liquor stores all over the country. Most bourbon—and all other spirits—is purchased in state stores. By the way, isn't it ironic you used to be part of JSOC and now you might work for a company that has the same initials?"

Paul nodded, "Mike and I have talked about that."

"Anyway, we've also contracted with a marketing company out of Louisville. They say we need to create demand for our product in these states to get on the state store shelves."

Obie pronounced Louisville the Kentucky way—Lull-ville.

"I agree with them on this. The plan is to use the unique packaging and product name to gin up sales in college towns. If we can stir things up, so to speak, in the bars and restaurants around college campuses it will create a grassroots movement and get us into the state stores."

Paul saw the logic. "Use the uhh, the *book bottle* to get people's attention?"

"You got it, Paul. The McClarys made sure I knew the bottle was your idea."

Paul nearly stammered, "It was really just an offhanded comment."

Obie held up a hand, "May be, but they told me you had the whole concept put together in five minutes...change the name from Peepaw's to Tutor's, tailor the bottle to the name, the whole shootin' match. By the way, Mike and Marge could've come to me and said the ideas were theirs, but they wanted to make sure I knew it came from, how did Mike put it? 'A washed up old Air Force guy with nothing better to do than ride his bike all day.'"

Paul laughed, "Yeah, that sounds like Mike."

"Your idea came to me year before last. These geniuses from Louisville came up with a list of possible names for the bourbon. One idea was to use my initials. 'O.J.'s Bourbon.' Can you believe that? For Christ's sake, haven't they ever heard of those murders out in California? Anyway, they were gonna let me go with the Peepaw name. After I shifted gears on them they acted like your ideas were *their* ideas. We've had a heart to heart and straightened that out by the way."

A knock at the door interrupted the conversation. Obie called out "Come" and two Tutor's employees—a young man and a middle-aged woman—entered pushing food carts.

"Right on time! Hope you don't mind an early lunch. I ordered for you. Garden salad and roast chicken. Sound okay?"

"Just fine, Obie."

Over lunch Obie explained that a distillery tour was starting at noon and he'd like Paul to join it. "Get a feel for what we do, and why it's special. You'll hear about mash bills, alcohol proof levels, and yeast strains, then come back here and we'll talk more."

Paul said that sounded fine. He had several questions and was eager to learn more about the company and the history of its bourbon.

They talked as they ate. Obie mentioned that the salad and chicken choices were mainly for his benefit. "Martha would have my hide if I brought in something fried." It turned out that Obie's family on the Johnson side had a history of heart issues. His father died of a heart attack before reaching the age of 60.

"My Momma's side was the opposite. Most of this land," he gestured toward an office window, "was used to raise oats a hundred years ago. My maternal grandparents—Meemaw and Peepaw in Kentucky-speak—ran the farm. Momma was an only child. All three of them ate oats every day. Oatmeal for breakfast, ground oats in their bread, oats baked into their desserts. Studies today show oatmeal helps keep a handle on heart problems."

Paul had read that oatmeal was a heart healthy food. He ate a good bit of it himself. He forked a bite of salad and nodded.

"So Peepaw, like pretty much every farmer in those days, made his own shine. One day he gets the idea to work some oats into his recipe and damned if the results aren't better... smoother. He's using water right out of the Cumberland River." Obie gestured again to the window. "Something about the combination clicks. Old Tutor then barrels the juice—he made his own barrels from white oak trees that grew right here on the property—and when it aged, it was even better. This here desk," he patted its top, "is made from white oak harvested 300 yards from here."

Paul listened closely, enjoying the story.

"So, fast forward a few decades. I made my pile of money in real estate development. Went to WKU on the other side of the state, met some lifelong friends from the Nashville area, then joined the Army. I started investing some of our family money with a couple of the Nashville contacts. Started making money hand over fist when I got out of the service. Have been at it hard for 45 years now. About ten years ago I got it in my head to try to make Peepaw's recipe well known."

Paul knew that any number of Kentucky bourbons came about from similar stories. The names of the old distillers populated labels in any liquor store: Jack Daniels, Basil Hayden, Jim Beam, George Dickel, Elijah Craig. The list was long. Perhaps the most expensive such product on the market, Pappy Van Winkle, drew the interest of investors and high-end collectors.

Obie set down his fork. He was into the story now.

"I decided to build a distillery right here on the family property. The Cumberland flows east to west and it meanders through Kentucky and Tennessee...squiggles back and forth. It pretty much divides its length equally on either side of the border. We already owned over 200 acres here on the south side of the river. The distillery construction started here almost eight years ago. In the meantime we started acquiring additional acreage on both sides of the river." Johnson hesitated before adding, "I happen to know a guy with a fair bit of business acumen when it comes to real estate."

He winked to make sure Paul knew he was talking about himself.

"Owning land along the river means we control and prevent any fertilizer or insecticide runoff into the river. Y'see, we did significant testing of the water and discovered a limestone shelf upstream gives the water the perfect PH for our bourbon."

Paul was impressed. *This guy is no dummy.*

"We raise corn, barley, and oats on most of the acreage—those are the three ingredients in our mash bill—using organic agricultural methods. The rest of the land is planted in white oak. Mature trees are turned into Tutor's Bourbon barrels."

Paul hesitated, "So...you basically have everything you need right here on the property?"

Obie nodded, "We do. We're about to release our first bottles that were completely sourced here. Up to now we've used a contract distillery up in Bardstown."

He explained that contract distillers set up their facility to use a recipe provided by another producer. The final product is theoretically the same as bourbon produced at the original location.

"The Tutor's on the market now is not the Tutor's that's about to be released. It's good, mind you, but it's not made with the same water we have here."

There was another knock on the door. Charlie Hunter popped her head in without being called.

"The tour's about to start Obie." She turned to look at Paul. "Well, you haven't left yet, I guess that means you're doing the tour?"

Paul removed a napkin from his lap and stood. He laid it on his plate and pushed his chair back in.

"I'm doing the tour."

CHAPTER FIFTEEN

"AAARRGH!!!"

"You can do it! That's it! *Twenty-eight!* Yes, two more!" Dom Santo watched as the stainless steel bar laden with 225 pounds of free weights settled back to Tanner Jelcik's chest. They were in the work bay area of Klean Sooner. It was just past 5 p.m.

"Come on Tanner-Boy, come on Tanner-boy...*Do it!*"

The bar, bowing slightly, contacted Tanner's chest and started back toward the ceiling, though not as quickly as it had for the first two dozen reps. AC/DC's "High Voltage" pounded from speakers mounted above the weight rack.

"AAAHHHH!!!" Tanner strained to push the bar all the way to its apex, allowing his elbows to lock in an extended position. His arms wobbled as if they were wooden stilts holding up a beach house in a hurricane.

Dom stood behind the bench with his hands palms up under the bar, spotting for the larger man. "That's twenty-nine! *One more!*"

The bar lowered back to Tanner's chest, Dom's fingertips now brushing the steel.

Can't let him get pinned. Tanner would kick my ass. Dom bent his knees slightly, readying his body to take on the full weight of the bar if necessary.

The bar reached Tanner's chest and he let it rest there for a few beats. Until the last couple reps he had employed a technique that used his overdeveloped upper body almost as a trampoline, the bar springing back up. He inhaled deeply and blew out the air forcefully. He did it again. His face was beet red, his eyes wild. On his third forced exhale he thrust upward with everything he had.

"AAAWWW!!!"

119

Dom watched in fascination, mentally crossing his fingers that Tanner would complete the thirtieth repetition. The Jelcik brothers had an ongoing—mostly friendly—competition. They had learned from watching the NFL Combine in early March that the average number of 225-pound bench press reps done by prospective linemen was 30 to 39. For tight ends and linebackers it was 25 to 30. For other positions the numbers were lower.

"Bet I can do thirty." It was Tanner who started it.

Three weeks before the Wells Fargo robbery Cole did 28 reps. Tanner topped out at 26. Tanner sulked for two days then visited three local gyms and got the names of contacts that could supply him with anabolic steroids. He started a cycle immediately and by the time of the robbery in Racine was seeing results.

The workout area of the building was outfitted with the weight bench under a wall rack bolted to the brick wall, stacks of steel plates in six sizes—10, 15, 25, 35, 45, and 55 pounds—a six foot wide, three-level storage rack filled with sweet-looking rubber coated hexagonal shaped dumbbells, and a pull-up bar, also bolted to the wall on one side. The other side was anchored to a steel support beam. The weights for the bench were Rogue Fleck Plates, specially painted and available from Rogue Fitness in six color schemes. The brothers had chosen the red and black combination—it was the closest match to the color of their trucks. All of the equipment was purchased from Rogue, a major supplier of workout equipment based right there in Columbus.

It had everything a workout freak required if he didn't care about developing his lower body.

The Jelciks didn't.

Dom also lifted. He'd taken up the activity while in Lebanon Correctional. Though not in the same class as the brothers, he was strong for his size.

The bar rose slowly. Perspiration beaded on Tanner's forehead. It collected in his eyebrows and the crinkles on the sides of his eyes. A drop rolled down one side of his face and fell to the rubber gym flooring that covered the concrete in the workout area. The drop joined several others, forming a miniature puddle.

Tanner's arms were now trembling. The upward movement of the bar slowed. His eyes, which had been locked on the ceiling, now flicked to Dom. They were the eyes of an animal caught in a trap. The left side of the bar seemed to freeze in place as the right inched up incrementally and locked in place.

Dom thought, *He's done. The left arm isn't going to make it.*

At that moment Tanner called out, "YES! Thirty!" Then, "Little help, Santo."

Dom was somewhat confused for a brief second as he applied upright force to the bar and helped it onto the rests at the top of the rack.

Then he got it.

Tanner had declared victory.

As Tanner padded off to the restroom to towel off—the Silverback Gorilla on his shoulder glistening with sweat—Dom reconfigured the weight bar. When he'd finished it had 60 pounds on each end. He stripped off his company work shirt, revealing his own tattoo, the flag of Sicily, on his right bicep.

Might as well get in a short lift before we head out.

Dom knew that Tanner would be in the restroom for some time. The man liked to lather up a washcloth with a bar of soap and wipe down his upper body.

He thinks it's a good substitute for a shower. Dom shook his head. *He's wrong.*

ZZ Top's "La Grange" was now playing over the speakers. Tanner's phone rested on a small table nearby. It was linked via Bluetooth to the sound system. Dom knew that Tanner, a country music fan like his brother, typically worked out to a playlist featuring classic rock. The Jelciks sometimes kidded that it was "Turk music," songs their daddy liked. It seemed to give them an extra ounce or two of aggression while working the weights.

Dom selected a pair of 25-pound dumbbells and began a series of curls. He watched himself in a mirror the brothers had mounted on the wall. He then set the dumbbells on the floor and spaced them two feet apart. He used the grips of the weights as a base for pushups. He did a quick 50, stretched for a minute, then did 25 more. He stood and returned the dumbbells to the rack. As he turned to the bench Dom took notice of the burial vault truck in the center of the work bay. He settled under the bar as his thoughts lingered on the truck.

Using the truck as a getaway vehicle had been a stroke of genius. Cole had come up with the idea. Dom took pride in the fact that he was the conduit that allowed it to happen. He settled back onto the bench and pushed the bar upward, beginning a set of slow presses.

Dom's thoughts drifted back to his time in prison. He had a sinking feeling the moment he entered the processing area of Lebanon Correctional Institution. He felt the eyes of predators from every direction. There were Aryan gangs, Black gangs, and at least two separate groups from Central and South America. Dom saw no chance of affiliation with any of them. This meant that in the eyes of most of the prison population he was one thing—*new meat.*

On his third day inside—exhausted from lack of sleep due to a constant state of vigilance—he felt someone slide into the seat next to him in the cafeteria. Dom flinched. He recoiled just a bit, drawing in his right arm protectively.

"Easy, amicu. You look like you could use a cumpari."

It was Tony Valenti. A man, Dom came to know, that had extensive connections to organized crime. He was in his forties with jet-black hair and a smile that he flashed when amused and, Dom discovered, provoked. His use of the Sicilian words for *friend* and *godfather* got Dom's attention.

It turned out that Valenti, who was doing eight years for racketeering after a plea deal, had noticed Dom's tattoo. The red and yellow Sicilian flag had the head of Medusa in the center with three human legs radiating outward. Most people didn't recognize it, asked what it was, and commented on its weirdness.

Not Valenti. He was from Youngstown, Ohio and was still very much connected. And everyone at LCI knew it. The moment he sidled up to Dom, the newcomer's troubled existence changed.

Nobody screwed with Tony Valenti's people.

When Dom was released he declined an invitation from Valenti to move to Youngstown and join his organization. He wanted to make a go of it in his hometown of Columbus. But Dom never really reconnected with his family and struggled to find work. It was at this point that he met the Jelciks. It was in a bar on High Street. The three men were trolling for women, and were more than a little drunk. They found themselves on adjacent barstools and struck up a conversation. Dom lamented over his employment situation. Cole offered him a job on the spot.

Dom didn't realize the Jelciks had a criminal past, at least not right away. A few months into his employment he came across a stash of weapons when he opened the wrong storage locker in the Klean Sooner building. He was astonished to see the Thompson, the carbine, several pistols, and another weapon that transcended all of them in its lethality and exotic nature.

It was a Barrett .50 caliber sniper rifle. It was big and bad and capable of firing a bullet several inches in length well over a mile. It could punch through two inches of concrete and steel plate.

As Dom stood transfixed at the locker, Cole approached. "Looks like we need to talk."

Cole had correctly surmised that Dom would not run to the police. Santo was thankful to have a job and enjoyed being part of yet another pseudo-family. It reminded him of his relationship with Valenti.

Dom learned that the brothers acquired the weapons in a home invasion. They used some of them in a robbery in Bartlesville before leaving Oklahoma and coming to Ohio.

They really had no use for the Barrett but couldn't bring themselves to dispose of it at the bottom of a central Ohio lake.

"I might know someone who will take it off your hands... probably make it worth your while."

Dom reached out to the people in Youngstown. It turned out that yes, they would be happy to have the weapon. They would even trade something of greater value for the $12,000 rifle. Six months earlier the gang had robbed a heavy equipment dealer outside of Philadelphia. They backed three long flatbed trailers up to the lot one night and made off with a Caterpillar bulldozer, two Kubota excavators, and another item.

Would the brothers have a use for a three-year-old Silverado Burial Vault Carrier? Complete with vault?

Yes they would, thank you very much. Cole told Dom "we'll use it for something...can't really use the Barrett."

The exchange was made in a truck stop parking lot off of Interstate 71 near Mansfield, between Columbus and Youngstown. Both the Jelciks and the Youngstown people were distrustful of the other side. Santo acted as the go-between. Cole and Tanner had come to trust him, and Valenti —who was still in Lebanon—had vouched for him.

The truck came back to the Klean Sooner building in Columbus.

Dom was starting a second set of presses as the guitar intro to "Runnin' Down a Dream" by Tom Petty began. It ended abruptly. Dom looked over to see Tanner holding his phone. He wore a company work shirt.

"Okay Santo, better get going. Cole's gonna meet us at the first garage." Then, "Don't know why I bothered to clean up... the parking garage jobs suck."

Being the first Monday of the month, this was the day the parking garage jobs restarted. The city of Columbus owned eleven parking lots inside the city limits. Six of these were garages. There were a number of privately owned facilities, but the primary contract that Klean Sooner had secured was with the city.

The dirty little secret—and it *was* dirty—was that homeless people in virtually every city in the United States large enough to have parking garages relieved themselves in the stairways. The garages were warm in the winter—well, warmer than the wind-whipped sidewalks—and cool in the summer. They were generally accessible to foot traffic. To street people who were often not welcome in the restrooms of downtown businesses they had tremendous appeal.

To be fair, the homeless could not be blamed completely for the problem. Patrons from local bars sometimes contributed, as did the occasional housewife or businessman who didn't think they could make it all the way home without going. *There's a spot right there between two cars and no one's around.*

The urine smell was bad enough, especially in the summer. But the number two, that was a real problem. Add the occasional residue from a sick-to-his-stomach Columbus Blue Jackets fan or Buckeye watch party reveler and you could have a real situation. City maintenance staff tackled the job of occasional clean up but they weren't happy with it. It was determined that a contract cleaner could be brought in to do the job, freeing up well compensated employees to tackle tasks they didn't feel were beneath them, at a cost that was acceptable.

The work went out to bid. Though the actual tasks were off-putting, a number of aspects of the job appealed to Cole. One, the city would pay by check, not a money transfer to a company bank account. This would allow Klean Sooner to make physical deposits with a check from the city, deposits that could be combined with significant amounts of cash taken from the Fireteam's robberies. Cole judged that the inclusion of these checks virtually guaranteed that the bank wouldn't question the cash.

Another benefit was that it allowed them to help themselves to license plates from the occasional Kia or Hyundai. The cleanups occurred after first shift workers—and downtown this was most everyone—had left the garage. Any vehicles remaining were easy targets.

Lastly, having the contract with the city legitimized Klean Sooner in the eyes of managers of privately owned facilities. There were over a dozen of these in the downtown area alone. Klean Sooner picked up more business with those that paid with checks. This meant more money laundering and more license plates.

All this was true, but as Cole drove Klean Sooner van number one, listening to Outlaw Country, into Columbus from Dublin, a few miles northwest of the city, he couldn't help grinning.

Just because these jobs are good for us, help us wash the cash, doesn't mean the guys like it. Especially Tanner. He absolutely HATES the work.

"Mama Tried" by Merle Haggard came up on the radio and Cole frowned. He didn't care for the song. He turned down the volume.

Cole had just finished an ozone job. A scam, really. Mold remediation had become an essential business in America in the last few decades. It was often mandated by buyers in real estate transactions involving homes of a certain age. Proper mold resolution involved physical removal of the growth by certified crews. They should be wearing approved personal protective equipment—or PPE—and the affected area should be treated with specific disinfectant products after the removal.

Some contractors—Klean Sooner was one—went with a short cut. They argued that their method worked just as well. It involved nothing more than plugging in an ozone machine in the area with mold and letting it run for a few hours while they sat in their van in the driveway scrolling on their phones.

That is precisely what Cole did all afternoon. He spent much of the time reading out-of-town newspaper websites looking for mentions of the Racine robbery. It was all routine stuff. If the FBI—Cole knew the FBI would have a task force looking at their robberies—had discovered anything that would lead to the Fireteam it wasn't mentioned in any of the stories. Cole was relatively sure they came away from that job without endangering themselves. Well, not any more than they already had...or than Tanner had.

He had to fire that goddammed shot into the ceiling in Peoria...just couldn't help himself. Gets a little lip from one teller and he loses it. Plus, he couldn't find the ejected shell casing.

Tanner had assured Cole that the casing was free of his fingerprints, but Cole was only about 80 percent sure Tanner was being truthful.

And 80 percent is probably too high.

The ozone jobs, in addition to being easy money due to the fact that they could underbid legitimate contractors that didn't cut corners, provided an additional benefit as well. They allowed the Klean Sooner members access to homes when the inhabitants were gone. Customers were told the ozone had temporary negative effects and no one could be inside other than "true professionals."

This gave Cole or Tanner—Dom was often on scouting trips out of state looking at banks—time to leisurely search for useful items that probably wouldn't be missed by the homeowner. It was how Cole acquired the ID that was stashed in the bolt bag in the storage unit out by the airport.

Eight months earlier he was contacted by a realtor that he'd worked with in the past to do an ozone mold remediation job in Gahanna on the east side of town. The sellers were an older couple. Originally from Canada, they were moving back to their native country after a tragic event. It seems their 35-year-old son had died suddenly in a car accident outside of Toronto. The couple had agreed to move to Columbus for two years so the husband could help facilitate an acquisition his company had made south of the border in Ohio. He would be paid a six-figure bonus to delay his retirement. The wife agreed and they bought the house in Gahanna.

When their son, Cormier Gullickson, was killed their world changed forever. They packed a bag and fled to Canada, and as it turned out, never to return. The husband's company hired a moving company to box up everything and the house went on the market. The realtor, his own best interests in mind, selected Klean Sooner to do the remediation when a home inspection red-flagged the mold. The deal was written in such a way that clean up fees would be taken from the realtor's commission, thus his motivation for a low cost—though not necessarily effective—option.

While inside the house Cole opened several of the moving boxes, looking for items of interest. He hit the jackpot in one. A large FedEx envelope with a Toronto return address was on top. It was unopened and dated the previous week. Cole opened it and discovered effects from the dead son. It included his wallet, which in turn contained his Ontario driver's license. It would not expire for two years.

Cole studied the photo on the license. Cormier Gullickson was 6'3" and weighed 215 pounds. The height was close enough to Cole's, the weight low, but that could be worked out. He was either naturally bald or shaved his head. Cole thought it would be easy enough to take that step if things became necessary. Cole tucked the entire envelope into the carrying case that housed the ozone machine when he left. Someone with the moving company had signed for the envelope. They would be blamed when it came up missing.

There was a problem with the eyes. Gullickson's were blue, strikingly so. Cole spent two days thinking about this. In the end he found a company online that sold non-prescription contact lenses in any number of colors. There were over a dozen shades of blue. Cole ordered three-dozen pairs of the shade—polar blue—that seemed to best match Gullickson's.

The contacts, along with scissors, a razor with shaving cream and a woman's compact mirror, went into Cole's bolt bag. A month later Dom used his contacts in Youngstown to acquire realistic fake IDs for himself and for Tanner.

If the Fireteam ever had to run, they would have a fighting chance.

Cole neared his destination—a downtown parking garage—and spotted the second Klean Sooner van just inside the entrance. Dom was unloading a commercial wet-dry vac while Tanner stood off to the side, hands on hips. He was staring in the direction of the stairway, shaking his head.

Cole turned up his radio as he approached the garage. He recognized the song, "Lord Have Mercy on the Working Man" by Travis Tritt.

He threw back his head and laughed.

CHAPTER SIXTEEN

Paul pulled out of the parking lot a few minutes after three. At the bend in the road a mile from the distillery he slowed and pulled to the side. He checked his mirrors and put on his flashers, then lowered the passenger-side window. Tutor's Bourbon Distillery lay in the distance, the Cumberland River in the background. It was quite a vista. Paul took several pictures with his iPhone.

He drove in silence for some time, lost in thought. The tour was interesting. Paul was one of a group of twenty people. He found himself paying more attention to the guide—a young woman named Callie Combs—than he had on similar tours he'd done with the McClarys. This one didn't follow the process of bourbon production from beginning to end. Instead it began in the main lobby and worked its way to the outer buildings before finishing back in the Visitors Center.

Combs covered the basics, explaining that all bourbon is whiskey, but not all whiskeys are bourbon. Legal requirements mandated that the mash bill, or mix of grains used to create the product, must be at least 51% corn for it to be considered bourbon. Other grains—usually rye, wheat, and barley—make up the remainder. Tutor's mash bill mix was 60% corn, 25% barley, and 15% oats. Combs repeated Obie's claim that the inclusion of oats resulted in a smoother bourbon.

A man in a blue and gold University of Michigan sweater asked, "If oats make the mash smoother, why don't other distillers use it?" All eyes turned to Callie.

"Mainly, it's because of the expense. Oats are a pliable grain. It's difficult to mill them to the proper consistency. Oats also generate more foam than other grains. You'll see that we have mechanical skimmers in place inside a number of the vats. This is an additional expense."

The man in the sweater nodded, seeming to accept the answer.

Combs added, "We'll try to prove to you that oats help smooth the bourbon when we do a tasting at the end of the tour." Several members of the group smiled and whispered comments at this point, something Paul remembered from other tours.

They visited the rickhouse, a seven story rectangular structure built of timber, early in the tour. Bourbon barrels were stored there horizontally in "ricks," or racks. A very regimented program was in place that determined when barrels were moved from one floor to another. Temperatures varied between the bottom floors and those on the top. Seasonal changes also came into play. The higher the location of the barrel inside, the warmer the temperatures. Barrels tend to age faster in higher temperatures. Callie said Tutor's started the aging process of all barrels by putting them on the top floor.

Combs explained "Angel's Share" and "Devil's Cut," two terms often mentioned in discussions about Kentucky's favorite spirit.

"The barrels contain a varying level of liquid. This is determined by the length of time each of them has spent aging. Angel's Share is the amount lost to evaporation through the oak barrels." Several in the group nodded knowingly, no doubt veterans of other tours.

Callie continued, "Some of the bourbon is trapped inside the wood staves of the barrel, this is the Devil's Cut."

Combs led them through buildings that were responsible for the different phases of production. They included cooking, fermentation, and distillation. She was personable and handled all questions with ease. Paul was impressed. In the rickhouse she was asked by the man wearing the University of Michigan sweater if it was difficult to remove barrels from the racks when rotating them.

"It surely is, but we take great care not to tump them. Too much work goes into producing them to take chances."

The man looked at her with confusion on his face. *"Tump?"*

Combs laughed. "Oh, sorry. That's something we say down here...means 'turn over by accident.' I guess it's a combination of 'tip' and 'dump.'"

The man grinned and responded, "I just learned a new word."

The entire tour group laughed.

They spent ten minutes in the barrel factory, a relatively small building on the Tutor's campus. Callie explained that much of the white oak used for the barrel staves was sourced right there on company property. She taught them about charring the barrels and passed around staves that had been charred to different levels. Each level helped produce different flavors in the whiskey.

After leaving this building she led the group back outside and took a paved path toward the river. It was a fine spring day in Kentucky. Combs was upbeat as she answered the occasional question. Paul was enjoying the tour and was glad he'd made the trip.

Combs stopped and gestured to a stand of trees. "These trees are white oak. They're left standing because, y'all saw the still in the lobby?" Several heads nodded. "Well the second original still is inside these trees." Heads turned.

Combs led the group a short distance and a still, nearly identical to its counterpart in the Visitors Center, came into view. It was under a protective structure made of white oak that appeared to be a modern addition to the site. Several in the group approached and took photos.

This was the final stop before returning to the Visitors Center for the tasting. On the way Combs pointed out an area a couple hundred feet away covered with trees that looked slightly different than the white oaks. "Those trees are burr oak. Bourbon barrels can't be made from them but we still utilize them here at Tutor's. All the decorative wood on the front of our buildings here is burr oak. Oh, and the facings of the buildings consist of fieldstones taken from Tutor's property."

Paul realized the location with burr oak trees was the same area he'd earlier noticed a glint. During a lull in questions as they neared their destination he asked about it. "What part of the bourbon process is done in the burr oak area?"

Several in the group turned with Paul to eye the area more closely. Combs stopped, then answered, "I'm not aware of anything related to production there." She turned and covered the last few steps to the door. Paul tilted his head slightly. *Was that a little abrupt?* He shrugged and followed.

The group filed into a room with two long semicircular burr oak tables. The one in front had eight chairs, the longer one behind it had a dozen. The seating was arranged so those in the group would be facing a smaller table made with the same wood. Behind the table were three long rows of glass shelves. Bottles of Tutor's lined the wall. The bottles were displayed exactly as they had been in the gift shop, most with the narrow side facing the room's occupants. Every few feet there was a break in the pattern and the wide side of a bottle faced out.

The group filtered in and found seats. Paul sat on an end seat in the rear row. There was a bottle of water and three small translucent containers, similar to those used in hospitals to dispense medicine, on the tables in front of each chair. Each medicine cup contained a small amount of brown liquid. Paul picked one up and saw by the graduated scale on the side that it held exactly a quarter ounce of bourbon.

"Okay folks, this is the part some of you have been waiting for." Combs smiled and leaned against the table at the front of the room. "Before we taste what came from those barrels let me give you a little history. We're located on the northern tip of McCreary County. The Cumberland," she gestured toward the windows on the rear wall that looked out at the river, "is the border between McCreary and Laurel County to the north. Laurel, by the way, is home to the 708,000 acre Daniel Boone National Forest."

A few heads nodded as Callie went on. "Our founder, Obie Johnson is well-off but there is no truth to the rumor that he owns the forest." Several in the group chuckled.

"Obie's maternal grandfather, Tutor Bishop, was born on this property in 1906. By the late 1920s he had perfected his bourbon recipe, using oats as a key component. Obie began to develop this property for bourbon production ten years ago. He was inspired by other successful Kentucky distillers who used family recipes."

"Like Tom Bulleit over at Bulleit Bourbon, right?" It was the man in the Michigan sweater. He was sitting front row center.

Callie nodded, "Mr. Bulleit is a good example. He has made his great-great-grandfather Augustus's recipe famous and his company quite profitable, but it took a lot of work. We're trying to do something similar here at Tutor's."

Combs turned and picked up a full bottle of Tutor's. "Now then, let's talk about the bottle." She glanced over at Paul and smiled slightly, surprising him. It was the first time that she indicated she knew he was anything but a random member of the tour.

"The shape of the bottle obviously is meant to replicate that of a book. From 1955 until the early 1970s Jim Beam released their whiskey in specially designed decanters. The shapes varied from San Francisco streetcars to bowling pins. They're still very collectible today. Rutherford's Scotch did something similar in their distillery in Edinburgh, Scotland. Some of the Rutherford bottles were shaped like books."

She held up the bottle of Tutor's. "Like this." Combs elaborated, "The bottle has a convex surface on one narrow side making it look like the spine of a book. The other side," she turned the bottle in her hands, "is concave. This makes it appear to be the 'page side' of the book."

"The bottle is relatively expensive to produce. Proprietary molds had to be created for each size of Tutor's. There are only two major glass bottle suppliers in the United States. As the popularity of bourbon grows it puts strains on these suppliers. Consequently their prices go up. Obie has made it a priority that these costs won't be passed on to you, the consumer. He's determined to keep pricing for Tutor's in the mid-range compared to other bourbons in the market."

135

Combs pointed out the labels on the front and the spine. Both featured blue lettering on a field of grey, the company colors. "The font is in something called 'Crimson Text Bold 700 Italic.'"

"That's a mouthful." The man in the Michigan sweater beamed. Paul noticed many in the group had lost some enthusiasm for his comments.

Combs tilted the bottle to show its top to the audience. "You'll notice that the bottle opening is offset to one side. The proper way to pour from our bottle is to position the opening at the top and tilt downward. This gives you a smooth pour." She removed the stopper from the top of the bottle, situated it over one of the translucent cups, and demonstrated. The bourbon flowed out evenly.

"If you try to pour with the spout on the bottom the whiskey glugs out." Combs demonstrated again. The liquid burbled out, a few drops landing on the table. "We certainly don't want to lose any of our Tutor's."

Michigan Sweater piped up, "Don't want it to tump!" Most people in the room snickered. He had regained a few of his admirers.

"The first bourbon we'll taste is the same Tutor's you can buy off the shelf wherever our bottles are sold." She picked up a cup. "Take a second to breath in the aroma first." She swirled the cup and inhaled. "Try to recognize flavors as you sip." She tilted the cup to her lips. The tour members all did the same.

"What do you taste? I get caramel, with a hint of coffee. Others mention black pepper, leather, tobacco...everyone's palate is different."

Several people in the room exchanged comments. A few scrunched their faces. Paul watched and remembered the first time he'd tasted bourbon. *It's definitely an acquired taste.*

Combs suggested they drink a bit of water to clear their palates. "Now you're in for a treat. These next two samples are not yet available on the market." The first was the original Tutor's recipe, but it had been barreled in the rickhouse on the property, not at the contract distiller in Bardstown. Paul tried it. He *did* detect a bit more smoothness.

Hunh, Obie was right about the effect of the water from the river.

The final sample was labeled "Volume Two." It was a variation of the recipe that contained rye in place of barley. Paul could tell the difference. He enjoyed this version as well.

The man in the Michigan sweater asked when these versions would be available to the public. Despite being tired of his voice, all in the crowd turned to Callie to hear her answer.

"Both should be available later this summer wherever Tutor's is sold. We are working every day to make it available in more and more markets." She glanced again at Paul.

Combs concluded the tasting. "Okay folks, that's the end of our tour. Our gift shop, if you're interested, is out this door to the right and down the hall. Restrooms are down the same hall. Thanks again for visiting Tutor's."

As the room emptied Paul approached Combs. "I couldn't help noticing you looking my way when you mentioned the bottle shape. I'm guessing Obie put out the word on me coming today?" Paul's smile was casual, not accusing.

Callie smiled back but shook her head. "Not Obie...but Charlie might have said something."

Paul continued, "Mind if I ask you a question?"

Combs looked over his shoulder, confirming that the last of the tour group had passed through the door. "Why did I avoid your question about equipment in the trees behind the Visitor's Center?"

Paul nodded.

"An area of the trees is cleared out. We have a playground there. That must be what you saw."

"Ooo-kayyy, so why not mention it?"

"We were told not to talk about the playground, or the daycare down the hall." Combs tilted her head to the left, the hallway opposite the gift shop. "I'm not really clear on why. I guess they want the focus to be on the bourbon."

137

"So why tell me now?"

"Charlie said to answer any questions you might have about Tutor's...anything."

Paul considered, "Alright, tell me one thing. How do you feel about working here? The full truth, nothing *but* the truth."

Combs grinned. "It's *fantastic!* I'm working almost every day with our master distiller, helping oversee all production. I hope to be one of the first women to do that job full time. The only reason I'm running the tour today is it's Obie's belief that everyone in the company do it at least a day a month. He says it keeps us connected to our customers."

Paul was impressed. This was a woman looking to thrive in a field that must be dominated by men.

Callie went on. "The daycare is great! Employees can keep their kids close by and even pop in to see them during the day. I'm a single mom and it means the world to me. My Jessy, she's two, is one building away from me all day. We can even have lunch together every day. I was with her right before this tour started."

Paul thanked Combs and wished her good luck. *Not sure she'll need it though, that's a woman that really seems to have a handle on things.* He made his way to the front desk in the lobby where he was again greeted by Charlie Hunter.

"Well, Paul, you got the grand tour, everything to your liking?"

Paul responded with a slight nod. "Very interesting." Then, "I loved the bottles."

Charlie laughed. "Thought you might...Obie said to send you back to his office when you finished. Go ahead and see yourself in, you know the way."

Paul walked to the office door and knocked in the same manner as the staff that delivered lunch a couple hours earlier.

He heard Johnson's voice, "Come."

Obie pushed his chair back as Paul entered and gestured to the two chairs in front of the desk. Paul selected one and Obie moved to the other.

"Well Paul, how did we do?"

Paul replied, "I have to say, it was impressive...everything about it. I see what you mean about the oats...and the difference the water from the Cumberland makes. It's subtle, but it's there. And your guide, Callie, she's a great spokesman, uh, spokes*person*, for your brand."

Obie agreed, "That she is. I have to keep reminding myself that she's not just one of our best female employees, but one of our best employees *period*. I'm old school when it comes to correct terminology."

Paul chuckled, "Me too. Just ask my wife."

Obie settled back in his chair. "What questions do you have, Paul?"

"A couple. If I *did* decide to come on board, what exactly would I do in these college town visits? But first, I'm curious, why don't you want visitors on the tours to see the daycare and playground?"

When Obie began, "Well," Paul realized the man began almost every sentence and answered almost every question with the word "well." *Where have I heard that? That...syntax?*

Johnson finished his answer, "it wasn't really my idea. The folks up in Louisville thought it would take away from the message we're trying to send on the bourbon." He paused and leaned forward. "What do you think?"

Paul didn't hesitate. "I think you should not only mention it, but *emphasize* it. Show that Tutor's is family oriented. I think the customers will think on-site daycare is a positive. If the bourbon is good, well, they were going to figure that out anyway."

Johnson grinned. "You have good instincts Paul. I like that about you."

Then, "The bourbon *is* good."

Paul reached Somerset before turning on his radio. The last podcast from his downloads still showed on his display. It was the *Hardball* episode featuring Nolan Ryan. Something clicked.

THAT's who Obie talks like, Nolan Ryan. It struck Paul that Ryan's first word when answering the interviewer's questions was "Well." *Like a good old boy trying to deflect a compliment.* Johnson had the same self-deprecating manner. Paul shook his head at the coincidence.

At the end of their meeting Obie spent several minutes explaining his vision of Paul's role. It basically came down to him spending two to three days a week at locations with the bar-restaurant-campus environments Tutor's was targeting. "Go to Morgantown, West Virginia...spend two-three days meeting bar owners...pass out some swag...tell them about us...get a read on how we might fit into their business. The next week, go to Indianapolis. Like that."

When Paul raised an objection, saying he really didn't know much, Obie waved him off. "You know all the important stuff. Talk about the bottle. *You* came up with the idea. We'll use the novelty to get our foot in the door. The bourbon will do the rest. The price point fits for these owners. It's slightly on the high end of what they'll pay to have it on their shelves, but if we can get a foothold now, we'll be in good shape when the juice from *our* rickhouse starts hitting the market."

Johnson said the arrangement with Jasper Spirits Consulting was to increase the annual contract with the McClarys by $40,000 effective the day Paul came on board. They would pay Paul $200 a day, plus expenses, for each day he was on the road. The expectation was that Paul would work a maximum of three days a week. Paul could take additional time off, if he liked, with a week's notice. The arrangement would last for six months. The McClarys would keep anything that remained from the original $40,000 and the deal would be reevaluated at the end of the six months.

Paul commented, "Seems like a pretty one-sided deal, and not in your favor. I'm guessing my wife will be happy with this."

Johnson waved a hand. "Not one-sided. I'll be the only distiller in Kentucky with my own Combat Controller."

Obie said he wouldn't ask for an answer today. He wanted Paul to discuss the offer with Lauren.

"Oh by the way, Charlie has a big box of goodies for you at the desk. Pick it up on your way out. There're shirts and such for you, whether you take the job or not. There's also some things for your bride." He gave Paul a conspiratorial look. "Marge McClary just happened to know her sizes."

Paul looked in his rearview mirror and saw the box. It was large enough to nearly block his view of traffic. Large enough that it wouldn't fit comfortably on the rear bench seat. He shook his head. *I think the fix was in on this deal from the start.*

He smiled then checked the queue on his screen. He was nearing Lexington. It was a fine late afternoon in Kentucky. The GPS told him he might catch the tail end of rush hour when he got to Cincinnati, but he should be home before 8:30. Plenty of time to talk with Lauren.

He started the next podcast. The subject was the U.S. Army's push toward Germany in 1945 at the close of World War Two. One segment covered the surprise capture of a bridge over the Rhine River at a German town named Remagen. Paul had heard the name somewhere but couldn't place it.

The Americans were seeking a way across the Rhine. The Germans had destroyed almost all of the bridges. When elements of the U.S. Army reached Remagen they were surprised that the bridge was still standing. They were able to cross under fire in a daring operation. The first man across was a sergeant, Alex Drabik. According to the podcast Drabik had been a butcher in his hometown of Toledo, Ohio.

Toledo...hunh.

Paul sensed movement in his rearview. When he focused on the mirror, the vehicle was blocked by the box from Tutor's. Paul turned to his side mirror, thinking the vehicle was moving fast.

Probably a Sierra pulling a U-Haul...or a kid driving one of those low-to-the-ground things with a rear spoiler.

Paul was surprised to see a silver Buick Lucerne flash past him doing at least 90. A silver-haired woman in her eighties was at the wheel. She was so short she appeared to be looking at the road through a gap between the top of the steering wheel and the dash.

Whoa! Paul watched her pull away, a look of surprise on his face.

Sometimes you don't see things coming.

CHAPTER SEVENTEEN

Tanner withdrew a can of Copenhagen from the left rear pocket of his jeans. He packed the tobacco in the can, producing the *slap-slap-slap* sound with quick movements of his right forearm. He did this without conscious thought. His focus was on the stairway of the parking garage. He opened the can and dug in with his thumb and forefinger, pinching a robust amount and slipping it between his lower lip and gum. He put his hands on his hips and shook his head.

I hate this part of our business.

Tanner turned his head and shouted over his shoulder at Dom. "Hurry it the hell up, Santo. Unload that goddammed wet-dry."

Dom was struggling with the machine, attempting to remove it from the rear of the van. It wasn't just the weight of the unit—nearly one hundred pounds—it was its bulk. It had a capacity of over twenty gallons. It was difficult to get a balanced grip that kept it from falling. He repeated the same plea Tanner had used earlier when finishing his lift in the Klean Sooner building.

"Little help?"

Tanner ignored him, speaking in a low tone. "It's a dirty job." He spat a glob of saliva flecked with ground tobacco to the floor. "A goddammed dirty job."

Both men looked to the garage's entrance as a vehicle pulled in. It was Cole in the second van. It stopped at the barrier gate long enough for him to take a ticket. The city had provided them with cards to slide in when exiting so they wouldn't have to pay when on the job. The van pulled in and parked next to its twin.

"Getting in a lift, Dom?" Cole smiled as he approached the pair.

Dom now had the wet-dry vac in a bear hug and was shuffling backwards attempting to get it clear of the van. His upper body was bent backward as if preparing to limbo. The machine was off-center, slightly higher on Dom's right side. He twisted from the van and bent his knees. When the vac was a foot from the concrete he released it. It clattered to the surface. The casters on the machine's right side struck first. It then lurched to the left. Dom bent and grasped the machine so it wouldn't tip completely and be damaged. He looked like a football player smothering a fumble. He held out his arms as he stood and looked from one side to the other. Both arms and the front of his cream-colored shirt were smudged with unidentified matter.

He frowned. *Great, we haven't used this thing since our last parking garage so I can guess what this stuff is.*

Tanner heard the bang and turned to Dom. "About time. Let's get this over with." Then, "Stop sniffing your shirt."

The city garage on Fourth and Elm was located a few short blocks northeast of the Ohio Statehouse. It boasted 682 parking spaces on its four floors and cost over $15 million to build. On this night Klean Sooner would be responsible for cleaning, disinfecting, and deodorizing stairways on the north and south sides. In addition they were to do the same to areas of the garage the city had received complaints about—an area near the northeast corner of the third floor and a spot on the second floor overlooking Gay Street on the south side of the building. The contract further specified the contractors "inspect the entire building visually and by the process of olfaction" to determine if other areas required treatment.

Cole had to look up "olfaction." It pretty much meant what he suspected. He, Tanner, and Dom would need to check the entire structure with their noses.

Cole had signed the contract after first insisting one other clause be changed. The original document stated that in addition to scheduled monthly cleanings for each garage, the contractor must respond to unscheduled emergency cleanings "as needed." Cole changed the wording to *if available*, arguing that the nature of a contract cleaner's business meant they were often already out doing unforeseen jobs. The city accepted the amended wording, no doubt persuaded by the bid Cole had submitted. It was substantially lower than all other bidders.

The change in verbiage had nothing to do with a possible conflict of schedule with other Klean Sooner jobs. It was Cole's way of assuring that the Fireteam could pull off multi-day robbery missions without losing the contract.

Cole devised the specific method used to clean the garages. He used the same linear logic for this problem that he employed for the robberies. After dropping off the wet-dry vac at the base of the stairway, the van would drive to the top floor of the garage and park near the entrance to the stairs. There they would unload a gas-powered pressure washer from the rear door of the vehicle. The unit was situated in front of the wet-dry before leaving the Klean Sooner building. A 55-gallon drum, formerly filled with degreaser but now containing water, was just inside the sliding side door of the van.

The first step in the actual soil removal was accomplished with a lithium battery powered leaf blower. One member of the team would start at the top and blow any loose debris to the platform on the floor below. While he did this, a second man started the pressure washer and made sure its draw hose was properly inserted into the drum of water. When the leaf blower operator returned, the pressure washer man began to blast away at the steps. The machine packed a punch—1500 psi—and easily removed any visible soils from the steps. By this time the third member of the team would have arrived at the top floor, having taken the elevator after prepositioning the wet-dry vac on the ground floor. He would retrieve a 24-inch wide heavy-duty floor squeegee from the van that was attached to a wood handle. Starting at the top of the stairwell he would walk backward and drag the excess water off each step with the squeegee.

The wand that the pressure washer operator held was attached to a fifty-foot hose that, in turn, was connected to the machine. Fifty feet was plenty long to do one flight of steps but no more. After reaching the platform below he would gather up the hose, climb back to the top, and pitch it back into the van. A stack of bright yellow Rubbermaid folding wet-floor signs were inside, enough to put one at the top and bottom of each flight of stairs.

There were also a half dozen 3-gallon pump-up garden sprayers in the van. They were filled with a mixture of water and a specially formulated disinfectant that also had an enzyme component that was very effective against odors, including urine and feces. After the steps were squeegeed one of the team would coat the surface with a light mist of the cleaner.

The pressure washer operator would drive the van down to the next level and meet the team that was working their way down the steps. Typically he would let the gas powered washer run while inside the van. Cole had joked, "I'll bet OSHA would lose their mind over that." But there were never any Occupational Safety and Health Administration inspectors in urine-soaked parking garages at night.

This method was repeated until the team reached the ground floor where the wet-dry vac would suck up all the liquid. It would be emptied in a drain if one was available or outside in the grass or into a street drain if not. This process was duplicated in all stairways on that night's list. The final step was to retrieve the wet-floor signs, hit any remaining damp spots with the leaf blower, and pack up. The team would then tackle the other reported problem areas before slowly driving through the entire garage with windows down, using their eyes and noses to detect other problem areas.

In this way they were able to comprehensively clear the building. Urine, the most common problem, was easy to eliminate. If someone had defecated however, the pressure washer would push—and liquefy—it all the way to the wet-dry at the bottom.

Or, as Tanner descriptively put it, "Shit runs downhill."

When Cole left Southeastern Oklahoma State University to return to Bartlesville, he didn't have a long-term plan. He just knew that with his mother gone and Turk God-knows-where he had to come up with a way to earn money. He and Tanner stayed with an aunt—Turk's sister—for a few months but it was an uncomfortable situation for all involved. Cole reached out to Cy Borgia, the man who had arranged cleaning jobs for Tammy years earlier.

Borgia started Cole as a cleaner and put him to work doing the same jobs he'd done years earlier when tagging along with his mother. He showed a talent for organization and seemed to have people skills that allowed him to relate to everyone from janitors to security guards to company presidents. Within six months Cole was promoted to supervisor of the night cleaning crews and had scraped together enough money to rent a one-bedroom apartment in Bartlesville. He and Tanner moved out from the aunt's place. It was now just the two of them.

Tanner insisted he should quit school and go to work with Cole. His brother wouldn't hear of it. There were arguments and, twice, physical altercations but Cole won out. Tanner would finish high school.

The younger Jelcik took out his frustrations on opponents on the football field. He racked up tackles—enough to be named all-league, all-district, and special mention on the all-state team. He was also flagged for unnecessary roughness a half dozen times and ejected from one game. Cole had been just as aggressive as Tanner on the football field, but had channeled it. Tanner was undisciplined.

Or, as an opposing coach was quoted as saying after a game in the Bartlesville Examiner-Enterprise, "That number 83, he's a maniac." It wasn't clear if the comment was a tribute to Tanner's intensity or a cautionary warning to the population of northeastern Oklahoma.

Cole became Borgia's right-hand man. He convinced the older man to aggressively advertise the company. He came up with marketing ideas, changing the name of the business to *CY-BORG Cleaning*. He conceived of a logo that was just enough unlike Arnold Schwarzenegger's character in *Terminator* to keep the company from being sued. The business took off. CY-BORG Cleaning became a member of the Building Service Contractors Association International—or BSCAI—an organization comprised of cleaning contractors from 15 countries. He attended the annual trade shows in several cities, including Las Vegas, where he networked with hundreds of others in the business.

By this time Tanner was working with Cole, having joined the business the day after his high school graduation. They got a bigger apartment—this one had two bedrooms and, it turned out, hot and cold running women—and despite Tanner being underage were regulars in what passed as the Bartlesville bar scene. No bartender refused to serve two drinks at a time to Cole, even though they knew one was going to find its way to his brother.

They pumped iron at a 24-hour fitness club and discovered it was almost as good a place to meet future hook-ups as the bars. It was here that they heard about the Arnold Sports Festival, an annual gathering for physique and strength sports in Columbus, Ohio that had a long-time association with Schwarzenegger, a former Mr. Universe. After Tanner had been with the company for nine months the brothers took a week of vacation and, in the first week of March, drove to Columbus to check out the festival.

They were blown away. The festival was Disneyland for the Jelciks. Most of the attendees were like-minded individuals, more concerned with the latest recovery drink than any politician's economic recovery program. The patrons of the show were overwhelmingly male but somehow there were enough women—Tanner referred to them as "Muscle-Bunnies" —to go around. They even got to see the great man himself one day when he visited the 500-booth Expo inside the Convention Center. They didn't get close enough to him to get a good picture. There were several hundred people swarming the man. They settled for selfies taken with the 8-foot bronze sculpture of Arnold just outside the building. The sculpture showed Schwarzenegger posing in his famous "twisted double biceps" position. Cole and Tanner removed their shirts and asked a buff woman in tights to take a few shots of them.

They performed the same pose. The statue was between them, framed by their biceps, triceps, and grinning faces.

They were less than halfway home when they formulated a plan to move to Ohio. They would start their own company. They weren't tied down to extended family, wives, or even serious girlfriends. Yes, they would leave Oklahoma behind and move to the Buckeye state.

They would need startup cash for the new business. They would also like to get back at the bank that foreclosed on their mother's house after her death.

These two things were not mutually exclusive.

CHAPTER EIGHTEEN

They would need weapons.

Not just the plink-around sort like the .22 rifles in the corners of half the closets in Bartlesville. No, they needed to arm themselves with hardware that would get the attention of anyone they targeted. Cole had definite opinions about this.

"We want to be taken seriously the second we walk into the place. Get people's attention on the guns, not us so much."

They were rolling through Indiana now. The road surface of I-70 had gone to shit the moment they crossed the state line from Ohio.

Tanner nodded thoughtfully. "Something that says, 'We are not to be fucked with.'"

"Yep."

Tanner considered, "You've been thinking about this for awhile." It was a statement, not a question.

"It's crossed my mind." Cole drove on. They were in a six-year-old Chevy Blazer from CY-BORG Cleaning. Borgia had allowed them to borrow the vehicle for the trip to Columbus. The company logo had drawn comments from several people attending the festival.

Tanner persisted, "So, were you seeing Drema just so you could get a handle on how things worked at the bank?"

Drema Johns was a buxom blonde with a gap the width of a nickel's edge between her two front teeth. She was four years older than Cole and had been married to her high school sweetheart Johnny Johns for three years. "John-John," as he was known around town, had lost interest in Drema an hour or so after the honeymoon ended. He spent most of his waking hours—when he wasn't working at the Tire Mart—chasing after Drema's high school football cheerleader squad-mates. He'd had her. He was collecting the full set.

Cole smiled, "Not *just* to get information on the bank. You remember her on the sidelines when she was in high school? She still fits into her cheerleading outfit." He smiled at Tanner conspiratorially. Both brothers remembered eying Drema during her senior year. Cole was in the eighth grade, Tanner the sixth—prime ogling years.

Drema went to work after high school as a trainee with a Bank of Oklahoma branch office in Bartlesville. By the time Cole connected with the lonely wife she was a full-time teller at the same bank. Another branch of the bank was across town next to Eastland Shopping Center. The Jelciks' parents, Turk and Tammy, did their banking at the Eastland location. The brothers focused their ire on this branch.

Cole assumed the security protocols were the same, or at least similar, at both locations. He very subtly extracted information from Drema over the course of their clandestine meetings. Sometimes these occurred in a cheap hotel room, occasionally in the back seat of Drema's Toyota Celica, and twice inside a thicket of trees at Bartlesville's Johnstone Park off Cherokee Avenue.

Tanner once asked, "How the hell were the two of you able to pull that off in the back of a damn Celica? I mean, there's like, *no* leg room in a Celica."

Cole answered, "We weren't concerned about leg room, T." Then, "Where there's a will, there's a way." He winked at his brother.

Over the course of their trysts Cole learned quite a bit. Some of it was about erotic body positions, much of it about bank procedures. He found out about exploding dye packs, baited money, and teargas inserts. Just as importantly he learned how the tellers were trained to act during a robbery.

As they neared Indianapolis Cole recited this information in as much detail as he could remember. Tanner listened intently, interrupting from time to time with questions. When Cole was tapped out Tanner sat back. He stared out the passenger window thoughtfully then turned to Cole with a solemn expression.

"So...," he began in a tone almost grave in its manner, "I guess you could say you were pumping her for information?"

Tanner couldn't wait for Cole's reaction. He burst out laughing at his own cleverness. Cole joined in. The brothers howled for thirty seconds, Tanner slapping the dash. When it subsided, Tanner, his eyes glistening, turned back to Cole.

"Let's rob that fucking bank."

Tanner had the idea for the weapons about the time they returned to I-70 after stopping at a Five Guys burger and fries joint in Terre Haute. They were discussing the difficulties of hiding their identity in any robbery in their hometown. Cole had ideas about masks and where to position their getaway car —they would leave the bank on foot and cut through several properties—but any local purchase of firearms would be remembered.

Between bites of a cheeseburger he remarked. "It just hit me, there was a place down in the Ozarks."

"Ozarks?" Cole was reaching into the bottom of the Five Guys bag with his right hand, fishing out fries. His left arm was draped over the wheel, fingers dangling down. He steered with the underside of his wrist.

Tanner elaborated, "Yeah. Remember when Turk took us and Mom to Bull Shoals Lake?" The brothers by this time had stopped referring to their father as anything other than Turk. "We stayed in that cabin for most of a week? We went to the fairgrounds one day and—"

Cole sat up. "And there was a gun show there. Yeah! We could check the schedule online, head down there on a weekend, buy what we need, be home the same day!"

Tanner stuffed the last quarter of his cheeseburger into his mouth and reached for his cellphone. He mumbled, "Might as w e l l   c h e c k   i t   r i g h t   n o w . "   I t   c a m e   o u t "Myahwhalchkkitryenaw."

They found that there was a two-day gun show three months later in June. Cole said, "Let me think. Got a dip?"

They rode in silence for ten miles. The *pwtt* sound of Copenhagen juice being spit out periodically interrupted the quiet. Cole spat into his empty Coke cup—he first rolled down the window and tossed out the ice—while Tanner made use of a small spittoon that was specially designed to look like a pineapple-style World War Two era hand grenade. It was a present from a cowgirl-type he dated a few months earlier back in Oklahoma.

"I think I got it." Cole laid it out.

They would start laying the groundwork with Cy Borgia about leaving, explaining that they fell in love with Columbus on their vacation and, besides, they thought it was time to get a new start, see what the world had to offer. They'd give him plenty of time—three months sounded about right—to get things in order and figure how to replace them. In the meantime, they would search the internet for a place to rent in Columbus and start researching cleaning bids and opportunities in central Ohio.

In June they would drive the four-plus hours to the Ozarks. The gun show at the fairgrounds was located in the town of Mountain View, Arkansas. There they would buy the most badass weapons available, pay with cash, and head home. Then, just before vamoosing from Bartlesville for good they would even the score with the Bank of Oklahoma.

That's just how it happened.

Sorta.

Donny Ritler was a gun dealer. Sure, he sold real estate—fishing cabins on the lake, 1,200 square-foot single story starter homes on country roads, like that—but in his heart and mind he was a gun dealer. He had a Federal Firearms License from the Bureau of Alcohol, Tobacco, and Firearms. He even followed all of their rules on gun sales.

Most of the time.

At gun shows it was often like the Wild West. Cash deals and sketchy paperwork were more common than any of the participants cared to admit. Ritler tried to hit shows as many weeks as possible between the months of March and October. He spent the winter in Florida in a house trailer outside of Winter Haven and got down to Key West every couple weeks. He'd spend his yearly profits then head back to Mountain View in the spring and start all over again.

He was a single man, 57. He had a paunch, strong opinions on politics and Razorback football, and most of his hair. His house two miles outside of town would be the envy of the late Charlton Heston, the iconic actor and NRA supporter. Ritler owned four large gun safes and, though they were usually full, still had firearms hanging on all of his walls. The only two items displayed that were not guns were a framed copy of da Vinci's *The Last Supper* and a slightly larger framed print of *Dogs Playing Poker*.

His friends and neighbors called his house *The Ritler Bunker*. Some used mocking tones, some admiring. Donny always took the term as a compliment, failing to see the ironic similarity to the "Hitler Bunker" of 1945.

He was unloading his truck after the local show at the fairgrounds on a Sunday in June. It had been a success. He'd sold a dozen pieces over two days. Seven were written up all nice and neat to keep Uncle Sam happy. The other five—well— the extra $2,100 in his pocket made him forget the details of those transactions.

He had gun cases in both hands and was sliding them from the bed of his truck when he heard a vehicle brake suddenly. He turned in time to see another truck—he later tried to nail down the model but wasn't sure—slide to the side of the road. It hit the wooden pole supporting his mailbox and snapped it in two. The mailbox pinwheeled for several feet as the truck came to a rest. The lone occupant, a large man, struggled to open the door and tumbled out, one arm gripping his chest. The man fell and lay there with his back to Donny.

"What the hell?" Donny released the gun cases and took a few tentative steps toward the road. The man was moaning.

Better call 9-1-1. Ritler reached into his pocket and withdrew his iPhone. When he was eight feet from the truck he

155

realized it had a set of rear doors. The one on the driver's side exploded open and another hulk of a man sprung out. He wore a red, white, and blue bandana and was pointing a handgun at Donny. The man on the ground sprung up. He was also now wearing a bandana that apparently had been tied around his neck.

The driver hissed, "Get him into the house. I'll move the truck."

The second man growled, "Get your ass inside. *NOW.*"

Ritler watched the man wave the pistol in his face and thought, *That's a Hi-Point JCP in .40 caliber. Nice piece for a hundred and eighty bucks retail. I probably could've sold them one for one-fifty.*

Then, *Goddammit.*

The Jelcik brothers went to the Mountain View Gun Show the day before, Saturday, intending to buy a couple mean looking handguns before turning around and returning to Oklahoma. They left early and made the 285-mile drive in less than five hours. It was an east-by-southeast route that put the sun in their face most of the way. They listened to CDs in Cole's used black Honda Ridgeline, mostly Jack Ingram and Cole Swindell with some Johnny Cash thrown in. They drank coffee, dipped Copenhagen, and commented on the pickups on the highway.

Tanner squinted as a Ford F-150 King Ranch came toward them in the westbound lane of Interstate-44. "Look at that rig...Damn! Gonna get me one of those some day."

Cole turned his head slightly and picked up the truck through his sunglasses. He nodded and smiled. Ingram's "That's a Man" flowed through the speakers.

At the show the brothers made the rounds. Cole honed in on a display of M1911 .45 caliber pistols at a booth run by a smiling, balding man that looked to be about 60. The price on the weapons was over $1,000 each—more than they could spend—but they would be perfect for the brothers' task.

Cole led Tanner a short distance away. "I have an idea."

They followed the man after the show and were pleasantly surprised to discover he lived just a few miles from the fairgrounds. He was outside the city limits. No houses were closer than a quarter-mile from his.

Cole drove his Ridgeline past the house and smiled. "Let's go see if Mr. Sam Walton has a store in this town."

It was Arkansas, so yes, there was a Walmart.

Cole bought a roll of dark grey duct tape, a can of black spray paint, two bandanas, and a 3-foot wide blue plastic kids wading pool. They found a place called Pizza Inn that had a buffet and filled up while checking their phones for a cheap place to sleep. They found one, the Dogwood Motel.

They checked in, paid the seventy bucks, and drug the pool into the room. Using tin snips from the truck they cut it into a half dozen strips of blue plastic. That done they watched *Top Gun* on TV before sleeping in their underwear.

They slept in Sunday, did a couple hundred pushups apiece in sets of 50, and took showers. Since they hadn't planned on staying overnight they wore their same jeans and shirts from Saturday.

Cole found an out of the way dirt lane that seemed to lead to nowhere. He pulled in and the brothers laid out the plastic strips and coated them with black paint. They left them there to dry before returning to the show at the fairgrounds. They killed a good part of the day there eating at the snack bar and surreptitiously watching the booth with the M1911s. At one in the afternoon Cole paid cash for a Hi-Point .40 caliber pistol and a box of ammunition. An hour before the show wrapped up the Jelciks left and drove back to the farm lane.

Cole held strips of what had been the pool over the Ridgeline's front bumper. Tanner tore pieces of duct tape with his teeth and stuck them on. When they'd finished the bumper was protected by several layers. They then drove to the gun dealer's house and pulled off the road a half-mile away. They waited.

When the man's truck came into view Cole instructed Tanner, "Do the plate."

157

Tanner jumped out and covered the rear plate—the only one required in Oklahoma—with pre-torn strips of the tape. He then got in the rear seat and knelt down. The dealer's truck was stopped in his drive.

Cole said, "Here we go, T," and they were off.

The rest was easy. Cole hit the mailbox post just right with the front left side of his bumper. The plastic strips cracked but minimized damage. Cole had the idea the day before when he saw that the wooden post looked weathered.

They got the man inside and quickly went through the place. They could hardly believe their luck. "It's a damn armory," Tanner exclaimed. They grabbed six M1911 pistols and an entire case of .45 rounds. They searched the dealer's pockets and took a roll of hundred dollar bills.

Cole realized the man must have more money stashed inside the house. They forced the dealer to give up his honey holes. After three rounds of playing *That's the last of it, really —Bullshit, where's the rest?* Cole believed he had all of the hidden cash.

The brothers were about to leave when Tanner found a hidden compartment in one of the gun safes. It opened to reveal reproductions of a World War Two carbine and a Tommy Gun as well as a large case with the biggest, meanest looking rifle inside that Cole and Tanner had ever seen.

"Hol—lee Shit" Tanner whistled. "Take it?"

Cole could see no possible use for a weapon like this in the bank job they had planned, but he couldn't pass it up. "Damn straight, the carbine and Tommy Gun too."

They left Donny Ritler on the floor, duct tape wrapped around his ankles and wrists, a strip across his mouth. He was despondent.

They got the Barrett. I'm not even supposed to have that. Oh shit...can I report this? Then, with tears forming in his eyes, *They took all my seed money for this winter, sixteen grand...all my Key West play money. Gonna be a long winter.* And finally, *Well, poop.*

The Jelcik's rolled back to Oklahoma. Tanner finished the count. "There's over $18,000 here!"

They had pulled off the plastic from the front of the truck and the tape from the rear plate and tossed it all into a ditch. Johnny Cash's "Orange Blossom Special" blared from the speakers.

Cole could still feel the rush. "Pretty good, huh?" He held out a fist and Tanner bumped it before pausing, his face turning thoughtful.

"Damn, forgot one thing."

Cole, wary, asked, What? What did we forget?"

"That picture on the wall. I was gonna take it...Did you see the bulldog was smoking a cigar?"

The next week they hit the Bank of Oklahoma branch near Eastland. Cole texted Drema a couple days before just "touching base." She was back with John-John, trying to make a go of it. He wanted to make sure she hadn't been transferred to Eastland.

Cole: *Still running the show at the bank downtown?*

Drema: *Yeah right. Like I'm in charge. Still working the window, LOL.*

Cole: *Bide your time. You'll get promoted. Can't keep a good woman down.* He included a devil smiley face emoji.

Drema: *LOL!!!*

Cole: *I guess you heard, me & T are moving to Ohio.*

Drema: *Sorry to see you go.*

Cole: *If you're ever in Columbus...*

The take from the bank was a little over $7,500. It was small potatoes compared to the home invasion in Arkansas but satisfying for the brothers. They felt like they'd gotten back at the bank for what it did to their family.

They were neophytes, having few of the techniques they would later develop and hone, but they were just good enough to pull it off and escape. They used two of the pistols—the long guns weren't seriously considered due to having to run through properties on their way out—and took the cash from the teller drawers. The vault was not a consideration.

A few days later they were back on the road to Columbus. Everything they owned was packed in the Ridgeline.

The Fourth and Elm parking garage stairways were finished. The trio from Klean Sooner packed up van number two. Tanner grabbed the wet-dry vac and easily hefted it into the rear of the vehicle. He looked at Dom.

"That's how it's done, Santo." Then added, "You pipsqueak."

Dom rolled his eyes.

Tanner then remembered something. He turned to Cole. "Guess what Big Boy? I did thirty reps of 225 today."

Cole looked at him with skepticism. He turned to Santo for confirmation. "Dom?"

Dom turned away, trying to avoid being put in the middle of the situation.

Cole interpreted Dom's reaction immediately. He looked at Tanner and said sarcastically, "Oh sure, I'll bet." This led to a fairly heated back and forth.

Dom turned back to the van and shifted the equipment around. *Fucking brothers.*

They made one last trip through the garage. It was after 10 p.m. Tanner and Dom rode in van two. Cole followed in van one. Their windows were down as they searched for additional trouble spots with dwindling enthusiasm. They stopped at the reported area on the south side of the second floor and sprayed it with the chemical mixture. They did the same to the spot on the third floor.

They were on the way back down intending to exit when van two braked suddenly on the second level. Cole, following, did the same. Tanner's head protruded from the driver's side window and he bellowed, "WHAT THE HELL ARE YOU DOING?"

Cole followed Tanner's eyes and saw a man in torn pants and a dingy jacket zipping his fly. He stood in the same spot they had treated ten minutes earlier.

Tanner put his van in park and strode to the offender. The man was obviously a street person. He had long stringy hair. The left side of his face was covered by a large burn scar. The right by grime and unruly facial hair. The result was a face of indeterminate race or origin. The man finished zipping and offered a weary smile.

"Jus hadda go, suh."

Tanner was incensed. "*Bullshit*, we just cleaned that spot. I oughta..." He took another step toward the man.

Cole got out of van one and approached. "Hold it, hold it. Calm down, T."

Cole had a bit of a soft spot for the homeless. He had a big one for victims of fires. A childhood friend had been burned badly in a house fire and had undergone painful skin grafts. This man obviously hadn't had proper treatment.

"What's your name, partner?"

"Rufus. Rufus Hendershot, suh. Jus hadda go."

Cole nodded. He tilted his head toward Tanner. "Get one of the pump-ups and spray this down." He pointed to a spot behind Hendershot.

Tanner was pissed. He walked to the rear of the van, muttering.

Cole turned back to the homeless man. "My name's Cole. Any chance we can get you to stop using parking garages as toilets?"

Hendershot bobbed his head. "Sure Mister Cole...just couldn't make it to the shelter and the library's closed." He sidestepped away from Tanner as the larger man approached with the sprayer. "Won't let it happen again."

Cole smiled and reached for his wallet. He opened it, intending to give Rufus a ten or a twenty then saw the two hundreds he'd won from Tanner and Dom when they guessed at the total take from the Racine robbery. He pulled one out and handed it to Hendershot. "There you go Rufus, get yourself some good food."

The man's eyes lit up. "You *serious?*"

Cole nodded, "Yep."

Tanner trailed over and looked at the bill. "You gotta be kidding me! A hundred bucks? To *this* guy?"

Cole frowned at his brother and extracted the second hundred. Handing it to Hendershot he said, "And get yourself a new pair of pants."

Tanner nearly squealed, "Hey, that's the money from..."

Cole shot him a look, quashing the end of Tanner's sentence. He glared at his brother. "Finish up. Then we're going to go back to the building and put 225 on the bar. We'll see what's what."

Tanner thought, *Oh shit.*

CHAPTER NINETEEN

Lauren put her hands on her hips and angled her face to the sky. She was breathing hard. It was a Tuesday in mid-May and the flowers were in full bloom, lending a faint aroma to the morning air. She stood and walked in tight circles on the sidewalk. She was on the corner of Greene and Wayne Streets in Piqua. Between breaths she was able to utter, "Oh wow, that seemed fast."

Lacey Billingham walked the same circle, but in the opposite direction. From a distance their counter-rotation might've seemed choreographed. In reality they were simply trying to catch their breath.

Both women ran with their smartphones in their hands, secured by sport bands that were designed for that purpose. Lacey checked her phone and broke out in a toothy grin. She stopped and let Lauren continue on her path until they faced each other. Lacey put her hands on Lauren's shoulders and said excitedly, "That was over a minute faster than our best time!" She beamed at Lauren, before adding, "You're doing so *well!*"

Lauren gave her a half smile, "It feels like I'm killing myself." But she knew Lacey was right. The women had enjoyed a growing friendship since Lacey started her job at the hospital. In the cafeteria one day she told Lauren she'd begun running a couple days a week in the morning before work.

"Matt is all for it, but he's a little leery about me being out on the street in the dark by myself. I told him he could come out with me and he just stared at me, like, 'What?'" She laughed, "Can you imagine, a diesel mechanic running through Piqua wearing tights?"

Lauren giggled. She'd met Lacey's fiancé two weeks earlier when he dropped off some paperwork for Kettering Health's Wellness program. It was designed to encourage healthy lifestyles for employees and their spouses. Though Lacey and Matt wouldn't be married until the following month the hospital encouraged Lacey to have him enroll. Lacey led Matt by the hand down to the lab and introduced them.

"This is my friend Lauren."

Lauren smiled remembering the burly mechanic in his work uniform, red-faced, being led around by the hand by the blonde who was a head shorter. The betrothed couple had found a small house to rent near downtown Piqua on Greene Street. Lacey confided that her parents seemed uncomfortable with the arrangement until she offered, "Would you feel better if I was living in a strange town by *myself*?" Her parents saw the logic. Matt would protect their daughter like a mother lion. They could live with the arrangement until the wedding.

Lacey threw out a question, "Would *you* be interested in running with me?"

Lauren was about to sip from her Diet Coke, the straw from her nugget-ice filled cup stopped an inch from her lips and hovered. "*Me?*"

Though her eyebrows were raised and her response indicated she thought the idea was ridiculous Lauren saw its appeal instantly. She'd felt for some time that she needed to break the cycle of work, sleep, work. The new hourly schedule for the lab had taken effect on May 1. Lauren now had stable hours of 7 a.m. to 4 p.m. during the week. Sure, there was overtime and the occasional weekend thrown in but she could now count on a regular starting time to her day.

They worked it out. Lauren would drive from their house outside of Troy to Lacey's place in Piqua. They met at 5:30 a.m., did their run, and Lauren drove back to Polecat Road to shower and dress for work. They quickly realized that as their capability to cover greater distances increased, the time allotted was just too short. Lauren had an idea. Over dinner one night she broached the subject with Paul, "What do you think about me joining the Piqua Y?"

She braced for pushback, imagining his response, "We have a full gym in the basement, why would you want to do that?" But Paul was one step ahead of her.

"It would be a good place to shower after your runs, right? Cut down on the driving before work?" He was on board.

"The Y" was the Piqua *YWCA*. The more common *YMCA* boasted nearly 2,700 locations in the United States. There were fewer than 200 YWCAs. Piqua had one of each. The YWCA building was on Wayne Street, just a few blocks from Lacey and Matt's rental.

The routine was modified. Lauren packed work clothes at night. She woke up at five and drove to the Y. She was usually stretching outside the building when Lacey came around the corner. They had a route that gave them the regimen that most runners craved but at the same time offered variation. From the Y they jogged three blocks north on Wayne and angled left on Riverside Drive. This street ran diagonally, southeast to northwest, paralleling the Great Miami River, which flowed beside it just to the north. They followed it a little over a mile until reaching the entrance to Forest Hill Cemetery on the left. The cemetery grounds were large with a number of loops and sections. Depending on how they felt, the women could stay inside a short distance or add extra mileage. Exiting Forest Hill, they linked up with neighborhood streets and worked their way back to Greene. Lacey continued past her house with Lauren until they reached the corner of Greene and Wayne. There they could chat and stretch before Lauren continued to the Y to shower and dress for work, while Lacey jogged easily back home. The drive to the hospital took less than 15 minutes.

Today's run had been encouraging. *A full minute faster than our best?* Lauren smiled. She'd come to cherish the runs with Lacey. On most mornings they loped along at a pace that allowed for conversation. Lauren found that despite the age difference she and Lacey had much in common. The younger woman was excited about her new job and her upcoming marriage. She looked forward to being a mom someday. She tentatively asked why Lauren and Paul had no kids and Lauren gave her the whole history of doctor consultation, testing, and artificial efforts that had ultimately been unsuccessful. That line of conversation had taken one entire run and parts of others.

It wasn't just the morning runs that had Lauren feeling more upbeat. Paul had accepted the position with Mike and Marge's company and was working a couple days a week. It involved overnight hotel stays, which had both positives and negatives. She missed him when he was gone but she was able to have some time to herself and work on projects around the house. There were enough of these to keep her busy until Paul's six-month period touting Tutor's Bourbon came to an end. She supposed they would reassess things after that.

The most important thing was that Paul actually seemed happy with the arrangement, which in turn made *her* happy.

Lacey removed her right hand from Lauren's shoulder and bent her right leg backward. She grabbed her toe and pulled upward, stretching the quad muscles above her knee. She braced herself by keeping her left hand on Lauren. The move was casual, something lifelong friends might do.

Lacey touched her toes then turned in the direction of her house, "Gotta tell Matt he might be marrying an Olympian." She giggled and began to jog home. Over her shoulder she called back to Lauren, "See you at lunch. Goodbye, Big Sis!"

It was a nickname Lauren's coworkers in the lab had playfully given her since she'd begun to meet Lacey in the cafeteria for lunch most days.

Lauren laughed.

"Goodbye, Little Sis!"

Paul's Tuesday morning had begun not unlike Lauren's, with a run alongside a river. In his case it had been the Scioto rather than the Great Miami. He was in Columbus. It was his third week working for Jasper Spirits. Paul drove to the city the morning before. His first appointment wasn't until 9:30 and since the drive time between Troy and Columbus was just an hour and a quarter he hadn't been rushed.

Charlie Hunter made a reservation for him at the Renaissance Columbus on the northern edge of downtown for Monday night. He was tentatively scheduled to be in Columbus for two days. Paul argued that the drive from Troy was short and he'd be happy to drive home Monday night—"Why spend the money for a hotel?"—but Charlie wouldn't hear of it.

"This is why Obie built expense money into your deal Paul. I'll get you a room and you won't have to rush through your day." Then, "I know a thing or two about men talking bourbon."

Paul laughed. *She's got me there.* If there was one thing Paul had discovered in the two-plus weeks of visiting bar managers and owners it was that they had no problem having long discussions about the whiskey.

Those that knew little about the product appreciated Paul's unintimidating method of delivering information about Tutor's. His line was, "I'm no expert, but let me tell you a few things about the company." The person he was talking with usually smiled and turned the Tutor's bottle in their hands. They then typically followed the opening line Paul had come to use. *There are no dumb questions when it comes to Tutor's Bourbon.* They seemed to open up and ask questions that, despite working in an establishment that sold alcoholic beverages—some of them their entire adult lives—they'd never felt comfortable asking anyone before. They felt, *shouldn't I already know this? I'd look stupid waiting until NOW to ask about it.* Paul seldom had the answer to any question that required any information that hadn't been covered by Callie Combs in the tour Paul did back in early April. But he always had the same response.

"I don't know, but I'll find out."

He did. Several times a day he would call one of the McClarys in Dayton or Charlie Hunter down in Sawyer. He peppered them with questions. Not just for the benefit of the bar staff member, but for his own. He always followed up with a call back to the person who asked the question. He felt they genuinely appreciated his effort.

The other type he ran into were the bourbon experts. Sometimes these were people who obviously knew the history of the spirit inside and out. They knew the mash bill grain percentages of every bourbon on the market and could calculate the price per ounce they would need to charge to make their desired profit as soon as they heard the cost of a bottle.

This group also seemed to have no problem with Paul's lack of knowledge. On the contrary, they enjoyed relaying information to him that would help him improve at his job.

There was also a subclass of expert—the Know-It-All. Once they detected that Paul was a newbie at this bourbon thing they went into lecture mode. Paul was able to withstand this— he *HAD* been in the military—and when the whiskey oracle had finally run out of facts and opinions, they took a liking to him.

Or as one pudgy bar owner in Athens near Ohio University admitted, "I like you, Pat. The liquor folks usually send some hot little thing in to see us bar owners. The last one stared at me all doe-eyed when I was talking at her but I could tell she didn't give a rat's ass about what I was sayin'...but you seem to really listen."

Paul simply nodded. The man had gotten his name wrong but had agreed to bring in a case of Tutor's for a drink promo. He supposed this made it a successful stop.

Once Charlie informed him that he would be staying in Columbus Paul decided to call his sister. Patrice lived in the Columbus suburb of Hilliard with her husband, Kevin, and two sons. Leo was 15, Frankie 12.

"Hey, Sis. I'll be in your neck of the woods Monday night. Mind if I come over for dinner?"

Patrice was two years younger than Paul. She was the Event Sales Coordinator for the National Veterans Memorial and Museum. This was a multi-million dollar facility just west of the Scioto River in downtown Columbus. Kevin was a structural engineer. Leo and Frankie were American boys, through and through.

Patrice didn't hesitate. "Bring wine."

Paul spent Monday making stops at several bars and restaurants. He was two hours into his day when he realized Columbus would require several trips. There were just too many establishments. High Street alone—the north-south artery that bordered Ohio State University's east side—was home to dozens of bars.

Paul worked the appointments that Charlie set up. He settled for a Clif Bar for lunch and made every meeting on his list. Tutor's had provided him with a significant amount of promotional material. In addition to three cases of 750 milliliter bottles of the bourbon, he had shirts, posters, boxes of drink coasters, and twelve-inch wooden rulers that boasted the Tutor's logo. The concept for the rulers—conceived by the marketing company in Louisville—was to give them to bartenders and have them act as though they would slap the fingers of any customer that ordered another brand of bourbon.

I'll have a Jack and Coke.

WHACK!

Paul thought this was funny. He didn't agree with everything that the firm came up with—he was pretty sure Obie didn't either—but this seemed like a winner to him.

After his last appointment Paul headed to Hilliard. He hadn't been to his sister's house for over a month. He pulled into the drive and saw that the front yard was pockmarked with three pizza boxes, a plastic baseball bat, and a Frisbee. He instantly interpreted that it was a makeshift wiffle ball field.

Attaboy Leo and Frankie.

Then he thought, *College is not that far off for them. Future Tutor's drinkers? Hmmm.*

He arrived bearing gifts, Air Force Special Operations shirts for the boys, a bottle of Meiomi Pinot Noir for Patrice that he picked up after his last meeting of the day and, for Kevin, a bottle from the sample cases of Tutor's. All seemed well pleased.

In return Paul received chicken breasts grilled by Kevin, a cross-examination by Patrice on the details of his new job, and a soliloquy on the relative strengths of Marvel superheroes from Frankie. For his part Leo, who was preparing to take the test for his temporary driver's permit, quizzed Paul on the study material.

"Unless it is posted otherwise the speed limit in a residential area is: A: 25 miles per hour, B: 20 miles per hour, C: 35 miles per hour, or D: 15 miles per hour?" Leo looked up from the booklet. "Wellll, Uncle Paul?"

Paul nailed the answer. On his third try.

He rose early Tuesday and put on his running shoes and shorts and an old 21st Special Tactics Squadron t-shirt. This was the unit to which he was assigned before he ascended to the Two-Four. He rode the elevator down from the eighth floor and crossed the lobby to an exit on the hotel's north side. Stepping out to the sidewalk Paul could see the sun's first rays of the day softly glistening off the dark grey glass of the upper floors of the 629-foot tall Rhodes State Office Tower two blocks to the southwest. Once said to be the largest granite structure on Earth, the building was named after Governor James Rhodes who was both the 61st and 63rd governor of Ohio, serving a total of sixteen years.

The sun didn't quite have the angle to reach the capital city's early risers at street level but that would be changing in the next few minutes. Paul set out at an easy pace, following Gay street west toward the Scioto a half-dozen city blocks distant. He caught most of the lights, crossing without altering his pace, but was halted by two—at 3rd Street and North High. He came to a complete stop at these, waiting for them to change like most other pedestrians. Paul had no inclination to try his luck dodging sleep-deprived motorists.

And he certainly wasn't one to run in place while he waited. You saw these people in every American city. Upon approaching a flashing "Do Not Walk" sign they slowed to a halt but kept their arms bent in running position, slowly undulating back and forth. At the same time, they would raise their heels, alternating from right to left, the balls of their feet not leaving the pavement.

They looked ridiculous.

Paul smiled, remembering the term used by a member of the U.S. Army's elite Delta Force for people who jogged in place while waiting for stoplights to change—*Wedding Dancers.*

The trooper—known as "Helipad" due to the fact that his high, wide forehead seemed large enough that a Blackhawk helicopter could land on it—explained the term to Paul during a down time between missions in Iraq. Paul was attached to Delta's B Squadron, a particularly effective collection of hard chargers tasked with killing or capturing high value targets—HVTs—in Iraq's Diyala Province.

"Y'see Sticks, these urban runners that stop at street corners and keep their arms and legs movin'—doesn't matter if they're men or women—they are basically rockin' the same body movements that an octogenarian shows off at a wedding reception."

This had caused Paul to pause in his task—replacing the batteries in the two PRC-152 radios he carried on each operation—and furrowed his brow. "How's that?"

Helipad elucidated. "You Air Force weenies aren't perceptive enough to see these things, so try to follow along. Every wedding with a D.J. has that moment when somebody's grandparent—doesn't matter if they're a man or a woman—gets out there on the dance floor and does a slow groove to "Love Shack" by the B-52's or "Getting' Jiggy Wit It" by Will Smith. You know, they're always surrounded by a circle of young women in dresses and bare feet and a buncha drunk Dude-Bro types with their ties loosened? Same moves as those runners."

Paul stared at the Delta trooper for a full five seconds before responding.

171

"That forehead of yours houses a massive brain, Helipad."

The light at High changed and Paul began moving again. He remembered another story about Helipad. He was shot through the left side of his upper abdomen with an AK-47 in 2014 while operating in northern Iraq. Despite the wound he continued to lay down covering fire as his teammates eliminated the shooter, an Iraqi wearing—of all things—an Atlanta Braves baseball cap. Helipad lost parts of two ribs and his spleen but returned to combat the following year.

While convalescing at Walter Reed Hospital in Bethesda, Maryland he checked himself out and made the short drive down to Virginia Beach. It was the weekend of the East Coast Navy SEAL Reunion, a rollicking affair held each year over three days in June. He signed up as a single for the golf outing and joined a SEAL Team Six compadre known as Dutch, who was entertaining a half dozen friends from his hometown. Helipad filled out their second foursome.

Golf, Paul had learned, was a game of failure. To keep one's sanity while continually falling short of expectations many participants found it necessary to have ready-made excuses for poor play. In this way it was not unlike fishing.

"The club face on my 8-iron is worn." "*My hooks aren't sharp enough.*"

"My grips are wet." "*I brought the wrong bait.*"

"The soft spikes on my golf shoes need replaced." "*This lure isn't the right color.*"

"Someone talked during my backswing." "*The barometer is rising.*" This fisherman's excuse is used interchangeably with *the barometer is falling.*

The golf and fishing worlds intersected at one of the most popular justifications of failure. "*It was just too damn windy out there today.*"

At Eagle Haven Golf Course on Little Creek Amphibious Base, Helipad's foursome teed off on hole number five—it was a shotgun start—with their carts laden with iced-down beer coolers. Dutch's first buddy hit the top of the ball and scalded a burner that stopped after 200 feet. He took a mulligan and repeated the shot, the two balls coming to rest within ten feet of each other.

"Damn...woke up this morning with a sore back." He rolled his shoulders and returned to his beer.

The next man sliced a drive into the next fairway.

"Awww, drank too much at the O-Club party last night."

Then it was Helipad's turn. He striped a drive that came to rest 220 yards distant in the middle of the fairway. Getting in on the act he turned to the group and raised his shirt revealing an evil-looking wound, a white circle of scar tissue the size of a bullet that was still red around the edges.

"I used ta hit it 300 before I got shot in Iraq."

The playing partners roared with laughter. Helipad didn't pay for a beer the rest of the weekend.

Paul contemplated the world he had been part of in Special Operations. It was a world where violent death was common, warrior skills were cherished above all others, and a bullet wound could somehow be viewed as humorous. In addition to a Combat Controller's expertise communicating with aircraft and guiding precision airstrikes, they were expected to hold up their end in ground combat with their personal weapons.

Paul's most embarrassing moment at JSOC occurred with Helipad's Delta B Squadron. It did not occur in Afghanistan or Iraq, but in a rural area near Lake Cormorant, Mississippi, just across the state line from Memphis, Tennessee. Since the 1980s military and law enforcement organizations have sent some of their best shooters to the facility. It was privately owned and had been founded by a World Champion shooter. The instructors taught techniques that could improve the performance of even the most elite combat shooters in the United States military.

The squadron was in Mississippi to hone their skills on the facility's shooting ranges and inside the "kill houses" built to replicate realistic target environments. On the squadron's last day at the site, each member was paired with a shooter from law enforcement for a friendly—but competitive—contest. The competition was on the 100-yard range and was judged on a combination of speed and accuracy.

Every member of Delta won their match. Paul did not. He was paired with an FBI sniper named Dez that won handily. Though Dez showed unusual talent, Paul would hear about the incident for the entire Iraq deployment. It bothered him so much that he'd mentioned it to Lauren several times over the years.

"For the love of God Paul, *get over it*."

Paul reached the end of Gay Street where it T'd into Marconi Boulevard. He crossed and came to an expansive grass area that rolled down to the river. This was Battelle Riverfront Park. The imposing figure of the United States District Court building was to his right. Beyond that, where the river began a bend to the northwest, was a rusty railroad bridge reaching across the Scioto.

Paul stopped, put his hands on his hips, and surveyed the area. A few morning joggers moved on a walking path down at the river's edge. A half-mile to his left was the Discovery Bridge, looking sleek as it carried Broad Street across the river. Paul could clearly see his sister's place of employment, the National Veteran's Memorial and Museum, across the river. Patrice brought Paul there to speak to a group of high school students the previous November for Veterans Day. The sun was up now, illuminating the scene before him. It was a fine morning, bordering on spectacular.

His first meeting today would be at an establishment on North High that was less than two football fields from the Ohio State campus and its 60,000-plus students. Bottles of Tutor's would be a perfect fit behind the bar.

Paul's lips were motionless, but his eyes smiled.

He headed off toward the path.

CHAPTER TWENTY

Dom Santo looked at the clock on the Cockpit Professional Multimedia screen of his BMW for the third time in the last minute. The numerals stubbornly refused to change, 5:44 p.m.

For shit's sake, what the hell is going ON up there?

He was stuck in the far left lane in a long file of pissed off motorists on I-80 westbound. He had just passed the exit for Anita, Iowa when the pace of the traffic first decreased to the speed of a slowed drain and then stopped completely, clogged. One of America's primary east-west arteries was in need of a God-sized plunger.

It had taken more than ten minutes to cover the last mile, which—after nearly twelve hours of driving—felt like an eternity. Dom departed Columbus at six in the morning and made the seemingly endless drive across the country's heartland all day. He sipped coffee, cursed himself for doing so at each restroom stop, and counted dogs inside vehicles he passed. So far there had been nine.

More hours driven than dogs counted. That's a bad ratio.

At each fuel stop Dom would visit any nearby chain grocery stores or big-box home improvement locations and purchase Visa prepaid debit cards. This converted a portion of the Fireteam's robbery take from cash to usable funds. It was a tedious process.

Dom made it a point *not* to stop at Iowa 80, billed as the World's Largest Truckstop, when he came upon its exit 220 miles back. He had done so a year and a half earlier when he scouted possible robbery targets in Des Moines. It made an impact on him.

A better description might be it *scarred* him.

The place covered 75 acres and had an above ground diesel fuel storage tank that held a million gallons. There was parking available for 900 semis. The main building—there were several others—was more mall than convenience store. It featured a restaurant that served 900,000 eggs a year. Dom stopped, got lost, and vowed never to set foot in the place again.

I suppose it wasn't as bad as Lebanon Correctional. Well, not quite.

Dom was bound for Omaha. It was an 800-mile slog that should have taken just over twelve hours. He still had 60 more to cover before he reached Council Bluffs and crossed over the Missouri River to Nebraska. It had been six weeks since the Racine job and the informal schedule to which the trio of robbers had gravitated suggested that it was time to line up the next one.

The Peterbilt in front of him released its brakes and rolled ahead a few car lengths before again coming to a stop. The BMW followed in kind, but not before Dom edged it toward the berm so he could peek ahead. The traffic snaked ahead for another half-mile until construction vehicles of some kind came into view.

How the hell do truck drivers do this shit every day? Compared to this, cleaning a turd-infested parking garage is a piece of cake.

The BMW helped make the drive somewhat easier. Well, it helped quite a bit. Dom loved the car. It was a three-year-old 530i, silver, and was loaded. If he were still stealing cars for a living he would've salivated over this one. But that was just a sideline to his main occupation now.

The Peterbilt driver opened his door, stepped down to the asphalt, and stretched. He moved to the berm before shielding his eyes and surveying the situation ahead. He then scratched himself, shook his head, and climbed back into his rig.

Dom watched the man before sighing and shifting the BMW's transmission into park.

That's right, I'm a glamorous and daring bank robber now. It's a thrill a minute.

He removed his sunglasses and rubbed his bloodshot eyes with the heels of his hands.

176

Dom bought the car for just under $40,000. It had low mileage but that was changing rather quickly as he scouted Middle America for the Fireteam.

The Fireteam. Pretty damn cool name.

The robberies, he admitted, were a rush. The actual takedowns were over in mere minutes. It was the planning and preparation that determined whether the team would be successful. Cole, Dom knew, was almost completely responsible for the team's success. Dom contributed in every way possible but he knew his role was to follow instructions. Lord knew Tanner wasn't coming up with any high level concepts. No, Cole was the driving force behind the Fireteam.

If it was possible Cole might be *too* careful when it came to the strategic nature of the robberies. Back at the beginning, over two years ago, Cole sat down with Dom and Tanner and laid out his vision. He explained that he and Tanner had been lucky when they robbed the Bank of Oklahoma branch building in Bartlesville. He'd thought long and hard in the time since and had hit upon some techniques that should minimize their chances of being caught.

The Carhartt bags, the Eisenhower jackets, code names, the elaborate process followed to take vehicles from airport lots, the vault truck switches in cemeteries, even the way they positioned their watches on the inside of their wrist, these were all carefully thought out aspects of Cole's vision. Combining these with the man's almost superhuman ability to read people and pick out the right bank employee to threaten with the driver's license ploy made the overall approach extremely effective.

But there was another component to Cole's system that dictated how the Fireteam operated. They never targeted banks in their area. All of the robberies took place in a vast circle that could be loosely drawn around Des Moines on the west, Indianapolis on the east, and extended hundreds of miles north and south of this line. Cole got the idea after reading about a serial killer from Alaska—Israel Something-Or-Other, Dom didn't remember the man's last name—that selected and killed all of his victims in the lower forty-eight states. The geographic distance between the killer and his unfortunate victims kept him off the radar of law enforcement for years.

Cole built this into his concept. They would live in one place but operate in a completely different area. Or as he put it, "We play all of our ballgames on the road, no home games."

This was why Dom spent so much time on the road. The banks he scouted were generally several hours from Columbus. Dom would drive to a city that was located near an airport in another state and visit several banks and S&Ls. He had an excellent sense of the building layouts and traffic patterns that fit the team's needs. Once he came up with a good candidate he would check out nearby cemeteries. Then he would examine the parking areas at the airport.

Thankfully Cole permitted him to take his cellphone on these trips. It allowed him to check overhead satellite photos of the target area, clarifying how the banks and cemeteries were situated. It also allowed him to stay in constant contact with Cole as they narrowed the search. Though Cole believed taking their phones along on the actual robberies was a practice that could lead to their capture, he thought one of them—Dom's—being in the area of a future bank job weeks or months ahead of the actual crime posed little risk.

Dom eliminated many of the possible victims without even walking into the buildings. There were several reasons for this. The most common was the amount of customer traffic. Too many vehicles through the drive-up area meant too many sets of eyes. Too many visitors inside the building decreased the ability of the two Jelcik brothers to control the situation.

Dom was particularly cognizant of this last consideration when evaluating targets. Too many people meant more stress for the two members of the team inside the building. Dom had complete confidence in Cole's ability to handle such a situation, but Tanner? Dom remembered waiting nervously outside the bank in Peoria for the brothers to return and hearing the gunshot from Tanner's carbine inside the building.

His eyes opened so wide that he later thought he must've looked like a cartoon character.

He remembered thinking, *Oh Shit!*

The last thing any of them needed was to increase the amperage of Tanner Jelcik.

The banks that passed the eye test from the outside qualified for the next step. Dom would enter the building and, in old-time movie lingo, "case the joint." He was adept at locating the vault—always the team's primary target—and had developed an excellent sense of how these establishments were laid out.

His purported reason for coming inside was always the same. He needed to purchase a prepaid debit card for a large amount, usually $500. While the teller was processing the transaction Dom would surreptitiously examine the area behind the counter. He made small talk with the employee.

"I just don't feel comfortable walking into a grocery store with all this cash." And, "Once I paid for a gift card at a Kroger and when my mom tried to use it, it didn't work...I just trust banks more, I guess." His smile was sincere.

As soon as he returned to his BMW he would sketch a diagram of the building's interior in a leather-covered binder. He added any notes that could be pertinent. In this manner Dom essentially compiled a dossier of potential targets.

This trip—if the traffic ever began moving—would be a challenge. After this long day of driving Dom would survey a dozen banks in Omaha and its suburbs tomorrow. Add the cemetery locations and a trip to the airport and it would be another full day. Cole had instructed him to also check out Lincoln, an hour to the southwest. This was home to the University of Nebraska. It was smaller than Omaha but was still home to upwards of another dozen financial institutions and, of course, cemeteries. In addition Lincoln boasted an airport that would need to be examined. That meant yet another full day. A fourth day would be wiped out by the long drive home. By the end of the week Dom would have whittled away at the extra $4,000 that Cole had set aside for this trip. In its place he would have a stack of prepaid Visa cards.

And a sore ass.

What a ball-buster! This will be the worst trip yet.

The success of the team meant that they were dealing with an ever-expanding geographic circle. Cole was pushing that rough circle out to the west. Up to now Des Moines was the furthest point in that direction they'd operated. By hitting a bank in Omaha they would stretch it another 130 miles.

Dom didn't know how to work the math, but he was confident that increasing the circumference of the team's area of operations grew the total square mileage inside the circle greatly.

The area the FBI had to worry about would increase... what was the word? Exponentially.

So there was logic in the decision to push the boundary. Dom had complete confidence in Cole. The man had given him a new lease on life. He hired Dom when no other employer would touch him. He also co-signed for the loan used to buy the BMW. When the car was paid off early with laundered stolen cash Dom's credit rating was back on the map. Cole set up the bolt bags for all three members of the team. Sure, Dom's Youngstown connections helped with the IDs for two of the bags, but they'd been Cole's idea and he'd taken care of stashing them in the storage unit. In addition to this money, Cole had another pile of cash—the team referred to it as their "cache cash"—tucked away for their use in a safe deposit box.

Still, these trips were wearing him down. He resolved to talk to Cole again about pushing their boundary to the east as well. It was something Dom suggested before the Peoria robbery. The discussion went nowhere mainly, he believed, because Tanner put a hole through the roof of the building on that job. Cole's attention was pulled toward his brother for several days. Dom's suggestion was pushed aside.

If we hit someplace east of Indianapolis wouldn't that ALSO expand the circle? Accomplish the same thing as

Omaha? There's gotta be places closer to us that would still keep Columbus outside the line on the FBI's map.

He would approach his boss in a respectful manner. Without Cole, Dom was convinced he would be a recidivist car thief.

In reality Dom actually *was* back to stealing cars. But it was just a sideline now.

The brake lights on the Peterbilt went out and the truck began to roll forward. Dom brightened. He would take care of business in Omaha and Lincoln then have a heart to heart with the man he'd known during robberies as Ike, the Supreme Commander. Maybe his job would get easier. The phrase that dragged itself through Dom's mind two minutes earlier appeared again, this time with more enthusiasm.

I'm a glamorous and daring bank robber now!

CHAPTER TWENTY-ONE

Cole guided his F-150 through downtown Columbus. The Klean Sooner custom decals were on the passenger seat, flipped upside down so the front side couldn't be read. He needed some cash for Dom and rather than take it from the backpacks being stored near the airport he decided to raid the safe deposit box.

He rented the box back in November using the Cormier Gullickson driver's license he'd acquired a couple months earlier and wearing a pair of the polar blue contact lenses. The box was located inside the Huntington Bank location at 600 South High Street in the Brewery District.

It would be a rainy day in Columbus. It wasn't yet, but it would be. Cole stopped at a red light and looked to the west. He saw a heavy line of nimbostratus clouds approaching. The wind was picking up, evident from the movement of an empty paper Starbucks cup as it rolled through the intersection. Cole watched as it passed in front of his truck from right to left.

I guess he had the right of way.

The Monday morning sun illuminated the cloud line leaving no doubt to the pedestrians below that they needed to pick up the pace if they were to avoid a soaking.

The light changed and Cole accelerated slowly, keeping an eye to the passenger window to make sure the Starbucks cup wasn't merely the point man in an all-out assault by discarded fast food packaging.

Dom had returned to Columbus at the end of the previous week on fumes, literally and figuratively. He told the brothers the next day that the low fuel warning light on the BMW came on while he was passing Springfield, some 45 miles from his apartment. He pushed on, unwilling to make yet another stop for gas and snacks.

"I just wanted to get home, y'know?"

When Dom switched off the ignition outside his apartment on North High the digital display that showed the remaining fuel range read four miles.

Cole didn't have to wait for Dom to arrive back in Columbus to know he was fried. He could tell during their phone conversation while Dom was still in Iowa, hammering toward Ohio 15 miles per hour over the speed limit. He answered Dom's call and asked his location.

I'm coming up to the Disneyland of truck stops in Iowa."

"The what?"

"Never mind. Listen...I gotta say, boss, it's a long-ass drive to get out here."

At first Cole tried to wave aside the younger man's concern.

"Well, we knew that goin' in. We'll have to plan any job there a little different...maybe build in a rest day after the drive out. So, no specifics over the phone, but did you find some candidates?"

Dom's answer was more positive than the tone in which it was delivered.

"Uh, sure. Three really good possibilities, but..." Long sigh.

"But it's a really long drive. Got it." Cole was trying not to lose his temper. For a second a thought flashed in his mind.

WWTD. What Would Tanner Do?

Cole knew his younger brother would've ripped Dom a new one the second that sigh bounced off a satellite tower and into his ear.

Tanner's been even edgier than normal lately. Could he be doing a cycle with the juice again?

The younger Jelcik brother used the injectable steroid Deca-Durabolin during his senior year in high school. It worked—as far as building muscle mass—but the side effects were frightening. In addition to the obvious ones like acne and a manic-depressive personality change, it came with the hidden dangers of liver cancer, stroke, and heart failure. These features were pre-installed in the drug like Apple Wallet and GarageBand were on a new iPhone. Cole found out and quashed it, telling Tanner that he had inside information the

184

Bartlesville Bruins would be drug tested during football season. It was a white lie.

The first drops of rain hit the windshield as Cole pulled into the bank's small parking lot. He used the rearview mirror to assist with putting in the contact lenses. He still fumbled with this, but it was getting easier. He thought about retrieving the collapsible umbrella he kept under the front passenger seat but elected to leave it. He was already wearing a waterproof jacket to hide the logo on his work shirt. He hunched his shoulders and tucked his chin as he crossed the lot and reached the entrance. Since he'd made the leap from prey to predator when it came to financial institutions he found that he had a different attitude when stepping inside. Maybe it was an air of confidence, maybe a feeling of contempt. Whatever the reason Cole now walked into the Huntington branch with an attitude that was apparent in his body language.

He first became aware of this when he stepped inside this building for the first time in November. One of the customer service women—her nametag read "Suzanne"—flirted with him unabashedly while he filled out the paperwork. He decided immediately to do nothing that would encourage her. The whole point of the safe deposit box was to set up a place to cache stolen loot under an assumed name. It would be impossible to carry on a relationship with the woman without her discovering his actual identity. Still, she persisted.

I should've worn a fake wedding band. Not that it would mean much these days.

Cole had not dated anyone on an extended basis for two years, and there were extenuating circumstances for that relationship. The woman was Kelly Petofsky, a petite brunette that worked in the Franklin County Title Office in the Whitehall section of Columbus. He met her when working through the registration process for the two brand new King Ranch F-150s. After the Fireteam acquired the burial vault truck they needed to somehow come up with legitimate paperwork that verified ownership if pulled over for a traffic violation or involved in an accident.

Cole turned on the charm after following Petofsky to Gramercy Books in Bexley, a quaint boutique bookstore with an attached coffee shop. After easing into the same aisle as her —the Self-Help section—he feigned surprise. "Heyyy, you work at the Title office, right? I met you a couple weeks ago."

Cole made sure to dress nicely, wearing a long-sleeved button-down shirt that accentuated his upper body and was in the same shade of mauve as the blouse Petofsky was wearing the day he visited her office. He'd purchased the shirt the next day.

They ordered lattes, sat in the shop and discussed books, and ended up at her place where Cole spent the night. In less than a month he had manipulated her into dummying up registration documents for the Silverado 5500HD. Two weeks later he broke off the relationship, leaving her with an implied threat that he could turn her in for her transgression.

He threw away the mauve shirt the following day.

Cole did a quick scan and was pleased to discover Suzanne was not on duty. He stepped to the station closest to the safe deposit box room, produced his Gullickson ID, and went through the process of signing in. A young man named Blair assisted him. Blair wore a short-sleeved dress shirt that was too tight at the neck, a tie adorned with buckeyes that exacerbated the condition, and a facial expression that Cole's heightened sense of observation interpreted as *I'm not doing this shitty job the rest of my life.*

Cole produced his key and Blair retrieved one with a matching number from within a compartment behind the counter. Cole followed the man into the room lined with stainless steel boxes and watched as he inserted the bank's key in one of the slots of box 51. Cole handed over his copy and Blair pushed it into the adjoining slot. He turned them both and stepped away. Before he left the room Cole asked, "First job out of college?"

Blair considered his answer, weighing whether an answer in the affirmative somehow made him look like a loser.

186

Cole watched Blair's eyes look up and to the left. Numerous psychological studies had determined that when a right-handed person looked in that direction after being asked a question they were contemplating telling a lie. Cole didn't know about the studies. Somehow he had always possessed the ability to interpret the phenomena, like a frontier tracker interpreting animal signs. He'd seen Blair use his right hand to sign him in and retrieve the extra key.

The man nodded while failing to conceal a frown.

Cole looked at the strangulation device masquerading as a necktie and ventured, "Go Bucks."

Blair's eyes lit up for a second, no doubt remembering the frat parties he attended just east of campus during his five-plus years as an undergraduate at THE Ohio State University. He gave Cole a thumbs-up and a wan smile before backing out of the room.

Box 51 was 10 inches wide, 10 inches tall, and 24 inches deep. This was the middle of three sizes offered by the bank. Cole pulled open the hinged door and grabbed the loop handle of the inner liner. This was known as the bond box. It was made of simple stamped metal and could be slid completely out of the box itself. Cole did so and set the bond box on a small rectangular table in the corner of the room. He lifted the top to reveal stacks of cash. Cole didn't need to count it. He knew it contained $181,250. He selected a stack of twenties—there are 100 bills in all standard stacks regardless of denomination—then counted out another thousand dollars from a stack of fifties.

Three grand. Dom ought to be able to find us a place or two to hit with that.

Cole pushed the bills into the front pockets of his jeans, returned the bond box to its place, and closed the outer door of the safe deposit box. He removed his key and stepped back to the lobby where he saw Blair at the nearest teller station. He was helping a grey-haired woman organize piles of rolled coins, a sullen frown on his face.

Attaboy, Blair. Only about 40 years to go before retirement.

At the entrance Cole saw that it was now raining steadily. He pulled up the hood on his jacket and jogged to the truck. He would be meeting Dom and Tanner at the Klean Sooner building. They needed to discuss their next course of action. Dom's call on his return from Nebraska had convinced Cole to at least consider targets on the eastern edge of the Fireteam's operating area.

The rain increased, beating down steadily. Cole turned on his wipers and punched up Outlaw Country. Chris LeDoux was performing the live version of "This Cowboy's Hat." Songs that included the word cowboy invariably made him think of growing up in Bartlesville and this one was no exception. The cowboy attitude was a much-valued trait in Oklahoma and Cole wondered how much it had influenced their path. He supposed there were three types of cowboys; the hard-working rancher, the lawman, and the desperado. He and Tanner obviously fell into the third group.

He was contemplating this as he steered the King Ranch back north on High. A block before the right turn that would take him to the Klean Sooner building he saw the back of a lone walker just ahead on his right. It was a man, head down, plodding tediously through the rain. He was pulling a two-wheeled aluminum cart with a cube-shaped plastic compartment affixed to the lower section. As Cole drew abreast he saw a burn scar on the left side of the man's face. Cole narrowed his eyes in thought for just a moment before it came to him.

Rufus?

Cole pulled the truck to the curb and slowed to match the man's pace. He lowered the passenger window.

"Rufus? Hey, RUFUS!"

The man continued to walk but turned his head toward the sound of Cole's voice. He slowed, wavered for two beats, then approached the truck. One hand was clutched across his chest as if to keep his jacket sealed tight. The other came up to his brow, guarding against the slanting rain. He squinted and tilted his head. Finally a spark of recognition flashed in his eyes.

"Mister Cole?" Then, "Your eyes okay?"

"What the hell are you doin', Rufus?" Cole glanced in his rearview before turning on his flashers. Without waiting for an answer he leaned across the passenger seat and opened the door. "Get in the truck, partner."

Unaccustomed to acts of thoughtfulness or even common courtesy, Rufus hesitated.

"Let's go Rufus. Jump in. Throw your cart in the bed of the truck. I'll give you a ride to wherever you're goin'."

Rufus, his need of relief from misery finally overcoming his stupefaction that the offer had been made, tentatively stepped to the side of the truck. He collapsed the handle on the cart before bending and grabbing openings on either side of the compartment. He strained for a second lifting it a foot before it slipped from his hands, its plastic surface slick from the rain. It fell to the sidewalk with a metallic rattle.

Cole quickly checked his mirror for traffic coming from behind. Seeing none he threw open his door while pulling up the hood of his jacket. He moved quickly around the bed of the truck and approached Rufus. The man was straining to lift the contraption a second time. Cole recognized the cart as the style often used by staff in offices to move stacks of files. "I got it Rufus, jump in the truck."

Cole bent to lift the unit and snatched it off the sidewalk as Rufus stepped aside, watching over the box like a mother hen. As he hefted it into the bed, Cole, surprised at its weight, angled his head toward the street person and asked, "What the hell's inside that thing?"

Rufus, not realizing it had been a rhetorical question, began, "Well Mister Cole—"

"Get in the truck, Rufus!" Cole raised his voice as he rushed back to the driver's side, again checking for traffic in the rain. He jumped behind the wheel as Hendershot pulled himself up onto the opposite seat. "Are you part fish? What're you doin' out in this?"

Rufus was thoroughly soaked and disheveled. He cocked his head and his face assembled itself into what Cole assumed was a smile. It had a jagged quality due to the fact that the scorched skin on his left side had lost its elasticity. Long stringy hair framed the face and acted as a conduit as rainwater fell from it to the F-150's leather interior.

Cole suddenly remembered carving jack-o-lanterns with Tanner and their mother as a kid. Tanner had once used a Van Dyke's taxidermy knife from Turk's shed to notch and sculpt a similar face on a pumpkin. They couldn't decide if it was comical or horrifying. Staring at Rufus now, Cole decided it was both.

Rufus explained, "I was working my fav'rit spot—panhandlin'—over on Fulton and Third. There's a ramp there that goes down to I-70. Good place to catch traffic when they're stopped at the light. Already made over seven dollars this morning when the rain hit. Headin' back to my crib now."

The spot Rufus referred to was a few blocks to the east. Cole was curious. "Where is your crib? What's in the box?" He tilted his head toward the bed of the truck.

Rufus was opening his jacket. It was the sort often sold in army surplus stores and was, Cole thought, too heavy for late May in Ohio. He extracted a piece of cardboard and became preoccupied with it as he answered Cole's questions. "The crib is close to the river. Best way to get me there—and I sure do 'preciate the ride—is to take me to the Marconi parking garage. You know where that is Mister Cole? Where the trains disappear?"

Cole had no idea about disappearing trains but knew the garage. He waited for an opening in the traffic and pulled from the curb, switching off the flashers. The Marconi garage was in the Arena District several blocks north of their present location. Cole had parked there a number of times and even done a complete walk through of the building a year earlier when Klean Sooner had submitted a bid to clean it. The

190

shortest route there would take the men through the heart of downtown.

"And the box on the cart?" Cole reached under his seat and withdrew a towel he kept next to the umbrella to cover his seat when he and his crew tackled dirty jobs. He handed it to Rufus.

Hendershot accepted the towel and wiped his face. Cole saw out of the corner of his eye that the layer of grime that set up shop on the right side of the man's face was removed. He was surprised to see that Rufus's race was still not readily apparent. He appeared to be a mix of black, white, and Asian blood. The facial scarring and slight disfigurement around the left eye eradicated some of the clues.

Cole thought *He's everybody...or nobody.*

Rufus had now completely removed the cardboard from inside the jacket. It appeared to be twenty-four inches square and was folded in the middle. He opened it like a book and smiled. "Still dry! Oh, sorry suh, I have canned food in the box, spoon and fork, can opener. You know, my stash. Can't leave it in my crib. Somebody'll take it."

Cole caught the light at Broad and continued north. "What about that?" He indicated the corrugated square that Rufus had protected from the rain.

Rufus turned the cardboard toward Cole and flashed another grin, this one even more misshapen than the last. There, in bold block letters, was written *HELP OUT A FELLOW BUCKEYE FAN.*

Cole smiled back, deciding that the man knew how to work a street corner in Columbus, Ohio.

They reached Nationwide Avenue three minutes later, took a left past the Columbus Blue Jackets hockey arena then made another left on West Street. Heading back south now Cole slowed and after a few hundred feet buttonhooked the truck to the left until they faced northeast. They were on Marconi Boulevard now. The garage, a modern six-story brick and glass structure that boasted 1,290 parking spots, rose before them on the left. Railroad tracks ran along the right side of the

191

street, bracketing motorists as they were funneled into the garage.

"You can pull over Mister Cole. I can walk from here."

Cole eased to the curb and turned in his seat taking in their surroundings. He saw no logical place that a street person could call their "crib."

"Where's your place Rufus?"

The rain was beginning to taper now. A car swept past them on the left and turned into the garage.

"Down the tracks...takes you all the way to the river. Got a nice spot there." Rufus pointed a thumb to the rear of the truck indicating the path that the tracks took to the southwest. Cole squinted through the rear window of the truck and made out a rusting railroad bridge in the distance, some 300 yards away.

"For Chrissakes Rufus, you can't manhandle that heavy cart all that way over railroad tracks in the rain."

Cole pulled forward and entered the parking garage. As he accepted a ticket at the electronic dispenser he could hear Rufus mutter, "Done it before...lotsa times."

Cole found a spot. He remembered the contacts. Adjusting the rearview mirror he pushed up his eyelids with his left hand and pinched out the lenses with his right. Hendershot watched him in silence. Cole reached under his seat for the umbrella and exited the F-150, glad to be under cover and out of the rain. Rufus followed him to the rear of the truck while tucking the folded sign back inside his jacket.

Cole handed the umbrella to Hendershot and ordered, "You hold this over us. I'll carry the box down to your spot."

Rufus began to protest and Cole cut him off. "Don't give me any shit Rufus...and don't open that umbrella while we're inside. It's bad luck." He winked.

They trooped outside, Cole clutching the heavy box with its attached handle and wheels, Rufus with one arm extended holding the umbrella aloft while the other pressed against his jacket to keep the sign dry. A wide sidewalk with a pedestrian crossing ran from the garage, past a twenty-foot tall art deco sign that featured a large red arrow and the word "PARK" arranged vertically in blue. The sidewalk continued to the railroad track and other parking structures and office buildings. They reached the track and turned right.

As they made their way southwest Rufus looked at Cole and cocked his head to their rear. "Back there's where the trains disappear."

Cole turned and saw that a couple hundred yards northeast of the Marconi garage the two sets of tracks went into and apparently through another parking structure. He'd never noticed this in his other visits.

"Damn, the trains *do* disappear."

They pushed toward the river. Two minutes later Rufus confided, "I bought that cart with some of the money you gave me Mister Cole. These new jeans too."

Cole realized for the first time the man was no longer wearing torn pants. He smiled, gratified that his two hundred bucks hadn't ended up in the cash register of a downtown liquor store. *Well, not all two hundred. I hear a couple bottles clinking around inside this box.*

They trudged on. The tracks crossed over two streets, Spring and Long. Cole stepped from one railroad tie to the next, Rufus keeping up. After a ten minute uncomfortable walk they neared the bridge. It was of steel construction, orange with rust, and from their vantage point appeared as a web-like skeletal box that stretched across the Scioto River below. Rufus collapsed the umbrella and made his way down the rock-strewn slope on the left side before exclaiming, "Home, sweet home!"

Cole surveyed the area. Concrete abutments supported each flank of the bridge where it connected to the bank. The ground sloped down to the river fifty yards distant. It was visible through a small stand of trees that hid their position from below. A walking path followed the river. It approached from Battelle Park on the left and disappeared under the bridge before continuing north. Cole saw a dry area under the bridge that reminded him of a small cave he and Tanner explored as boys in Bartlesville.

The blunt, dark grey leading edge of the raincloud was now east of downtown, its trailing mass broken into smaller cells as if attempting to better keep up. The rain lessened, the drops seeming to fall slower, almost hesitating in their journey to the ground where they would eventually be drawn to the river. Shafts of morning sun poked through the gaps. Somewhere behind them a blue jay jeered.

"You have a nice spot here, Rufus."

CHAPTER TWENTY-TWO

Tanner turned his left forearm inward and checked his watch. *What the hell is taking him so long?*

He and Santo were waiting for Cole to return from the bank. When he hadn't shown a half hour earlier as expected Dom decided to head to the weight bench and get in a lift. Tanner's watch read 10:19 a.m. He was impatient. He re-crossed his arms and looked down at Santo from behind the bench. Technically he was spotting for the smaller man but to an observer he would've appeared like an executioner watching a transgressor who was strapped under a guillotine.

Dom was working through a set of presses with 120 pounds on the bar. His upper body displayed almost no fat. The Sicilian flag moving up and down—full-staff, half-staff, full-staff. After 15 reps Dom seated the bar back in its rests without requiring assistance.

"Bout time, pipsqueak. Move aside and let me show you how it's done. Help me load the bar to 225."

Tanner was determined to top Cole in their NFL Combine-inspired contest. He had just reached 30 reps—Santo was his witness—the day that they encountered the homeless man taking a leak in the city garage. Cole became angry at something he said to the man—Tanner didn't remember it being too offensive—and they returned to Klean Sooner. Cole proceeded to push up 32 reps nearly an hour after midnight to retake the lead.

Sonofabitch!

Tanner's decision to do a cycle of "muscle fuel" *did* seem to be paying off though. He had duplicated the 30-rep feat twice since and had topped out at 31 two days earlier.

There's a reason bodybuilders do the drugs—they work!

In high school Tanner used Deca-Durabolin. Being a newbie he did not realize that the maximum benefits of the drug came

195

when the user also took testosterone. Consequently Tanner saw an increase in mass but not all of the gain in strength he'd hoped for. He did, however, see one of the more unfortunate side effects—Deca Dick. The lack of sexual pizzazz he usually possessed in spades with the fairer sex of Bartlesville High was gone, replaced by embarrassment and a more-surly-than-normal attitude. When his brother hinted that the football team might be drug tested he gave it up. The drug test was his stated reason for this but Deca Dick—DD—was the real motivator.

Now he was more astute when it came to pharmacological "helpers." He was using trenbolone, another steroid, in oral form. "Tren" in its injectable form was developed for use as a growth promoter and muscle builder for beef cattle. Bodybuilders typically took 25 to 150 milligrams every other day. Tanner was taking an amount he considered judicious, 100 milligrams every other day. Though Tren could also lead to erectile dysfunction—quite sensibly called "Tren Dick," or TD—and a nasty cough after a dosing, Tanner outsmarted the process by injecting 150 milligrams of testosterone each week. He was lifting more often and recovering faster. It was just a matter of time before he surpassed Cole's high-water mark of 32 reps.

The weights added to the bar, Dom headed to the restroom while Tanner linked his phone to the sound system and pulled up a playlist he'd named "Turk Rock." He scrolled through the list searching for an appropriate banger to accompany his lift. Still scrolling, he settled under the bar. He stopped and smiled a few seconds later.

Dom was standing over the toilet relieving himself when he heard the opening riff of Judas Priest's "You've Got Another Thing Comin'" blast through the wall. It was followed by Tanner's agitated roar.

"Goddammit Santo, get your ass in here and spot for me!"

Dom sighed.

Tanner's shirt was off as Dom tentatively approached the bench. The big man lay under the bar, his heels bouncing at twice the beat of the music.

Tanner's been wired lately.

Dom mentally recounted the list of infractions he'd noticed from Tanner in the last few days alone.

On the way to an ozone job he'd seen a man with shoulder-length hair loping across Sawmill Road. He exploded, "Those fuckin' long-haired bastards bounce on purpose when they walk so the hair in back floats up and down...they do it on *purpose!* If you cut their hair they would stop doin' it and walk normal." Then, still thinking about the man two blocks later, "Sonsabitches!"

Tanner became red-faced on a late night floor strip and re-wax job at a Walgreens on the city's east side when he saw a single-use plastic dental floss pick laying outside the front door. "Jee-zus *Christ!* Why the hell do I see one of these goddammed things on the ground outside the door of EVERY —SINGLE—BUSINESS I walk in these days? Just what the fuck is *wrong* with people?"

And just this morning while switching channels on the office television he came across an old episode of *Law & Order* and completely lost his shit when he saw Detective Lennie Briscoe tip a coffee cup to his lips inside the interview room of the NYPD's 27th Precinct. "The cup is empty...the fuckin' cup is *EMPTY!* Why do they fake it and act like the cup's fulla' coffee? It is *goddammed EMPTY!*"

Dom took up station behind the bar and assumed a positive tone toward the larger man. "Okay big man, it's all you. Fire when ready."

Tanner scrolled through the playlist and selected a song. Bachman Turner Overdrive began to crank out "Takin' Care of Business" and Tanner began to pump along rhythmically.

Dom called out *"One...Two...Three..."*

Cole left the Marconi garage and turned in the direction of the Klean Sooner building. He gave the railroad tracks a final look and cast his eyes toward Rufus's bridge before leaving the area. Cole's walk back to the garage took less time and effort than the approach he'd made carrying Hendershot's stash. He left his umbrella with the homeless man.

"Keep this Rufus, in case you get caught in a storm again. And here, hope this makes up for you gettin' rained out today down on Fulton and Third." He handed over fifty dollars.

Rufus accepted both. "I sure 'preciate it Mister Cole. You a good man...they don't make 'em like you anymore."

The episode with Rufus had put Cole behind schedule but it wasn't a huge concern. One of the day's tasks was to meet Tanner and Dom at the building to organize equipment and prep the vans for another after-hours floor waxing job. The main reason for the rendezvous, however, was to determine a target area for the eastern edge of the Fireteam's operating area.

Cole had mulled over Dom's argument that stretching both sides could be a benefit, further confusing the FBI. After careful consideration Cole agreed. He would not budge from one stipulation. Their target area had to remain west of Columbus. This was a key component of Cole's overall plan. It derived from a book he read a few years earlier.

American Predator: The Hunt for the Most Meticulous Killer of the 21st Century was published in 2019. Cole came across the book soon after he and Tanner made the move to Columbus. It was in the apartment of the first woman Cole dated in Columbus, Roxy Tinkers.

Roxy was a hot "gym-sis" Cole met in a Giant Eagle Supermarket. She had a cart full of eggs and carb-rich cereals, a dazzling smile, and wore an Arnold Sports Festival workout shirt tight over hard abs and obviously fake boobs. One thing led to another and Cole ended up at her place, a loft apartment in the Grandview section of the city just southwest of the Ohio State campus.

Roxy's real name was Beatrice. Few people in Columbus knew this as she used her nom de guerre in every personal interaction and on her social media platforms. She thought the name she'd chosen was exotic. Most everyone else thought "Roxy Tinkers" sounded like the name of a stripper. Cole discovered her given name one night when he got a glimpse of her driver's license. She told Cole she was "way into" him.

Cole admitted to himself that Roxy checked most of the boxes for him as well. She was hot, available, and a demon in the sack. But she had one fault; she used the word "evidently" in nearly every other sentence.

When asked if she would be working out on any given day her answer was "Evidently."

She started sentences with the word. "Evidently this restaurant doesn't clean their restrooms often." "Evidently the Buckeyes have a game today."

She also ended sentences the same way. "That dog is a Golden Retriever, evidently."

It drove Cole batty. He lasted much longer with her—two months—than Tanner would have. *T would've gone apeshit on day one.* But the relationship did produce one thing of incalculable value. He came across the *American Predator* book—which featured a killer named Israel Keyes—in her apartment. It turned out that Roxy was a fan-girl of serial killers—not nearly as much of a deal-breaker as overuse of an adverb. The small bookshelf in her bedroom was chock full of works on Ted Bundy, Jeffrey Dahmer, and John Wayne Gacy. Tucked away in one corner was the volume featuring Keyes.

Israel Keyes lived in Alaska and worked as a carpenter. He was intelligent, good looking, and appeared to be unassuming. But Keyes had a dark side and led a shadow life as an arsonist, sexual offender, burglar, bank robber, kidnapper, and serial killer. He selected random victims, prepared for his crimes meticulously, and—most fascinating to Cole—committed his crimes far from home.

The great majority of his victims were in the lower 48 states. Keyes would fly to say, Chicago, rent a car, drive to Vermont, break into the house of his victim, and return to Alaska in the same manner. He was believed to have killed 11 people in states as scattered as New Jersey, Florida, and Texas.

Keyes committed the majority of his crimes from the late 1990s through his apprehension in 2012. This would almost certainly not have happened if he hadn't changed his tactics and murdered an 18-year-old coffee booth attendant near his home in Anchorage. Law enforcement officials developed evidence that pointed to a local connection. Keyes was tracked and arrested in Texas months later while on yet another spree. He committed suicide in his cell in Anchorage with a concealed razor blade. Before bleeding to death he painted 11 skulls on the wall using his own blood.

Cole had no desire to kill people. He was sure Dom was of a similar mind. *But Tanner? Hmmm, sometimes I wonder.*

It was possible that Keyes would never have been caught if he hadn't diverged from his usual methods. Cole made the "play no home games" mantra a top priority in the team's approach to robberies. The fact that when he was apprehended, Keyes was in possession of a significant amount of dye-stained currency did not escape Cole's notice. His practice of singling out a bank employee and overtly threatening their family was designed to minimize the chances of being saddled with booby-trapped stacks.

So far—for two-plus years—this game plan had worked. Now Dom wanted to mix in a job closer to home. Dom had done everything asked of him, and more. Cole decided that as long as a robbery that happened closer to home was counterbalanced by one out west, the Fireteam would not increase their chances of being captured.

Cole came into the office at twenty till eleven. Both Tanner and Dom sat at desks poking at their cellphones. Tanner had an oversized dip of Copenhagen inside his lower lip. He looked up as Cole entered and spit into his hand grenade-shaped spittoon.

"Bout time big brother. We've been sitting on our asses for two hours."

Cole glanced at Dom who gave a barely perceptible shake of the head.

Cole pulled off his rain jacket and hung it on a hall tree in the corner opposite the TV. He turned to face Tanner. "Things took a while at the bank". Then, "Lift today?"

His brother nodded. "Yeah, thirty-one again today. I'm right there, ready to be top dog."

"Well, T, make sure to let me know when you catch up." Without waiting for Tanner's response he continued. "Let's look at these towns...anybody print the maps?"

"Right here." Dom gestured to four sheets of 8.5 x 11 printer paper that he'd arranged into a square on his desk.

Cole dragged a chair over. "Gather round, gents."

The first sheet was a printed map of the United States. The others were of three different Ohio cities, Toledo, Dayton, and Cincinnati. Cole asked the other men to prepare the maps for the meeting the day before. He suspected that Dom did all the work.

The map of the U.S. was dotted with red specks indicating robberies the team had committed the last two years. They arranged themselves across Middle America like pellets from a shotgun blast. A line drawn freehand in pencil formed an oval. Des Moines was on the left edge of the oval, Racine the north, Indianapolis the east, and the Ozark area of Arkansas—where the Jelcik's robbed the gun dealer—the south. Off to the left flank was a blue checkmark that cut squarely through the word "Omaha." Cole examined the map for most of a minute before setting it aside and arranging the other three maps in a line.

All three cities had airports, meeting the requirement for vehicle theft. All would have dozens of possible target buildings and cemeteries to leave the burial vault truck. Cole saw that all three were located along I-75, the major north-south highway that ran from the Michigan state line in the north to the Ohio River in the south.

Cole picked up the U.S. map and laid it above the other three. Both Tanner and Dom leaned in. Santo spoke. "Doesn't seem to matter which one we pick...all of them would stretch our area the same distance. Columbus stays outside the line no matter which one we pick."

201

Cole was reminded of something he came across over a year earlier. The FBI had just established the term "Fireteam" for them. Their use of World War Two weapons and the Eisenhower jackets were a significant reason for this. Cole thought it prudent to read up on the war. He found an article online that described the process American planners used to select the targets for the first atomic bombs.

Two nuclear weapons were dropped on Japan. The first, on August 6, 1945, was a uranium bomb nicknamed "Little Boy." The target was Hiroshima. Three days later a plutonium bomb, "Fat Man," destroyed Nagasaki. What fascinated Cole was the fact that several cities were considered. These included Kyoto, Kokura, Yokohama, and Niigata. Late in the process Kyoto was removed from the list due to its cultural significance. Kokura was actually the primary target for the second bomb. The city avoided annihilation when poor weather caused the B-29 carrying the weapon to divert to Nagasaki.

One city lives because cloud cover keeps the bombing crew from seeing its target. A second city is vaporized.

Cole stared at the maps of the three Ohio cities. The Fireteam was choosing a primary target of its own. The banks in two of the cities would be safe...for now.

He turned to Tanner. "What do you think, T? Any preference?"

Tanner shrugged. "Ain't much difference far as I can tell." He spit into the novelty spittoon, sat it on the desk, and picked up a blue Sharpie. He knitted his brow and examined the three city maps before reaching toward the map of the United States. The marker hovered over Ohio.

Tanner lowered the Sharpie and drew a checkmark.

CHAPTER TWENTY-THREE

Paul held his cellphone to his ear and listened to a recorded message. In it, different voices related facts about Tutor's Bourbon. He thought one of the voices belonged to Callie Combs, the budding master distiller who led the tour Paul joined in Sawyer the first week of April.

He was on hold, sitting in the ground floor bedroom that he and Lauren converted to an office. He was surrounded by Tutor's literature, maps produced by his printer, and lists of contact names and numbers arranged by city. Several of the stacks were arrayed in a semi-circle on the floor behind his chair.

It was late afternoon on the first Friday in June. Paul had spent parts of two weeks making in-person calls with prospective Tutor's customers in Columbus. He needed to finalize his schedule for the following week. Both McClarys were on a Zoom call with the management team of a California wine producer that was looking to expand their distribution east of the Mississippi. Paul decided to try to catch Charlie Hunter before Tutor's closed for the day. Charlie answered and sounded happy to hear from him.

"Paul Hull! So glad you called. Were your ears burning?"

"Ma'am?"

She laughed. "Obie was just telling me today that he wanted to touch base with you. I get the impression you've been a busy man?" She posed it as a question rather than a statement.

Paul began, "Well I—"

"Oh sorry Paul, I have another call. Can you hold for a bit?"

She was gone before he could answer. The Tutor's recording took her place. Paul slowly spun his chair, taking in the walls of the office. His four Bronze Star certificates hung there, as did the one denoting his Purple Heart. A number of photos adorned the walls. Several included men he'd served with in the Global War on Terror. His fellow Combat Controller Gatewood Dowdell appeared in two of them.

Paul continued to spin, careful not to disturb the papers at his feet. He could hear Chappy pawing at the outside of the door. The Hulls kept it closed at all times to prevent the cat from adding to his impressive total of chewed charger cords. Paul was about to open the door to shoo Chappy away when the recording stopped.

"That you, Master Sergeant?"

It was the unmistakable voice of Owen Johnson. Paul laughed, "Reporting for duty, Cap'n Johnson."

"Good to talk to you Paul. Sorry about the wait. I was on the phone with our bottle manufacturer."

Paul remembered Combs's comment during the tour that the design of the bottle added production expense to Johnson's product. "I guess my bottle idea ended up costing you money."

Obie chuckled. "Not a problem, Paul. What do they say, 'we'll make it up in volume?' Now tell me, how's our arrangement working out from your point of view?"

Paul considered, "Well sir—"

Johnson cut in, "Please Paul, call me Obie."

Paul began again, "Okay Obie. I have to say I like the job more than I thought I would. I've met some good people and gotten to see a few cities I haven't visited before. I still have plenty of time to do what I want at home." He deliberated. "I guess it's about the best setup a retired old ground pounder like me could ask for."

"*Good,* good, glad to hear it Paul. Now let me tell you how *we* view things. We're getting excellent feedback on your meetings. People seem to like you and respect the way you go about your business."

Obie paused.

Paul felt like he should fill the void but could think of nothing better to say than "Oh...Okay."

"The bottom line indicator of how this little promotional gig is working is the visibility of our product. That's a hard thing to measure. You're not in sales...if you were we would have an easy way to evaluate your performance, cases sold, revenue generated. You're doing something a touch different...and however you're doing it, it's working."

Paul was confused. "I don't think I've done all that much. I feel like I'm wandering around out here, trying not to lie to people when I'm not sure of an answer."

"Exactly!" Then, "Do you remember meeting a man at someplace called the Mohawk Restaurant?"

Paul was mystified. The Old Mohawk Restaurant and Bar was in Columbus's German Village neighborhood. It was south of downtown, a few miles from the Ohio State campus area establishments where Paul was concentrating his efforts. The area wasn't on the priority list that was supplied to Paul by Charlie Hunter. He'd heard from his brother-in-law Kevin that the Mohawk had excellent food and he'd carved out an hour the previous Monday to try it out. While there he met another customer, a former Marine Corps cook, and spent twenty minutes BS'ing with him over one of the restaurant's Mother Mohawk sandwiches.

"Uh, sure. I met an old cook. Good guy. Said he'd been in the Corps."

Obie chuckled. "Well Paul, what you did that day was meet yourself a multi-millionaire. That was retired Brigadier General Mackenzie Blackborough, 'Black Mac.' He owns restaurants near USMC bases in four states. Has a cooking show on cable TV. He was the top logistics man in the military before he retired. Among other things he oversaw all of the food service specialists in the Corps."

Paul was flabbergasted. "*What?!?*

Johnson continued, "Talked a little Tutor's Bourbon with him, didn't you?"

"Well, I was wearing a logo shirt...yeah, it came up. Mainly we talked military chow. That, and the Mohawk sandwich. He was eating the same sandwich I was."

"Welllll Paul," Obie drew this "well" out longer than most, "Black Mac got on the horn and gave us a jingle. He got through to Charlie, who was perceptive enough to push the call through to me. Long story short, all six of Mac's restaurants will be serving Tutor's by this time next week."

Paul was speechless. Finally he stammered, "But I didn't know."

"Ha Ha Ha! Doesn't matter. By the way, my Martha loves Mac's TV show. She's *really* impressed that you connected us with him. If this were a movie some character would be saying '*You have made a powerful ally.*'" He laughed.

"Now then, the *other* reason I wanted to talk to you is this. There's a new development in Toledo around their university. Fella named Carlucci is renovating most of a block. It's walking distance from the campus and would be a real feather in our cap. I was hoping to convince you to pay him a visit. I took the liberty of placing a call directly and he has some time next Thursday. If it fits for you I'll have Charlie book a room. Maybe you can hit some spots in Bowling Green too."

Paul looked at the papers near his feet. One pile had contact information for every bar and restaurant in northwest Ohio.

"Roger that, Obie."

After completing the call with Johnson Paul stood and stretched. The annoying pawing seemed to have stopped. He opened the door slowly and saw that Chappy was gone. Stepping into the hall he realized why. He could hear the garage door being raised.

Momma's home, Chappy.

The cat stood at attention near the entry door. When Lauren entered Chappy immediately stepped to her. He raised his back and rubbed against her legs. Lauren offloaded her purse and workout bag onto the dining room table. She knelt and scooped up the feline.

"Hello Chappy, did you miss me?" She scratched his ears and was rewarded by purring that Paul could hear from across the room.

Paul approached and gave her a kiss. "Good day today?" Then, glimpsing at her workout bag, "Good run with Lacey this morning?"

"Yes and yes. Good day, *fantastic* run! We did five miles this morning. Lacey wants us to do a 5K before her wedding. That's the end of this month so we need to find one fast."

Lauren's eyes were bright. Paul marveled at the difference between the Lauren that typically came in the door at the end of a workweek and the version he saw now. Running and enjoying it with a new friend were definitely agreeing with her.

Lauren continued to pet the purring Chappy. She walked through the kitchen as she talked, stopping to hold him up to the window overlooking the back yard. "And we're going try to run the 10K in Minster in October...look at the birds, Chappy... can you believe it? A 10K. I haven't run a 10K since I was stationed in New Mexico!"

The corners of Paul's lips turned up as he watched Lauren move around the kitchen before returning to the dining room. "Well you're certainly jazzed—wait a minute...what're you doing?"

Lauren was now next to the table. She reached out and let Chappy step onto its surface. "Let me show you something. Chappy and I have been doing some training while you've been out working the last few weeks." The cat took a few tentative steps before stopping. His tail swayed back and forth as he looked first at Paul and then at Lauren. Then, to Paul's astonishment, Chappy jumped back to the floor.

You've gotta be kidding me.

As Chappy again brushed against her legs Lauren turned to her husband, beaming. "Reverse psychology...it works!"

Paul spent a good amount of time over the weekend going through the material on Bowling Green and Toledo. Both cities boasted college campuses with enrollments of over 15,000. The athletic teams of both institutions were in the Mid-American Conference, or MAC. The schools had many similarities but there were differences as well. The most

207

significant was that Bowling Green was a city of barely 30,000 while UT was situated inside of a city of a half million. A healthy rivalry had developed between the two over the years.

There was a vibrant bar scene around the BGSU campus. Hot spots included Kamikaze's, Tubby's, Campus Quarters, and two long-time favorites, Howard's and Ziggy Zoomba's.

Choices around the Toledo campus were less robust, possibly due to the dozens of options dispersed throughout the much larger city limits. A developer named Clint Carlucci was trying to change that. Carlucci and his wife Gwen were both UT graduates, having attended during the late 1980s. In their day a strip of college bars existed on Bancroft Street just east of campus. Charlie's Blind Pig was the anchor on the corner of Bancroft and Westwood. The Stein & Pitcher was next door. Across the street and further east was the Ottawa Tavern. They were all gone now but the Carluccis were bringing back bigger and better versions of them using passion, investment capital from friends, and a fair percentage of their own personal funds. These were boosted spectacularly at the tail end of the COVID-19 pandemic when the Carluccis sold their medical equipment business that serviced patients with acute respiratory issues.

Paul put together a tentative schedule for the trip. He decided the most sensible idea was to make the 100-plus-mile drive to Toledo on Wednesday, stay overnight, and do the Carlucci appointment and as many other stops as possible on Thursday. He could stay a second night and leave early to catch owners and managers in Bowling Green Friday before they got busy with the weekend crowds.

I could maybe check out that restaurant in Toledo they used to mention on M*A*S*H. What was it? Tony Packo's. That would be a good place for dinner Wednesday.

The skeleton of a three-day schedule assembled, Paul emailed Charlie Hunter and the McClarys to fill them in on his plans. By the end of the day Monday he would receive confirmation of a hotel reservation. Before hitting "send" on his email Paul checked with Lauren.

"This one will be a three-day trip, are you sure you're okay with that?"

She rolled her eyes. "Seriously Paul, you'd think I was helpless! I'm perfectly capable of functioning without having a former commando around to look after me."

Saturday was a day of domestic tasks. It was seasonably warm. Temperatures hovered in the mid-seventies. Paul mowed the lawn with his 30-inch wide walk-behind mower—he refused to buy a rider on principle—while Lauren transplanted potted starter plants she'd kept in the house all winter to their back patio. The area was constructed of pavers and ran the full length of the house. Planters covered the top of the 24-inch retaining walls. Paul planted tomatoes and peppers earlier in May. Now that the final frost of the season was past Lauren could move the cilantro, dill, parsley, and thyme starts outside as well. She worked cheerfully, noting that the buds on the rose bushes that ringed the patio were full and should bloom in the next week or two.

This task complete she decided space remained for a few additions. She walked out into the yard and positioned herself in Paul's path. When he came to a stop she leaned in and spoke over the noise of the mower.

"I'm going to run into town to get a few more plants for the patio, Text me if you need anything."

Paul nodded. "Let me guess, you're looking for catnip?"

She gave him a look that said *please* and headed for her Jeep. As she backed down the drive she thought, *Catnip!*

Paul returned the mower to its spot in the garage. As he entered the house he had a thought. *What was the name of that soldier from Toledo that crossed the Rhine?* He wracked his brain, finally coming up with it. *Alex Drabik. I should check on the net to see if there are any sites in Toledo related to him. I'll have some time to kill.*

This was a common occurrence. Paul routinely checked out museums, gravesites, and locations relevant to people he considered interesting. Often these were military figures. Sometimes athletes. But always people who had experiences he believed were significant. Paul had a long history of this. So much so that Lauren now took it for granted that if they were traveling there was a better than even chance her husband would turn down a country road to investigate a hidden treasure. Though usually harmless, the practice had been nearly disastrous the previous August.

Paul picked up an old towel from a shelf then grabbed a cold Corona Light from the garage refrigerator. He removed the cap with an opener that was attached to the wall and took a long pull as he entered the house. Glancing down he was just able to see Chappy positioning himself for a dash outside. Paul shifted his foot to block the feline and, in so doing, spilled an ounce or so of beer on his shirt.

Damn cat.

Paul gently directed Chappy backward with his foot and closed the door. He headed to the office and closed the door. The pawing started immediately. Paul sighed, wiped sweat from his face with the towel, and opened his laptop. He selected a browser and took another swig of the beer while waiting for the wifi connection. He entered *a-l-e-x d-r-a-b-i-k* in the search bar and waited for results. There were over 200,000 results. Paul was about to take another sip of Corona when he saw this. The bottle stopped halfway to his lips.

Two hundred thousand results?

He set the bottle on a coaster and began to burrow in.

Drabik, Paul found, was a true American hero. He was one of the millions of "citizen-soldiers" that formed the backbone of American military might in World War Two. These were men who left their homes and families to travel half a world away and fight against totalitarian regimes. Paul had the utmost respect for these people.

These were the men who saved the world.

As a boy going to school in Holland, Ohio near Toledo, Drabik was one of the larger kids in his class. Paul read that in a 1955 interview Principal Matthew Reed said, "He was a big boy, although I never saw him start a fight. Lots of times I saw him beating up bullies who pestered smaller kids. That's why I'm not surprised about his heroism." A teacher identified only as "Mr. Teransky" said of young Drabik, "He was modest and fearless."

Drabik left his job with the Folgers Meat Packing Plant in Toledo to join the Army in 1944. The United States had endured nearly three years of war and needed bodies. Alex distinguished himself during training in California. He was credited with rescuing 120 recruits who were lost in the desert. Despite this he was referred to as a small town "plough jockey" by members of his company who hailed from cities in the Northeast.

Drabik was assigned to Able Company of the 27ᵗʰ Armored Infantry Battalion, a 2,000-plus-member component of the 9ᵗʰ Armored Division. The unit arrived in Europe in late December, in time to participate in weeks-long hellacious fighting against Nazi forces in Belgium. Known as the "Battle of the Bulge," fighting raged across hundreds of square miles. Much of the terrain was inside a massive wooded forest known as the Ardennes. Americans withstood sub-freezing temperatures and fanatical attacks before outlasting their foes and pushing them back toward Germany. Drabik sustained a shrapnel wound from artillery fire but refused to be evacuated.

This last nugget struck a chord with Paul. Several of the Special Operations personnel he fought alongside in the war on terror replicated Drabik's action, demanding to stay with their brothers-in-arms after suffering what they considered minor wounds. *This guy was the real deal.*

American and British forces slugged it out with the Germans, advancing toward the Rhine. The river defined much of the border between Germany and several other countries, including France. As the Germans retreated they destroyed bridges, assuring that Allied forces could not get a foothold on the eastern bank. American and British commanders were resigned to the fact that all the bridges would be destroyed and their best course of action was to push to the Rhine and cut off as many enemy troops as possible, trapping them on the western side. After consolidating, they would cross the Rhine at a still-to-be-determined point in an amphibious assault—Operation Plunder—that could be very costly in men and material.

On March 7, 1945 elements of the 27th Armored Infantry approached Remagen and from a position overlooking the town saw to their surprise that a bridge was still intact. This was the Ludendorff Bridge, a 1,066-foot structure built nearly 30 years earlier during World War One. Its purpose then was the same as in 1945—to carry German men and supplies to and from the western front in France.

News of this startling discovery made its way all the way up the chain of the American command structure. General Dwight Eisenhower concurred with subordinates—the Americans on the scene should improvise and attempt to take the bridge intact.

Drabik, now a sergeant, was at the tip of the spear. The Germans attempted to blow the bridge with prepositioned explosives as the Americans approached. It was later determined that the explosives were of construction—rather than military—grade. The bridge sustained significant damage but still stood. American infantrymen braved rifle, machine gun, mortar, and tank fire as they fought their way through the deadly funnel that the bridge had become. They took the bridge and withstood desperate counterattacks for the next several weeks as thousands of Americans were rushed across and into Germany.

The German efforts to eliminate this American foothold included Panzer and Tiger tank units, Luftwaffe bombers and the first jet aircraft used in combat, combat swimmers with demolition charges, and even V-2 ballistic missiles. The Americans held the bridge and pushed on to Berlin, shortening the war and preserving thousands of lives.

And Alex Drabik was the first man across.

Damn! Why is this guy anonymous?

Paul thought of the term some in the know used to describe modern American Special Operations personnel. They were "Pipe Hitters."

Alex Drabik was one of the original Pipe Hitters.

Paul drained the last of the Corona and stood. *I gotta dig into this. Are there any relatives of Drabik left in Toledo? Is he buried there?* He pulled the door open, contemplating a second beer. Chappy sat in the hall, his green eyes staring up accusingly.

Paul nearly snorted. "Jeez Chappy, chill out. It's your own fault you're not allowed in that room." He bent and picked up the cat. "Come with me and show me your new trick." He walked to the dining room table and let Chappy step onto its surface. The cat glared at him, circled, and tucked himself into a tight ball. He was going nowhere.

Paul began, "But I just saw you—"

Realizing he was trying to reason with a domestic animal, Paul cut his accusation short. He suddenly remembered an old Warner Brothers cartoon in which a construction worker discovers a frog at a building site. The creature wears a top hat, carries a cane, and belts out ragtime tunes. Hoping to profit from his find the man takes the frog to talent scouts only to discover it will not perform in front of anyone else. The creature—named "Michigan J. Frog"—simply utters a croak. This drives the man nuts.

Chappy remained perched on the table, observing Paul with apparent disdain. The cat was unwilling to repeat the dismount from the table he'd performed for Lauren. Paul had one thought.

Chappy is my Michigan J. Frog.

CHAPTER TWENTY-FOUR

On Tuesday the three members of the Fireteam met at the Klean Sooner office. Dom had completed the drive to Toledo, the recon of the banks, airport, and cemeteries, *and* returned to Columbus the previous day. It had been a long ten hours but, in his words, "A helluva lot better than that boring-ass drive to Nebraska."

Over coffee and a dozen of Buckeye Donuts' finest Dom laid it out.

"So I left my apartment about seven in the morning—"

Tanner interrupted, "For Christ's sake Santo, we don't need that kinda detail." He suddenly began to cough violently and his face reddened. Settling down he continued, "I mean, what are you gonna tell us next, how many ounces you pissed out when you woke up?"

Dom wasn't in the mood to take any shit from the younger Jelcik. Cole was in the room and Dom was sure the boss would want to hear his report more than Tanner's grousing. "What crawled up your ass, Tanner?"

Tanner pushed his chair back and made a move to get up but Cole, sitting on the edge of a desk, motioned for him to sit back.

"Calm it the hell down, T. This is business." He watched his brother ease back and suppressed a smile. He was pretty sure he knew what had Tanner in such a pissy mood. Last night after cleaning the windows of the local Jeep dealership the brothers returned to the office and hit the weights. With the "Turk Rock" playlist thumping through the sound system Tanner finally caught Cole, pushing out 32 reps of 225. He strutted around the work bay like a banty rooster for five minutes as Motley Crue's "Kickstart My Heart" blasted the walls. At the end of his celebration he jumped toward Cole, landing in a crouch, then turned his shoulder and flexed.

"Gorilla power, BAY-BEE!"

Cole bent and picked up Tanner's phone. He scrolled through the list by artist, came to Aerosmith—one of Turk's favorite bands—and turned to his brother.

"Get over here and spot."

Cole hit play and flipped the phone to the rubber mat. The driving guitars of "No More No More" came through the speakers as Cole laid back and took a series of deep breaths followed by forceful exhales. He narrowed his eyes at Tanner and started rhythmically pushing out the reps. The song ended as he surged through number 24. "Last Child" came up. By the time Brad Whitford was cruising through his first guitar solo Cole was whipped, his arms loaded down with lactic acid.

But it didn't matter. He'd completed 33 reps. He crawled out from under the bar and turned to his incredulous brother.

"Grizzly Bear beats Silverback Gorilla."

Dom saw Tanner ease back into his chair and let out a slow breath. He continued with his report.

"So it takes a good two and a half hours to get up there. I visited five banks and bought debit cards—used most of the cash—and have diagrams of all five buildings." He pointed to the leather binder on the desk. "Basically there were three buildings with good layouts, but only two of them have cemeteries positioned the way we like 'em. Of those two, one has a shit-ton of traffic in and out of the building—pretty good amount of window traffic too—sooo—"

"So there is really only one choice, right?" It was Cole.

Dom nodded, "Yep, that's my take."

Tanner, calmer now, asked to see Dom's drawing of the interior of the prospective target. "Looks doable. These are offices here, right? Restrooms down this hall?"

Dom nodded, "Yeah, and here's the vault." He indicated a rectangle with an "X" through it.

Cole examined the drawing, "How many tellers?"

"Five counter stations, two dedicated tellers—both women—another floater that comes and goes from this office." He indicated a larger square at the opening of a hallway.

Cole and Tanner gathered round the drawing, any friction from the night before was gone. The Grizzly and the Silverback came into contact through the Klean Sooner shirts as the brothers brushed against each other.

"The cemetery near this bank looks good?" Tanner's index finger was on Dom's diagram, his eyes on his teammate. All of his bluster had seemingly disappeared.

"Yeah, it's located well. Not that many trees on the property, which isn't exactly, uh..."

"Opportune?" This from Cole.

"Uh, yeah, I guess. Anyway, the cemetery should work. For a location inside the city limits it doesn't have much traffic nearby. There's a highway a coupla' miles away that gets us on the road to Columbus." He hesitated before adding. "We should be able to make it work."

Tanner picked up the binder and nodded. "What else?"

"The airport is small. I mean, really small. There's no shuttle from the terminal to long-term parking. Passengers get off the plane, go to baggage claim, then walk out to their car."

Cole rubbed his chin. "So we take a cab to the airport, wait for a flight to come in, and file out to the lot with them."

Tanner added, "Hang back, let them flow out to their cars then hit one of the Kias or Hyundais that are left behind."

Cole nodded, "We've done it that way before." He looked up.

Both Tanner and Dom said "Columbia." The team had hit a Savings & Loan in Columbia, Missouri during a heat wave the previous summer. They'd walked out of the terminal of Columbia Regional Airport the night before and directly into the parking lot where Dom smashed the window of a Hyundai Tucson in record time.

Tanner winked at Dom and held out his fist.

Dom bumped it and thought, *Fucking Tanner.*

Cole looked up from the materials on the desk. "Good report Dom, nice job. I think we go ahead with Toledo...save Omaha or Lincoln for the next one. Any objections?"

Dom was relieved. He thought there was a good chance Cole would opt for the plan to push farther west. "Not from me, that's for damn sure."

Tanner agreed, "Let's do it." Then, "When we goin'?"

Cole considered for a few seconds. "We have a walk-through tomorrow at Ohio State's baseball stadium. They want to pressure wash all the seats since the season is over...not sure why their maintenance people aren't tackling the job but we can't skip it. Could lead to more business there. Friday we have two ozone jobs. I'm thinking we drive up tomorrow night, grab a vehicle at the airport, and hit the bank Thursday morning."

"Sounds good." Tanner's coffee cup was empty and he reached into his back pocket for his Copenhagen. "I'll prep the guns and the truck."

Cole nodded, "Good. Dom, sit down and help me pick a hotel. We'll reserve it with one of the prepaid debits...get that set up. Then we'll run out to the storage unit to grab the Carhartts and pick out plates for T's bag...probably go heavy on Ohios." He was referring to the backpack Tanner would carry to the airport filled with license plates, one of which would be used as a replacement on the vehicle they would steal.

Tanner stood and made for the work bay. He stopped and turned while spitting into his Buckeye Donuts cup. "What's the name of this place again?"

It had slipped Cole's mind as well. Other than the Huntington Bank in Columbus where they had stashed bricks of stolen money, all financial institutions had devolved into mere targets.

Dom answered, "Fifth Third Bank."

After falling behind his brother once again in the bench press contest Tanner made a decision on the spot to up his trenbolone dosage from 100 to 150 milligrams every other day.

As he made his way to the truck his mind was on the contest, not the upcoming robbery. *It's bullshit. I paid that guy at the gym five hundred bucks for a couple bottles of tren and the testosterone and Cole is still kicking my ass. It's BULLSHIT!*

He pulled himself up onto the bed of the Silverado and used his key to open the lock. He lifted the heavy lid until it locked in an upright position. Reaching in he fished out the carbine and the Thompson and leaned them against the vault. He then bent to retrieve the three .45 pistols. Their relative small size forced him to lean over the vault's rim to reach them. His upper body blocked the overhead lighting in the work bay, throwing his shadow inside the rectangular vessel.

"Goddammit! Fuckin' shadow!" Tanner swore out loud and shifted his body to allow more light to enter the vault. In so doing he extended his right leg as a counterbalance and it contacted the Thompson. He'd just located the pistols in the right rear corner when he heard the Thompson and the carbine crash to the steel bed of the truck.

Oh for Christ's sake!

He reacted without thought, popping up from his awkward position, and struck the top of his head on the edge of the heavy lid.

"GODDAMMIT!" He drew back a fist with the intention of punching the lid.

"Everything alright out here, T?"

It was Cole. He'd heard his brother's cursing from the office.

Tanner touched the growing lump on his head with three fingers and winced. When he pulled his hand back he saw a trace of blood. *Sonovabitch!*

"Yeah, all good. Bumped my head on the lid."

Cole nodded and turned back to the office, attempting to hide a smirk. From his vantage point he couldn't see the two long guns on the truck bed.

Good thing. Cole would've lost his mind if he knew what happened. The elder Jelcik brother was a stickler for gun safety. When they were young their father drilled it into them.

219

One of Turk's taxidermy customers—a man named Jay Gault—had leaned his Winchester Model 1200 12-guage shotgun against a fencepost while easing through two strands of a barbed wire fence. He was deer hunting north of Bartlesville. The loaded weapon tipped and discharged, sending a slug through Gault's left tibia. He lost the leg below the knee and hobbled around on a prosthetic device for years afterwards, sometimes rapping his kids and grandkids on the head with his cane to get their attention.

Tanner had just repeated Gault's mistake. He thanked the man upstairs that his brother had insisted on unloading the weapons in Racine before storing them.

Pushing on the lump with the palm of his left hand, Tanner pulled out his iPhone and opened the Flashlight app. He used the light to locate and remove the .45s. Before tucking the phone back into his pocket he pulled up a playlist to link to the sound system. He selected one that he'd labeled *Cowboy*. It was heavy on Kenny Chesney, Alan Jackson, George Strait, and Toby Keith. Tanner had assembled the list without consciously realizing that every song on it was performed by a man wearing a cowboy hat. Ironically, his next thought was, *Gonna have a bump on my head for a week. When we get back from Toledo I might bust out my Stetson and wear it to hide the damn thing.*

Tanner spent the next fifteen minutes in a corner of the work bay cleaning the weapons and checking their actions. He wore thin cotton gloves and wiped every centimeter, removing prints. Even though the guns had not been fired in Racine, Tanner made sure to apply a thin coat of gun oil inside and out. When he handled the carbine he remembered pulling its trigger in Peoria and pushed it out of his mind. Finished with his task, he returned the weapons to the vault and slammed the lid before locking it.

Take that, you bastard. Tanner liked to joke that "inanimate objects *can* feel pain." Sometimes he really believed it. He hoped his heavy-handed treatment of the lid would make it think twice before screwing with him the next time. He jumped down from the truck bed with a degree of satisfaction.

Tanner made his way to the office, turning off the music as he left the work bay. Cole and Dom were gone. He checked the door to make sure it was locked. The nature of their business as a cleaning contractor meant there were very few visitors but Cole insisted that whenever they were prepping for a robbery the doors would be locked. The team kept the backpacks used in the car thefts inside a locked closet in the office. To avoid confusion Cole made sure they were a different size and brand than the bolt bags kept in the storage unit.

Tanner opened the bags and withdrew the walkie-talkies and headsets and laid them out on one of the desks. Cole insisted on new batteries before each job. It seemed like a waste of good batteries to Tanner but he knew what would happen if they had a communications failure during a robbery. *Cole would have my ass.* Before sitting, Tanner spit once more into the coffee cup then reached behind his lip to remove the tobacco, pinching what he could and dropping it into the makeshift spittoon. He used his tongue to push the remaining flecks into place then expelled them as well.

Nasty habit...oh well, time for another dip.

Tanner removed the can from his pocket and noted its slightly reduced weight. *Gonna need to take a new can to Toledo.* Whenever possible the brothers bought their preferred tobacco product in 10-can rolls. Tanner packed the dip, the *thwack-thwack* sound reminding him of a similar noise that came from Turk and Tammy's bedroom on occasion. He once approached the door at the age of five and leaned his ear to the crack. When the sound stopped he pressed harder. Seconds later the door swung open and he tumbled inside. A pissed off Turk—Tanner didn't understand why his dad seemed so upset —stood over him wearing nothing but a pair of ratty boxers.

"What the hell you doin', boy?"

"Just heard a noise, dad. Wanted to see what was makin' it."

Turk simply stared at him before he uttered a phrase that stuck with Tanner the rest of his life. "Just knockin' boots, boy, just knockin' boots." His father closed the door in his face.

Tanner smiled and inserted a healthy pinch inside his gum before settling behind the desk. He used the remote to turn on the small television. The cable system they used had their proprietary news station appear by default whenever a set was activated. This was fine with Tanner as he just used it as background noise. He busied himself with the communications gear, pausing when the broadcast cycled to the weather. He watched, curious to see if rain was in the forecast. The Fireteam had avoided jobs on days that featured severe storms. Assured of a good outlook by the odd-looking weatherman Tanner was about to return to his task when a paid political ad appeared on the screen. It was a sappy piece extolling the virtues of a candidate running for office in the fall. Tanner rolled his eyes. *Asshole...the other guy is just as much of an asshole.*

Tanner gave the screen a derisive sneer. He wasn't political, far from it. While millions of Americans were apolitical, allowing others to choose the candidates that ran the country, Tanner took it a step further. He was *anti-political*. He hated all the sonsobitches. *All these people running for office are out to screw the common man. What we need is a guy like George Patton.*

The World War Two general was just the kind of man that should be in the White House. He was a hard charger that took no shit from anybody. Tanner had never heard of the man when his brother suggested "George" as his code-name.

"Who the hell is George Patton?"

Cole simply suggested, "Let's watch the movie."

They streamed *Patton* at the house on Bruck Street one night and Tanner was captivated. The actor that played the general was also named George—George C. Scott. He seemed like almost as much of a hard-ass as the real Patton. When the general slapped one of his soldiers and accused him of being a coward, Tanner was convinced. *George* was the perfect code name for him.

He went back to preparing for the bank robbery.

CHAPTER TWENTY-FIVE

The FBI Task Force broke the case on Tuesday afternoon. Rita Kekich called Tyson Foxx's office line a few minutes after 2 p.m. When he picked up she sounded like she was in mid-sentence with another person.

"This is Foxx."

"—it all needs to happen fast because—Oh, hello, this is Kekich. I think we might have something here." She was rushing her words. "Can we come up?"

Foxx raised an eyebrow. "Who's we?"

"Me and Remick...Remick and I...whatever. Can we come up?"

Foxx didn't hesitate. "Yeah, get up here." He rose from his desk. He'd been looking at a list of recovered baited bills that had been part of the robberies pulled off by the Fireteam. There were remarkably few considering the large quantities of cash the team had pulled out of vaults and teller drawers the last two years. Foxx attributed this to the point man's gambit of threatening the families of his victims.

There *were* bills with recorded serial numbers that had been taken by the men but few had turned up. Those that had were spread across the country. Recovered bills had the most evidentiary value when they were discovered while in the possession of a suspect. This linked them directly to a robbery. More often the cash was spent several times before it came to rest with another financial institution or law enforcement entity that could compare the numbers with those taken in a heist.

A thief could pay his drug dealer with a hundred dollar bill. The dealer could use it to buy drinks at a strip club. The strip club owner could pay a dancer cash under the table to avoid taxes, and the dancer could slip it into a birthday card for her son living out-of-state with his father. By the time the bill was scanned it may have paid for diesel fuel at a truck stop, beers at a ballgame, or chicken feed at a country store.

The variables resulted in exactly what Foxx saw on his screen—a kaleidoscopic pattern of red dots spread across a map of North America, each representing the eventual resting spot of a stolen piece of currency. Most were located in a dozen states in the center of the country. But some were as far away as Canada and Mexico.

Foxx situated three chairs around the small conference table in his office. Kekich, he knew, was liaising with some of the analysts on the sixth floor. Judging by her tone he didn't think it would take her long to reach him on eight. He was standing, taking in the view of Chicago and Lake Michigan beyond when he heard the rap on the door.

"Yeah, come in."

Kekich rushed in. She wore a dull green pantsuit that complimented her auburn hair. The jacket was cut to allow for a shoulder holster that concealed a nine-millimeter Glock-19 Gen 5 service pistol, a slightly smaller version of the Glock-17. The 19 was preferred by many of the Bureau's female special agents.

Kekich was followed by a large man carrying a laptop computer. He wore a white dress shirt with a loosened tie, a grey Fu Manchu, and a facial expression that projected a message to any perceptive observer that its owner would tolerate zero bullshit.

This was Scott Remick, a former special agent that now worked as an analyst. Remick had a colorful history in the Bureau. He played amateur rugby, shaved his head, and rode a Harley-Davidson Softail Standard motorcycle painted vivid black. All of these attributes made him the perfect choice sixteen years earlier to be placed into a Tampa-area pawn shop in a wide ranging operation designed to foil illegal activities by a Florida biker gang. The gang—known as the Bell-Tollers—ran a drug operation in the western and central regions of the state. They supplemented this by rolling tourists outside of St.

Pete and Clearwater Beach nightspots and clubs on the periphery of Disney World near Orlando.

They kept the cash obtained in the robberies and pawned most of the watches and jewelry—that which wasn't doled out in the form of gifts to their women—in Bay Area pawn shops. Remick assumed a position in a shop and soon gained favor among the gang for his knowledge of motorcycles and, more importantly, proclivity to pay what the bikers believed was a fair price for the goods. He was a tough negotiator, not giving in easily in the transactions. Several times he turned away from purchases telling the seller to "get the hell out of my shop." This caused his superiors no little frustration as—watching remotely through hidden cameras or after the fact on video—they witnessed evidence walking back out the shop's door.

In the end this technique paid off with sensational results. Remick's hardline realistic approach ingratiated him with the gang. It reached the point where he began to buy drugs from them and he passed himself off as a mid-level dealer, one who'd earned their complete trust.

Remick's subsequent testimony in the many racketeering and drug trials resulted in nearly twenty convictions, gutting the gang. For the remaining Bell-Tollers, however, he was a mortal enemy who was marked for death. His FBI superiors thought it best to pull him out of Florida and remove him from fieldwork completely. He resisted this, insisting he had "no problem with any of those assholes showing up on my doorstep...I play rugby." But the Bureau was adamant. The impasse ended when Remick was offered a position as an analyst. He was intrigued and agreed to it. He worked in counterterrorism cells for several years until the wars in Iraq and Afghanistan wound down and the Bureau reorganized. Remick was plucked by Tyson Foxx who put a smile on the big man's face when, during the interview, he uttered a phrase Scott would never forget.

"You think like a criminal Remick...I want you on my team."

Kekich and Remick stepped quickly to the table as Foxx moved aside. He didn't waste words.

"Whatta you got?"

Remick nodded at Foxx, uttered a curt "Hey Foxxy," opened the laptop, and hit the spacebar. The screen brightened to reveal a page featuring a number of rows and columns. There were dozens of check marks spread throughout the squares formed by the vertical and horizontal lines. Remick remained silent, angling the computer toward his boss.

Foxx registered the "Hey Foxxy" greeting but didn't react. The FBI was notoriously formal, particularly inside the walls of their buildings. Remick was flaunting custom by not wearing a suit coat or sport jacket and having his tie loosened. He was on the verge of insubordination by calling his task force commander by a nickname. Foxx ignored it. He was concerned with results.

"Talk to me Scott. Show me what you found."

"Rita explained that regular search parameters were not working in the hunt for these"—Remick searched for a word, considered offenders, and went with—"cats." I ran the data through a couple of our programs to find any anomalies occurring near the targeted banks for thirty days preceding each robbery. After the algorithm spit out most of these," he pointed to short phrases in the far left column, "I added a few oddball possibilities I thought of myself." He looked at Foxx with a twinkle in his eye.

Remick elaborated that the vertical columns represented robberies believed or suspected to have been committed by the Fireteam. Both Foxx and Kekich were relatively sure that two of the robberies represented at the top—Indianapolis and Detroit—were not pulled off by the trio they were seeking. There were just too many discrepancies, the most glaring being the number of perpetrators—four in Indy, just two in Detroit. Nevertheless Foxx was fine with leaving them in the "maybe" category.

Foxx squinted slightly and read a few of the phrases on the left side of the screen:

Suspicious Activity Reported at Cemetery
Moving Violation Issued Within 5 Miles of Bank
Nearby Arrest for Solicitation of Prostitution

There were several more. Remick explained that each square could be clicked on to reveal expanded information. He demonstrated this by moving the cursor to the *PEORIA* column and pulling it down to the row that dealt with prostitution arrests. He clicked on the square and two names appeared.

"We checked out all solicitation arrests in all twenty towns. We were able to eliminate all offenders as suspects in the robbery."

Foxx showed a rueful smile, "Not surprising. These guys are too smart to make a mistake like that when they roll into town to pull a job."

Both Kekich and Remick nodded in agreement. Left unsaid was the fact that a number of offenders in previous crimes were caught after committing just such a mistake.

Kekich piped up, "We left off 'Vehicle Stolen at Airport' and 'Stolen Vehicle Found in Cemetery.' We already knew these things happened."

"Not in Indy or Detroit." It was Remick.

Foxx waved a hand. "Forget about those two for now. You're building up to something here."

The big analyst smiled and reached to the keyboard. He took the cursor down to the bottom row and said, "Be my guest, click on any city in the bottom row."

Kekich interjected, "Other than Indy and Detroit."

Foxx did so and was amazed. The row was labeled *Incoming Cash at Bank*. Eighteen of the cities showed multiple cash purchases for prepaid debit cards. In all eighteen the purchases were for exactly the same amount, $500. The eighteen banks victimized all had transactions and, in every case, nearby institutions experienced the same activity.

Foxx let out a low whistle. "HOLLL-LEEE SHIT. This is them! It's them casing the banks!" His head snapped up, turning from Remick to Kekich and back again. "Have we pulled video? Tell me we have video of these transactions."

Kekich answered, "We've requested the video for these specific transactions from every bank. All the card purchases occurred within two weeks of the corresponding robbery. We've already received emails from Des Moines, Columbia, and Terra Haute. It's the same guy in all three...not the point man or the tail gunner that we see in the robbery videos—too small—but it's the same brah buying the cards."

Foxx ran a hand through his hair. "Gotta be the driver, gotta be."

Remick gave Rita a quizzical look, "Brah?"

She smiled and flashed him a shaka sign. "Island talk."

The *Incoming Cash at Bank* row had been Remick's idea. He later said he wasn't exactly sure of what might turn up. "I don't know, maybe they come in with coins from a piggy bank and spend ten minutes rolling pennies while they look for the vault."

It was inspired by his time masquerading as a pawn shop employee. "People come in, look around, act like they have a reason to be there...you can just tell there's something hinky with them." He reasoned that the gang could be doing something similar and took a stab at how they might disguise their activity.

"That's great work you two, great work!" Foxx was effusive.

Kekich admitted, "It wouldn't have happened if you hadn't shifted our focus from following the money after the robberies to looking at what happens beforehand." She thought it odd that the mantra stressed at the FBI Academy was the exact opposite of the approach that seemed to have put them on the Fireteam's trail. *Hell, even the movies tell you to do it.* She thought back to the line from *All The President's Men*, the 1976 movie about the Watergate scandal.

Follow the money.

Foxx scrambled the entire task force. There would be little sleep this night. Facial recognition software was examining images of the card buyer in an effort to identify him. Every member of the unit mentally crossed their fingers, hoping the man had a record and would be in their database. A priority message was composed and transmitted to all financial institutions on the master list maintained by the Bureau. It requested information on any and all purchases of prepaid debit cards. The FBI's Data Collection section processed responses as they rolled in, pulling all transactions for $500 into a separate folder. At 6:11 p.m. Central Time, less than four hours after Kekich and Remick entered Foxx's office, the task force received a report that a $500 debit card had been purchased recently, matching the profile they'd assembled.

The special agents and analysts went into overdrive. Jackets came off, shirtsleeves were rolled up, and coffee makers—generally dormant at this time of day—could barely keep up with the demand. Scott Remick's tie was still loose but he no longer looked out of place. By 7 o'clock they'd identified two more $500 purchases in the same area and they were sure.

The Fireteam was preparing to hit another target—and soon.

Foxx was put in touch with the local authorities and alerted them, passing on their findings. A call was placed to HRT, the FBI's elite Hostage Rescue Team. They were among the best in the world when it came to resolving high-risk situations—often with appropriate and necessary violence. HRT's building assaulters and sniper teams had few peers. After much consideration Foxx decided to rely on the city police force tactical teams rather than HRT.

The locals made another suggestion that intrigued Foxx. They recently put in place a program involving private drone owner-operators. In some ways it mirrored the relationship from past decades between police and private ham radio operators who were sought out to help with communication during emergencies. In the current program, drone operators agreed to lend their hardware and expertise to police

231

personnel to literally give them "eyes in the sky." After receiving Foxx's blessing, the Chief of Police "activated" enough drones to blanket every cemetery in the city. They might not catch the Fireteam at a bank but, as Remick said, "We'll sure as hell get them when they do the vehicle exchange at the cemetery."

Representatives from the Chicago task force would be in the air within the hour. They would link up with special agents from the local FBI field office. City and state law enforcement were scrambling. Assets would be in place by tomorrow morning. The task force had performed beautifully in a few short hours. But there was one glaring problem.

They had the wrong city.

CHAPTER TWENTY-SIX

Paul drove north on I-75 on Wednesday. He hadn't left Troy until Lauren came home from work. In the past this may have been problematic due to her many hours of overtime. Since becoming a regular morning runner with Lacey, she tended to leave the hospital at, or shortly after, her designated clock-out time of 4 p.m. Unless she ran errands or went shopping, she was home well before five. Today she breezed in at 4:30 and—after greeting Chappy—gave Paul a rundown of her day as he finished packing a small suitcase.

After telling him that she and Lacey had an easy run in the morning she asked if Paul would be eating dinner before he left.

"No, I want to try that Tony Packo's place...they're supposed to have hundreds of autographed hotdog buns framed and mounted on the walls."

Lauren looked at him as if a horn had sprouted from his forehead. "What? You're kidding, right?"

Paul snickered, "No, seriously. Signed by politicians, rock stars, ballplayers...anybody famous that comes through Toledo. All the old actors from that show M*A*S*H."

She looked at him doubtfully, not sure if she was being teased. "Anywayyy...we've picked a 5K race. It's this Saturday in Dayton. It's a Brewery Run. We figured you and Matt could hang out and try some of the beers while you cheer us on. That is, unless you want to run with us."

"The run might be fun but my vote is for the beer...I can run anytime." Paul added, "I guess I'll leave it up to Matt. His call."

Lauren looked amused, "If it's up to Matt you won't need your running shoes." She held her hands out to each side, palms up, and moved them up and down pantomiming a scale. "Beer versus running...beer versus running...hmmm." They both laughed. Lacey's fiancé had a well-known aversion to any exercise that didn't include a ball or a barbell.

After a kiss and hug Paul was out the door. The drive would be easy. It was a calm 80-degree day with routine weekday traffic. He planned to be at Packo's by 7:30 and check into his hotel before nine. Once on the highway he started an episode of the *Uncommon History* podcast entitled "The History of Kentucky Bourbon." Paul thought of this as continuing education. He knew his knowledge of the whiskey was limited and believed it was a weakness he could work on.

Soon after beginning the pod his mind began to wander. Something in the host's introduction of the subject matter made him think of Tutor's. Paul had received a form in the mail from the distillery two days earlier explaining optional health insurance plans. This was something he didn't need due to his coverage based on military service. He also had secondary coverage through Lauren's plan at the hospital. As his hand hovered above the wastebasket Paul saw the postmark on the envelope—*Somerset*.

The next day Paul drove to the McClarys' to pick up additional bottles of the bourbon to dole out as samples in Toledo and Bowling Green. He asked Mike about the postmark.

"Just curious, Tutor's is outside of Sawyer. Why is their mail postmarked in Somerset?"

Mike laughed, "Because Obie knows the little post office in Sawyer—supposedly the smallest one in the country—is a point of pride to some of the locals. Between shipments from the gift shop, and mailers from their promotions department, Tutor's sends out dozens of items every day. If it went through Sawyer, that little office would have to be expanded."

Paul followed, "And Sawyer could no longer claim"—here Mike joined in and they spoke in unison—"*the smallest post office in America.*"

They both laughed, then Mike added. "You know what he does? He sends a Sprinter van all the way to Somerset every day with their mail...sometimes twice a day."

Paul shook his head slowly, "Just so Sawyer keeps their bragging rights?"

Mike nodded, "Just so Sawyer keeps bragging rights."

Paul realized the podcast was thirty minutes in and he couldn't remember anything that had been discussed. *Oh well, maybe I'll learn by osmosis.*

He passed Wapakoneta, the hometown of Neil Armstrong, the first man on the moon, and saw the Armstrong Air and Space Museum on his left. Its shape gave the observer the impression of a moon sinking—or rising—on the horizon. Paul had visited the facility but it'd been a couple years earlier. He thought it might be time for a refresher. *I wonder if Wapakoneta has a 5K?*

An hour later Paul came upon the exit for Bowling Green. The university and most of the town were to his left. He could see a football stadium from the highway and knew the school colors were brown and orange. There did not appear to be many buildings taller than the stadium. BGSU had a reputation as being a college town and the bars supposedly reflected this. He would find out Friday when he made his scheduled stops.

As Bowling Green receded in his rearview mirror Paul disengaged the overhead sun visor and swung it to the left. The sun was beginning to dip toward the western horizon and he felt the glare on his left eye. He adjusted the angle of the visor and made a quick check to see if it needed further tweaks. In doing this Paul caught sight of the flat, open farmland of northwest Ohio that seemed to have no end. The experts said a series of glaciers—the last occurring 25,000 years ago—ground through this region, leaving behind a sweeping topography that was as level as it was bland.

Paul believed the glacier story. There was overwhelming scientific proof. But now, gazing out at the vast plane, he would've also believed that a God-sized concrete block was accidentally dropped here while being transported west where it was meant to flatten Kansas.

Paul parked his Escape outside of Tony Packo's at twenty after seven. He'd navigated through the south and central parts of the city before angling northeast and crossing the Maumee River, which cut through the city on its way to Lake Erie. The bulk of the metro area east of the river was officially designated as the city of Oregon. However there was a narrow, few-blocks-wide strip east of the river that was claimed by Toledo. Paul wondered if this was contrived by gerrymandering politicians from a past administration for the sole purpose of claiming tax dollars generated by the restaurant.

The building was a pleasant combination of quaint, rustic, and cheerful. It was two stories of oddly angled walls that fit onto a corner formed by streets that did not meet at right angles. Paul was reminded of overhead views he'd seen of Fenway Park in Boston, whose builders had to make it fit into the surrounding neighborhood. Green and white striped canopies both protected and flattered the antique window frames. Hues of orange, yellow, and muted green were complimented by rust-colored exterior light fixtures that lined the building's crest. The fixtures consisted of curved metal arms that connected to buttercup-shaped shrouds.

They look like those instruments used to snuff out candles in church.

Paul entered through the south-facing door and was immediately hit by aromas that, rather than competing with each other, had assembled themselves into a potion for the hungry. Paul detected spice, meat, the soft fragrance of bread, and something peppery. His mind went back to the bourbon tasting with Callie Combs at Tutor's as she attempted to sort through the flavor traces of the whiskey.

Paul was greeted by a pleasant woman behind the wooden bar who drew him a beer from the tap—he selected Packo's Golden Ale—and pointed him to a table. The restaurant was known for its Hungarian hot dogs. Paul had two, plus an order of German Potato Salad. He promised himself he would come back with Lauren so he could show her the place and try one of the stuffed peppers he'd noticed on the menu. *Looks just like the ones Mom used to make.* But the highlight was the autographed buns. There were hundreds of them. They covered long stretches of the walls as well as crooked nooks and crannies. After finishing his food Paul ordered a second beer and spent twenty minutes playing *First-Time-Packo's-Visitor,* wandering through the restaurant and seeing the signatures of six presidents, entertainer Bob Hope, and dozens of rock stars. There were several signed by the cast of M*A*S*H. The show helped popularize Packo's when it was mentioned in several episodes by the fictional Corporal Max Klinger. The character was played by Toledo native Jamie Farr.

Paul left Packo's later—and fuller—than planned and headed for his hotel, a Hampton Inn on Secor Road near the university. He'd been in Toledo for a little less than two hours and had checked off one of the boxes on his to-do list. Tomorrow, after his appointments, he hoped to accomplish another. He wanted to visit Alex Drabik's grave.

But that would have to wait.

He had work to do Thursday.

Cole, Tanner, and Dom spent most of the morning at Bill Davis Stadium on Ohio State University's main campus. They were walked through the entire facility. In addition to taking bids on the pressure washing of stadium seating, the university was open to outside cleaning of other areas of the stadium. A recent $500,000 donation by a former player, Nick Swisher—who went on to play in the major leagues—had provided artificial turf. Hundreds of thousands of small black rubber chunks resided at the bottom of the green strands. The particles—known as infill—boosted safety for players and durability for the turf itself. During competition the particles migrated across the surface, resulting in uneven coverage. This was difficult to detect visually.

Regular maintenance consisted of spreading extra infill from time to time. The athletic department was considering having all of the rubber removed and brand new product spread evenly, in effect to give the surface a "reset." Klean Sooner did not own the wide-area vacuum equipment required for such a job but Cole wanted the seat-cleaning piece of business so the team dutifully walked the entire facility and listened to a low-level member of the athletic department explain the parameters of the bid process.

Near the end of the tour the Jelciks and Dom stood near the pitcher's mound as the man pointed out areas of concern in the seating sections above. Cole followed the narrative, taking pictures with his phone. Tanner asked to use a restroom, was directed to an opening through the third base dugout, and was joined by Dom. After using the facilities in a men's room down a short hallway, the two men returned to the dugout. Dom spied two batting practice balls under the bench in a corner and picked them up.

"Hey Tanner, I bet I can throw a baseball farther than you." Dom played organized baseball until the seventh grade.

"Get the hell outta here, pipsqueak." Tanner climbed the dugout steps and looked toward the mound. Cole was walking toward them. The man from the athletic department was disappearing through an opening beyond the other dugout.

Dom scampered up the steps behind Tanner. "Come on T, I'm tired of lifting around you...feeling like a weakling...let's see if I can compete with you in something else."

Tanner paused, hands on hips, and surveyed the smaller man. "Whaddya got in mind?"

Dom gestured to the large electronic scoreboard in right-center field. "We each get one throw toward that"—he gestured at the scoreboard—"furthest throw wins twenty bucks from the other guy."

Tanner considered, "Well, that'll buy me a coupla cans of Cope." He shrugged, "Your funeral."

Dom windmilled his arm, gripping the ball in his right hand. He stutter-stepped toward his target—in baseball

238

parlance it was a "crow-hop"—and let it fly. The ball sailed toward the scoreboard, losing momentum as it neared, and landed fifteen feet in front of the warning track. It took one bounce off the turf, banged into the wall, and settled to the outfield surface.

Ten yards away Cole stood, clapping slowly. "Impressive, Dom. Very impressive."

Dom turned to Tanner, "Let's see what you got, big boy."

The larger man pushed past Dom while mimicking the winding arm motion to loosen up. He took one step and brought his arm forward awkwardly. In addition to the lack of fluidity, Tanner held onto the ball too long. When it was finally released it skittered toward the left field foul pole.

Dom reacted without thought. "HAH! Omigod you throw like a g—"

He stopped just before finishing the sentence, realizing he was, very possibly, a dead man. In an attempt to spackle over his comment, he shifted gears, "guy I used to know...You throw like a guy I used to know!" His eyes showed fear.

Tanner wasn't buying it. He knew what Santo was going to say. He was furious. He began "You mouthy little Sicilian—" That was all he got out before he began to cough. It turned into an extended jag as Cole interceded.

He put an arm on Tanner's shoulder, "You okay, T?" As Tanner continued to cough Cole turned and mouthed, *Get in the van!*

Dom turned and, as announcers say when a game is wrapped up, headed for the exit.

They ate lunch at a wing joint called Roosters a few blocks from campus. Cole ordered for the group, requesting 50 wings —half Nashville Hot Dry Rub, half Carolina Gold—and three Cokes. They sat at a booth away from other customers. Dom hung back until Tanner selected a seat then slid in on the opposite side. They reviewed the upcoming schedule for Toledo. Cole explained that there was an Allegiant Air flight due into the airport at 9:35. He wanted to be checked into their hotel by eight, giving them plenty of time to take a taxi to the facility and find the baggage claim area.

Dom was squeezed against the wall by Cole's upper body but didn't complain. Tanner—still pissed—stared lasers at him as Cole moved from tonight's schedule to action at the bank the following day. The plan was routine, containing elements the men had utilized several times, but Dom kept his eyes on the older brother as if hearing the instructions for the first time. By doing this he was able to avert Tanner's glare. When the food came, Dom sat back and watched the devastation.

The team left Columbus at 5 p.m. after meticulously assembling their gear and loading it into the cab of the truck. The weapons went inside the burial vault. Tanner snapped the lock shut and gave it several tugs to make sure it was secure. After topping off the tank with diesel they maneuvered their way through rush hour traffic.

Cole drove, with Tanner in the front passenger seat. Dom sat in the rear seat behind Cole, happy to be more than an arm's length from Tanner. This made up for the fact that— unable to listen to his preferred music through earbuds due to Cole's "no phones" rule—he had to endure Outlaw Country the entire duration of the trip. The seat to his right was crowded with backpacks, travel kits, and the Eisenhower jackets. Sticking near the speed limit the trio made it to their hotel—a Best Western—a few minutes before eight.

At 9:07 p.m., the exact minute that Paul Hull walked through the entrance of the Hampton Inn near campus, the Fireteam exited the Best Western on the southwest part of town and approached their waiting cab for the short ride to the airport. Just before piling in Cole reminded the other two, "Remember, we use code names from here on out." Minutes later they approached the airport's access road and saw a sign that read:

Eugene F. Kranz Toledo Express Airport

Tanner was in the back seat with Cole. He furrowed his brow and asked of no one in particular, "Who the hell is Eugene F. Kranz?"

Before Cole or Dom could answer, the driver, a dark-skinned man in his forties, looked over his shoulder and said You doh know? Apollo Tirteen! Dee movie. Dee man in mission control dat was in charge...*Gentlemen, I beeleeve dis will be our finest hour.* Dat was Gene Krantz. Dat was Gene Krantz!" He seemed insulted that the question had been asked.

Tanner eyed the man and asked, "Where you from, partner?"

"Senegal."

Both Cole and Dom burst out laughing. The fact that an immigrant was aghast at Tanner's lack of knowledge about a less-than-well-known American historical figure struck them as hilarious. Tanner's eyes narrowed for the briefest of moments then he joined them. As the three howled, the driver pulled to a stop in front of the terminal. Cole paid the fare and gave the man an extra twenty. The cab pulled away, its driver mumbling "*Eeet was a goddammed Tom Hanks movie...Tom Hanks!*"

As the cab disappeared around a curve Cole turned toward the long-term lot. The smile faded from his face.

"You weren't lyin' Audie. That lot is damn close to the terminal. Looks like less than a hundred cars there. Might be tough to find a Kia or a Hyundai."

Dom stepped to Cole's side. They stood shoulder to shoulder, scrutinizing the lot. Dom's backpack was slung over his right shoulder, mimicking how Cole wore his. He liked it when his boss called him by his code name. Audie Murphy—Dom had learned—was definitely a man to be admired. He'd been small in stature, but fearless in battle.

Dom would do anything possible to prevent the Fireteam from failing. He remembered again how Cole had helped him get on his feet after leaving prison. How the big man's guidance allowed Dom to grab his share of the American Dream.

241

"Don't worry Ike. If there aren't any Korean rides out there we'll be okay. I have some other tricks up my sleeve." He patted his backpack. Cole turned and grinned. Dom executed a very Cole-like mannerism—he winked.

The plane from Richmond was five minutes late. The three bank robbers split up and wandered through the baggage claim area. Each of them made a restroom pit stop to kill time. Minutes after the plane taxied to the terminal the first squirter hurried toward the building's front exit. Not only did he meet all of the expectations for *First Man Off The Plane* with his trendy carry-on and sporty upscale attire, he bore an uncanny resemblance to the first man off the plane in Milwaukee. The man breezed past baggage claim and checked his phone. Dom watched as Tanner fell in step behind the man, balled his fist, and set his jaw. He took two quick strides in the man's wake before breaking away. Tanner then looked toward Cole who was leaning against a support column, watching intently.

Dom waited for Cole's reaction, expecting the worst. Instead he saw the boss cover his face to hide a laugh. Tanner was doing the same.

Fucking brothers.

The vehicle heist was good—Dom quickly smashed through the rear window and the Jelciks performed their tasks in choreographed fashion—and bad—there were no SUVs that met their requirements. They settled for a white Hyundai Sonata, a four-door sedan.

The exit gate from the parking lot was automated and the owner of the Sonata made things easy for them by leaving her ticket on the dash. Cole was sure the owner was a young woman because the seat was positioned as close to the steering wheel as possible and there were decorations resembling Hawaiian leis hanging from the rearview mirror. Cole once sat next to a body shop owner in a bar in Bartlesville who told him, "Half the cars that come in my shop are driven by young women who have Hawaiian leis hanging from their mirror. They pull out in front of other drivers cause they can't see 'em."

Two miles from the airport they pulled into an abandoned gas station. They unscrewed the Michigan plate from the rear of the car and replaced it with one Dom stole the year before from a grey Sonata at the Columbus airport. It was, they believed, a close enough match for the short time they would need the vehicle. The broken window glass was tossed onto the cracked concrete of the lot and plastic was stapled over the window opening.

Ten minutes later they were back at the Best Western. Cole backed the Sonata into a tree-shrouded corner of the parking lot to hide the missing rear window.

They had work to do Thursday.

CHAPTER TWENTY-SEVEN

Thursday began in unremarkable fashion. Paul was up at 5:45. He completed a series of calisthenics in the room before heading down to the hotel's small workout area. He did twenty-five minutes on the treadmill while watching the TV in the corner. The first five were spent catching up on the news, the next twenty part of an old episode of *Leave It To Beaver*. In the episode, Beaver—played by Jerry Mathers—and his friends make a prank phone call to Don Drysdale, a star pitcher with the Los Angeles Dodgers in the 1950s and 60s. Paul paid little attention to the plot, though he was sure wackiness ensued. His attention was on scenes featuring Drysdale. Paul enjoyed cameo appearances like this on old shows.

This episode had to be filmed at least a decade before I was born.

Partway through the show Beaver's mom is shown working in the kitchen wearing a dress and a strand of pearls. Paul realized the characterization was ridiculous but found himself smiling. There was something quaint, almost reassuring about the way women were portrayed in the old shows.

Paul detected movement out of the corner of his eye and turned to see a twenty-something woman two treadmills over. He hadn't noticed her come in. She looked from Paul to June Cleaver and rolled her eyes.

Paul decided it was a good time to wrap up his exercise session. He stepped off the machine and wiped it down before setting the remote within reach of the woman. She didn't meet his eyes.

I guess June and I made her mad.

Stopping at the small breakfast area Paul microwaved oatmeal in a Styrofoam bowl and grabbed a banana. He filled two of the small cups with coffee, attached lids, and stacked one on top of the other. Balancing the cups in one hand and the food in the other Paul moved cautiously to the elevator. He approached, calculating how he would push the "Up" button. Turning slightly he was able to depress it with his elbow. When the elevator arrived he stepped in and knelt, lowering the coffee cups to the floor. He poked "4" and squatted back down to grasp the cups. When he reached the fourth floor he repeated the procedure at his door.

After eating and showering Paul spent a half hour on his phone. He had emails from three of the bar owners he'd visited —two in Columbus and one in Morgantown—asking for specifics on promotional materials. He decided to try calling the McClarys to get the answers. Marge picked up.

"Hey Marge, it's Paul."

"Good morning world traveler! How are things in exotic Toledo, Ohio this fine day?"

"So far, so good. I've had two cups of bland lobby coffee and might slug my way through another."

Marge was sympathetic. She'd had more than her fair share of hotel breakfasts. "Just think, Paul, what would you have given for some bad coffee on some of those nights you had overseas?"

"Good point...maybe I'll have *two* more cups. Listen, I have calls from some of the owners and managers. Sounds like they want to get started with the kickoffs. They're requesting the cardboard stand ups of the Tutor's bottle for their bar. They also want—"

"Let me guess, more of the wooden rulers?"

Paul chuckled, "Nailed it."

Marge joked, "I hope those things don't lead to lawsuits. I think bartenders might actually be slapping customers' fingers. Text me the addresses. What time is your appointment with the Carluccis?"

"Leaving in ten minutes."

The Carlucci property was adjacent to the university. It was located on the corner of West Bancroft Street and Westwood Avenue. Paul cruised east on Bancroft and eyed the 206-foot

Gothic clock tower that rose over University Hall to his right. If he hadn't known it was part of a university he would have guessed.

No doubt about it, that thing belongs on a college campus.

He stopped at a red light at the next intersection and got his first glimpse of the area the Carluccis had developed. Charlie's Blind Pig, a rectangular building, was on the corner. Next to it was The Stein and Pitcher. Beyond that Paul could see the sign for the Ottawa Tavern. They shared a large parking lot in the rear. Paul turned in.

The interior of Charlie's was decorated to look like a 1920s speakeasy. Paul, carrying a leather sample case, walked to the bar where a tall man in his twenties was stocking the coolers. The man looked up and asked, "You the bourbon guy?"

Paul nodded and said, "I'm the guy from Tutor's."

"Gwen and Clint are in the office." The barman pointed to the rear of the building.

Paul wandered back and came to an open door. He rapped on the frame and poked his head inside. A man with salt and pepper hair combed straight back looked up from a desktop computer. He removed a pair of tortoise shell glasses and squinted in Paul's direction.

"That you, Hull?"

Paul nodded and asked, "Mr. Carlucci?"

"Call him Clint...I'm Gwen." This from a woman sitting at a second desk. She rose and stepped toward Paul with her hand outstretched. Clint Carlucci rose and approached with her. Both Carluccis appeared to be in their mid-fifties. Paul saw that Gwen was two inches taller than her husband. Her chocolate-colored hair was shoulder length. She had smile lines around her eyes. They shook hands and Clint pulled a chair from the corner, situating it between the two desks.

"I apologize for the lack of amenities, we've been open for a month but we're still in construction mode." Clint was 5'7". He wore a golf shirt not unlike Paul's but rather than displaying a Tutor's logo Carlucci's featured script lettering that read *The Ottawa Tavern.* Paul noted that his wife sported a light pullover that displayed a tall beer mug overflowing with suds and the words *Stein & Pitcher* underneath.

"No worries. Thanks for making time for me. I know it must be hectic." Then, instead of launching into a sales pitch, Paul asked, "Can you tell me about your businesses?"

This broke the ice and the Carluccis led Paul on a tour of all three establishments. Clint explained that the term "Blind Pig" was used during Prohibition to refer to a place that sold alcohol illegally.

Paul nodded, "That explains the speakeasy décor."

Gwen smiled and led the way toward the east side of the building. She gestured to a stairway that led down and, seemingly, beyond the wall of the building. "That's what gave us this idea." She stepped down and with a cheery expression prompted Paul to follow, "Check this out."

Paul trailed her down the steps and into a short hall. Clint brought up the rear. They climbed another set of stairs at the end of the hall and when they rose Paul saw he was in a pub-like restaurant with a long wooden bar that was backed by an enormous mirror. Gwen turned to him, "Welcome to the Stein and Pitcher."

Paul discovered that a second underground passage led further east to the Ottawa Tavern, which had a stage for bands and more of a club feel than the other two bars.

Clint explained, "The tunnels give the places a different vibe. Speakeasies back in the day sometimes had escape tunnels. We thought it would be a cool idea. We think they'll come in handy during the Ohio winters...walk in one door, visit three different places." He added, "It would've been prohibitively expensive—pun intended—to put in tunnels after we built the three bars. But since we had it done during construction it was doable."

Paul grinned, "If you were shooting for cool, I'd say you hit the target."

Gwen explained, "Clint and I met at UT and used to come to the Blind Pig. We both had a soft spot in our hearts for the place—the Stein and the O.T., too—and hated to see them torn down a few years ago."

Clint continued the narrative. "After we sold our respiratory business we traveled for six months, played golf for a few weeks, and realized we were bored to death. Sitting around with some old college friends one night we talked about how much fun the three bars used to be. They were all gone. Seemed a shame."

Gwen added in a mock flirtatious tone, "Where would this generation's couples meet?"

They returned to the office in the Blind Pig and Clint, looking at his watch, asked, "Can you tell us about Tutor's in ten minutes? I hate to rush you but we have a problem with the walk-in cooler at the Stein and the company rep called just before you got here to say he was on his way."

In the short time that Paul had done this job he'd come to realize that restaurant owners dealt with pop-up emergencies on a regular basis. They, and anyone who wanted to do business with them, had to be flexible when it came to their schedules.

"Let me give you the five minute version."

Paul returned to his Escape with a sample case that was considerably lighter. He'd left behind three of the 750 milliliter bottles of Tutor's—one for each building—as well as stacks of imprinted coasters and half a dozen rulers. His five-minute filibuster on Obie Johnson's dream turned into fifteen. When the man from the walk-in cooler company arrived he was told by Clint to wait at the bar.

At some point in the discussion Paul realized he knew more about Tutor's than he'd believed. He spoke about the bourbon itself and the family recipe that used oats to smooth out the final product. He touched on the distillery, the bottle, the company day care, and Obie's inclination to preserve Sawyer's claim of having the smallest post office in America.

"I have to tell you Paul,"—it was Clint—"I was skeptical. Toledo's a blue-collar city and the college kids mostly drink

249

beer. Pretty sure when Gwen and I were coming to the *old* Blind Pig the only liquor they ever served was Jack and Coke." He looked at his wife.

She smiled, "I may have had a Sloe Gin Fizz or two."

Clint waved off her comment, "Eighty-plus percent of sales back then had to be beer. Our thought was it would be about the same now that we're up and running, especially with all the craft beers out there," he gestured in the direction of the bar. "But I see the potential of that bottle around a campus... and the marketing stuff looks good. We *do* sell a fair number of old-fashioneds. We'll try a bottle at each bar if you can leave them." Carlucci turned to his wife, "Anything else, honey?"

"Yeah, can we get a few of those rulers? We have a couple regulars that need their hands slapped."

The visit with the Carluccis lasted less than an hour. Paul had allotted the entire morning to the three businesses. He knew that Obie viewed them as a prime target in Toledo due to their proximity to the university and potential to be a hot spot. The fact that they'd recently opened meant that Tutor's could get in on the ground floor. Paul was refilling his sample case with bottles of Tutor's when he groaned, realizing he'd inadvertently produced a bad pun of his own—using "ground floor" outside a line of bars connected by tunnels—not unlike Clint Carlucci's "Prohibition" and "prohibitively expensive" remarks.

Have to remember to tell Lauren about this...well, maybe not.

He secured the sample case in the cargo area of the SUV then covered the cases of bourbon with a blanket to hide them from sight—Lauren's idea, *you can't be too careful*—then got behind the wheel and started the engine. Paul planned to visit Alex Drabik's grave in the evening. He checked his watch and realized he had nearly two hours to kill before his next scheduled stop. He reached for his phone and thumbed the photos app. Before leaving Troy he'd taken a screenshot of a page from *findagrave.com* that showed the address for

Resurrection Cemetery, the final resting place for Sergeant Drabik and his wife Margaret.

He found the address—5725 Hill Avenue—punched it into his navigation system, and saw that it was less than ten minutes away. Paul put the Escape in gear and headed west, once again passing the clock tower at the university.

Resurrection Cemetery was Toledo's newest and largest—in terms of ground space—Catholic Cemetery. It covered 235 acres. Consecrated in 1985 by Bishop James Hoffman, it served Catholic families from Toledo and the surrounding area.

Paul approached the north entrance and turned in. Stone walls stood on either side of the drive and extended for thirty feet before being replaced by a four-foot line of hedges. The hedges appeared to ring the entire property. Paul's eyes were drawn to a colorful religious symbol—he didn't know its significance—that was inset into the wall. One component of the design appeared to be the turret of a castle.

That looks similar to the towers on the Ludendorff Bridge that were defended by German machine guns...the guns firing at Alex and his men as they made the crossing.

Paul eased past the wall and continued for several yards before coming to a fork. He brought the vehicle to a stop and tried to get his bearings. A second screenshot on his phone listed the section in which the plot was located. Paul pulled it up and read, *SECTION 6A.*

The majority of the cemetery appeared to be on his right so he went that way at the fork. Easing forward he looked for any kind of signage that might reveal his current location. Gravestones flanked both sides of the drive. They dotted the landscape to his left for hundreds of yards. A warren of narrow drives wound through the area. Markers were also on Paul's right. They filled the space—perhaps 150 feet—between the line of hedges that flanked the property and the paved drive occupied by the Escape. Well ahead of him, perhaps two hundred yards west, was a cluster of large mausoleums. They were modern in design and left Paul with the impression that they housed thousands of crypts.

Big place...not Arlington, but big place.

Paul had attended several military funerals for comrades. A number of these were at Arlington National Cemetery. He'd been part of the honor guard for two of them.

Paul saw metal poles a couple hundred feet ahead on either side of the drive. Green signs hung from them. He had a clear view of the one on the left but the characters were too small to make out. The sign on the right was blocked by two vehicles—a cemetery maintenance truck and a Jeep Grand Cherokee—that had eased their passenger-side tires into the grass to keep the roadway relatively clear.

As he crept past Paul saw that the Jeep was similar to Lauren's, though, he thought, a couple years newer, and red, rather than white.

The sign on the left was now close enough to make out. Paul was gratified when he read *SECTION 8*. He had spent a fair amount of time in cemeteries over the years and knew they were often laid out in confusing fashion. He had to be close to section 6.

And he was. Once he'd completely cleared the vehicles on the right he could read the sign ahead of them. Paul was happy to see that it read *SECTION 6*.

Okay, now what? This is a big section. Gotta be a couple hundred markers here.

He glanced again at the pictures on his phone. He had little expectation that the information there would help him locate the World War Two hero's grave. Paul had been surprised that the *findagrave* site did not include a row number. He'd searched for a frustrating hour the previous weekend for any information that could help him nail down the specific location but came up dry.

Seems like Alex is a forgotten man.

Paul decided his best course of action was to pull over and walk the entire section until he found the Drabik monument. The website did have a photo of it. To Paul's eyes it was unremarkable, a simple granite marker with Alex's name as well as Margaret's. Viewing it online, the monument was so unexceptional that Paul thought part of the gravesite was missing from the photo. Surely a man of Drabik's accomplishments would have a more conspicuous final resting place. Trying to find the unpretentious monument in this sea of similar ones could be a challenge.

As the SUV came to rest on the right side of the drive Paul became aware of a man further to the right and a few dozen yards ahead. He was tall, trim, and had a full head of fine white hair that seemed to be at the mercy of the late morning gentle breeze. He wore khaki pants and a white button-down dress shirt that was appropriate for both the eighty-degree temperature and the solemn surroundings. His back was to Paul, his hands apparently clasped in front of his body.

Paul stepped from his vehicle and took a few tentative steps toward the stranger, thinking he might be associated with the maintenance vehicle pulled off the drive to the rear. As he drew within a dozen steps he realized the man was talking softly, directing his attention to a monument in front. Embarrassed, Paul began to back away when the man turned.

Their eyes met. Paul held up his hands and began to apologize. "Sorry to interrupt, sir. I thought you might be with the cemetery." He gestured to the truck, noticing for the first time that it had a flatbed that held a large burial vault.

"No, no, no, you're fine. I don't work here. There must be some staff members around but I haven't seen anyone since I've been here." He had a hint of the south in his voice. Not a twang. Something softer, more soothing.

Paul saw the man held the bill of a baseball cap with both hands. He wore glasses and had the faraway hawkish countenance that Paul had observed in other times and places on many occasions.

He has the warrior look.

Paul decided to take a shot.

"Do you mind if I ask you a question?"

The man smiled slightly, then surprised Paul.

253

"Would you be looking for Alex Drabik?"

Paul was taken aback. His eyebrows shot up. His expression must've confirmed the older man's suspicions as he began to chuckle.

"You had the look, son." Then, "What branch of the service were you in? Don't tell me, let me guess." He put the cap on his head and adjusted it so the bill cast a shadow over his eyes. "Hmmm, not a pilot...probably not a Navy man...still in good shape. I'd say Marine Corps or Army infantry...maybe a Ranger?"

Paul laughed, "Close, Air Force Combat Controller. Name's Paul Hull." He held out a hand.

The man accepted it and said, "Combat Controller? Wow, that makes you the real deal. I'm Jim Harvey, glad to meet you, Paul."

Paul squinted at Harvey's hat and saw a sewn patch of a cartoonish helicopter with the words *Flying Banana* embossed underneath. He pointed to it and simply said, "Okay, I gotta ask."

Harvey laughed. "I flew this odd looking thing back in the sixties," he pointed to the hat. "It was the Piasecki H-21. It was supposed to be referred to as the 'Workhorse' or the 'Shawnee' but everybody called it the Flying Banana."

"I can see why." Paul saw that the shape of the craft was elongated with the fuselage curving upward near its center. It had two rotors and insect-like stabilizers protruding near its rear.

"It was built for the arctic but there sure wasn't any freezing weather where we were." Harvey had a distant look in his eyes. Again, Paul recognized it.

He asked, "Vietnam?"

Harvey nodded, "How about you, Paul? Afghanistan?"

Paul nodded in return, "Yep, and a few other places."

Harvey stared at Paul for a few seconds then offered, "How 'bout we go visit Sergeant Drabik and his bride?"

Harvey explained that he grew up in Tennessee, attended the state university in Knoxville, and joined the Army after graduation. "Went to flight school and was sent to Vietnam early on. Things got a lot hotter after I left, but it was plenty hot enough for me."

Paul had an excellent bullshit detector and noted that its needle hadn't moved an iota. Harvey, he suspected, was humble to a fault. The man continued.

"After the service I worked in the auto industry. My wife and I ended up in Toledo. I worked in purchasing for Jeep." He gestured to the Grand Cherokee parked in front of the truck. "She took care of the kids and the house."

Paul interjected, "My wife drives that same model."

"Fine vehicle. Anyway, one day back in the early eighties I was reading a book on World War Two—can't remember the title—and I come across the story of the bridge at Remagen. Alex is mentioned and the author mentioned he was a butcher from Toledo. I dug out the phonebook—still had 'em in those days—and who do I find still listed in the D's"?

Paul stood with his arms crossed, a slight smile on his face. "Alex Drabik."

"None other. I get it in my head that I want to shake his hand so I drive to the address on Dorr Street that was in the phonebook, knock on the door, and this older gentleman in a work uniform answers the door. I ended up staying for an hour."

Harvey said Drabik was a quiet man with a sense of humor. He adored his wife, wore his work uniform for years after retiring, and kept in touch with Army buddies by attending reunions. Harvey and his wife Judy visited the Drabiks several times in the 1980s.

"He didn't think he was anything special. He and Margaret raised a daughter and kept to themselves. When Margaret passed in '93 it really affected him. Folks said they saw him sitting in the back pew at church looking lonely as a man could look. He died a few months later in a car accident in Kansas on his way to a reunion."

Harvey added, "I was proud to know him."

Paul nodded once. "You should've been."

A siren wailed somewhere in the distance. Harvey pointed to Paul's shirt and remarked, "Enough about me. Tell me, what's a Combat Controller doing with a bourbon bottle on his shirt...and a square one, at that?"

Paul gave him the two-minute version, and handed him two business cards and a pen. "If you don't mind giving me your phone number, jot it on one of these and keep the other. I'll be back up this way later in the summer and I don't know anybody here. I'll take you to Packo's."

Harvey grinned. "Bring your wife. Sounds like a plan. Alex is right over there," he tilted his head to the Drabik monument, "you have a good visit." He strode toward the Jeep.

Paul walked to the monument and stood in front of it, looking at the name—*DRABIK*. In his mind's eye he could hear the machine gun fire on the bridge, the men screaming, the tank shells exploding.

This man made history...this—

Paul sensed something was out of place. The sound of the single siren was joined by several more. He heard tires squealing and turned in time to see a white sedan bolt through the opening at the cemetery's entrance and tear through the grass before veering back on the drive. It sped toward Harvey's Jeep and the truck parked behind it. Harvey froze ten feet in front of his vehicle. The sedan came on and skidded to a stop next to the truck.

Paul's mind registered the movement, the obvious threat, and the potential danger to Jim Harvey. He also recognized something he hadn't seen since his last deployment overseas.

The front left fender of the sedan was smeared with blood and the windshield was pockmarked by bullet holes.

CHAPTER TWENTY-EIGHT

In the room at the Best Western after returning from the airport the three members of the Fireteam ordered pizza and a six-pack of beer—it had become somewhat of a tradition—and worked on the last key piece of information they needed for the next day. This was determining the channels on the scanner that were used by the Toledo Police Department.

By the time the pizza arrived Cole had pretty much figured it out. He reviewed it with Dom, who would be responsible for keeping the team abreast of developments while he waited outside the bank in the Sonata.

Tanner flipped channels on the TV for ten minutes, finally selecting a broadcast of Georgia Championship Wrestling, which he left on until a commercial appeared. He then switched to a *Baywatch* rerun in hopes of seeing the women run on the beach in their swimsuits. He employed the "last" button several times to bounce back and forth between the two channels.

After the pizza was eaten and the beer drained the men got ready for bed. Dom typically occupied a segment of Tanner's bed on these trips. But after the baseball throwing incident earlier in the day Dom thought it prudent to settle in with Cole. No one said a word. It was assumed by all three that this was judicious.

After the beer and pizza, which followed the destruction of the 50 wings earlier in the day, Dom assumed there was a better than even chance that the room could devolve into a flatulence-filled cube. In this he was not disappointed. Well, he *was* disappointed—but he was right.

The main culprit seemed to be Tanner, though once the Jelcik brothers fell asleep, all emissions were silent and Dom couldn't be sure. He suspected that Tanner was doing some sort of performance-enhancing drug. It seemed like he was coughing a great deal. Could an overabundance of gas be another symptom?

Dom didn't know. He tucked his nose into the crook of his elbow and hoped it helped to filter out the poisonous air.

They were up at 7 a.m. and walked a hundred yards to a Bob Evans. Cole and Tanner ordered Original Farmer's Choice breakfasts—1500 calorie plates loaded with eggs, sausage, hash browns, and pancakes—while Dom got buttermilk hotcakes topped with roasted apples.

When the waitress reached for their menus Tanner pulled his back, held it so Dom could see, and pointed to the kids menu. "Damn Audie, if I knew you wanted hotcakes I'd've ordered this for you." He pointed to a picture of "Little Piggy Pancakes," which consisted of pancakes of different sizes stacked to resemble a face, snout, and ears with blueberries for eyes and banana slices for nostrils. A single sausage link was situated below to represent the mouth.

"Very funny, George." Dom acted annoyed but he took Tanner's jibe as a sign the big man was cooling off after yesterday's unfortunate occurrence at Bill Davis Stadium. They lingered over coffee and Cole decided the channels they would use on their walkie-talkies would be 15 and 25. Before leaving they discussed the "Ten-Codes" used by Toledo PD.

Back at the Best Western they took turns in the restroom. Tanner went first and took an unusually long time. Dom, who had to offload most of a pot of coffee, waited patiently. When the big man came out Dom expected to enter a room infused with noxious fumes. He was pleasantly surprised when he found it was not so.

The window of time Cole targeted for the robbery was 10 to 10:30 a.m. The Fifth Third building was located in a commercial area on Reynolds Road, a wide street in the western part of town. The area was dotted with drug stores and gas stations. The bank was on the east side of the street, across from a strip of shops known as the Reynolds Corner Plaza.

The escape route had them driving south on Reynolds for several blocks, taking a right on Hill, and after barely a half-mile, ducking into Resurrection Cemetery on the left where they would've prepositioned the truck. After switching vehicles the team would follow the cemetery drive past a cluster of large mausoleums before reaching Holland Sylvania Road and turning south. Two minutes later they would be on the I-475 beltway, moving around the city and on the way home.

At 9:15 the trio left the room after removing all traces of their stay. In the lot they transferred their weapons from the truck to the Sonata. Cole loitered nearby watching for prying eyes while Tanner climbed up on the Silverado's bed and unlocked the vault. He nonchalantly passed the guns down to Dom. The Thompson and carbine were wrapped in separate blankets. A third blanket held all three M1911A1 .45 caliber pistols. Tanner paused after handing down the Thompson, coughing so violently his face turned red.

Below, Dom thought, *Damn T, what the hell?*

Cole drove the truck, Dom the car with Tanner riding shotgun. They entered the cemetery from Hill Avenue on the north side and followed the drive as it curved right, away from the entrance gate. The Silverado slowly eased past rows of monuments for nearly a full minute. Cole surveyed the area and decided to leave the truck partially in the grass on the right side of the asphalt.

Come back through the gate, pull to the truck, follow the drive past the mausoleums and onto Holland Sylvania.

He visualized it in his mind, looked at the route, and nodded. "Load up, guys."

Ten minutes later they sat in the parking lot of the Reynolds Corner Plaza. Dom was behind the wheel. When he pulled into a space between two pickup trucks, Cole—from the passenger seat—told him to keep moving. "If anyone comes back to one of those trucks they'll be able to look right down into this thing." He directed Dom to an open area of the lot outside of a discount tobacco and vape shop called the Smoke Shack.

259

Fifth Third Bank was directly across from them. Reynolds Road had two northbound lanes, two southbound, and a dual access turning lane between them. Vehicle traffic was light. They sat with the car running and watched for 15 minutes. In that time they saw two cars and an SUV pull to the drive-up area. A woman driving a van parked on the side of the building, entered, and returned to her vehicle five minutes later.

The weapons were ready, the jackets were zipped, masks rolled up on their heads, throat mikes adjusted, walkie-talkies switched on, watches turned to the inside of their wrists. Despite the air conditioning all three men were perspiring, as —like a soldier following orders—the sun climbed toward its late morning station. The thermometer on the Sonata's display read 84 degrees. There was next to no traffic coming across the scanner.

Tanner, growing irritable, began to rock back and forth in the rear seat. He felt crowded. The Sonata was not built with the intention of making a man of his size comfortable in the back seat. Particularly when a slightly larger man sat in the seat in front.

"Whaddaya think, Ike? Time to rock and roll?" Tanner wiped sweat from his right eyebrow.

Cole took one last look at the bank before glancing at the traffic. "Okay Audie, ease up to the road." Then, "After that garbage truck on our right passes by..." He paused, waiting for the truck. "Let's do it! Masks!"

All three men pulled down their ski masks.

In the back Tanner's voice rose, "GIDDY-UP!"

Diane Crenshaw sipped from the Starbucks cup then set it on the desk. The iconic green, white, and black logo, she knew, was meant to depict a mermaid-like creature. The idea was that the Starbucks beauty was a metaphor for the allure of caffeine. Like the fabled seagoing sirens that drew unfortunate sailors into the rocks, caffeinated beverages from the ubiquitous coffee joint would pull the weak-willed through its doors, enticing them to spend six bucks on a Grande.

Well, something sure does it. The damn places are everywhere.

Her eyebrows knitted and she reached again for the cup, turning it slightly to better view the logo.

MY God! This girl has two tails and she's pulling one up with each hand, spreading them to the sides. Looks almost pornographic. Maybe now I know why people pay six bucks for a cup...the guys, anyway. Why the hell did I?

Diane was doing two jobs this week, her own duties as head of the commercial loan department and that of the branch manager, Courtney Czaben, who was on vacation. Diane was between appointments. She spent 20 minutes on a Zoom call walking through the finer points of a small business loan with a couple in Sylvania that were starting, of all things, a coffee shop. *There must be a dozen of them in Sylvania already.*

She glanced again at the Starbucks cup. She couldn't get the phrase *Small Business Failure* out of her head.

Well, they are putting up a significant amount of their own money...the rate is favorable to the bank...our risk is minimal.

She looked again at the cup. She knew of at least three Starbucks locations within a mile of the couple's proposed site.

"Damn...they're toast."

Diane had another Zoom call at eleven in her office. For now she was in Czaben's office, whittling away at the "To-Do" list left for her. When Courtney informed her that she'd be heading to Vegas for a week, Diane said, "Oh, fun!"

"Not really, Bill convinced me to go before I knew he bought tickets to watch a pickleball tournament there all week. *Pickleball!*"

Diane laughed then. She laughed again now. "Better you than me."

Czaben then put a sly grin on her face and vowed, "Ain't no way I'm going to that tournament. I'll find something else to do out there."

Crenshaw nodded, "What happens in Vegas..."

Czaben told Diane to ignore the emails that came to the manager's computer. "If anything earth-shattering comes through I'll see it on my phone in Vegas and take care of it. The main things to accomplish are on a list on my desk."

Going through the list now, Diane saw that she was down to number 7, *Coordinate Luxury Box at Ballpark for Out-of-Towners*. Fifth Third Bank owned the naming rights to the Toledo Mudhens' ballpark in downtown Toledo. The Hens were the Triple-A affiliate of the Detroit Tigers. The ballpark opened in 2002 and helped revitalize a challenged area of the city. Fifth Third controlled some of the luxury boxes. Czaben had a list of potential clients outside of Toledo that were interested in seeing a game.

Diane picked up the contact list and saw the first number was for a developer in Dayton. She'd just started to dial when the open doorway to the office darkened and she sensed movement.

"Put the damn phone down, Courtney."

Diane was confused. *Courtney?*

She looked up to see a nightmare. A giant of a man wearing a black mask was pointing a rifle at her.

She froze for a second, her brain seemed to shut out the danger and focus on the man's words. "Courtney?"

The man sneered through his mask and nodded to the open door that bore a nameplate proclaiming *COURTNEY CZABEN*.

"Oh, I'm not Courtney, I'm—"

"*SHUT THE FUCK UP AND—*" The man stopped screaming and began to cough. It was a deep, violent episode that lasted just a few seconds, but in that time Diane came to her senses. She still had the cellphone in her hand. She'd dialed the first digit of the 937 area code for the developer in Dayton. She quickly hit 1-1 before sitting the phone next to the Starbucks cup.

Days later, remembering the incident, Diane realized the stressful situation must've heightened her senses. She clearly remembered hearing the faraway voice on the phone through the robber's coughs.

Nine-One-One, what is your emergency?

Tanner finally brought his cough under control.

Sonofabitch! This goddammed cough! Maybe should've waited until after the bank job to dose.

In the bathroom of their room at the Best Western Tanner had popped 150 milligrams of tren. He dropped one of the tablets and spent two minutes finding the damn thing before rinsing it off then downing it with the others. After that he removed the testosterone from his travel kit and prepared the syringe. He spent some time with his pants down, turning so he could see inflamed areas in the mirror caused by previous injections. He selected a clear spot on his left thigh and, with a wince, pressed the needle home.

When Dom crossed Reynolds and pulled in front of the entrance to the bank all three men started the stopwatch feature on their digital watches. The two passenger side doors opened simultaneously and the brothers jumped out. The Carhartt bags were attached to the carabiners. Their long guns pointed to the ground.

Tanner saw Cole raise the Tommy Gun and move directly toward the teller windows. Two employees, both women, had their backs to the men. Tanner moved toward the offices, thinking, *those chicks are in for a surprise.* He smiled through his mask.

The door to the first office was open. Tanner saw a nameplate that read *DIANE CRENSHAW*. He raised the carbine to his shoulder and sprung into the doorway. He kept his finger on the trigger, completely disregarding his brother's rule. The office was empty but showed signs of being occupied recently. A laptop computer was open. Tanner saw a blue icon and the word *Zoom* on its screen. He backed out of the doorway and turned toward the next office.

Sensing that this one was occupied Tanner eased into the doorway, reading the nameplate, *COURTNEY CZABEN*. He raised the rifle.

"Put the damn phone down, Courtney." Ordinarily Tanner would've used the last name of the office's occupant but he wasn't sure how to pronounce *Czaben*. He wanted to come off as an intimidating badass, not a moron.

The woman had a cellphone in her hand. She looked at him, her mouth forming an "O." Then, apparently confused said, "Oh, I'm not Courtney, I'm—"

Tanner, already in an agitated state, went off. He began to scream, bringing on the coughs. Getting himself under control, he motioned with the carbine.

"Up! You go for a silent alarm and I kill you and everyone in the building." As the woman complied Tanner demanded, "The other manager where is she?"

Stammering, the woman answered, "Vegas, she's in Las Vegas."

"She's not here?" It was, Tanner supposed, an inane question. *Dumbass, if she's in Vegas she's sure as hell not here.* Still, he had to account for everyone.

"You walk to the lobby. Do what you're told by the big guy." A terrified look now appeared on the woman's face as her mind had seemingly caught up to events happening around her.

Six miles away in the block and glass five-story quasi-fortress known as the Lucas County Council of Governments building, a veteran 9-1-1 dispatcher named Rob "Buzzsaw" Brzycki answered the call from Crenshaw. After the standard *Nine-One-One, what is your emergency* opener, Buzzsaw resisted the temptation to pepper the caller with questions—something a less seasoned dispatcher might do—and listened to the entire exchange between the caller—a woman—and a man who threatened her. The man, Buzzsaw's experience told him, seemed highly stressed.

Buzzsaw opened a second line to the Toledo Police Department as the facility's equipment continued to record the call. The conversation coming through the caller's phone had ended, replaced by ambient noise. Buzzsaw looked quickly to the screen that used GPS data to triangulate the location of cellphones. He saw a blinking red dot on Reynolds Road.

After explaining the nature of the call to his counterpart at Toledo PD, Buzzsaw added. "Looks like the phone is on North Reynolds...sounded like it was happening in a bank...my system puts it at...hold on...1308 North Reynolds, better get some people in that area ASAP."

The police dispatcher, also experienced, decided to err on the side of caution and made the mental leap of classifying the occurrence as a robbery in progress. The message went out over the Toledo PD radio net.

All units, vicinity of 1308 North Reynolds Road, Code 10-42.

CHAPTER TWENTY-NINE

OH SHIT!
Dom's eyes locked on the scanner in disbelief.
Ten forty-two? That's Robbery in Progress! They gave this address. How in the fuck—
Dom recovered a bit of his cool and spoke quickly, the throat mike picking up his words and conveying them to the men in the bank, "Cole! I just heard a 10-42 code over the scanner. Cops are coming! Cole?!?" In his excitement Dom completely disregarded the code word protocol. He looked at the running chronograph on the inside of his wrist, seeing *2:41*. This time he said it out loud.
"How in the fuck?!?"

As Cole approached the counter he already suspected neither of the two tellers would be the team's ticket to the vault. Both were still turned away from him facing out the drive-up window, apparently in conversation. He could tell that the one on the left was young—early twenties.
She's too young. Wouldn't be trusted yet.
There was something about the second woman's hairstyle that suggested to Cole that his threat-by-driver's-license method might not be effective with her. Cole didn't know *how* he could tell these things; he just knew he *could*. He needed to see her face.
"Keep your hands where I can see them." He raised the Thompson.
The women turned in unison. Cole saw smiles freeze on both faces. The woman on the left locked on Cole's mask, then the Thompson, and back to the mask. The woman on the right did the same thing but looked at the Thompson first. As he suspected the woman on the left was young. Her counterpart was in her late twenties, her hair was cut short and spiked. She

wore a seafoam green blouse with an open collar. As she turned Cole saw a small neck tattoo depicting a bird of prey with claws extended, swooping toward a coiling snake. The woman's overall look was one of defiance.

Cole had two quick thoughts. The first was *nice ink*. The second, *how the hell did she get a job at a bank?*

He repeated the command. "Hands where I can see them! Out here, NOW!" He nodded toward an opening at the left side of the teller counter and gestured with the Thompson. The women complied. The younger woman shuffled out with a look of terror on her face. As the second woman emerged Cole saw that her look of shock was already turning to insolence.

This woman might actually be happy to give me her address hoping I show up later...it would give her a chance to kick MY ass.

He smiled. If they were to get into the vault his threat would have to be made to one of the managers that Tanner was rounding up.

"On the floor! Hands stretched out where I can see them." Cole looked over his shoulder expectantly. The first of Tanner's targets should be coming soon. His eyes came back to his watch, *1:22*.

Seconds later a petite blonde in her forties moved cautiously into the lobby. Cole swung the Thompson toward her and she nearly jumped. He saw through her frightened expression, detecting competence, intelligence, and somehow, a person that had a lot to lose.

She'll have a family, two or three kids...she'll get us in the vault. He waited for Tanner to finish clearing the rest of the building as the seconds blinked on the watch face.

Tanner watched the woman who wasn't Courtney walk toward the lobby. It struck him that his outburst toward her followed by the coughing jag probably alerted any remaining employees to his presence. He needed to get to them before they tripped an alarm or placed a call for help. He moved quickly through the remaining areas of the building, clearing an empty office with its lights out, a break room with small restrooms—men's on the left, women's on the right—and a supply room holding stacks of copy paper and miscellaneous janitorial supplies.

Tanner smiled, *they should hire a contract cleaner. They'd get much better results than trying to clean themselves.*

Cole stepped toward the woman. He towered over her. His read was that he probably didn't need the gun. She would do what she was told. Even if Tanner returned with more employees they already had their ticket to the vault.

"What's your name?"

She blinked, not processing the question. "My...?"

"Your name, what's your name?"

"Uh, Diane. Diane Crenshaw."

"Where's your driver's license?"

Crenshaw stared at him with a look of complete incomprehension. "In my purse...my office."

Cole nodded. Seconds later he heard Tanner's voice over the walkie-talkie. "Building clear, George returning to lobby."

Cole spoke, "George, I'm sending the woman back to you. Get her purse."

Tanner moved toward the offices, responding to his brother, "I copy, Ike." He met the woman who wasn't Courtney in the hallway.

He hissed at her, "Get your purse!" He fought the urge to cough.

The woman entered the first office, the one with the open laptop. She stepped to the desk then hesitated. "I have to open the bottom drawer." Left unsaid were the words *don't shoot me.*

Tanner nodded. "Do it! Let's go!"

Tanner and the woman returned to the lobby. Cole was ten feet from the tellers on the floor, pointing the Thompson in their direction. He paid no attention to the building's entrance, knowing Dom would call out if a threat developed from that direction.

269

"Okay Diane, I want your driver's license. No arguments."

Crenshaw, baffled, complied with the demand, searching through the purse and unsnapping the clasp on a leather wallet. Her hand emerged with the card. And Cole snatched it from her.

After two seconds of examination he lowered his voice. "You are getting us into the vault. If you don't, I'll be paying a surprise visit to 2222 Berdan Avenue."

Crenshaw's eyes widened as she processed the threat. She nodded once. "I know the combination."

Cole smiled. "Let's go."

The vault was built into a wall to the left of the teller counter. It was accessed through the same opening the tellers passed through on their way to the lobby. Cole motioned in that direction and turned to Tanner.

"Toss your Carhartts in front of the vault door then guard the tellers," Then, voice lowered, "*especially the chick in the green blouse.*"

Tanner tucked his carbine between his left arm and upper body and quickly opened the carabiner. He removed both bags, tossed them in front of the vault, and turned to the women on the floor. His carbine was already back in position, finger on the trigger.

Cole followed Crenshaw to the vault door and watched as she worked the combination dial. His watch read 2:27. Crenshaw finished working the dial and stepped back.

Cole snapped, "Open it!"

She depressed a heavy bar and inched backward, pulling the massive door open. Cole put a hand on her shoulder and directed her inside. He could feel her trembling. Once she was inside Cole bent and grabbed Tanner's bags then tossed them in front of Crenshaw.

"Fill 'em. Big bills first. No goddammed baited bills or dye packs." Crenshaw picked up the first bag and moved to the rear of the vault. Cole was following when he heard Dom's panicked radio call. He froze for a beat then responded.

"Say again...Audie, say again!"

270

The next sounds came to Cole in stereo. First over the Midland X-Talker on his belt, a fraction of a second later more muted, through the open door of the vault. His brain correctly processed both, meshing the two versions.

They were gunshots.

Jeter Coy of the Toledo Police Department guided his patrol vehicle, a pursuit-rated Ford Police Interceptor Utility Vehicle, north on Reynolds Road. The vehicle was based on the Ford Explorer and boasted a number of upgrades over stock models sold to the general public. These included upgraded suspension and braking systems. Coy knew he was unlikely to make use of any of these features on his present call. He'd been directed by dispatch to track and pull over a garbage truck that apparently had a defective gate on its rear trash hopper. The department had received cellphone calls from several motorists reporting trash spewing from the truck as it made its way up Reynolds.

Ah, well, you do what you gotta do.

Coy was two years out of the police academy where he graduated first in his class. Word from the old-timers was that used to be called the class *Honor Man*. Political correctness mandated this term be retired and replaced by *Honor Person*. Most of the rank and file called bullshit on the term. The best the PCers could hope for in actual practice was *First in the Class*. That's what Coy was.

Coy's father was a Yankee fan. He named his son after Hall of Fame shortstop Derek Jeter. Some from the younger Coy's generation might have had a problem with being named after a baseball player. Not Jeter. He loved the sport and knew that inadvertently it had led to his chosen profession.

During Jeter's youth, the Coy family's next-door neighbor was a Toledo Police Detective named Rick Molnar. In his high school days at Oregon Clay, east of the river, Molnar was a rough and tumble defenseman on the hockey team and tough-nosed third baseman on the diamond. He went on to play four years of baseball for the University of Toledo Rockets. After

271

college Molnar joined the Toledo PD, working first as a patrolman before earning the coveted detective's badge.

Along the way Molnar gained a reputation for sacrificing his body in front of bad-hop groundballs to the hot corner, not shying away from a fight while on patrol, and drawing confessions from suspects as a detective. Colleagues raved about Molnar's ability to gain the confidence of a suspected pedophile in the interview room.

"Go ahead, you can tell me...the kid was begging for it, right? Didn't give you a choice. You just did what any of us would've done...yeah?"

After getting an admission Molnar would burst from the room, furious at the offender, looking for something to punch. *"That son-of-a-bitch is going to JAIL!"*

Molnar coached Coy's Oregon Youth Baseball team for three years, imparting baseball knowledge and telling a few cop stories. Young Jeter wanted nothing more than to follow in the man's footsteps.

So far he'd been remarkably successful. He also played third base for the Rockets, once challenging the entire Central Michigan Chippewa team to a fight from his position, 40 feet from their dugout. After his success at the academy Coy gained a reputation as a tough customer on the streets, one that could be counted on to put an end to altercations. Some by de-escalating the situation before it redlined. Some with his fists after it reached the point of violence. Coy was a crack shot and in excellent physical condition. The garbage truck situation could be easily handled by any officer on the force.

The situation at the bank would require someone with Coy's talents.

Jeter heard the dispatcher's 10-42 code and became instantly alert. He checked his location and realized to his amazement that he was less than half a block from the reported address. He sat up straighter and scanned ahead, locating the Fifth Third branch. A late model sedan, a Hyundai Sonata he thought, had backed to the front of the building in a handicapped spot. Coy keyed his mike to report he was responding to the scene and required backup.

He stomped the accelerator pedal.

How in the fuck?!?

Dom didn't understand it. After the Jelciks exited the Sonata Dom backed it into the handicapped space nearest the entrance. He reached under his seat for the .45 pistol and waited nervously, following the narrative coming through the X-Tracker in the cup holder. He visualized Tanner's trip down the hall and Cole's approach to the counter—the same counter he'd stood at days earlier when he paid for a prepaid debit card.

Dom heard Tanner shout at someone and cringed as a series of violent coughs were picked up by the man's throat mike and broadcast over their net. He imagined Cole entering the vault and then—

The call came over the scanner.

After making his rushed warning call to Cole, Dom searched Reynolds frantically, looking first to his left, then his right. He pulled back the slide of the pistol, jacking a round into the chamber, and released the weapon's safety. On his fifth scan of the street he missed the movement of the police vehicle coming from his left. He looked right—*still clear*—then back left.

The Interceptor swerved into the lot and screeched to a halt directly in front of the Sonata. Dom saw a single police officer throw open the driver's side door on the far side of the vehicle. He had a single thought.

Gotta protect the guys.

Wordlessly Dom threw open his own door and raised his pistol in a combat stance. As he began to squeeze off rounds, he saw the officer disappear below the hood. Dom stopped firing and moved the pistol from side to side. His eyes were wide, pupils dilated.

Coy ducked behind the engine block to give himself protection. He'd felt one of the .45 slugs crack past his left ear, but he was unharmed. He didn't consider making a *Shots Fired* call. No time. Thinking tactically he duck walked to the rear of the Interceptor, staying low, out of sight of the masked shooter. He reached the rear of the vehicle, took a deep breath, and quickly sprung around the Interceptor's rear hatch. Coy brought the front sight of his Sig Sauer .40 caliber service pistol up to the center mass of the target and began pulling the trigger.

The first round struck the man in the shoulder spinning him slightly. Three of the next four rounds caught the man center mass and he was thrown against the Sonata before slumping. As he was trained, Coy continued to fire as his target dropped. A number of rounds struck the side of the Sonata.

Satisfied that the shooter was eliminated as a threat, Coy turned his attention to the front entrance. He saw a large man, also wearing a mask, burst through the door and raise a rifle toward him. Coy swung his Sig toward the man but was too late. He saw the rifle barrel flash and felt a powerful impact to the ballistic vest covering his chest. As Coy saw the sky he realized he'd been knocked off his feet. He didn't register the fact that four more bullets filled the space where he just stood. Jeter lost his grip on the Sig as he hit the asphalt. Scrambling frantically he came up with it.

Weirdly, a memory popped into his head. His chest felt exactly as it did when the three-hole hitter for Kent State hit a smash at him that skipped off the turf and caught him flush. He'd recovered to throw the man out at first. He could do it again.

Coy gripped the Sig and sat up. The big man was advancing toward him in a crouch, his rifle tucked into his right shoulder. The two men fired simultaneously. For an instant, Coy saw the man flinch. At the same moment he felt another vicious blow to his chest. From his sitting position his upper body snapped

274

backwards, his head bouncing off the parking lot. He was dazed.

I think the vest held...probably just bad bruising on the chest...might have a concussion but...

The sky above him darkened. He looked up to see the big man, a growing blood stain high on the left side of his chest. His rifle pointed directly at Jeter's face. The man spoke.

"You killed my buddy Dom...You son of a bitch."

Jeter Coy saw the flash.

CHAPTER THIRTY

Cole froze as Crenshaw spun around. She had also heard the gunfire. Their eyes met momentarily and, had Cole's face not been masked, would have mirrored each other. Their eyes were wild, Crenshaw's with terror, Cole's with foreboding. He quickly shifted to action.

He leveled the Thompson at the waist and hissed, "Don't fucking move!" He backed out of the vault, leaving the Carhartt bags on the floor inside. Moving quickly through the opening to the teller counter, Cole entered the lobby. With little conscious thought he thumbed the safety lever above the rear grip of the Tommy Gun from "Safe" to "Fire," something he had not done in the two years the Fireteam was active.

More gunfire.

To this point all of the reports were heavy *Pop-Pop-Pops* of pistols. This new barrage featured the *CRACK* of a heavier caliber. Cole counted five of them. He recognized the fact that his brother was no longer inside the lobby and stepped toward the front entrance. He could just make out Tanner, his carbine raised, moving left and away from the building, out of Cole's line of sight. *Was that blood on the side of the Sonata?*

Cole moved toward the entrance, crouching reflexively. Steps from the door he detected movement to his left and swung the Thompson in that direction. The younger woman was curled in a fetal position, sobbing. But the second teller was drawing herself into a sprinter's stance.

Cole, instantly furious, leveled the Thompson at the woman. The blood drained from her face as Cole squeezed the trigger. At the last possible instant he diverted the barrel of the weapon slightly and watched as a .45 slug tore into the terrazzo floor next to her before deflecting into the far wall. Miniscule bits of stone and concrete flew from the gouged floor. A few of them peppering the woman's left side.

"I said *on the goddammed FLOOR!*"

Cole watched her drop back to the terrazzo face first. His brain began to catch up to the sensory input, processing at an accelerated speed. He saw specks of red appear on the left sleeve of the seafoam blouse.

POP-CRACK

The two shots were nearly instantaneous. Cole left the women on the floor and reached for the door, dreading what he would see.

In the split-second before he burst through the door Cole remembered a debate with his brother at the beginning of the Fireteam's series of robberies. Tanner wanted to wear bulletproof vests. Cole argued against it, citing the fact that it would diminish their maneuverability. The real reason was something much different.

In 1997 in Los Angeles a two-man robbery team, Larry Phillips Jr. and Emil Matasareanu, engaged in a running gun battle with LAPD in the city's North Hollywood district after a robbery gone bad. The pair was armed with illegally modified fully automatic weapons and carried an enormous amount of ammunition. They also wore body armor.

The episode, captured live by hovering news helicopters— some of which drew fire from the gunmen—lasted an hour and featured indelible scenes as they walked through the streets unleashing streams of bullets on the outgunned police.

Phillips eventually shot himself. Matasareanu, shot 29 times in the lower body, bled to death. Twelve police officers and eight civilians were wounded. The incident led the LAPD and other departments to upgrade their weapons. Standard small-caliber police pistols were ineffective against the body armor.

Cole feared that Tanner, fortified with body armor, would become even more aggressive. As much as he hated to admit it he could see Tanner turning into an unhinged gunman like the pair in the North Hollywood Shootout.

Cole heard one more *CRACK* and pushed through the door. The number of possible scenarios he might find combined to momentarily overload his ability to process, much like a pilot burdened by an overabundance of information during a cockpit emergency. He failed to register Tanner's final words to the police officer when they came over the X-Talker.

He emerged into a world of chaos. The first thing that struck him was the odor. A miasma of gunpowder, car exhaust, and something else—blood—seemed to hang over the front parking area of the building. Cole sensed, rather than consciously viewed, people crouching behind cars in the Reynolds Corner Plaza parking lot across the street. Two were holding up cellphones. A bullet hole spider-webbed the glass front door of the discount tobacco store a hundred yards distant. A pickup truck on Reynolds slowed. The driver gawked, then sped away.

Dom's body lay in a heap near the Sonata, several bullet wounds visible. His left arm was bent under his torso at an impossible angle.

He's gone.

Cole saw Tanner spin away from a figure lying on its back at the rear of a police Interceptor Utility Vehicle that was blocking in the getaway car. His brother's face was set in a mask of rage. Cole saw the figure was that of a police officer—his head ruined—and he realized that life as he knew it was over.

Sirens intruded, several of them. He quickly swiveled his head up and down Reynolds then returned to Tanner. He saw that his brother was indeed bleeding. He'd been shot high on the left chest but it didn't seem to slow him down.

"T, MOVE THE COP'S CAR!"

Tanner looked at him, uncomprehending, then got it. He darted to the open door of the still-running vehicle as Cole screamed the command a second time. Tanner slid behind the wheel and put the Interceptor in gear. As it shot forward Cole stepped over Dom's body without giving it a second look. He got behind the wheel, propping the Thompson in the footwell near the gas pedal. The cuff of Cole's sleeve caught and the hot barrel slid up his right forearm, singeing the skin. He didn't feel it.

Tanner jumped into the passenger seat and Cole floored the accelerator. The shootout had now log jammed traffic near the bank to the north and south so there was no cross traffic to deal with. Cole swung the wheel left and shot south on Reynolds.

A trail of white smoke marked the path of the speeding Hyundai. Cole had no way to ascertain if it was from the squealing tires or damage to the engine from the policeman's weapon. There were two starburst-like bullet holes in the windshield, a third strike appeared to have glanced off the glass—scoring it—as if deflected from its original path. One of the holes was tinged with a sticky pink residue.

Cole, glancing frantically from the mirrors, to his bleeding brother in the passenger seat, to the windshield, thought, *Dom's blood.* He blew past a dozen vehicles pulled to the side of the road. Those in front were trying to avoid becoming part of the shooting gallery they detected as they neared the bank. Those behind were simply playing *Follow the Leader.*

All looked as if they were pulling over to show respect for a funeral procession. None of the drivers yet knew their maneuver was prescient. A half dozen of them captured video of the getaway vehicle as it rocketed south. The route to the cemetery was barely two miles. The Fireteam's members had all been aware that after fleeing the robbery those two miles would be fraught with danger.

The surviving members were experiencing something beyond their worst nightmares.

The first leg of the run to the cemetery—the mile straight south—took the brothers past a handful of side streets and one larger intersection. This was Nebraska Avenue, a half-mile south of the Fifth Third building.

Cole was doing 60 miles per hour as he approached the intersection. He saw the light turn red and watched as vehicles ahead of him in both southbound lanes braked and coasted toward it. Cole began to tap the Sonata's brake pedal while assessing the eastbound and westbound traffic that now had the right of way.

"HOLD ON!"

Cole punched the accelerator and adjusted course slightly left into the northbound lane. Both Jelcik brothers leaned forward slightly as a pincer movement of traffic began to close their escape route. The Sonata hurtled through the intersection, narrowly missing the cab of a semi tractor-trailer on the left and two eastbound SUVs on the right. Horns blared. Cole caught a flash of a black man—his face incredulous—pumping gas at a corner Sunoco station on the right. He cut back to the southbound lane and drove on, for the first time hearing the annoying chimes of the seatbelt warning system. The scanner added to the confusion as responding officers—some obviously in a state of extreme agitation—sought to maintain radio discipline as the radio net was bombarded with calls.

"There were cops on the right coming toward the intersection!" It was Tanner, who saw flashing lights on Nebraska, approaching Reynolds from the west. Cole's eyes bounced from the road ahead to the rearview mirror, noticing for the first time that a bullet had exited the clear plastic sheet they'd installed after it penetrated the windshield. Tanner turned in his seat to watch for the pursuers. He winced and pressed on his wound.

"AAAGGGHHH."

Cole shot him a look then quickly flicked his eyes back to the mirror. He saw the traffic at Reynolds and Nebraska come to a halt in all four directions. Several police vehicles—lights and flashers on, sirens screaming—cut aggressively through the intersection on a diagonal path and headed north toward the bank.

Tanner shouted, "They're going to the bank! We have a shot!"

Cole knew they may have just escaped the inner ring of the police cordon. He also knew that Toledo PD—or any police department for that matter—would pull out all the stops when it came to hunting cop killers. There was no shortage of witnesses—including the man pumping gas—that had seen the speeding car with bullet damage. Their window of opportunity for escape would close quickly. He tore off his mask and tossed it in the back seat. Tanner did the same.

Gotta get to that damn cemetery.

Before reaching Hill Avenue the Sonata raced past an Urgent Care Clinic. Cole thought, *What the hell am I going to do about T? Can't go to a hospital.*

Without looking at Tanner he tried to get an assessment of the wound. "How bad is it?"

Tanner made a weak attempt at humor. "Heh, at first it felt like you punchin' me. So, it didn't hurt none." He winced and sucked air through his teeth, trying to smile at the same time. It gave him the look of a crudely carved jack-o-lantern. "Now, though, it hurts like a *sonuvabitch.*"

Cole chanced a look at his brother and saw that the bloodstain on the Eisenhower jacket had grown to the size of a pie plate. There was an ugly black-ringed hole two inches from its top edge.

Goddammit.

Mercifully, they caught a green light at Hill. Cole took the turn doing forty and Tanner looked north as they slalomed through the intersection.

"I see flashers way back. Looked like they might be heading this way."

Cole buried the gas pedal and the Sonata was willing.

They streaked west, the entrance to Resurrection Cemetery coming into view.

It was Tanner's idea. Looking back on it Cole blamed himself, but it was his brother that made the suggestion.

"We gotta hide this car."

"What?" Cole saw the entrance 300 yards ahead and he moved his right foot from the accelerator to the brake pedal.

"As soon as they find this car they'll know we've switched vehicles. It'll be out in the open if we dump it where the truck's parked. We need them to keep lookin' for this thing...it'll buy us some time."

Cole considered as the stone gate of the cemetery took shape on the left. "T, we don't have time to look for a place—"

Tanner cut him off. "There's those buildings in the cemetery..."

Cole knew he was talking about the large mausoleums. "Yeah?"

Tanner removed keys to the truck from his jacket and held them up. "Drop me at the truck, take the car behind the buildings...I come pick you up." Tanner winced again.

Cole shot a look at him as he braked hard and pulled the wheel to the left. Tanner's face seemed pale. Both men were pushed to the right as the Sonata fought to make the turn. The sedan's momentum carried it through the opening between the stone walls before it left the asphalt and cut through an open grassy area. Cole braked hard and turned the wheel to the right, gaining control.

The truck was now dead ahead, no more than 150 yards to the west. Cole made his decision.

"Okay T, get ready." He accelerated again and skidded to a stop seconds later next to the vault truck. Tanner jerked open the door with his right arm. He held his carbine tight against his left side with the other. Wordlessly he pushed himself out of the Sonata. Sirens were clearly audible.

Tanner turned, yelled "*GO,*" and kicked the door shut.

Cole immediately took off for the mausoleums, remembering from their prep that there was a crescent drive on the far side.

That should be a good place to—

Cole was on top of the vehicle before he noticed it. It was a red SUV. He continued west but reduced speed slightly. Then, ahead, he saw another SUV, this one grey. As he neared the second vehicle Cole glanced in his mirror and saw movement.

What the fuck?

Tanner kicked the passenger door shut after pulling himself from the getaway car. He was beginning to feel lightheaded. He felt his heart racing as the pain from the bullet wound increased. *Gotta get the hell out of here...FAST!*

Fumbling with the key, he leaned the carbine against the truck. As he reached for the door he felt movement to his left. He saw a red Jeep in the grass in front of the truck. And there, near the front of the vehicle stood a tall white-haired man.

A witness.

Tanner thought, *Well I'll be god damned.* He reached for the carbine and raised it unsteadily. The old man was quicker than Tanner expected and ducked for cover in front of the Jeep's grill. Tanner stepped in the grass between the two vehicles and moved quickly to the right.

No time to screw around with this guy...the sirens are gettin' closer...gotta kill him fast.

Tanner took a step, almost had the angle, took another step. The act of holding the carbine in a firing position with his left arm was agonizing, but...there was the target.

Tanner squeezed the trigger.

Paul Hull hit the big man with a flying tackle as the carbine discharged. The bullet creased the hood of the Jeep before plugging into the turf some 30 yards away. The man's head slammed into the tapered edge of the Jeep's roof above the driver's door. He lost his hold on the weapon, his hands slick with blood, and went to one knee.

Paul saw the attacker pull at the waist of his jacket, revealing a holster. As the man began to withdraw a pistol, Paul snatched the carbine from the ground and drove its stock into the assailant's temple.

Paul drew the rifle back, in position for another blow should it be necessary. It wasn't. The bloody attacker slid to the grass as the first Toledo Police vehicles entered the cemetery.

Tanner opened his eyes. He sensed figures above him. At first there was just a single man holding the carbine. Then a second figure—the white-haired man—joined him. Tanner heard sirens—it seemed like dozens of them. The pain, he realized, had faded. He was cold. And dizzy, so dizzy. He looked to the sky and squinted. Could it be?

There were birds gathering—thousands of them. They moved as one massive colony, forming a vortex. Cole taught him the word—it was a *murmuration.*

Tanner smiled, *so unusual to see one this time of year!* His pain faded more. It was completely gone now. The swirling birds drew closer, blocking out the sun...

Darkness.

Cole saw the entire incident. He first sighted the white-haired man through his rearview mirror. He braked and turned to see more clearly through the plastic that covered the window opening. He watched a man attack his brother—his *wounded* brother—and viciously drive the stock of Tanner's own weapon into his head.

Enraged, Cole grabbed the barrel of the Tommy Gun with his right hand while spinning the steering wheel with his left.

I'm comin', T!

Then the police came through the cemetery entrance. They swarmed the area of the burial vault truck. Several officers jumped from their vehicles and raised weapons towards the man who struck Tanner.

Cole wavered, slammed the wheel with a fist, and punched the accelerator, heading for the west entrance.

CHAPTER THIRTY-ONE

Tyson Foxx stood bleary-eyed in the Fifth Third Bank parking lot, staring at the spot where Jeter Coy was executed. There was no chalk outline—modern investigators almost never used the technique favored by moviemakers—just a bleak asphalt surface surrounded by four orange safety cones that acted as supports for the yellow crime scene barricade tape. The cones were weighted, assuring they would stand undisturbed by the gusts that greeted this Friday morning.

Foxx watched as the tape bowed to the westerly wind, fell for a few seconds, and bowed again. A front would be moving through Toledo later in the morning, bringing rain that would wash away the stain in the middle of the square that was barely perceivable on the dark surface.

FBI and Toledo PD Crime Scene Units were still working the site in an effort to collect as much evidence as possible before the rains came, but some part of Foxx's brain would be happy when the physical reminders of the tragedy were washed away.

It would be a long time before other reminders faded from Foxx's memory.

"I didn't add any cream or sugar."

It was Kekich. She wore the same navy blue windbreaker with the yellow block-letter FBI identifier on the back as Foxx. She handed her boss a Styrofoam cup with a plastic lid.

Foxx accepted the cup. "I think black is appropriate." He inhaled and let it out in a sigh as he cast his eyes to the dark clouds forming in the west. "It's a black damn day." Foxx sipped the coffee.

All of the FBI Task Force members who had flown from Chicago to Omaha on Tuesday night were now in Toledo. News of the shootout and chase reached Foxx and his team on Thursday afternoon. They scrambled to repack all of the gear they'd offloaded from the plane and set up in the Omaha field office.

They'd made use of one of the FBI's Gulfstream G5 Bombardier aircraft when flying to Omaha. The business jet was capable of transporting 16 passengers in luxury. The dozen members of the traveling party spread out, enjoying a comfortable flight.

The G5 left Omaha's Eppley Field minutes after offloading Foxx's team, adhering to the tasking schedule assigned to it by FBI headquarters in Washington, D.C. But there were no direct commercial flights from Omaha to Toledo. Nor were there any indirect flights that would get them to Toledo on short notice. The best option was to have the team board a 9 p.m. Delta flight to Detroit—bumping several pissed off travelers in the process—then drive an hour south to the Ohio city. Personnel from the Detroit field office met them at the airport and handled the driving duties but it was an ill-tempered group that checked into their hotel after midnight.

They found that their nasty mood was surpassed by that of the rank and file members of the Toledo Police Department. Their officers and detectives had torn the city apart looking for the stolen Sonata used in the robbery. The Lucas County Sheriff's Department and the Ohio State Patrol assisted in the search but it was to no avail. The vehicle, and the surviving member of the Fireteam who drove it, had vanished.

Kekich brought more than coffee. She had information. "For what it's worth, it looks like the analysis of the... Fireteam's methodology that we used to lead us to Omaha was correct." She hesitated before using the designated FBI nickname for the robbery team, knowing Foxx hated it.

He spun to her, one eyebrow raised. "How so?"

"It turns out that one of the team, we think it was this guy," she pointed to a second set of cones and barricade tape a few feet away where Santo's body was found, "was inside the bank Monday and bought a prepaid debit card."

Foxx was about to take another sip of coffee. The cup froze, inches from his lips.

288

"*What?* Why didn't we get the report?"

Kekich configured her face to display a rueful smile. "You're not gonna believe this...the bank manager was on vacation and told the assistant to ignore emails to her account...said she'd handle them remotely from where she went."

Foxx couldn't resist. "Which was where?"

Kekich's smile disappeared. "She was in Vegas...watching a pickleball tournament."

Foxx opened his mouth slightly but could think of nothing to say. He turned back to the spot where Officer Coy was killed. The two agents stood in silence for a full minute, taking turns sipping coffee.

Kekich broke the silence. "There's no guarantee it would've made a difference. The gang *did* do the same prep work in Omaha. They even did it a few days earlier, which means Omaha, logically, *should've* been the target. We still would've sent people out there if we'd known about this buy."

Foxx stared at her, his look of disbelief transforming to one of determination. Left unsaid was the fact that the task force would've sent personnel to Toledo as well. And, more importantly, warned the Toledo Police Department that a bank in their city was about to be robbed.

"Let's go to work." Foxx walked to the bank's entrance, Kekich in tow.

Four hours later Foxx, Kekich, and several other members of the task force convened in a hastily arranged conference room at the FBI Toledo field office. It was located on the eighth floor of the 120-year-old Ohio Building on Madison Avenue in downtown Toledo.

While at the scene of the shootout Foxx and his agents conducted interviews of the bank's personnel and watched video of the incident from several camera angles. Detailed analysis of the video would be completed by the Bureau's technical staff in the coming days and weeks. Foxx insisted on watching the different camera feeds on iPads. This allowed his team to stand at a number of vantage points in and around the bank while watching the incident on the devices. The technique often gave them different perspectives and sometimes led to revelations.

They also witnessed evidence collection by the crime scene teams. They viewed bullet impact points, making videos of their own that they could consult as the investigation progressed. Nothing collected at the scene gave them the current location of the car or its driver. That didn't mean there was a dearth of evidence. On the contrary, the scene was dripping with it. Quite literally.

The deceased member of the Fireteam whose body was found outside the bank was Dominic Gabriel Santo, 28, a convicted car thief who'd done a stint in Ohio's Lebanon Correctional Institution. His driver's license was found in his wallet. His identity was further confirmed when his fingerprints matched those in the Integrated Automated Fingerprint Identification System—or IAFIS. This was accomplished using a handheld biometric device on the body while it was still in the parking lot.

Upon leaving the Fifth Third location Foxx and his team drove to Resurrection Cemetery. A second suspect, tentatively identified through his driver's license as Tanner Lynn Jelcik, 28, was found at that location. Two witnesses were standing over the man when police arrived. Both men, Jim Harvey of Toledo, and Paul Hull of Troy, were interviewed extensively Thursday by Toledo Police detectives and special agents from the Toledo field office of the FBI. Foxx would interview both of them shortly. After viewing the scene at the cemetery most of Foxx's task force made the trip to the Ohio Building.

Harvey and Hull were led into the interview room at 12:30 p.m. Foxx, Kekich, and Scott Remick, the analyst, greeted them and shook hands. A stenographer from the Toledo office, Kathy Rachuba, attended as well.

Foxx began, "Well you guys had a helluva day yesterday, didn't you?"

Both men smiled and nodded. Harvey added, "That we did." Then, "Did the guy you caught at the cemetery give up the third man?"

Foxx looked at his colleagues before clearing his throat. "He didn't make it...died on the way to the hospital...he bled to death. We haven't released that to the media yet." He looked at Paul. Left unsaid was the fact that the blow to the head by the rifle butt could have contributed to the death. Foxx noted that there was no trace of regret in Hull's eyes, *You gotta do what you gotta do.*

Foxx continued, "You notice I'm interviewing you two at the same time. The usual procedure is to interview witnesses separately so the response of one doesn't influence or," he searched for a word, "*corrupt* the other one's recollections. But I know our local people already talked to you separately. I thought I'd try something different."

Hull spoke, "Maybe something one of us says jogs the memory of the other?"

Foxx pointed at Hull and winked. "So, why don't you lead it off, Paul? Why were you there? What did you see? What did you do?"

Hull cleared his throat. "I was there to visit a grave."

Foxx prompted him, "Family member?"

"No, a soldier from World War Two I read about. Never met him. Just wanted to pay my respects."

Remick, sitting to Foxx's left, shuffled through some papers, selected one, and slid it in front of Foxx.

After scanning it for twenty seconds Foxx looked back at Hull. "You have *four* Bronze Stars?"

Hull looked confused at the non sequitur.

Foxx continued, "You're a patriotic guy and you just wanted to visit the grave of another one, right?"

Embarrassed, Hull shrugged, "Something like that."

Harvey chimed in. "I can vouch for that, Agent Foxx."

The task force commander looked to the bespectacled man. "You and Mr. Hull are friends?"

291

Harvey didn't hesitate. "We damn sure are now. He saved my life." Then, "I never set eyes on Paul until yesterday. But I'm a pretty good judge of character. You got it right—he's a patriotic guy."

Hull explained that when he recognized the danger he ran east, parallel to the cemetery drive, staying as low as possible behind rows of grave markers. When he was nearly even with the gunman he sprinted toward him and launched himself just as the man raised the carbine. He finished with, Foxx thought, a ridiculously understated line.

"Seemed like the thing to do at the time."

Hull and Harvey were led through the incident and questioned in minute detail. Neither of them offered much information on the driver, other than the fact that, as Harvey said, "He looked a good bit like that so-and-so that tried to shoot me." The agents had seen the video from the bank and knew the man and Tanner Jelcik shared similar characteristics.

Kekich asked about the conclusion of the action when the police showed up. Hull was still holding the carbine when they came through the entrance. He tossed the weapon aside and was bending over Jelcik when officers surrounded him and Harvey, screaming at them to get on the ground.

"What did you intend to do to him?"

Hull, with no hesitation, said, "CPR."

Kekich raised her eyebrows, "You're serious?"

Hull nodded. "He had obviously lost a lot of blood...and I hit him pretty hard...if he was going to make it he'd need help."

The agents knew from preliminary autopsy reports that the bullet fired by Officer Coy had nicked Jelcik's left subclavian artery. He bled both externally and internally. There were indications that substances found in his blood may have contributed to the bleeding.

Kekich probed. "And you were kept from doing that when the responding officers told you to get down?"

Harvey interjected, "They *were* pretty insistent, Miss Kekich." He added, "Damn shame all those guns were on *us* when the third man was driving out of the cemetery a few hundred yards away."

Foxx observed, "Just doing their job, Mr. Harvey. Following procedure." But inside he lamented the lost opportunity.

The interview lasted an hour. At the end of it Foxx felt he was no closer to finding the third member of the gang—strongly suspected to be Tanner Jelcik's 31-year-old brother, Cole—but he felt better about the quality of people randomly going about their lives in America.

Hull was a hero overseas. A decorated Combat Controller. They are some of the best we have. He took on a 240-pound killer yesterday to save a man he'd never met...and all because he was paying his respects to ANOTHER hero.

Foxx remembered a line from an old William Holden Korean War movie, *The Bridges at Toko-Ri*. A character, speaking about American aircraft carrier pilots who were willing to sacrifice everything for their comrades and their country, stares out to sea and asks, "Where do we get such men?"

Hull—and Harvey—seemed like such men to Foxx. The third member of the Fireteam—Foxx reflexively frowned when the word popped into his head—was nothing like these men.

Foxx wanted him.

The interview wrapped up. Kekich looked at her watch and suggested to Foxx and Remick, "Lunch? It's twenty till two."

Foxx turned to Hull and Harvey. "You guys had lunch?"

The Brick Bar was directly across Madison from the Ohio Building. It was situated in part of the lower floor of a monolithic cube-like building that mirrored the Ohio Building in many ways. It had a gritty feel, live jazz bands at night, and excellent food. The FBI contingent, plus Paul—Harvey begged off, he and his wife had a scheduled meeting with their financial advisor—trooped across Madison and were seated at a table near the back wall. They ordered sandwiches and soft drinks.

The conversation became more informal. Foxx discovered that Hull worked with FBI agents overseas on some of the operations the Combat Controller participated in with the Army's Delta Force and the Navy's SEAL Team Six. One of the agents, Grady Jenks, was the godfather of Foxx's son.

Foxx smiled warmly when Jenks's name was mentioned. "Grady likes his coffee."

Paul nodded, "He had an espresso machine in his tent at FOB Rushmore." He was referring to a Forward Operating Base in Afghanistan's Paktika Province. "I ran into him last Veterans Day at an event my sister put on at the National Veterans Museum in Columbus." He smiled, "Pretty sure he was drinking coffee there too."

When the food came, Paul asked. "How are you going to catch Jelcik's brother...if it's him?"

Foxx didn't hesitate. "It's him. The truck they were using for their getaways was registered to Cole. There's something hinky about the paperwork—we'll get to the bottom of that—and we think it was stolen."

Remick, chewing on a pulled pork sandwich, added, "Pretty slick idea. Leave the truck in a cemetery...nobody pays it any attention. It appears they were using the vault on the truck bed to hide their weapons and the stolen money. They hid right out in the open."

Kekich, looking for a waitress to refill her Diet Coke, added, "Looks like the rifle and the pistols were stolen in a home invasion from a gun dealer in Arkansas. The descriptions the dealer gave match up with the Jelcik brothers."

Foxx continued, "We put out an APB on Cole at noon. He and his brother run a commercial cleaning company in Columbus—Santo worked there too—and they lived nearby. Agents from our Columbus field office are watching those locations, hoping he shows up."

Kekich added, "We're tearing his life apart electronically... looking for safe deposit boxes, friends, female acquaintances... any place he might have money stashed."

Remick added matter-of-factly, "He'll run to the money."

Foxx looked from the burly analyst to Hull, "You can count on that...Scott thinks like a criminal." They laughed.

It was nearly 3 p.m. when they said their goodbyes.

Foxx asked, "Where to now, Paul?"

"If you folks are finished with me, I have some business to catch up on down in Bowling Green. I need to call my wife again on the way home. She was pretty, uh, *disturbed* about this whole thing when we talked yesterday. She thought all my combat was behind me."

Foxx looked at his watch. "We'll be in touch if we need you. You have our contact information. Pick up the phone if you think of anything that might help us...anything at all." Then, "We have a press conference in five minutes. The media is all over this thing." They shook hands.

"It was a pleasure meeting you, Paul."

Foxx turned away, already reviewing his answer to one of the questions he anticipated from reporters. *Why haven't you caught the third member of the gang?*

CHAPTER THIRTY-TWO

Five hours earlier, at 10 a.m., Cole Jelcik stepped into the back seat of a taxi outside John Glenn International Airport in Columbus. He caught sight of his reflection in the door window and nearly did a double take. He'd never before been completely bald. The condition, combined with the polar blue contact lenses he now wore, altered his appearance drastically. Cole closed the door and spoke the only words he would utter during the ride.

"Bus Station, one eleven East Town Street."

The driver was an overweight white man with tired eyes. He said *his* only words of the drive.

"You got it."

Cole had tossed three backpacks onto the seat before entering. He stared at them—the bolt bags. He fixated on them until tears shone in his eyes. They were tears of anger, not of grief or sorrow. Something inside of Cole had decided that he would not blame himself—*could* not blame himself—for what went wrong. To do so would be too overwhelming. He would not be able to live with himself.

So the fiasco in Toledo had to be someone else's fault. *What was the term soldiers used in all the World War Two books to describe a screwed-up situation? FUBAR. Fucked Up Beyond All Recognition.* The Toledo job was FUBAR.

Cole reviewed the previous day in his head. After the shit-show at the bank and the wild ride to the cemetery, he witnessed Tanner attempt to take out the white-haired man near the truck.

How the hell did we miss that guy?

Just as his brother was about to pull the trigger he was blindsided by another man. *That guy came out of nowhere... still, we should've seen him. There was just too much shit going down...the sirens...* He shook his head.

297

But then came the most painful memory. The man used the rifle to deliver a savage blow to Tanner's head. *T would've made it out if not for that.*

Cole had no choice. He punched the accelerator, flew past the crescent drive near the mausoleums, and followed the cemetery roadway to Holland Sylvania Road. There was no traffic within 200 yards in either direction. He went left—knowing he had no chance of evading the cops while inside the Sonata—then jerked the wheel right at the first turn.

It was Reo Street, a residential strip with numerous mature trees that provided privacy for the homeowners. Unfortunately for one resident, this privacy doubled as cover for a criminal who was capable—and desperate.

Dal Harrelson was an 81-year-old widower. He attended mass at Our Lady of Lourdes Catholic Church on Hill Avenue —less than a mile from his house—on Friday and Sunday mornings. He volunteered at nearby Resurrection Cemetery, trimming grass around grave markers. He paid special care to the stone his beloved Gertrude rested under, finishing each working day at that location. It didn't feel the least bit unnatural to him to see his name on the face of the stone each day. It was right there next to that of the love of his life.

When not giving his time to charitable endeavors Dal enjoyed fishing and tinkering in the two-car garage that stood detached from the house at the rear of the property. He was there, sitting on an automotive mechanic's roller seat, cleaning the tires of his 2010 Mercury Grand Marquis, when Cole Jelcik rolled up his driveway.

Dal saw the blood and the bullet damage on the Sonata through the open overhead garage door and knew he was in deep trouble. He saw the driver, a giant of a man, spring from the car and stride quickly toward him. The man carried a pistol in his right hand. The roller seat featured a tray just above the casters. It was a handy feature that allowed the user to store tools and miscellaneous items within arm's reach. Dal reached into the tray. His eyes stayed fixated on the brute as his hand moved frantically across the tray, finally gripping the handle of a large flathead screwdriver. He raised it and—

The man swatted the screwdriver from Dal's hand, hitting it with the flat side of the pistol. Dal felt pain shoot up his arm and was sure some of the bones on the top of his hand were broken. He let out a short *oooh* sound and pulled the injured hand to his body. Dal stared up at the dark, ugly barrel of the pistol. The man spoke.

"Where are your keys, old-timer?"

Cole saw the old man's eyes flick to the car and just as quickly flash back. He'd been reading people his entire adult life and he knew what this meant.

"They're in the car, huh? Good. How 'bout duct tape? Where's your duct tape?" Cole looked around the interior of the immaculate garage, every tool in its place, fishing poles, rakes, and brooms in a line as straight as a hound dog's pecker, a phrase Turk used often—the origin of which escaped both Cole and Tanner. "I'll bet you have six different-colored rolls in here somewhere."

He saw the man fight his eyes as they again sought to betray him. He lost. His eyes glanced momentarily at a drawer in a nearby workbench.

Cole kept the .45 trained on the old man and backed to the drawer. He found his estimate wasn't far off. There were four different colors of duct tape inside—two rolls of each—arranged in rows as neat as everything else in the garage.

"You're pretty particular, aren't you, partner?" He selected a roll of standard grey two-inch tape that had been partially used, noticing that when the man returned it to the drawer after its last use he'd bent a quarter inch of the leading edge back over the sticky side to allow for an easy start on its next use. *Convenient.*

Cole returned to the man on the stool, his mind calculating his next few moves with the focus of a blackjack player counting cards. His natural inclination was to think long term.

Now, he concentrated on just the next few moves. Nothing mattered if he didn't get out of Toledo safely.

He still wore gloves. After tearing off the first strip of tape he would need to start the second strip with his teeth—this meant leaving behind his DNA—or his fingernails. *Fingerprints.* He considered. *The cops have Tanner. He'll keep his mouth shut but they'll ID him. Santo's gone. They'll have his ID too. They'll find the common link to Klean Sooner, they have video of the other robberies. It won't take a rocket scientist to figure out I'm the third man.*

Stepping closer to the man, Cole kept the pistol up while using the thumb of his right hand to peel off the left glove. He let it fall to the floor. He quickly shifted the pistol to his left hand and bit down on the cuff of the second glove while pulling that hand free. He spat the glove to the concrete.

A step closer, Cole turned his attention to the act of taping the man. *I set down the pistol, he might run. I can catch him, no problem, but...* Sirens wailed in the distance, coalescing into a continuous squall. *No time to screw with him.* He transferred the pistol back to his right hand and took the final step.

He swung the pistol in an arc and struck the man above the left ear.

CRACK

"Lights out, old-timer."

Cole quickly taped the man's wrists and ankles. He noticed a two-inch-long rectangular lump above the ear. The combination of steel grey hair and the small amount of blood that leaked from the wound resulted in an ugly-looking blotch. Cole started the Grand Marquis and backed it out of the garage. He cut the angle too tightly and the right rear fender scraped along the Sonata's rear bumper. Cole hit the brakes and adjusted the wheel slightly before continuing. The scraping resumed. Cole was reminded of documentary reenactments of a killer iceberg tearing a crease in the side of the Titanic.

300

"Screw it...no time." He increased pressure on the gas pedal and the Grand Marquis lurched past the Sonata, becoming free of the newer sedan as Cole completed the arc. He put the car in park and jumped in the shot-up getaway car. As he pulled it into the garage he heard yet another police vehicle scream past Reo on Holland Sylvania. The window was closing on his escape. *Will the cops set up checkpoints?* He didn't know.

Quickly checking the interior of the Hyundai, Cole grabbed Dom's walkie-talkie from the cup holder—it had apparently been separated from his throat microphone cable when he left the car to engage the police officer at the bank—as well as the police scanner and the Tommy Gun.

Cole hopped out of the Sonata without bothering to switch off the ignition. Santo's USB cable still dangled from the column. He walked to a standard-size door next to the larger opening and pulled it open, then twisted the inner lock so no one could get through without a key. Cole turned to the unconscious man. In the process his eyes fell on the scraped fender of the Grand Marquis.

"Tough break old-timer, but you can probably buff it out."

He grabbed a floppy hat from a hook on the wall beside the fishing poles, hit the down button on the overhead, and closed the smaller door behind him.

Cole eased the Grand Marquis down the driveway, pulling the hat low over his eyes. He adjusted the seat back as far as it would go and slouched down. He saw that some of the neighbors had begun to gather in their front yards, their attention directed toward Holland Sylvania Road. Cole pulled down the visor, hoping to find a pair of sunglasses to help hide his identity. Nothing. He reached across the passenger side and popped open the glove box. He saw the folded arms of a pair of glasses amidst the well-organized contents.

Excellent!

Cole pulled them out and discovered they were the oversized dark lens style favored by some octogenarians. They had wide side shields and looked to Cole like they were designed to fit over another pair of glasses.

Perfect.

The big Mercury rolled to the end of the street. Cole kept his head still but used peripheral vision to scrutinize the neighbors as he passed. Only one, a woman walking a small dog, paid him the slightest bit of attention. She raised a hand to him automatically then placed it next to her ear. Cole realized she was in mid-conversation with someone on her cellphone.

She might not even remember this car driving past.

At the stop sign Cole waited as a van sped past from right to left. The side of the vehicle was covered with a large blue and white *13 ACTION NEWS* logo. He went right on Holland Sylvania, keeping at or below the speed limit the entire way out to the expressway. He monitored the mirrors the entire drive and, as he'd hoped, the further he got from Resurrection Cemetery, the less sign there was of police presence. Once on I-475 he turned up the scanner. He heard mentions of an ambulance and his thoughts turned to his brother.

Cole knew that Tanner would dread a life in prison. The subject came up once when Dom was telling stories of his time in LCI. Tanner said if it came to it, he would never be taken alive. "No damn way I'm spending the rest of my life in a box."

But Cole suspected his brother would eventually grow used to life inside. Lord knew he would not be screwed with in there. Tanner, he expected, would become one of the Alphas behind the walls of any prison. If there was a chance of someday being released he felt Tanner would adapt to the life. *I could even figure a way to send him Copenhagen.*

A slight smile crossed Cole's lips before quickly fading. He realized there were cameras at the Fifth Third branch that covered the exterior of the building. Tanner's execution of the cop would've been recorded.

They'll play that goddammed video at every single one of his parole hearings...T will never get out.

He drove on. When he reached I-75 he merged into the southbound lanes and soon moved out of range of the Toledo Police broadcasts on the scanner. Cole switched it off and turned on the Grand Marquis's radio. It was tuned to an AM station. Thinking of the old man that owned the car this did not surprise him. He listened through multiple news cycles. After an hour he learned little more than what was in the first report: a bank robbery had been interrupted by Toledo police, one officer and one suspect were killed in the exchange of gunfire, a car chase ensued that ended at Resurrection Cemetery, a second suspect was taken into custody there, and a third suspect was at large.

Cole exited the highway at Findlay nearly an hour after leaving Toledo. He took State Route 23 south and passed through several small towns. At 12:30 p.m. he reached Marion, a small city of 35,000. It was big enough to have a Lowe's. Cole parked in a far corner of the lot, pulled the hat down further, and walked in, still wearing the glasses. He was out of the store in eight minutes, having purchased the largest pair of bolt cutters he could find and a heavy lock that looked to be the right size for his purpose. He risked a second stop, going through a Taco Bell drive-thru, and was back on the road. Columbus was just over an hour away.

He reached the northern edge of the I-270 beltway that circled the city and followed it clockwise, passing the Anheuser-Busch plant and, a few miles later, the airport. Ten minutes after exiting the beltway he was punching in the code at the storage facility gate. When it rolled open Cole steered the Grand Marquis through and cruised slowly to the proper unit, thankful that he'd had the sense to rent it under the Cormier Gullickson identity.

He parked next to the heavy metal overhead door and got out. Acting like he was checking his tires Cole surreptitiously confirmed the location of the security camera in this section of the facility while at the same time making sure he was alone. After establishing that he was, Cole reached through the open window and retrieved the bolt cutters. The lock on the unit required a key, which was in the Klean Sooner building. Cole would not be returning to that building or, for that matter, the house he shared with Tanner.

303

I'm losing everything...the business...everything at the house...my truck.

Cole felt the anger spiking in his brain. *My truck!*

The lock was heavy-gauge steel, but Cole was motivated. He turned his back to the camera and took out some of his frustrations. The device was no match for a 30-inch bolt cutter wielded by a man that could press 225 pounds thirty-three times without stopping.

Cole raised the door partway and the motion activated light came on. He gathered the Tommy Gun, scanner, and walkie-talkies from the Mercury, and ducked into the unit. Once inside he found one of the chairs and unfolded it. He closed the door before sitting. After a while the lights went out. He sat that way for a long time, running through the events of the day and weighing his options. Eventually he made his way to the rear corner of the unit, moving stacks of boxes in the process. The lights back on, he found the hidden handles at the top of the modified steel drum. He removed the top and sorted through the backpacks, selecting his.

Cole removed the woman's compact and set it on a box. He spent 15 minutes cutting his dark black hair as close to the scalp as he could manage. He then covered his head with shaving cream and used the razor to render himself bald. This took much longer than he expected. He found that he really needed two mirrors, one set up in his line of sight and one he could angle to reflect a view of the back of his head. He had to remove and reapply the shaving cream several times. He also did not have a towel. He resorted to wiping his head with the edge of a large rolled-up floor mat he'd brought from Klean Sooner months ago and tossed on the pile of boxes to help give the contents of the unit a seedy look. Cole made no effort to conceal the hair—a source of his DNA—littering the floor of the unit, figuring that if the authorities somehow discovered its connection to him he was already hung.

Next he selected a pair of the polar blue contacts and used the mirror to fit them over his eyes. The change in his appearance was significant. Cole fished out the Cormier

304

Gullickson Canadian driver's license and compared the photograph to the image in the mirror. It was a strong resemblance. Cole decided that if he lost some weight the similarity would border on uncanny.

He had an overwhelming need for information. He was of a generation that had it at their fingertips all hours of the day. He, Tanner, and Dom had left their cellphones in Columbus when they left for Toledo. Cole mentally subtracted the phone from his dwindling list of resources. His thirst for an update on the situation was so strong he wondered if he could resist utilizing the phone if he had access to it.

Probably a good thing I can't get to it. I'd be tempted to sit and scroll through the damn thing until the FBI showed up to toss my ass in prison.

A plan was beginning to take form. He had the Canadian license. There was over $100,000 in cash and debit cards in the bolt bags. If he could get to Canada...

He removed $2,000 and several Visa cards from the bag and put them in his wallet, then replaced his driver's license with the one featuring Gullickson. He removed the holster from his belt and tucked it into his bag. Cole lifted the door a few feet. He knelt and peered out, half expecting to see the gun barrels of a police tactical team. He exited the unit and opened the trunk then quickly loaded all three backpacks inside. He placed his pistol under the seat. Next he removed the new lock he'd purchased at Lowe's from the Mercury. After attaching it to the unit he pocketed the keys.

Cole drove out of the storage facility. The Marquis was low on fuel. He didn't plan to drive it much longer but thought it prudent to have a full tank in case things took yet another wrong turn. He filled up at a Speedway station using one of the debit cards. He pulled a few wipers from the dispenser near the pump then, after wiping an imaginary spot from the windshield, balled the paper around his license and nonchalantly dropped the bundle into the wastebasket.

The FM radio stations were worthless when it came to news updates. The AM options were better, but concentrated mainly on Columbus happenings. Cole heard a brief mention of the shootout on 610 WTVN, but it included few specifics. He longed for the days of cruising in his truck, listening to Outlaw Country.

If there was ever a time to listen to a station with that name, this is it.

He drove to the bus station on East Town Street, parked, and entered. He wore the floppy hat he'd taken from Dal Harrelson's garage.

It was a long, narrow structure. The interior walls featured blue tile that rose six feet from the floor, topped by drywall that continued to the high ceiling. Steel benches were spaced every few yards down the center of the open floor plan. A dozen people were inside. A few milled about. Most sat on the benches looking at their phones and keeping their possessions close. The floor was worn out terrazzo that reflected almost none of the meager overhead lighting.

Needs a few coats of wax.

Cole used the restroom then found a board showing the bus schedule and studied it. He considered his options, quickly arriving at a decision. He walked to the ticket window and paid $91 for a ticket to Buffalo. It left the next day at 11 a.m.

Back in the car, Cole went through a Chipotles drive-thru and ordered two burritos with chips and the largest drink they offered. He cruised back to the storage unit, eying an apartment complex across the street as he entered the gate. After transferring the backpacks and food inside the unit he drove the Grand Marquis across the street and parked. The car could not stay at the storage facility overnight. He locked it and made his way back to the unit on foot. While waiting for a break in traffic he turned to assess the vehicle's hiding spot.

The damn thing is basically invisible. Bland as hell...I can't tell if it's beige or grey...blends in perfectly.

Cole returned to the unit with the pistol tucked in his belt. He ate the burritos and threw in an oversized dip of Copenhagen. He spent some time planning his next several moves while sitting in the folding chair. The lights switched off. The only sound was the occasional *thtt* of the tobacco juice leaving his mouth and splattering onto the ice that remained in the cup.

Cole stayed inside the unit all night. He was mildly concerned that the exterior of the unit could attract curiosity since it had no lock, but there were a few empty units in the facility that also weren't locked. He banked on it being ignored for the one night he would hide inside. He slept on the floor, first laying down the large floor mat. It had spent years in front of the entrance to one of Klean Sooner's customers and smelled like it. The floor surface was still uncomfortable, his thoughts more so. He could not get the image of the man striking Tanner out of his head. He saw the man's face, the thrust of the rifle, his brother going down.

Cole slept fitfully. He changed positions on the mat several times in an effort to get comfortable. At one point he woke and, out of habit, engaged the backlight feature on his watch. The face was, as always, situated on the inside of his wrist. He stared at the changing figures in confusion for a few seconds, not comprehending. The watch read 14:37:22. Then he got it. It was after one in the morning. The watch was still running in the stopwatch mode he and the other members of the Fireteam utilized on jobs. He stopped the counter.

The mission was over.

It was just past 6 a.m. when he woke on Friday. His need for information had not dissipated. He heard people outside, nearly panicked, and waited in silence while gripping the pistol. He pressed his ear against the door and heard two men haggling over the price of a riding mower. Seconds later an engine was started and the sound drowned out the voices. After more discussion, now muffled, a price was apparently agreed upon. Cole heard the men straining to push the mower up what was apparently a steep ramp—*"this is one steep goddammed ramp"*—followed by the sound of heavy objects sliding across metal. A door slammed. One man said *"call me if you come across another'n,"* and two vehicles drove off.

307

Cole lifted the door a few inches and saw the area was clear. He went through the tedious process of opening the front gate, crossing to the apartment complex, and driving back to the storage unit. There he reloaded the bolt bags into the trunk before leaving again.

He took State Route 33 east for twenty minutes to the small town of Canal Winchester, again listening for updates on the radio. He'd visited the town with Tanner, checking out its large craft beer brewery and taproom, BrewDog. He found a Walmart and bought two sweatshirts, a travel kit, several travel size necessities to fill it, and a visor that read Titleist across the front. On the way to the self-checkout he added boxes of KIND and Nature Valley snack bars.

In the car he changed into one of the sweatshirts and slipped on the visor. Anyone examining him would still see a bald pate rather than one covered by dark hair. He filled the travel bag with the necessities before popping the trunk and tucking it into his bolt bag. He tucked the extra sweatshirt into Dom's. He took a gamble with the pistol, stuffing it and his extra magazine into Tanner's backpack. Cole read somewhere that there were hardly ever security checks of bus passengers' luggage. He'd seen no metal detectors in the station the day before. He decided it was worth the risk.

He drove back to Columbus and pulled the Grand Marquis into long-term parking at the airport. One bag went on his back, the others on each shoulder. He marched to the terminal, not wanting to expose himself to close scrutiny on a shuttle bus. Once there he repeated the Fireteam's tactic of blending in and made his way to the taxi stand.

At the bus station the driver struggled to turn in his seat, his girth limiting his mobility. "That'll be twenty-six fifty."

Cole handed over two twenties. "Keep the change."

The cabbie, happy to have been paid in cash and even happier with the tip, offered, "Safe travels, now."

Cole, now out of the vehicle, grasping his bags, turned to the station, not giving the driver a second look.

He wiped moisture from his eyes.

"Yeah."

CHAPTER THIRTY-THREE

The bus was a Greyhound, one of the iconic companies made famous in the days of yesteryear. Images of snub-nosed silver buses transporting excited vacationers to the Grand Canyon or Mount Rushmore were part of the country's collective memory. Greyhound reeked of Americana.

Right now, approaching Buffalo on I-90, *this* Greyhound reeked of something decidedly less glamorous. The distance from Columbus to Buffalo was 330 miles. By car this could be knocked out, conservatively, in five hours. The bus had been on the road for seven and a half hours. It made several stops, taking on a few passengers here, dropping off a few there. Cole stayed on board the entire time, never once taking advantage of the short respites.

Before they left Columbus Cole slipped the driver two fifties for him to look the other way when it came to enforcing Greyhound's baggage rules. The policy was one piece in the passenger compartment under a seat or in the overhead bin, one piece in the baggage compartment under the bus. There was no way that Cole would let himself be separated from the bags, especially since one of them held a loaded weapon in addition to its store of cash and debit cards.

Once again Cole's knack for reading people paid off. He saw by the man's scuffed black oxfords, threadbare collar under his uniform jacket, and worn tie that there were circumstances in his life that diverted his salary elsewhere. He gestured for the driver to step to the side as the other passengers waited to stow their bags under the bus.

"Hey partner, how 'bout you let me buy you a new pair of shoes?"

Cole selected a seat in the rear near the restroom. This gave him a degree of privacy and a few more options to find spots for the three backpacks. But it also exposed him to that well-known peculiar fragrance best described as *public restroom.*

The seat location did allow him to jump into the restroom at his leisure without undue worry that the backpacks would disappear. A few riders cast judgmental looks at his extra baggage but the challenging stares they received in response from Cole put an end to any possible official complaints.

Cole was in no mood.

The lengthy trip did allow him time to work through his situation. The Gullickson ID was key. It would allow Cole to easily cross into Canada where he could further establish the identity by applying for credit cards. He would join random clubs and organizations, those that offered membership cards. He wasn't looking to become sociable, he simply wanted supporting documentation that he could carry on his person—wallet detritus.

Cole believed that Dom's prison contact, Tony Valenti, was now out. Though he'd never met the man—Valenti was still at LCI when the Fireteam exchanged the .50 caliber rifle for the burial vault truck—Cole understood enough about the criminal mind to know that Valenti almost certainly would have returned to a life of crime upon release.

You don't trade for the Godzilla of sniper rifles, a stolen one at that, if you're planning to walk the straight and narrow.

Maybe Valenti would have some ideas that would help a fugitive stay hidden from the law. He may even have interest in expanding his illegal activities north of the border.

I could be Valenti's Canadian point man.

At some point Cole would make a short return to Columbus to retrieve the cash from the safe deposit box at the Huntington bank. The box, like the storage unit, was paid for in advance for the entire year by Cole—or more accurately, by Cormier Gullickson.

The trip came to a merciful end at 6:40 p.m. Cole waited for all of the other riders to leave. He smiled, remembering how

312

he and Tanner zeroed in on the assholes at airports that pushed their way to the front of the exit line on planes.

The smile was a rare flash of the good times with his brother. Cole's memory of Tanner was quickly replaced by the scene of the man in the cemetery hammering him to the ground with the butt of the carbine.

His smile disappeared.

Cole made his way to the front of the bus. He winked at the driver and the man gave a short nod in return. Transaction complete. He stepped down and squinted into the sun's reflection off of several downtown buildings. Cole found himself in the middle of a modern American city. He scanned the buildings, looking for a hotel. There were several. He chose an Embassy Suites a few blocks away and began to walk.

It was an eight-story building with all the upscale amenities that professionals accustomed to frequent travel expected. After checking in with the Gullickson ID and one of the Visas, Cole asked about a business center. He was directed down a hall to an out-of-the-way room with two desktop computers, a printer, and counter space along one wall with faux-leather office chairs. There was no one in the room. Cole selected a seat in front of one of the computers. He dropped the three backpacks to the floor and sighed. Cupping the mouse, his hand traced a series of circles. The computer screen came to life.

Cole typed in *toledo bank robbery,* hit "enter," and waited.

After a second day with no sign of Cole Jelcik, FBI teams in Columbus entered the Jelciks' house and business as well as Santo's apartment. Over $17,000 in cash was recovered, a fraction of the amount they were suspected to have stolen in the series of robberies. The FBI Task Force stayed in Toledo for two days. When it became apparent that Jelcik had been able to evade apprehension and escape the city they began to trickle back to Chicago.

The first to leave was Remick, late Friday. He wanted to get back to the office, saying, "I can't do much here...I need to get back to the data."

Foxx and Kekich followed on Saturday after lunch. The return trip wasn't deemed a priority rising to the level that would require use of a Bureau jet. Rather than fly commercial out of Toledo or Detroit they requisitioned a vehicle from the Toledo field office. They were halfway into the 250-mile drive —passing a sign near Elkhart, Indiana, advertising the Recreational Vehicle/Mobile Home Hall of Fame and Museum —when Foxx took a call from the Toledo Chief of Detectives.

"You might want to get back here."

The body of Dal Harrelson was discovered by a woman who had been the best friend of his deceased wife, Gertrude. Abigail Donofrio had grown concerned when Dal missed Friday mass at Our Lady of Lourdes. She began to call his phone the minute she returned from church that day. After leaving several messages that went unreturned she decided to stop at the Harrelson house on her way home from buying her weekly groceries just after noon on Saturday. When there was no answer at the front door Abigail walked behind the house to the garage. She knocked on the door before trying the knob. Finding it locked she cupped both hands to the window and peered in, squinting as her eyes adjusted to the darkness inside.

She first saw the unfamiliar car. Confused, she concentrated on it. Her heart began to race when she noticed the bullet damage and bloodstains. Her eyes frantically darted across the garage's interior and rested on a pair of legs that were duct-taped at the ankles. They weren't moving.

"Oh my."

Back in Toledo Foxx and Kekich went directly to the Harrelson house on Reo. They were both in rotten moods, particularly Foxx. They found that their dispositions were matched by Toledo Police personnel on the scene.

The lead investigator, a detective named Whiting, met them in the driveway. Without preamble Whiting reported, "He was beaten and duct-taped, then left to die. Just to make sure an old man in his eighties wouldn't suddenly turn superhero and tear through the tape, our boy Jelcik left the Hyundai with its engine still running. Its tank is dry now—no telling for sure how long it ran—but our people had to open the garage doors to knock down the carbon monoxide level."

Foxx inquired, "Is that the cause of death?"

Whiting sighed, "Doc Brumenshenkel hasn't ruled on it yet...says Harrelson took a significant blow to the head that cracked his skull...hard enough that bone probably penetrated the brain. If that didn't kill him it would've left him with some level of impairment. Whatever...the air inside the garage was poison."

Foxx slowly shook his head. "We have to catch this son of a bitch."

Whiting concurred. "We've updated the APB on Jelcik... added the information on Mr. Harrelson's car. Hopefully it turns up soon so we run down this..." Whiting turned to stare at the garage, which was swarming with activity, "animal."

He led Foxx and Kekich toward the crime scene. Nearing the door he stopped and turned to the pair.

"Oh yeah, we have another problem."

Muncy Zlotnik was a pain in the ass.

Anyone who spent more than five minutes in the same room with him could confirm this. Muncy was 34 years old, a graduate of Toledo's Woodward High School. He did not attend college—not officially—but he spent more time at the University of Toledo's Student Union and the bars surrounding campus than the great majority of those that did. He worked in a computer repair shop in a strip mall three blocks west of the university. When he wasn't snooping through files and emails on laptops and tablets that were brought into the shops, he was trolling for college-age women. Muncy had little success. It wasn't that he lacked looks completely. His shoulder-length, flowing brown hair was parted in the middle and feathered back, evoking comparisons to 1980s actors Leif Garrett and Shaun Cassidy. The twenty-something college women of the present had no idea who these actors were, but a small percentage of them were intrigued enough to give Muncy a second look.

It was his rat-like eyes that turned away virtually all who had given him this second look. They were slightly smaller than they should've been and flicked from side to side. Upon focusing on a potential mate the eyes bore in, causing most on the receiving end to recoil. Any women who were exposed to these charms and were somehow able to achieve a level of attraction to Muncy generally changed their minds after a short conversation. He asked questions like, "You ever think about getting your front teeth fixed?"

Muncy was a pain in the ass.

He had it in his head that he would become successful by running a popular regional website that could drive traffic to advertisers. He knew that clicks were generated by dirt—sex, violence, corruption, conspiracies, like that—but he also knew that to get access to information from legitimate sources he had to assume the persona of a nice guy.

Muncy started a letter-writing campaign with members of local government with the intention of securing a press card that would give him access to various official functions. Once successful, he would pepper the internet with stories of police corruption and government ineptitude. He zeroed in on one particular female Toledo town council member. After getting a favorable response from her on his initial email he began to send her stories he wrote for a dummy newsletter, *Glass City Musings*. These were fluff pieces on school art projects and obviously inane city programs. Muncy's stories showed them in such a positive light that the councilwoman lobbied for the special access that he craved.

Two days after receiving the press pass Muncy changed the name of his newsletter to *Dirty Toledo* and began to post hit-pieces on the corresponding website. He excoriated cops, firefighters, and even the councilwoman who had been unfortunate enough to vouch for him.

On the day after the bank shootout on Reynolds, Muncy attended a press conference at the FBI building on Madison. The Chief of Police spoke first, lauding the actions of Officer Coy. An FBI Agent from Chicago also spoke, giving some interesting details about the robbery gang. He reported that a second suspect had been pronounced dead after leaving Resurrection Cemetery and hinted that evidence strongly suggested the surviving—and missing—member of the gang was Cole Jelcik, the brother of one of the deceased suspects.

During the question and answer portion of the conference a reporter from the Toledo Blade asked about the involvement of two private citizens at the cemetery, a man from Toledo and another from Troy. A rumor was circulating that the man from Troy was involved in subduing the suspect at the cemetery. The police chief deflected the question and all follow-ups on the same subject. Muncy decided to take a different line of questioning. He raised his hand and asked, "Is it true that Officer Coy had a history of altercations...that he liked to fight?"

All eyes turned to Muncy. The Chief of Police put his hand over the microphone, turned to the FBI Task Force Director, and mouthed the words, *"That guy is our resident asshole."*

While heading back to the shop from the press conference Muncy decided to make a detour to Charlie's Blind Pig, the reconstituted bar near the university that was part of a promising new development. Muncy had become a bit of a regular. He took a seat at the bar and motioned to the bartender, "Jack Daniels, on the rocks."

The bartender was a head taller than Muncy. He reached for a glass and filled it with ice. But rather than pulling the bottle of whiskey from its position in front of the mirror at the back of the bar, the man reached for something near the beer taps. He stepped to Muncy with the object and whacked him across the fingers.

"Owww! What the fuck, Barry?!?"

317

Muncy pulled back his hand, more shocked than hurt. The bartender laughed. "Looks like you've been Tutored, Munce."

Barry went on to explain the marketing campaign of the new bourbon the Blind Pig had brought in for trial the previous day.

"What the hell," said Muncy, "I'll try it."

It was not yet Friday-night-busy in the bar so Barry stayed close to Muncy making small talk. "Whaddaya think, Munce?" Barry nodded to the glass, already less than half as full as it had been five minutes earlier.

Muncy held up the tumbler, "Not bad, not bad at all." He stared at the book-shaped bottle on the liquor shelf. "Weird-ass bottle, though." After another sip he asked, "You say this Tutor's guy was from out of town?"

Barry scratched behind an ear. "Wasn't actually from Tutor's. Worked for," he turned to a collection of cards near the point-of-sale screen the three new bars used, "someplace named Jasper Spirits Consulting." He handed the card to Muncy who accepted it and scanned the information on its face. His eyes stopped on the bourbon rep's home address, *Troy Ohio.*

Muncy's eyes seemed to go full-vermin. "When *exactly* was this guy in here?"

"Yesterday. Musta been," he paused, "well, it was not too long before all those sirens started because of the shootout, whatever time that was."

Muncy downed the remaining Tutor's in one pull. He wiggled the glass. "Tutor me again, Barry. Then come here and answer a few questions."

Ten minutes later Barry moved toward the other end of the bar. "Gotta go get their orders, Munce." He gestured toward a group that just walked into the Blind Pig.

Muncy nodded. He'd wrung all the information out of the bartender that could be expected. He looked again at the business card then checked his phone for the time.

Hmmm, ten till five. Maybe they're still open for business.

Muncy dialed the office number on the card. He was pleasantly surprised when it was answered. A woman said "Jasper Spirit Consultants, this is Marge. Can I help you?"

"Uh, yeah, I'm calling from a bar in Toledo and I'm trying to get in touch with a," he glanced again at the card, "Paul Hull." To this point, technically, everything Muncy said had been the truth.

"I'm sorry sir, Paul is unavailable. Is there anything I can help you with?"

"Well, yeah, I had an appointment with Paul yesterday afternoon and he didn't show up. I thought I'd call to reschedule." Before the woman could answer Muncy added, "Is Paul okay?"

The woman was professional. "Yes, Paul ran into some... unexpected events yesterday and wasn't able to make it to all of his appointments. I thought we'd contacted everyone to reschedule, sorry. Can I get the name of your business so we can work you back on the schedule the next time Paul's in northern Ohio?"

Muncy smiled, "No, that's okay. I'll be in touch."

He looked back at the card and found Hull's cell number. The call went to voicemail. Muncy left a message. "Hello Mr. Hull, this is Muncy Zlotnik with," he hesitated, thinking the name *Dirty Toledo* may not carry the same cachet as more traditional news institutions, "with a news organization in Toledo. I'd like to talk to you about the role you played yesterday when Tanner Jelcik was subdued in Resurrection Cemetery. Please call me back." He left his number.

Muncy thought it was fifty-fifty that he heard back from Hull. There was a chance that he wanted nothing to do with his name being linked to a case with a fugitive on the loose. There was also just as much of a possibility that the man was like a high percentage of Americans these days. They were the type that, as the kids say, *lived for the gram*. They wanted nothing more than to trend on social media. Whichever camp Hull fell into Muncy was going to run with the story.

He drained his glass and headed for the door.

319

CHAPTER THIRTY-FOUR

The stories Cole read while sitting in the Buffalo Embassy Suites business center on Friday night were from the traditional media. Muncy Zlotnik's story would not be posted until the next day. What Cole saw, though, was revealing enough.

Tanner's dead?!? How the hell?

Cole immersed himself in the stories. The cop was lauded as a hero. The stories did not reveal how he was able to appear at the scene so quickly. Cole wondered if the officer—his name was Coy—showed up out of dumb luck. This was something he'd always worried about. It was something that even the most meticulous planning could not prevent.

Dom died at the scene of the robbery. This did not surprise Cole. His last memory of the undersized man was looking down at the bullet-riddled body as he stepped past it to drive away the getaway car. Cole closed his eyes and tried to shake away the memory. He preferred to remember Dom as the loyal teammate that, on jobs, was known as Audie.

The event at the cemetery was documented in detail. The *Toledo Blade* website had the most comprehensive coverage. A map was included that showed the route from the bank to the spot where the burial vault truck was positioned. There was a brief allusion to civilian witnesses in the cemetery but no mention whatsoever of one of them being involved with Tanner's apprehension or, Cole thought, *murder.*

Cole had been identified as the third suspect. This was expected. He was wanted on a number of charges including bank robbery and felony murder. Cole stared at the screen dumbly. He had taken great pains to minimize the possibility of gunplay during the robberies. Most of the precautions were geared toward his brother. But a deadly shootout had still occurred and he, Cole, hadn't fired directly at anyone. The death of the cop meant that anyone involved in the crime could be charged with a capital offense in Ohio. That meant the death penalty.

Cole shook his head. *I might as well have shot that chick in the green top at the bank. Would've gotten my money's worth.*

Cole walked numbly to the bank of elevators. He was overwhelmed by the events of the past two days. He thought he'd come to grips with the enormity of the situation during his flight from Toledo to Columbus and even gotten ahead of things somewhat on the bus ride with his plans for a future as Cormier Gullickson. The death of Tanner, though, came to him as a gut punch.

His room was on the fifth floor. He let himself in and dropped the backpacks on one of the beds. He unzipped Tanner's bag and removed the pistol and extra magazine. These went under the mattress of the far bed, within easy reach if he needed them quickly in the middle of the night. Though there was no mention of the man on Reo Street, or his car, on the news reports, Cole did not rule out the possibility that the FBI might track him to Buffalo.

He removed the travel kit from his backpack and set it near the sink. After that he turned on the television and bounced between news stations as he ate three of the snack bars. He mechanically drank several glasses of water from the tap, knowing how important it was to stay hydrated.

But his mind was on Tanner.

The news stations were local—or national—and included nothing about the Toledo robbery. *Apparently the robbery and gunfight were REGIONAL events...too big for the local stations, not big enough for the national boys.*

Even though he had seemingly drained the internet of information in the business center, Cole felt secluded, paralyzed by an inability to connect to the information sources he needed.

Tomorrow is Saturday. First thing, I find a mobile phone store. Have to be able to get on the damn net to see what's happening.

He was whipped. Beat. The sun had not yet set but the TV was doing him no good and he needed rest. He turned it off. He engaged the security safety swing bar on the door and pulled the curtains shut. After stripping to his underwear he got in the bed, checking to make sure he could easily retrieve the pistol.

Memories of Tanner swam into his head. They were not sequential, coming to him in random order. There was Tanner next to him in the tattoo parlor in Bartlesville, proud as hell of his Silverback Gorilla, giving Cole shit about his "pussy Grizzly Bear." Then came the steamy Saturday in July when they climbed to the attic and found Turk's stash of *Penthouse* magazines. Cole was 10, Tanner 7. Neither knew what to say at the time so they both wordlessly threw them back into the box and continued to look for treasures that held more interest.

Cole remembered wrestling with his brother in elementary school, junior high, and—when things got testy at times—in high school. Cole began to slide into that state of consciousness that wasn't quite sleep, but would not be remembered the next morning. He saw himself at age eight. Tanner was five. They were picking apples from the tree in the back yard near Turk's taxidermy shed. In an instant they were in the kitchen, helping their mom cut slices for apple pie. Then, the next second, the pie was coming out of the oven. The crust rim, pinched by Tammy's index and middle fingers to form a crown-like pattern while still doughy, was now golden brown. Tammy cut the first slice, slipped it on a small plate, and set it in front of Tanner. He looked from the steaming delicacy—a rare treat in their house, and demurred. He pushed the plate toward Cole.

"Here Cole, you're the oldest."

Just as Cole nodded off, the final image came to him. He saw the rifle butt strike Tanner's head.

323

At 7:30 the next morning Cole rode the elevator to the lobby carrying two of the backpacks, Tanner's and Dom's. He wore the third. He asked the concierge, who had just come on duty, to store them for him. Cole was not about to trust these bags full of cash to a random housekeeper and her sticky fingers. He gave the concierge a look that told the man he'd *better* be trustworthy.

In the breakfast area he selected two bagels and poured a cup of coffee. He walked back past the front desk, fired a second visual warning salvo at the concierge, and found his way to the business center. He was again the sole occupant of the room. He made a quick check online about the robbery and manhunt. Seeing little additional information, he spent 15 minutes on *apartments.com* jotting down phone numbers with the courtesy pen and notepad next to the keyboard. Ten minutes in, a man entered the room and sat at the second computer. He navigated to the Delta Airlines website, printed a boarding pass, and left wordlessly.

Cole's goal was twofold. He wanted to find a place to live— at least temporarily—that was close enough to the American border to allow for quick transitions between the two countries. Secondly, he needed to establish an address in Canada that would accept mail. He would have credit cards and miscellaneous membership cards sent to the address. Most important for the task at hand, the address could be used when signing up for a phone plan.

Before leaving the business center Cole spent an additional five minutes researching rental car policies for customers without credit cards. *I should've applied for a couple of the damn things a year ago.*

He grabbed a second cup of coffee and returned to the room on five. At 8 a.m. he started to make calls from the room phone. He began each call by apologizing for the early hour interruption on a Saturday. Cole struck a deal on his fourth try. It was a two-bedroom unit on Victoria Street in Hamilton, Ontario that cost $1,600 a month Canadian. Cole did the math and determined that this was less than $1,200 in American dollars at the current exchange rate. The location was barely an hour's drive from Buffalo.

When the woman on the line explained it was a monthly rental Cole agreed to pay a pro-rated amount for the remainder of June as well as all of July, saying his employer would reimburse him. "My boss wants me to get started there right away. He'll want to send some things to the address immediately. Is that a problem?" Assured that it was not, he paid with several of the $500 Visa debit cards. This took some time to process. Cole heard background music as the woman typed in his card numbers and asked about it.

"I'm sorry, I can turn that down, it's Elton John."

"No, no, no, don't bother. I was just curious. I love music, all kinds."

"That's nice, Mr. Gullickson. What's your favorite?"

Cole hesitated, hearing the use of his new name. His previous pseudonym, Ike—one he loved—would never be used again.

"Well, I listen to a lot of Ootlaw Country on satellite radio. He pronounced "Outlaw" like a life-long Canadian.

Minutes later he left the room with the third backpack. The pistol was inside. He asked at the front desk for directions to a cellphone store. Ten minutes later he walked into a T-Mobile store. The transaction was surprisingly smooth. He gave the Hamilton mailing address. He apologized for not having an email address—"My company is still in the process of getting that set up"—and paid in cash. Before leaving the store with the brand new iPhone he asked if there was a car rental company nearby.

The helpful sales associate—smiling as he counted the hundred dollar bills—nodded. "There's a Hertz three blocks north on Pearl Street."

He rented a full-size SUV, a GMC Yukon, black, and paid in advance. Rental companies, he had discovered, allowed you to rent without a credit card if you provided a debit card to keep on file. Airport locations required two forms of identification but here, downtown, this did not apply. He gave the Hamilton address and informed the associate that he would be returning the vehicle to a Hertz location there.

"No problem, Mr. Gullickson. Let me get you that address."

By the time Cole rolled out of the Hertz lot it was nearly 11 a.m. He drove around the downtown area for twenty minutes, familiarizing himself with the vehicle and—more importantly—the freeway access points that would provide for quick exits out of the city if the need arose. According to the signs, one of these routes, Interstate 190 North, would take him to the Peace Bridge, which crossed over the Niagara River into Canada. Cole noted that the Niagara Falls itself was barely 15 miles further north of the bridge.

Cole had no interest whatsoever in seeing the Falls. He felt hunger pangs and remembered a sign near the Hertz location.

A short time later he pulled into the lot of Dinosaur Bar-B-Que. *I shouldn't have any problem getting my protein here.*

Cole wore the backpack inside. He ordered a full rack of ribs and spent the time loading familiar apps onto the phone. The aromas coming from the kitchen had him primed for the meal.

When the food arrived, though, Cole's appetite disappeared. The colossal plate of ribs reminded him of the 50-wing lunch he'd enjoyed with Tanner and Dom after the walk-through at the Ohio State baseball stadium. *When was that? Wednesday? Just three days ago?* He saw their faces and remembered Dom challenging his brother to a throwing contest. Cole smiled sadly. He ate half of the ribs and asked for a doggie bag.

On the way out of the restaurant he passed the merchandise area and had a thought. *Maybe get some local gear?* He bought two logoed t-shirts and a short-sleeved button-down mechanic shirt. They were all in black, all XXL.

Back inside his room at the Embassy Suites he went to *Craigslist* on the iPhone. He checked out vehicles for sale by private owners in the Hamilton area. An 8-year-old Lincoln Navigator caught his eye. The mileage wasn't terrible—109,000—and the asking price seemed low to Cole, $7,500.

Must be some reason for that.

326

If he were to live in Canada, Cole would need an appropriate full-time vehicle. He had plenty of cash for now but—until he was able to retrieve the money from the safe deposit box—he thought it prudent to buy a used vehicle rather than pay $200 a day for the rental.

My guess, the seller is motivated. I can probably get that thing for less than he's asking. Especially if I pay with American dollars.

Cole screenshotted the ad for the vehicle and saved it to his photos, making a mental note to contact the seller when he got to Hamilton. He wasn't yet sure when that would be. Certainly in the next day or two. He still had some prep work to do for the crossing into Canada. At check-in he was told he could extend his stay each day by simply informing the front desk.

He started searching again for information coming out of Toledo, The *Blade* had details on the planned funeral for the cop. Cole read the first sentence then swiped to the next story. There was still no mention of the stolen Grand Marquis. This comforted Cole, convincing him that he was at least two steps ahead of the FBI. It would be three steps if he made the crossing to Hamilton before the missing car came to their attention.

Looking for other sources Cole returned to the original search page and saw a choice for something he hadn't noticed before. It was a link to a website named *Dirty Toledo*. The headline read, *Good Samaritan Thwarts Killer's Escape.*

"What the hell?"

Cole clicked on it. The story, under a byline by Muncy Zlotnik, began:

A highly decorated former Special Operations veteran is credited with subduing the armed gunman apprehended by Toledo Police Thursday in Resurrection Cemetery after a botched robbery. The hero, Paul Hull of Troy, Ohio (see accompanying photo) has not been publicly credited by police officials. Dirty Toledo staff members learned of Hull's actions yesterday and want to be the first to offer congratulations. The suspect, Tanner Jelcik of Columbus, received a gunshot wound while engaging, and killing, Officer Jeter Coy. Jelcik subsequently died of the wound after being confronted by Hull, who, while serving as an Air Force Combat Controller in the Global War on Terror, was highly trained in hand-to-hand combat techniques. Hull, now a representative for Jasper Spirits Consulting of Dayton, was working in Toledo at the time of the incident.

The accompanying photo showed a brown-haired man at a podium. Cole flashed back to the cemetery.

That's the sonofabitch that put Tanner down!

CHAPTER THIRTY-FIVE

Paul returned to Troy on Friday after eating lunch with the FBI agents. As soon as he got in his vehicle he texted Lauren to tell her he was leaving Toledo and would be available to take a call if she wanted to talk before he made it back. He was barely ten miles out of Toledo when he decided to skip any stops in Bowling Green. This deep into the afternoon the chances of having productive meetings had dwindled. He knew that Marge would have called the businesses to explain he may not make it today. On the way home he ran the incident from the previous day through his head.

What were the chances of me being in that cemetery at that exact time? One in a zillion?

No matter, he was glad he was able to keep Jim Harvey from becoming a victim of the robber, Jelcik. At 4:01, as Paul neared Findlay, his phone rang. It was Lauren, calling exactly one minute after her shift at the hospital ended. "Hey babe."

"So you decided to actually come home, not stick around and break up a drug ring or maybe foil a terrorist plot?"

She sounded more under control today, not as distressed as she was when Paul called yesterday to explain what happened.

"They decided to bring in the Avengers to take my place. It's a step down, sure, but they think Iron Man and the boys might be able to fill my shoes."

Lauren laughed. "Lacey said we can cancel the 5K tomorrow with everything that's happened."

"No, not on my account. I think having a couple beers might be just what I need. What time is the race?"

Lauren gave him one more chance to back out, "You're sure?"

"Absolutely."

Lauren, noticeably brighter, remarked, "Excellent! I'll let her know. She and Matt will pick us at 3:30 in the afternoon. The race is at 5."

Paul, half-joking, declared, "I'll be day-drinking tomorrow. You and Lacey can take your time in the race. It'll give me and Matt time for an extra cold one."

Paul called Tutor's and got Charlie Hunter.

"Oh, Paul! Are you okay? We heard you were somehow tangled up in that mess in Toledo."

Before Paul could answer Charlie cut him off. "Don't answer that. Obie wants to talk to you and he has to be in Somerset at 5. I'll put you right through. He can fill me in later. Really hope you're okay." With that Charlie was gone. Seconds later Obie came on the line.

"Paul! What in the world? I'm hearing things went cattywampus up there. You alright?"

Paul gave a short laugh. "I'm fine, Obie."

"Word we got was the police had you tied up all afternoon. You were a witness to a robbery?"

After a pause Paul began the story. "It was a little bit more than that."

He was halfway through the story when another call came to his phone. Paul glanced at the unfamiliar number and let the call roll to voicemail. Finished with Obie—the Tutor's founder was going to be late for his five o'clock—Paul checked the voicemail. It was from a member of the media asking Paul to call about his involvement with the suspect inside the cemetery.

That's the LAST thing I need. Didn't sound like he wanted to tell me who he works for. Sounded...sketchy.

Paul deleted the message.

A few minutes after 5 as Paul neared Piqua he called Mike McClary. The call was answered after one ring.

"You okay?"

"Yeah, Mike, I'm fine. Sorry about the appointments, I'll have to make another trip—"

"Forget about that! What the hell happened?"

Again Paul ran through the story. When he finished, the line was silent. Paul thought the call might have dropped. "Mike?" "Yeah I'm here...Just what is it with you and cemeteries?"

The next day went well. The Hulls, Matt, and Lacey enjoyed the day in downtown Dayton. Microbreweries offered their products for sale under tents. The weather was warm, the sky clear, and the crowd enthusiastic. While the women ran, the husbands talked about Matt and Lacey's upcoming wedding. That lasted two minutes. Then, being guys, they talked about the different beers until the race was nearly over. Matt asked Paul about the incident in Toledo. After hearing a concise description of the events Matt nodded.

"So, this third guy, the guy that got away...any chance you need to be worried about him?"

Paul's plastic beer cup stopped on its way to his mouth. He considered, "I don't think so. The guy is on the run. Besides, he has no idea who I am." He brought the brew the rest of the way and sipped. "I kinda like this one."

Matt eyed Paul's cup. "Ironic I asked about the guy when you took a sip of that." He indicated the screened logo. The beer was from Branch & Bones Artisan Ales on Wayne Avenue. It was called *Big Black Cloud Stout*.

Lacey finished third in the extremely competitive 18-24 age group. Her finishing time was just under 23 minutes. Lauren surprised herself by running a time of 26:45. She was flabbergasted to hear her name called during the awards ceremony. She also earned a third place medal.

By this time the McClarys had wandered downtown—their South Park home was within walking distance—and joined the two couples. The evening was shifting to party mode. As Lauren returned from the awards stand she asked Paul to take a picture of her and Lacey together with their medals.

Paul removed his phone from his pocket as the smiling women leaned toward each other and held up their medals. He saw three missed calls from Rita Kekich.

331

Uh-oh.

Paul selected the camera app and pointed it at the women. He took the picture.

Minutes later, under the guise of needing to use the restroom, Paul walked toward the port-a-johns and dialed Kekich. She picked up.

"Thanks for calling back, Paul. There have been some developments."

She explained that the body of an 81-year-old man had been recovered within blocks of Resurrection Cemetery, He'd been beaten and duct-taped, then left on the floor of a closed garage. The Fireteam's stolen Sonata was inside the garage, the ignition switched on and the fuel tank empty.

"Damn." It was the only word that Paul could summon.

"The victim was a widower named Dal Harrelson. Mr. Harrelson's 2010 Mercury Grand Marquis is missing. We have law enforcement agencies from Ohio and every surrounding state actively searching for the vehicle. We're hoping," she hesitated, "we're *anticipating* that it will turn up soon."

Paul considered his words. "Agent Kekich, what's to say that car isn't already in *another* garage somewhere and this guy Jelcik has himself a different vehicle?"

Kekich let the question slide past. "There's another reason we've been trying to reach you. There has been a post on a popular Toledo-based website identifying you as the person who confronted and subdued Tanner Jelcik."

"*What?*"

Paul heard Kekich take a deep breath and let it out. "I'm sorry, Paul. We're not exactly sure how this guy...Zlotnik, got the information but we're checking. He's screaming about being harassed, threatening us with an attorney, the usual ho'opunipuni."

At the mention of Zlotnik's name Paul's chin quickly rose an inch. He remembered the voicemail from the man yesterday. He'd deleted it. *Had to be the same guy.*

He began, "What are the odds," then hesitated. "Wait, what was that word you used? All the usual...what?"

"Oh. Ho'opunipuni...it means 'bullshit' in Hawaiian."

Paul frowned and started again. "What are the odds that *Cole* Jelcik sees that report?"

"No way to know. Our people think he's running and won't have the time or the means to try anything with you. Still, we're contacting the authorities in your town and your county to make sure their eyes are open." After a hesitation Kekich went on. "There were some pretty specific facts about you mentioned in the post. You'll want to check it out."

"What's the name of the site?"

"*DirtyToledo.com.*"

Paul rolled his eyes. "Wonderful."

Lacey and Matt dropped off Paul and Lauren a few minutes after ten. Paul, who had made an effort to hide any concern while with the younger couple, was surprised when Lauren closed the door and demanded, "Okay, what's bothering you?"

"You could tell?"

Chappy came out from an unknown hiding place, walked past Paul without as much as a glance, and rubbed against Lauren's legs, arching his back. She bent to scratch under his ear.

"Well, let's see. You were scanning the crowd like some sort of Terminator. And you held that last beer in your hand without drinking for 45 minutes. It had to be warm by the time we left."

Paul's face assumed a resigned expression. "It was."

Lauren stood, both arms around Chappy. "So? What's up?"

Paul related the details of the phone conversation with Agent Kekich, touching on the man's body being discovered and the missing car. He finished with the information about the website.

She made the connections immediately. Pulling Chappy closer she hypothesized, "You think the missing robber might see the report and come here? My God Paul, did you see any sign of him at the race?"

"No, none at all...and I wouldn't have missed him. The guy that went after Jim Harvey in the cemetery was a monster. Huge. He was bigger than most of the operators I worked with on deployment. His brother, Cole, is supposed to be even bigger. A guy like that would've stood out at the brewery event."

Lauren wasn't completely assured. "But you were watching for him. If you're concerned, I'm concerned."

Paul thought the best approach at this point was to gather information. "Why don't we check out this website and see how bad it is?"

It was bad.

DirtyToledo.com, they found, had categories across the header that left little doubt about where the site stacked up in the world of legitimate journalism. They saw, *Pothole of the Week, Top 10 Most Corrupt City Officials,* and *Stupid Police Tricks.* This last choice apparently featured cellphone videos made by citizens during interactions with police officers. There was a virtual black banner across this category with an accompanying headline reading, *This feature disabled until after Officer Jeter Coy's funeral. Check back every day for updates.*

Lauren frowned, "Looks like some real class acts run this."

Paul smirked, "I think the technical term is *assholes.*"

They found what they were looking for below the header.

Good Samaritan Thwarts Killer's Escape.

Lauren leaned in as Paul, under his breath, muttered, "Oh boy."

They read in silence until Lauren, unable to contain herself any longer, exclaimed, "They printed your name, your picture, our *town!* They practically give a road map of how to find you!" She took a breath before asking, "Where was that picture taken? How did they get it?"

Paul, still scrolling, answered, "it was taken at that Veteran's Day thing I did back in November for Patrice. I think it was on the Museum website for a while. They must've taken it from there...had to dig for it." Before Lauren could comment Paul had a thought.

"Does Patrice know about this thing in Toledo?"

Lauren nodded, "I called her after you filled me in the day of the robbery but I haven't talked to her since."

They called. Patrice answered, mildly concerned that the lateness of the call meant trouble. Two minutes into the conversation she realized her concern was justified. Paul and Lauren had her on speakerphone and she went online to see the story as they explained.

Patrice was outraged. "*I took* that picture and posted it to our site myself! They can't just pull it from us and use it on their damn scandal site!"

After hanging up with Patrice they discussed the situation.

"I'm going to cancel my trips for Tutor's this week. We'll stay in touch with the FBI...see how their hunt for Jelcik progresses. They said they've alerted Troy PD and the Miami County Sheriff's office. I don't want to go too crazy over this but I think we need to be cautious.

Lauren, remembering the situation the couple faced the previous summer, had to agree.

CHAPTER THIRTY-SIX

Cole holed up in the hotel. On Sunday morning he saw an update on the *Toledo Blade* website that revealed the body of Dal Harrelson had been found.

The old-timer?

Cole was somewhat surprised that the old man didn't survive. *He looked like a tough old bird. I didn't think I hit him that hard.*

An examination of the article revealed that carbon monoxide poisoning was a contributing factor in Harrelson's demise and may yet be determined as the official cause of death. A detective named Whiting was quoted in the article, saying,

> *Mr. Harrelson sustained wounds consistent with having been beaten with a heavy object. He was subsequently restrained with duct tape and left inside the garage—an enclosed space—with the vehicle used in the bank robbery, which was running. When discovered, the vehicle, a 2021 Hyundai Sonata stolen from the airport parking lot Wednesday night, had an empty fuel tank. Cole Jelcik remains the prime suspect and an additional count of aggravated murder will be added to the charges that are pending.*

Cole was perplexed. Had he left the old-timer's garage without switching off the ignition? A thought, not quite a revelation, swam into his head. *That damn car didn't have a key. Dom's USB cable started it.* Cole had not intended to let the engine run. He was sure that if the Sonata had a key in the ignition he would've removed it without a thought.

So the old-timer died because of that? Cole pondered this for five seconds. *Oh well, I guess you just had to take one for the team, old-timer.*

Cole knew the importance of preparation. He'd stressed it for over two years to Tanner and Dom before each robbery. He planned to give himself every opportunity to make his disappearance into Canada successful.

He researched the mechanics of physically passing back and forth over the border. His Canadian license would suffice to get him into the country but to get back to the States he would need a passport. The steps to acquire one in Canada were different than in the U.S. He made notes. Using the address in Hamilton as a base, he should be able to secure the documentation within a few weeks. Once he had the passport he could come and go as he pleased. At some point he would make the drive back to Ohio to get the rest of the money.

Ohio. The thought led him back to the fiasco in Toledo and his brother. Cole returned to the *Dirty Toledo* website and read the article for the umpteenth time. He focused on the picture of the man, Hull, standing behind a lectern, a smile on his face. He screencapped the image on his iPhone and saved it to his photos.

Good Samaritan...Hero.

At the bottom of the article was the comment section. Cole read through them, feeling his temperature rise.

Glad we still have people who know how to treat scum like this Jelcik character.

Attaboy, Air Force. Aim High...Fly-Fight-Win!

Oh, NOW you're pro-police? Your site rips them every day but Officer Coy dies and you're all about the clicks. F*ck you.

Enjoy your time in hell Jelcik. Say hi to Hitler and Manson...watch out for that Dahmer guy.

Cole renewed his reservation at the Embassy Suites every morning. By Wednesday he'd become familiar with the layout of Buffalo and the surrounding area on the U.S. side of the border. He plugged the address of the Hamilton apartment into the navigation system of the Yukon and saw that drive time was 68 minutes. He weighed the advantages and disadvantages of buying an E-ZPass from the state of New York. This would speed up any border crossings he needed to make but would create electronic data that could be used against him. There was a fine line between establishing a realistic identity for Cormier Gullickson and a trail that led to Cole Jelcik.

He decided against the pass.

He contacted the owner of the Lincoln Navigator in Hamilton via text. They messaged back and forth about the vehicle. Cole suggested meeting so he could check it out. The man—Cole hadn't asked his name—said he worked second shift. Could Cole come Saturday afternoon? Cole agreed and got the address. He'd rented the Yukon through Saturday. If he bought the car and had to wait for possession until all the paperwork was processed, Cole would extend the rental of the Yukon for a few days, or simply rent another vehicle.

It was all coming together. Cole called the desk and extended his stay again, asking for Saturday check out.

It *was* all coming together, but at night just before nodding off, the image would come to him. Tanner being hammered to the ground. Hull standing over him.

Paul took the entire week off. The folks at Tutor's were very understanding. Obie told him to take as much time as he needed.

"You take care of things at home, Paul. Things are starting to roll for us and we appreciate your contribution. I expect you'll pick right up where you left off when you get back to it."

Charlie Hunter told him to give her a call if there was *anything* the company could do for him. He had been planning a swing through western Indiana that week that included West Lafayette, the home of Purdue University.

"Those Boilermakers can wait for you to come another time." Then, in a conspiratorial tone, Charlie added, "You know they'd just pour beer on our Tutor's, right?"

Paul got the joke three seconds after hanging up. *Beer, whiskey...Oh, Boilermakers!*

He called Mike McClary. Marge was with him and they put Paul on speakerphone. They discussed the upcoming weeks. A pattern of responsibilities had developed. Paul typically discussed the general travel schedule and key targets in each area with the couple at Jasper Spirits. Once this was agreed upon, Marge sent a synopsis of the plan to Charlie Hunter who, in turn, took care of the hotel reservations and shipments of marketing materials and bourbon samples to Paul. It was working well despite being more of an evolution than a structured plan.

Paul explained his concerns over the manhunt for the fugitive and the unwanted disclosures on the *Dirty Toledo* website. The second he finished Marge exclaimed, "You are *certainly* not going to Indiana this week. You stay home with Lauren."

Mike agreed, "Absolutely, Paul. We'll reassess the following week. What did we have planned...?"

"Pittsburgh," Paul filled in the blank.

"Yeah, Pittsburgh. Hopefully the guy is behind bars long before then. Does the FBI still think he's running?"

"That's what they say." Paul tried to sound hopeful.

Marge chimed in, "So you're back to being a house husband for a week. Any plans? Bike rides? Maybe hang out with Chappy?"

Paul laughed, "I ordered some books a couple days ago... catch up on my reading, I guess."

At 5 a.m. on Monday morning Lauren turned off the light in the master bathroom and twisted the doorknob before exiting into the bedroom. She went out of her way to avoid waking Paul before leaving to meet Lacey for their morning run. She was surprised to see her husband awake. He was sitting on the bed tying his running shoes.

"You're getting an early start to your week off. Going down to the basement to work out?"

Paul shook his head. "Nope. Thought I'd tag along with you and Lacey this morning."

Lauren's eyebrows rose. "Seriously?" Her immediate reaction was less than positive. She'd come to enjoy the time with Lacey. The run jump-started her day. The physical aspect gave her a sense of accomplishment and more energy throughout the day. But it was the companionship that she'd developed with the younger woman that was now the main motivator to get up early in the morning. She found herself making mental notes throughout the day. *I need to remember to mention this to Lacey tomorrow morning.* They chatted and laughed as they made their way through the streets of Piqua. The addition of Paul, bless his heart, would completely change the vibe.

Then she got it. Paul wasn't in it for the conversation. Or even the exercise. He was coming as a bodyguard. That man, Jelcik, was affecting their lives in ways that were becoming less and less subtle.

They drove separately. Lauren would stay at the YWCA to shower after the run while Paul would return to Polecat Road. After finding spots on the street they stood in front of the Y and stretched. Paul asked, "So, Lacey will just run here from her place to meet up?"

Lauren checked her phone and nodded. "She should be here in a minute or two."

Lacey appeared on cue, rounding the corner of Greene and Wayne. She was not alone. Loping along beside her was her fiancé. As they approached Paul couldn't help himself. He burst out laughing.

"Thanks Paul, I really appreciate the moral support." Matt feigned offense, a smile on his lips. He bent at the waist and put his hands on his knees as he caught his breath.

341

"Wow, Matt, a whole two blocks. You should take a break." Paul put the needle to the younger man. They'd now had beers together. Step two in the male relationship was sarcastic banter.

Matt rose. "Thought I'd see how the skinny people started their day."

Though Matt was trying to downplay his appearance, Paul understood exactly why he'd accompanied Lacey that morning. It was the same reason Paul was there—to make sure the women were safe. His respect for Matt went up a couple notches. "No need for you to tag along, I'll hang with the ladies this morning."

Though Matt didn't have a complete understanding of Paul's military background, he knew enough to realize his fiancé would be in good hands. "You sure?"

Paul nodded. "Absolutely."

Matt sighed. "Good! It wasn't going to be much fun running in these." He lifted a foot, displaying a pair of high-top basketball shoes. "Had these since high school."

Paul and the women were still laughing as Matt disappeared around the corner at a dead walk.

Gatewood Dowdell showed up at the Hulls' house Monday night unannounced. He was still in uniform, having apparently come direct from his job at Wright-Patterson Air Force Base.

Greeted by Paul at the door, Gatewood extended a hand that held a zippered black case.

Paul reacted by asking, "What's this?" despite recognizing the size and shape immediately. It was a ballistic nylon handgun case.

"It's our new pistol, the Sig."

The Air Force began to procure Sig Sauer M18 9-millimeter pistols for their combat units in 2020. They replaced the all-metal Baretta M9, which had been in use for decades. The Sig was made of lightweight polymer materials and had an adjustable grip to fit different-sized hands.

Paul stared at his friend. He and Gatewood had spoken on the phone twice since the Toledo incident. There had been no mention of weapons. In the Special Operations community there were two mindsets among those that had completed their service.

Paul fell in one group, those that laid down their weapons for good when the missions ended. Gatewood was in the second. These operators continued to have a close relationship with weapons, often owning several. They were never going to be in a position where they felt outgunned.

Paul accepted the case and unzipped it. He removed the pistol, noting the desert brown color and plastic-like composition. The weapon was introduced just as Paul was recovering from his leg injury so he'd never deployed with one.

"Light." He hefted it, appraising the features.

"Thought I'd loan you one of these for a week or so." Gatewood continued, "There's a couple extra magazines in the case. Feel free to come to the range with me if you like."

Paul, still examining the pistol, asserted, "I'm pretty sure I can figure it out, Woody"

Nodding, Gatewood responded, "Yeah, as I recall, you were pretty damn good with the pistol, not that they got used much in combat. But you held your own in training with the customer units we worked with." He hesitated and let a broad grin spread across his face. "Unlike that time on the rifle range in Mississippi with that FBI agent."

"Christ Woody, give that a rest."

When Dal Harrelson's body was discovered, the hunt for Cole Jelcik intensified. The tape that was used to bind the victim was tested for traces of DNA. The results showed a definite relationship between the fugitive and Tanner Jelcik, whose DNA, in addition to obviously being recovered with his body, was abundant inside the Sonata.

The BOLO—or, *Be On the Look Out*—alert that was generated to locate Harrelson's Grand Marquis resulted, within a few days, in a cascade of information that flowed to

Foxx's task force. Beginning on Sunday there were a rash of reported sightings that were run down by local law enforcement agencies from Missouri to Maryland.

It was Scott Remick, the FBI analyst, who had the idea to send out specific requests to airport security departments asking them to comb the parking lots and garages of their facilities to try to locate the vehicle. He reasoned that the gang had become adept at obtaining stolen vehicles in these environments. Why wouldn't Jelcik do the same thing in reverse and stash a car there? Or, in his words, "Airports have been their honey hole for two years. It stands to reason that he might fall back on an area of familiarity, especially in a time of stress."

On Monday night members of the Columbus Regional Airport Authority Police Department discovered the stolen Mercury in the long-term parking lot. Columbus Police, agents from the FBI's Columbus field office, and units from the Ohio State Highway Patrol swarmed over the vehicle. Additional DNA was recovered and sent to the lab at Ohio's BCI—Bureau of Criminal Investigation—in the nearby town of London. The results were pending.

But there was little doubt. Cole Jelcik drove the car to the airport.

Investigators were perplexed by the timing of the car's appearance at the airport. Electronic records showed that the Grand Marquis entered the lot at 9:47 a.m. Friday. There was no sign that the fugitive spent a significant amount of time at Harrelson's residence the day before. To the contrary, all signs pointed to the fact that he left in a hurry. Drive time from Toledo to the Columbus airport was two and a half hours. If Jelcik left the Reo Street address around noon on Thursday, where had he spent the next 22 hours? Surveillance teams had blanketed Jelcik's house and business as well as Dom Santo's apartment. There was no indication of a current girlfriend. Checks on the backgrounds of all three suspects were run. There was no evidence of relatives living in the Columbus area.

It appeared that the Jelciks had moved to Ohio several years earlier from Oklahoma, leaving all extended family behind.

All flight manifests for Friday and Saturday were pulled. Jelcik's name did not appear on any of the passenger lists. A fake ID was a possibility, but it was remote. Records showed only two passengers purchased a ticket on Friday or Saturday for outgoing flights on those days. Both travelers were tracked down and ruled out as suspects. All other tickets were bought well in advance. Jelcik would have had to purchase the ticket in advance under the fake name. He would have no way of knowing that the robbery would turn disastrous and he'd need to flee.

This time Foxx made the leap of logic that kept the task force from losing the scent. If Jelcik didn't leave the airport on a plane, then how *did* he leave, and where did he go? He could've gotten a ride, but the gang's social circle, based on the available information, was extremely small, one could say nonexistent. If a friend didn't pick up Jelcik, he needed to arrange for a ride from a service. Uber and Lyft were ruled out as FBI evidence collection teams by now were in possession of Jelcik's phone. Next they looked at taxi companies. They found a hit. A driver reported taking a fare from the airport Saturday morning to a bus station on East Town Street. The trail wasn't yet hot, but it was getting warmer.

CHAPTER THIRTY-SEVEN

The research of Canadian laws and regulations seemed never-ending. Holed up in the hotel room, Cole put his time to good use. He figured out how he would renew the Cormier Gullickson driver's license before it expired. He went on the Toronto Maple Leafs' website and joined their Leafs Insider Club just to get a card that he could carry in his wallet. While on the site he checked out the merchandise and, finding all items 25% off, bought a jersey in XXXL as well as a knit cap—he couldn't bring himself to buy the version with the fluffy white pom on top—and a baseball cap. *That blue is dark, like the label on a bottle of Labatt's beer. But it should go well with my new eyes.* He smiled.

Credit cards were easy. He found online offers for both Visa and Mastercard that seemed happy to send high interest cards as long as you had an address and a heartbeat. The heartbeat requirement, as far as he could tell, was optional. Cole didn't give a rat's ass about the rate. He needed the cards. He had them mailed to the Hamilton apartment. Once he had them in his possession he would begin to make small purchases to build credit and establish a buying history.

Three times a day he stopped to work in some exercise. Two of the sessions were in the room and consisted of stretching, pushups, and sit-ups. In between the two he hit the hotel fitness center. He used the weight machines but also made sure to do at least 20 minutes on a treadmill. Aerobic exercise was relatively uncommon for Cole but he wanted to try to reduce bulk somewhat to better match the photo on the Gullickson license. At least once a day he felt himself being checked out by female employees or guests. He reacted cordially, but kept his distance. He had retrieved the backpacks from the concierge and stowed them in the room, leaving them only when he was in the fitness center.

347

He kept the Grizzly tattoo covered at all times. The description of him that the FBI was circulating did not mention it. He hoped they didn't know about it. The tattoo parlor in Bartlesville that did the work went out of business a year after the brothers had them applied. But the employees of the shop had no doubt scattered to other similar businesses and may remember the artwork. The authorities had Tanner's body and knew about his gorilla, but no one had yet made the link to Cole's Grizzly and he wanted to keep it that way. People might see it today, if he wasn't careful, and report it much later when the FBI added it to his list of distinguishing characteristics.

Never having shaved his head before, Cole found that he was continually running a hand over his scalp, assessing the level of the nubs. He vowed to eliminate this habit, thinking it could be a "tell" to others that he only recently began the process. He shaved a second time on Monday morning and by Wednesday night decided it needed to be done again.

He thought about Dom at least once a day. Tanner, though, was on his mind almost constantly. More and more the childhood scenes in Cole's head were pushed aside by the memory of the blow to the head of his wounded brother by Paul Hull.

This was exacerbated when he checked out updates on the robbery and manhunt. The old man's car had been located at the Columbus airport. There was no indication in the stories that the cops or the FBI had made the connection to the next step he'd taken in his escape, but Cole was savvy enough to know they weren't likely to divulge everything they'd learned to the media.

It appeared that the investigation was now centering on Columbus so Cole turned his attention to media outlets in that city.

But not completely. He still felt compelled to check out the *Dirty Toledo* website. On Wednesday afternoon an updated story was posted, again under the byline of the writer named Muncy Zlotnik. From all indications Zlotnik had reviewed the comments at the bottom of the original post—there were now well over a hundred of them—and got a good read on what types of takes would be well received by the site's readers.

He blasted Tanner. Terms like *white trash* and *cop-killing scum* were used in the story itself, not just the comment section. Cole felt his temperature rise as he read.

Zlotnik now mentioned the presence of a second witness at the cemetery, one that, according to unnamed sources, was about to be *mercilessly executed* by Tanner.

Hull was mentioned in glowing terms. He was the *vigilante that was in the right place at the right time to bring the miscreant to his knees...a guardian angel with an attitude.*

Cole took a deep breath, stood, and paced back and forth between the window and the door. Unconsciously his eyebrows lowered slightly. His jaw clenched, one side of his mouth pulled back.

Back at the computer he noticed a sidebar article titled *THE REAL LIFE ACTION HERO?* He scrolled to the story and saw that it was packed with more idolization of Hull. There were two additional pictures. One showed him in a group photo of men in uniform at attention. They were wearing red berets. The second was a studio shot of Hull in dress uniform. His chest rack had several rows of ribbons. He still wore the beret. Under each picture were the words *Obtained through the Freedom of Information Act.*

Cole stared at the pictures for a long time.

Late Wednesday, after finishing a room service salad, Cole flipped channels on the TV and came across a rerun of *Patton.* He was mesmerized by the actor's portrayal of the general's swagger and take-no-bullshit attitude.

I really picked the right code name for Tanner. A smile came to his face as he thought of his brother. It disappeared when the memory of Hull cracking Tanner's head with the rifle came to him. That vision was now the first recollection that came to mind when Cole thought of Tanner. It was infuriating.

Cole reached for his can of Copenhagen and pinched a third of the dwindling contents. He inserted it behind his lower lip then got back on his phone. The screen brightened, returning to the picture of Hull in his dress uniform.

Hmmmm.

In Chicago on Wednesday morning Rita Kekich came into the task force conference room. It looked like a command center for an army planning an invasion. Whiteboards were set up on easels. They were situated throughout the room in a seemingly random fashion. Open laptop computers were sprinkled across the large rectangular table. Printouts and coffee mugs hid much of its surface. Foxx sat at the head of the table talking on a cellphone. Kekich took a seat. As she waited for Foxx to finish his call she looked around the room. There were a total of twelve people working in this project room. They flowed in and out as various tasks were designated. It reminded her of how big city newspaper rooms were portrayed in old movies.

"Morning Rita, what do you have?" It was Foxx. He'd finished his call.

"We may have found the bus driver."

Foxx set up straight. "Do tell." His eyebrows were arched.

The FBI was looking at all bus departures from the Columbus East Town Street bus station on Saturday, the day a suspect matching Jelcik's description was driven there by taxi from the airport. The challenge was tracking down the drivers. They were spread all over the country.

"The driver of an 11 a.m. bus to Buffalo was tracked down late last night in Rochester, New York. He told the agent that interviewed him that a man matching Jelcik's description boarded the bus."

Foxx grew excited. "Was he shown a picture? How sure was he?"

Kekich nodded, "Yeah, he's 80 percent sure. Says something about his face was different than the picture. He says he remembers the man because he brought three backpacks on board the bus and refused to put any of them in the cargo area. The driver decided to let it slide since the bus wasn't full."

Foxx leaned in.

Kekich continued, "The man was wearing a hat so the driver couldn't remember hair color...but he's 80 percent."

"That's 80 percent better than we have now. Let's get everyone looking in that direction."

Kekich held up a hand. "There's something else."

"Uh-oh." Foxx looked apprehensive.

"Our agent says the driver seemed evasive when he talked about the three bags. I talked to Remick about it and he has a theory."

"Which is?"

"He thinks the backpacks were full of cash and Jelcik bribed the driver to bring all three on board."

Foxx stared at Kekich for ten full seconds.

"That damn Remick...glad he's on our side."

In the weeks that he'd been employed by Jasper Spirits Consulting, Paul had gotten used to a day with structure. Though the activities varied, shifting from preparation, to time on the road, to face-to-face meetings, the fact that the days were full had subtly adjusted his mindset. His days had a purpose. He found that the time spent home by himself since the Toledo incident seemed to pass slowly. Much slower even, than it did before he took the job. He supposed he'd gotten used to the retired life after recovering from his leg injury. The job had jumpstarted his internal clock, sped it up.

What the hell am I gonna DO all day?

He made phone calls, staying in touch with the McClarys and Charlie Hunter down in Sawyer, but they had work to do and he felt he was intruding on their day. He exercised. He ran in the mornings with Lauren and Lacey but was increasingly getting the feeling that he was interfering with their normal dynamics. There was road construction on part of their regular route, Riverside Avenue, and they had to modify their runs.

They adapted by both starting and ending on the long stretch of Greene Street. Paul sensed his addition to their already disrupted runs was not particularly well-received.

He did laundry. He'd already developed a slight case of cabin fever when, late Monday afternoon, the books that he'd ordered were delivered to the house.

They all had Alex Drabik as subject matter. Well, they all recounted the action at Remagen in March of 1945. Historical works that centered on Drabik's role didn't exist. To come to a full understanding of the man's actions one had to read accounts from several different publications and piece them together. That is exactly what Paul did over the next few days.

He started with *The Remagen Bridgehead*, a publication put together by the U.S. Army's Research and Evaluation Division. This was a bit technical and contained a number of obscure military terms and concepts but Paul, with his background, understood it well enough.

Next he perused *Crossing the Rhine: Remagen Bridge*, by Andrew Rawson. He skipped through a good bit of the text, concentrating on the section that described the actual day of the crossing and Drabik's heroics on March 7, 1945.

There was significantly more detail in *The Bridge at Remagen* by Ken Hechler, who was an Army combat historian at the time of the action at Remagen. The book, published in 1957, included hour-by-hour details of the fighting.

Paul started the Hechler book Tuesday morning after returning from his run with Lauren and Lacey. He was halfway through it by late afternoon when UPS dropped off a related item he'd purchased on eBay. This was an out-of-print magazine called *AFTER THE BATTLE,* which was published in Great Britain in the 1970s. Each issue featured photographs taken during World War Two. The magazine's staff traveled to the specific location of each photo, captured a modern image, and included both versions in the publication. In addition to dozens of these "then and now" comparison images, the text that ran throughout—Paul would find—was extremely well researched and detailed. The specific magazine that Paul bought was Issue 16. It was titled *Crossing The Rhine*. On the cover was a 1970s era photo that showed the bridge towers that still stood, long after the bridge collapsed during the war.

Paul alternated between the Hechler book and the magazine. He compared photos and crosschecked them with maps he found on the internet. He moved from the living room recliner to the office, and back again. This greatly frustrated Chappy, who tried to follow Paul inside the office each time, only to have the door closed in his face.

Wednesday was a virtual repeat of the day before. By that night Paul had nearly finished the book and the magazine. It took his focus away from the manhunt for Jelcik. He wasn't sure if this was good or bad. He kissed Lauren goodnight and told her he'd see her in the morning. He wanted to finish reading and would do it in the living room.

"Okay, if you fall asleep out there you want me to wake you up early to run, right?"

"You won't have to do that. I'll come to bed in an hour or so when I finish and get up when your alarm goes off."

Lauren looked doubtful. "But if you don't...?"

He grinned. "Wake me when you get up...bang pots and pans together if you have to...but it won't happen."

Paul read military books in a different way than most in the general public. His combat background came into play. He inserted himself into the action, trying to imagine the sounds and smells. The smoke of gunpowder and haze from explosives were a difficult thing to forget. As was the smell of blood.

He read into the night. His eyes grew tired as he turned the pages. Chappy perched on the arm of the recliner, content to observe. Sometime after midnight he nodded off. The Hechler book was in his hands, turned to the index at the end. The magazine was open, spread across his chest with the photo of the Ludendorff Bridge towers facing up.

CHAPTER THIRTY-EIGHT

March 7, 1945

Sergeant Alex Drabik trudged toward the company command post. It was a cold, grey morning. Low clouds hung in the air. They wouldn't be visible until the sun came up in an hour but Alex knew they were there. They'd released a chilled, light rain on him all night as he curled in a poncho under a grove of walnut trees. A canopy of branches and leaves was the only protection from the elements for him and his squad from 3rd Platoon.

Drabik reached a paved road and paused for a few seconds to scrape mud from his boots before angling left on the hard surface. The senior enlisted members—sergeants—of Company A, 27th Armored Infantry Battalion, had been instructed the night before that they were to assemble at the command post in the morning to get the straight dope on the day's objective. Alex knew it would be more of the same—push toward the Rhine—but he had a couple unusual motivations to attend the meeting. First, it would be the initial briefing by the new Company Commander, Lieutenant Karl Timmermann, a man Drabik admired. And second, there was a rumor that hot coffee would be waiting.

Drabik approached the command post, a lofty term for what amounted to little more than a group of smoking, hacking soldiers standing at the rear of a deuce and a half, the Army's workhorse two and a half ton truck. As Alex neared he saw one of the group break away and extend his arm. It was Staff Sergeant Joe DeLisio, another 3rd Platoon non-commissioned officer, who hailed from the Bronx. DeLisio's hand held a steaming tin cup filled with coffee.

"Here ya go, ya plough jockey." DeLisio's voice was a blend of Italian, New Yawk, and Army-tough.

Drabik smiled and reached for the cup. "Thanks Joe."

DeLisio held a second tin cup in his left hand. He turned and ambled back toward the truck, stopping a few feet outside the semi-circle of men. They stood silently, DeLisio and Drabik, sipping the morning brew, looking for all the world like a couple of characters from a Bill Mauldin cartoon. Drabik, tall and thin, was a head taller than the more animated DeLisio. Neither had shaven that morning. The stubble combined with tired eyes to make them look exactly like what they were—war-weary veterans.

They had met in training back in the States. Their battalion and the other elements of the larger 9th Armored Division had been assembled to buttress Allied forces pushing toward Germany. The entire division—5,000 men strong—had made the crossing from the United States to Scotland in August of 1944 on board the RMS Queen Mary, which had been converted from a luxury liner to a troop ship. Drabik remembered laughing along with DeLisio as they sat through a mandatory lecture on the ship. The subject matter was venereal disease and the dangers of unprotected sex with the women of Great Britain and the European continent. The lecturer—a major—had referred to pubic lice as "mechanized dandruff."

They made the English Channel crossing at the end of August and by December were in position near the Luxembourg-Belgian border when German forces struck the American line with everything they had. What followed was a bitch of a six-week slugfest in sub-freezing temperatures. Drabik was hit by shrapnel but stayed with his men. Thousands of his comrades, he reasoned, had endured much worse and stayed in the fight.

The German Army was in full retreat now, attempting to retract as many men and as much equipment east, over the Rhine, as possible, giving them a chance to recover from the Allied onslaught. They were pulling back everywhere, blowing the bridges behind them.

"Here comes our West Pointer." DeLisio smiled and indicated with his tin cup. A lone soldier stepped briskly toward the truck.

Drabik, in on the joke, grinned at DeLisio's comment. There was a class of professional officers in the Army that graduated from the United States Military Academy located at West Point, New York. The greatest percentage of officers, however, attended civilian colleges before being granted a commission. The remainder of officers did it the hard way. They joined the Army as enlisted men and were selected to attend Officer Candidate School. This last method was how Lieutenant Timmermann earned the bars on his shoulders. His hometown was West Point, Nebraska. Veterans in the company, therefore, referred to him as a "West Pointer," in a joking manner.

Timmermann, though, was no joke. He'd earned everything he was given and both DeLisio and Drabik knew it. They had the utmost respect for him as a leader in combat. Someone called out "Ten-shun."

Timmermann stopped at the edge of the group. He wore the same boots and fatigues as the rest of the group and, like most of them, had netting stretched over the outside of his helmet to allow tree bark or leaves to be attached for camouflage.

"As you were." Timmermann got right to it. "I guess you've all heard the scuttlebutt. Captain Kriner was wounded yesterday during our fight in Stadt Mechenheim. He's being sent home. Even though a captain is supposed to lead a company, we're fresh out." He looked into the eyes of several of the sergeants. "They needed to pick a lieutenant to do the job and I guess that's me." Before anyone could offer congratulations he went on. "We're about ten miles from a town called Remagen. The Krauts are trying to push everything they can across the bridge before we get there and cut off their escape. Word is they have some kind of experimental rocket launcher on our side of the river they want to save."

A sergeant asked, "We walkin' or ridin', sir?"

357

"Good news boys. We'll roll out on trucks and half-tracks. Expect to dismount and fight through pockets of resistance, though." He looked in the direction of Drabik and DeLisio. "I'll want 3rd Platoon on point."

The two sergeants, in unison, said "Yessir."

The men saddled up and were moving southeast on the road to Remagen less than an hour later. Two men in a reconnaissance car led the way. The column was escorted by a company of the Army's new Pershing tanks, formidable beasts armed with 90-millimeter cannons developed to duel with the German Panzer and Tiger tanks. The rain halted and the clouds hung low. Rifle and machine gun fire caused the column to halt several times. Drabik, carrying his M1 Garand semi-automatic rifle, dismounted with his men each time as the Americans worked to outflank their adversaries and cause them to pull back.

The stops, starts, and firefights continued into early afternoon. With the vehicles halted at a bend in the road, the reconnaissance car probed ahead. The car drew fire and stopped. Both men—Drabik knew them only as Penrod and Munch—exited the vehicle and crept to a tree line. Moments later they waved and yelled, getting Timmermann's attention. He hustled up and—to his amazement—saw below and a mile distant a railroad bridge clogged with vehicles and pedestrians.

The Ludendorff Bridge, the last remaining bridge spanning the Rhine, was still standing.

Excited radio calls went up the chain of command as the men climbed down from their vehicles. They ate, smoked, and took turns peering through the trees at the town of Remagen below. Though they could see a bend in the river well to the north, the men had no way of knowing that this geographical feature caused the water to accelerate as it flowed past the town. The bridge had three spans with two tall towers on either side. Soldiers were just visible in the towers. The Germans had covered the entire length of the bridge with wood planking, thus allowing wheeled and tracked vehicles to pass over the tops of the train tracks. On the far side the tracks disappeared into a massive basalt ridge known as the Erpeler Ley.

As the men waited, the American high command debated what to do. Some wanted to destroy the bridge, others wanted to try to seize it. In the end the decision was made. Timmermann was ordered to make an attempt to capture it. He quickly devised a plan. Three columns of infantry would move down the slope. One would clear out the center of Remagen, the other two would be on the flanks. DeLisio and Drabik were on the left, meaning they would move down the slope to the river north of town and make their way along the bank to the bridge. This would put them under fire from German guns across the river for most of their approach.

The Americans worked their way down. German fire from the east bank and the towers on the far side of the bridge rained down on them. The American Pershing tanks in elevated positions on the west side of the river fired back. A few minutes past 3 p.m. word came down that a German prisoner captured south of Remagen claimed the bridge—which was packed with explosives—would be blown at 4 p.m. The tanks were ordered to fire white phosphorus shells around the bridge to provide cover for the infantry positioned below.

The Americans would try to rush the bridge.

Minutes before the order was given an explosion rocked the American side. A large demolition charge exploded under the approach to the bridge. It created a crater that would prevent any supporting vehicles from making the crossing. It was an infantry show now.

As the men prepared to climb onto the structure a second blast went off. This one shook the entire bridge, covering it in smoke and haze. It seemed to lift into the air several feet before settling back. The Germans had detonated the demolition charges.

"Well that's that." A relieved Alex Drabik stared at the cloud as it began to drift in the wind away from the point of the explosion.

And then, amazingly, the spans of the bridge reappeared. The Ludendorff was still intact!

The Americans reorganized. They didn't know how long the bridge would stand. There was a real danger that even if they made it across, the bridge would collapse behind them, leaving them to the mercy of the Nazis across the way. After a quick reorganization, Timmermann called to the men of the lead platoons.

"Git Goin!"

Alex, a quiet man by nature, eyed his platoon and said simply, "Who's coming with me? I'm going across." Several men later reported these words. Alex did not remember saying it.

The men leapfrogged under fire from one rusting steel girder to the next. Bullets ricocheted off the span with a *SPANGE* sound causing the men to duck. DeLisio screamed "Keep moving!"

The towers on the other side opened up on the Americans. The turreted tops of the towers were manned by crews firing MG-42 machine guns. The fearsome weapon—nicknamed "Hitler's Buzz Saw" by American soldiers—fired 20 rounds of high velocity 7.92-millimeter bullets a second. It made a distinctive ripping sound that sent fear through the souls of the Americans. Still, the men of A Company came on.

A shell from a German artillery piece screamed down from the top of the Erpeler Ley. It struck one of the support girders and cut through it without exploding. Its trajectory altered, the projectile continued on to the western side of the river and detonated inside Remagen. Every soldier on the bridge ducked instinctively, though the shell was well past them by the time they reacted. A neat round hole was left in the steel. Still, the Ludendorff Bridge stood.

Drabik's helmet fell off his head as he passed the halfway point of the crossing. He continued on, attempting to close on the towers before the gunners above could depress their weapons enough to bring him down. General William Hoge would personally hand the helmet back to Alex the following day.

Most of the fire came from the tower on the right. DeLisio entered the tower to clear it. Drabik ran on. He reached to opposite shore with Timmermann behind him, leading the remainder of the company. Drabik saw movement to his left. Bullets continued to strike the steel supports he'd just passed, *SPANGE, SPANGE.*

The movement to Drabik's left was a German soldier. Alex swung his M1. The soldier dropped his rifle, put his hands in the air, and pleaded, "Kamerad! Kamerad!"

It was a cry of surrender.

Drabik raised his M1...

SPANGE, SPANGE, SPANGE.

Paul jerked and reluctantly opened his eyes. He saw a magazine open on his chest. The Ludendorff Bridge towers caught his attention. A book, *The Bridge at Remagen,* was in the crook of the recliner between the left armrest and his leg. He stared up to see Lauren holding metal pots in each hand.

"What the hell?"

She smirked down at him. Her words had a singsong lilt, "You saiiiiid..."

CHAPTER THIRTY-NINE

Cole woke up Thursday morning with a new purpose. The image of Hull hammering Tanner was never going away.

I have to do something about this guy.

He went online with his phone and began to research. He started by going back to the original article on the *Dirty Toledo* site. He reread the article with a new purpose. This time he wasn't looking for specifics on the robbery investigation, he was looking for details on Hull.

What, exactly, is a Combat Controller?

Cole spent a half hour on websites that helped him understand. Air Force Combat Controllers were the real deal.

Okay, so he's tougher than he looks. Gotta be smart about this. If I go after him I'll need a plan. If I come at him head on I'll take him out, but it could get messy.

The ideal situation would be to have Hull in a position of weakness. This would not be easy. Cole continued to research. He went to the second article and brought up the picture of Hull in his dress uniform. He looked at the photo for a long time.

He's got some Boy Scout in him. Hard eyes...but a Boy Scout.

Back to the first article, Cole saw that Hull lived in Troy, Ohio. He had an idea of the location and confirmed it by checking online. Next he typed in *Paul Hull Troy Ohio*. There were a few hits, not many. One caught his eye. It was a reported burglary from the previous summer in the Troy newspaper. The victims were Paul and Lauren Hull. Their address on Polecat Road was listed.

He's married!

Cole smiled. This opened up a whole new set of possibilities. He began to search for mentions of the wife. There were a few references related to a hospital in Troy. Apparently she worked in the lab.

Dark parking lot at night? Hmmm, maybe.

He continued. There was little else. He was about to move back to the husband when his scrolling stopped on an article from *OHIO RUNNER*, a website featuring race event calendars and results. There, in the results for the Downtown Dayton Brewery Run, he saw:

WOMEN 40-50 AGE GROUP
1st Place: Erin Dinzeo, Dayton: 23:58
2nd Place: Terrie Schwaiger, Sidney: 24:41
3rd Place: Lauren Hull, Troy: 26:45

Hull's wife was a runner.

A smile formed on Cole's face.

He spent the next 15 minutes back on *Craigslist.* He decided it was too risky to cross the border to buy the Lincoln Navigator and then try to get back into the U.S. Getting back would require documentation that he didn't yet possess.

The Navigator was out. He would buy something on this side of the border. He found a silver 2016 Chevy Traverse—a mid-sized SUV—listed with an asking price of $9,800. The mileage was nearly 150,000 but the owner claimed it was extremely well maintained.

We'll see.

The Traverse was located in Tonawanda, just north of downtown Buffalo. Cole punched the number into his phone and composed a text.

Interested in the Traverse. Would like to check it out. If I pay cash can we expedite title transfer?

His iPhone dinged less than ten seconds later. A thumbs-up emoji appeared on the screen.

Cole's grin had a wolfish quality. He was still going to make the move to Canada, but first he was going to tie up a loose end.

The owner of the Traverse was a man named Rick Timm who worked for a construction company. Cole drove to Timm's house in Tonawanda Thursday after the man returned from work. The vehicle was as described, though Cole thought it could use a new set of tires.

"How about nine thousand even?"

Timm shook his head. "Ninety-eight is a bargain. It's my bottom line. Gotta have ninety-eight."

Cole eyed the man. "Ninety-two hundred...cash. You make out the bill of sale for eight thousand and I pay less tax."

Timm, without a hint of shame, declared, "Deal."

They shook hands.

Timm said he'd taken the liberty of scheduling an appointment at the Erie County Department of Motor Vehicles the following day—he'd taken a half-day off work—anticipating that they would close the deal. Could Cole meet him at 2 p.m. the following day at the 170 Pearl Street location?

Cole now knew the layout of Buffalo well enough to realize the address was barely a half-mile north of the Embassy Suites. He could walk there easily. He didn't want Timm to know where he was staying and simply said, "Sure can."

The men met the next day in the DMV parking lot. Timm arrived in the Traverse while his wife, Diana, drove a second vehicle, a Lexus ES Hybrid sedan. The car was jet black, brand new, and gleamed in the afternoon sun.

Cole nodded toward the Lexus as he counted out 92 one hundred dollar bills. "Construction business is good these days, huh?"

Timm smiled, accepting the cash. "Diana had a good day last week at Buffalo Creek Casino." After a pause he added, "*Real* good day."

A half hour later, the paperwork complete, Cole accepted two sets of keys from Timm and they shook hands again outside the front entrance. Cole would register the vehicle in Canada using the address for the Hamilton apartment. He didn't have insurance yet—he'd work on that after returning from his errand in Ohio—but if stopped for any reason by a police officer he'd show the title and explain the registration and insurance documents hadn't yet arrived in the mail. If that didn't suffice, well, he had the .45.

He would return to the Embassy Suites and make final preparations for his departure Saturday morning. He wanted to do more research on the Hulls. The Traverse started, its engine sounding powerful and efficient. Cole saw that the fuel tank was just over half full. He picked up his phone and found the number for Dinosaur Bar-B-Que.

I think I'll have another go at that full rack of ribs. Got my appetite back.

On Thursday morning after returning from the run with the ladies, Paul made coffee and settled in the recliner to dig back into the Drabik material. There seemed to be two versions of what occurred immediately after Alex reached the far side of the Ludendorff Bridge.

In one, the sergeant fired on German soldiers, joining with his comrades in clearing the area around the bridge approach. In the other, though, Drabik is said to have motioned for a surrendering German to accompany him and his squad as they assumed a position 200 yards north of the bridge and dug in, preparing for a counterattack.

Paul sipped his coffee. *Hmmm. Why would—*

His cellphone rang. It was Rita Kekich.

"Good morning Agent Kekich." He paused for a quick second then asked, "What happened?"

Kekich gave a short laugh before beginning. "Nothing earth-shattering, I'm afraid...which might be a good thing as far as you're concerned. We located the car Jelcik stole from the house in Toledo. It was in a parking lot at the Columbus Airport."

Paul thought for a second. "He flew somewhere?"

"No, but he did leave Columbus." Kekich explained how the FBI had traced the fugitive's path from the airport to the bus station. "He took a Greyhound to Buffalo, New York Saturday morning. We're going with the assumption that Jelcik may try to cross into Canada. We've alerted Canadian officials and we're moving significant assets into the Buffalo area."

Paul asked, "How sure are you?"

"We were eighty percent yesterday. Today," she paused, "ninety-five percent. He's there. We have a sniff of him now. We'll pull out all the stops in Buffalo. I just wanted to notify you. We know you've put your life on hold since that... *journalist* started posting your information online." The word had perhaps never been used in a more pejorative fashion.

"Great news, Agent Kekich. We'll be following the hunt. Hope you get him soon and none of your people get hurt." Then, "It'll be nice to have things get back to normal around here."

Kekich disconnected the call and walked to Foxx's office. She rapped once on the doorframe and waited for her boss to react. Foxx was sitting at his desk, leaning in toward his computer screen. Without looking up he spoke one word, "Come."

"I just notified Hull." Kekich approached the desk and settled into a chair.

Foxx looked up. "Good. He sound relieved?"

"Actually, yes. I was a little surprised."

Foxx raised an eyebrow. "Why is that?"

Kekich explained, "I thought there was a possibility that a guy like Hull might look forward to going head to head with Jelcik."

Foxx considered. "He's more than capable of taking care of himself. Just the same, I don't think he goes looking for a fight. I think he'll be happy to let us take it from here."

They were discussing which task force members to send to Buffalo when Remick entered the office. He didn't knock. Without being asked he sat in the second chair in front of the desk.

"Come in, Scott." Foxx said it with an amused look on his face. Remick, as was his habit, eschewed established FBI customs, even when walking into another office.

He began without preamble. "I was just talking to one of my compadres in Quantico..."

Kekich interrupted, "You have compadres?"

Deadpan, Remick nodded, "I have beaucoup compadres."

Kekich gave a short laugh. "Compadres is Spanish, beaucoup is French. You're mixing metaphors."

Remick smiled, "This from a Colorado girl who talks like a Hawaiian?"

Foxx broke up their banter. "*Anyway*...what's up?"

"So, late yesterday Ricardo Maroney was cleared of all charges."

Foxx and Kekich regarded him with blank looks. Ricardo Maroney was wanted for the execution-style murder of an armored car driver in Arizona. He had, so far as they could determine, absolutely nothing to do with the Jelcik case.

Remick continued. "Information has come to light that Maroney was definitely in Alabama at the time of the murder. An informant in Phoenix has fingered another suspect."

Foxx asked, "So?"

"So Maroney is being removed from our Ten Most Wanted list."

The FBI Ten Most Wanted Fugitives list was instituted in 1950 following a conversation between FBI Director J. Edgar Hoover and William Kinsey Hutchinson, editor-in-chief of the International News Service. The intent was to raise public awareness of the fugitives and increase law enforcement's ability to capture them.

Kekich interrupted, "Well, that breaks the tie."

"What the hell are you talking about?" Foxx was becoming annoyed with the seemingly irrelevant track of the conversation.

"There have only been ten women on the list...ever. Until Maroney was cleared there had only been ten suspects removed from the list because the charges were dropped."

Remick nodded.

Foxx spread his hands. "I don't see how this has anything to do with our hunt for Jelcik."

Remick explained. "It does...because my contact says it looks like Cole Jelcik will take Maroney's place on the list."

Kekich quickly shifted her head back an inch and raised her eyebrows.

"Wow, our boy just made the big time."

After speaking to Kekich, Paul weighed his options.

I can stick around here, keep an eye on Lauren, or I can get back to work. I wonder if my appointments for next week have been canceled?

He decided to do some checking. First he called Charlie Hunter to see if his hotel reservations were still in effect. Told that they were, Paul asked her to leave things as is until he could have a discussion with Lauren.

Next he called Marge McClary.

"Have you canceled the appointments in Pittsburgh yet?"

"I'm putting together an email right now. Should have it ready to send in a few minutes."

Paul deliberated. "Maybe hold off for now."

Marge was confused. "Really? Why?"

"I just heard from the FBI. Jelcik is in Buffalo. Sounds like they're closing in on him."

"*Buffalo?*" She paused. "That's good, right?"

"For us, yes. For Buffalo...not so much. Anyway, I haven't talked to Lauren yet but I might still make the trip. If I do I'll need some more samples."

Marge seemed to brighten. "Why don't you and Lauren come down to our place Saturday night. We're having brisket sandwiches. You can grab the samples. We can have a fire, maybe invite the Dowdells."

"Sounds great, Marge. Plan on us coming by. I'll talk to Lauren and let you know about next week."

When Lauren got home from work Thursday night Paul related the new development in the FBI manhunt. When he finished he posed a question. "So I was thinking, maybe, if you feel okay with it, I go ahead and make the trip to Pittsburgh next week. You don't have to answer now, you—"

Lauren perked up. "YES, yes go to Pennsylvania!"

Paul was mystified. "You're okay with that?"

"For God's sake, Paul, you're cramping our style during the morning runs! Lacey is getting married in nine days and we're dragging you through the streets of Piqua with us. We haven't been able to have quality girl talk since you joined us. Go...go to Pennsylvania!"

CHAPTER FORTY

Cole pulled the Traverse out of the Seneca One Stop gas and convenience store Saturday morning and steered toward the entrance ramp for I-80. He would stick to this route until it reached a point several miles northeast of Pittsburgh near Williamsburg, Pennsylvania. From there I-80 bent due west and eventually entered Ohio near Youngstown.

Wish I had a number for Dom's buddy Tony Valenti. I'd ask for a job application.

At the Seneca station Cole had topped off the tank of the Traverse outside before heading into the store. He made sure to hear the chirp of the remote door locks. The three backpacks full of cash were in the back seat. The .45 pistol was resting under the front seat where it was within easy reach. Inside the store Cole bought an array of snacks, a Gatorade, a large coffee, and the last four cans of Copenhagen visible in the display rack above the cashier.

It was 8:40 a.m. and it had already been a productive day. He'd gathered his few possessions and stuffed them inside one of the backpacks. While checking out of the hotel he thanked the young woman at the desk for allowing him to keep a second vehicle in their parking garage the night before.

"Absolutely Mr. Gullickson! Please come back and see us!"

Cole—wearing the Titlcist visor, jeans, and the black Dinosaur Bar-B-Que mechanic shirt that showed off his biceps —beamed. His polar blue eyes seemed to draw the attention of anyone he spoke to—especially the women.

"Will do," he eyed her nametag, "Cici."

Cole stashed the backpacks in the Traverse, pulling the cargo shade cover over them to hide them from view. He then drove the rented Yukon back to the Hertz location before walking quickly back to the Traverse.

371

He'd decided to take the route down through Pennsylvania rather than the shorter drive along the southern rim of Lake Erie. His chosen drive would take considerably longer—seven and a half hours rather than six—but there would be no tollbooths. This meant no cameras. He was relatively sure he was still well free of the FBI but decided there was no reason to take a chance.

Cole was already thinking several moves ahead. After he'd taken care of Hull he intended to drive due north on I-75 and make his way into Canada at Windsor, Ontario. He would then drive east until finally reaching Hamilton and the new apartment.

Why drive back up through Buffalo? That's where the FBI will be looking for me.

He'd worked out the sequence in his head. Most of it. He knew how it would play out, how and where it would end. He just didn't know how long it would take. He needed access to Hull's wife. Once that happened Hull would have no choice. He would have to follow instructions. Cole was sure that a man like Hull was willing to put himself in harm's way to save his wife. He counted on it.

The night before, Cole had searched further on the web and found that the picture on the *Dirty Toledo* website of Hull standing at a lectern was taken in Columbus at the National Veterans Memorial and Museum. He smiled.

Right in my back yard.

Cole now had the site for the endgame. He moved on to other details. He would need a burner phone, one he could use for a few days before discarding. That was no problem. There were dozens—maybe hundreds—of places he could stop to buy one between Buffalo and Troy. He would pick one up somewhere in Pennsylvania or Ohio when he stopped again for gas.

He also needed a place to hole up while stalking the wife. It could take a week, possibly longer. Ideally it would be somewhere off the beaten path...and not *too* close to Hull's home. Cole had used Google Earth to view a satellite image of the Hull house outside of Troy.

Thank you, Dirty Toledo and Muncy What's-Your-Name for giving me the address.

He found the perfect place. Twenty miles north of Hull's place, just outside of Sidney, was a weather-beaten, single-story motor inn called the Motel LaBelle. It didn't have a website but Cole found pictures on *yelp.com* that showed a thoroughly depressing L-shaped building with no interior hallways. The doors opened directly to the outside and—theoretically—to a less dismal future. It had easy access to and from I-75, sitting just 300 yards north of an exit on County Road 25A. A search online showed mentions in the Shelby County Sheriff's log for drug arrests, assaults, and reports of overdoses.

Yeah...perfect!

Cole called and reserved a room for a week, casually mentioning that he would be in town to work on a construction project. The disinterested woman on the desk phone took down the numbers of one of his debit cards. Cole noted that the price he was charged for the week was barely more than he'd paid for one night at the Embassy Suites in Buffalo.

Cole made it to Ohio and passed through Youngstown and Akron. He listened to country stations on the radio and made a mental note to activate SiriusXM as soon as he set up shop in Canada. He missed Outlaw Country. Fifteen minutes after passing Akron he jumped on southbound I-71 and pushed through another 20 miles before pulling off at Ashland. He had driven just over 250 miles.

He topped off the tank then walked quickly inside looking for the restroom. He was grateful to see that it was unoccupied and proceeded to relieve his bladder for a full minute.

There was a Walmart nearby and he spent fewer than ten minutes inside buying a phone, a set of binoculars, a half dozen sheets of lime green poster board, and an assortment of markers. He hurried out, anxious to leave a building with

373

security cameras and concerned about leaving the backpacks in the Traverse. Before getting back on the highway he cruised the drive-thru at a joint called The Burger Den and ordered something called a Feel the Burn Burger with onion rings and a Diet Coke.

Gonna be hard to get down to Cormier Gullickson's playing weight eating this stuff.

When the food was handed to him, he sat the bags on the passenger seat. The Diet Coke went into one cup holder, a can of Copenhagen—in ready position—in the second.

The Traverse rolled back down the ramp to I-71 at 1:45. An hour later it approached the I-270 beltway that circled Columbus.

Memories of Dom and Tanner swam through Cole's head as he skirted the city. A kaleidoscope turned in his head, flashing through scenes from the weightlifting area in the Klean Sooner work bay, the Arnold Sports Festival, and the twin F-150 pickup trucks. Some, like Tanner bitching about the parking garage jobs, brought a smile to Cole's face. In his mind's eye he saw Dom's reaction to Tanner's errant throw on the Ohio State baseball field and laughed out loud. Inevitably, though, the kaleidoscope stopped on the scene of a bleeding Tanner being battered by Hull.

The smile disappeared. Cole wiped his eyes and drove on.

He followed the beltway to the west side of the city where it merged with I-70. Now heading west toward Dayton, Cole felt some reluctance leaving Columbus. This had nothing to do with thoughts of the past. It was because he had some tasks to complete in the city before he delivered the final payback to Hull. He glanced at the city skyline in his rearview.

I'll be back.

He allowed himself a small smile, realizing his thought was a classic line spoken by Arnold Schwarzenegger in *The Terminator*.

An hour later he reached Dayton and merged onto I-75. He'd driven north just 15 minutes when he saw a sign indicating Troy was five miles ahead. He'd entered the Motel

LaBelle address into his navigation system with little thought to the Hulls' relative location. Now he was within a few miles of their place. He couldn't resist doing a drive-by.

Cole pulled off at the first Troy exit and ducked into a gas station parking lot. He punched the address—880 Polecat Road—into the system and saw he was just minutes away. Following tree-lined streets to the center of town, Cole negotiated a traffic circle that surrounded a large water fountain. He drove south for two miles, leaving the city limits, and saw the turn for Polecat on the right.

Cole, his heart rate quickening, took the turn. There was a horse farm on the right. It was surrounded with pearl white fencing that contrasted with the green grass of June that had not yet turned brown under the early summer sun. A partial canopy of trees shaded Polecat for a half-mile until the road bent to the left, out of Cole's line of sight. Farm fields were visible through the trees on the left. Gravel driveways emerged through them on the right. Cole cruised slowly to the third drive and noted the *You Have Arrived At Your Destination* notification on the navigation system screen. He hit "end."

Passing the drive Cole saw a single-story house with a garage on the left. The garage door was up and two SUVs—one grey, one white—were visible. An older black pickup truck was parked outside the garage, off to one side. Cole continued east on Polecat until it curved to the northeast. Just as he was out of sight from Hull's house he swung the Traverse into a farm lane and reversed course. The view of the house from this direction was virtually clear of trees. As Cole approached he saw a man and a woman emerge from the house and get into the white SUV. His view of the man was fleeting, but Cole was sure. It was the man who pummeled Tanner.

Hull!

He reached under his seat for the .45. Before closing his hand around the grip he knew it was a terrible idea. A car had appeared in his rearview mirror, winding through the curve. Cole's fingers touched the cold steel of the pistol, hesitated, and rose back to the steering wheel.

He headed for Sidney.

Paul skipped the morning run with the ladies Friday. This was due to two factors: Jelcik was two states away with the FBI closing the net, and Lauren and Lacey obviously wanted to start their day without the testosterone that he apparently brought to the table. Still, he followed Lauren's progress on Find My iPhone on his phone. Lauren had insisted they add the app to their phones when Paul began to spend more time out on his bike. Paul rarely checked on her, but did so today.

He prepped for the Pittsburgh trip for a good part of the day and worked in a long bike ride. That night he and Lauren started the latest season of *Reacher* on Netflix and finished three episodes. They made popcorn and—other than the several times Chappy stood on the cabinet under the TV and stretched up to paw the screen—had an uneventful evening.

Saturday was also low-key. They worked in the yard for much of the day and split a frozen pizza for lunch, saving room for the bigger meal they would have at the McClary house later in the day. They showered and dressed for the evening. It was late afternoon when they pulled out of the garage in Lauren's Jeep.

The get-together at the McClarys' was enjoyable. Gatewood and his wife, Roberta, brought Kentucky football t-shirts for the Hulls and Mike and Marge. The sandwiches were excellent and Mike opened a bottle of Tutor's. Paul realized he'd hardly had any of the whiskey since starting his job and mentioned it.

"Then you can consider this research, right?" Mike said this as he handed Paul a tumbler of the bourbon, a smile on his face.

They watched the fire and sipped their drinks, enjoying both. Mike added wood to the fire periodically. At one point, a half hour after sundown, he pulled two chunks of wood from a stack near the firepit and brushed past Roberta. She looked up from her seat as he passed and sucked in her breath.

"What the hell is *that*?"

She pointed up, past Mike's head. All eyes turned to see a possum tightroping across a wire 20 feet above them. The creature paused for a second and regarded them before continuing on his way. Lauren and Marge cried out, "Perry!"

Roberta gaped at them, stupefied. "What? Who?"

Gatewood laughed. "Honey, that's just Perry, he's a member of the South Park neighborhood M.S.F."

"The what?"

"The Marsupial Special Forces." The entire group burst into laughter.

Paul stuck to his limit of two bourbons, declining a third before he and Lauren said their goodbyes. As he thanked Gatewood for the shirts, Paul mentioned that he would get the Sig Sauer back to him soon.

"Hold on to it for now Sticks....You never know."

Cole walked into the office at the motel. A chubby balding man with a cigarette tucked behind his ear looked up from his cellphone and raised an eyebrow. "Help you?"

"Yeah, checking in...Gullickson."

The man punched a few keys on an ancient desktop computer and squinted at the screen.

"I see you here. What's that first name...Korm-ee-er?" He attempted to pronounce it phonetically.

Cole corrected him. "Corm-ee-ay, it's French-Canadian."

The man grunted. "You say so."

He opened a desk drawer and rattled around inside before producing a room key. It was attached to a credit card-sized piece of plastic with a number stamped on one side. He slid it across the counter and, in an authoritative tone, said. "There's no smokin' in the room Corm-ee-ay."

Cole turned the plastic in his hand to see the number was either a "6" or a "9." There was no line below or above the number.

He asked, "Is that a six or a nine?"

The man gave a mocking smile and answered, "It sure is."

Cole's eyes narrowed. ""What?"

"It sure is a six or a nine." The man's smile widened.

Cole, after the events of the week and the long drive, was not having it. He felt the Jelcik temper rising.

"Look here, partner, I'm in no mood." He leaned in, putting his elbows on the counter. His biceps were now inches from the man's face, the polar blue eyes boring in. "Tell me what fucking room I have in this shithole and then stay the fuck away from me, got it?"

The man nodded. "Nine."

Cole walked out. The man in the office stared at his back as if he wanted to set him on fire.

CHAPTER FORTY-ONE

The previous year Cole dated a woman named Jade that he met at a Columbus bar frequented by bodybuilders. She was actually more into CrossFit, having been a competitive runner before developing iliotibial band syndrome and a lower leg stress fracture. Like many runners, she'd become more than a little obsessive about her daily exercise. The term "positive addiction" was a common description of this mindset. When the injuries came about, Jade attempted to power through, pushing herself through the discomfort. She told Cole she could deal with the pain but feared she would eventually do enough damage that she wouldn't be able to run at all. This was unacceptable.

She searched for another way to achieve the endorphin release offered by running and discovered CrossFit, an activity that seemed to draw participants from the mostly unrelated disciplines of running and weightlifting. That is what put her in the bar the night Cole met her.

One of the things Cole learned from her—there were many and most had nothing to do with traditional exercise—was that runners are creatures of habit. They will not only run through injuries, but are not deterred by things like shitty weather. And, most relevant to Cole now, often started their days at a ridiculous hour to get in their daily workout.

Though there were other options, Cole had determined that the most likely way to get at Hull's wife was to catch her during a run. He knew she worked in the local hospital so runs during the day were out. That left early mornings or evenings. Cole hoped for the former but was determined to make either fit into his plans.

Cole was familiar with the drive to maintain and ramp up a continuous exercise program. Both he and Tanner had it when it came to weightlifting. Even with the strain of staying ahead of the police and FBI he could feel a niggling compulsion in the back of his head, pushing him to get his ass back inside a gym. He and his brother, in fact, had been driven toward specific exercises, all involving the upper body. They spent almost all of their workout sessions concentrating on this, virtually ignoring any muscle group below the hips.

Occasionally Cole wondered what path his life would've followed if he'd been more well-rounded with his workout regimen. When he was at Southeastern Oklahoma State it was only after he'd followed the recommendation of the strength coach and worked harder on his lower body that talk of a possible NFL future began. The death of his mother and Cole's subsequent return to Bartlesville to stay with Tanner had ended that possibility. It had also marked the end of the leg workouts. Cole was left with the classic Jelcik body, an oversized upper torso supported by comparatively thin legs.

Cole secretly wondered if this tendency to practice strengths rather than work on weaknesses had somehow contributed to the disaster that his Fireteam met in Toledo. Had they become too predictable? Had the routine of stealing a vehicle from an airport somehow led the cops to them? Were Dom's scouting trips and debit card purchases somehow tracked? Should he have varied their tactics to make them more unpredictable? Cole made an effort to push these thoughts away. To face them was too painful. He might see that *he* was culpable in putting Tanner and Dom in their graves.

No, it was Hull that was responsible, at least in Tanner's case.

It was Cole's knowledge of the obsessive exercise mindset that found him sitting in a grove of trees off Polecat Road Monday at 4:30 a.m. He wanted to see if Hull's wife was a morning runner.

Cole had spent Sunday familiarizing himself with the burner phone, shopping, and looking more closely at Google Earth views of the area around Paul and Lauren Hull's house. He also spent 45 minutes experimenting with the markers and poster board he'd purchased at the Walmart in Ashland. The plan that was evolving in his head required some thought. He applied his problem solving abilities to it throughout the course of the day.

He had the phone figured out in an hour. Afterwards he drove the Traverse through Sidney for some time noting landmarks and escape routes, exactly as he'd done in Buffalo. The closest option was the ramp to I-75 that was visible outside the window of Cole's room, but there were others.

The shopping proved productive. Sidney had a Walmart on the west side of town but Cole, still leery of cameras, searched further and found a shop downtown called Ron and Nita's that sold durable work clothing and had a large selection of footwear. They were having a weekend sale and Cole spent nearly $400 on Dickies and Carhartt pants, shorts, and shirts. He also picked up a pair of size 14 New Balance cross-trainers that he felt might be more practical for his needs than the boots he'd been wearing since the robbery.

The Carhartt gear made him think of the bags he'd left inside the vault at the Fifth Third Bank. Inevitably his last memory of Tanner followed. *That goddammed Hull!*

Cole left the store carrying two large shopping bags. He stared across the street at the impressive Shelby County Courthouse before getting back in the Traverse. He needed to find a hardware store.

A few blocks north of downtown Cole spied an older two-story building that housed an Ace Hardware store. He pulled into a diagonal parking spot and entered. Fifteen minutes later he exited with a bag that held plastic zip ties, duct tape, a couple screwdrivers, and a pair of wire cutters. He picked out the roll of duct tape from a section that included several sizes and colors. He did not give Dal Harrelson a second thought when he did so.

After examining satellite views of the area around Hull's house, Cole arrived at the conclusion that there was only one location that allowed for a clear view of the place while providing a high degree of cover. This was the spot near the

381

bend in Polecat Road he'd seen the day before. The farm lane he'd pulled into to turn around actually curled behind a stand of trees before disappearing into a field that—in the photo—appeared to be planted in corn. There was no way to tell how old the photo was and Cole hadn't paid attention yesterday to the particular crop that was currently growing there.

Well, it's the only spot. Gotta get down that lane at oh dark-thirty so the Traverse is hidden.

He'd done just that. By 4:30 he was sitting in knee-high foxtail grass, tucked in close to the trunk of a mature maple tree. He had a couple protein bars left over from the drive from Buffalo, the binoculars—useless so far in the darkness—and the .45. Headlights from the occasional vehicle drove past, taking the curve at modest speeds. The Hulls' house was, he figured, a little less than a quarter-mile away.

As his eyes grew accustomed to the low light, Cole realized the field behind the trees was planted in soybeans this year. They had germinated and the shoots were just visible, defining rows that extended from his view until they disappeared into the darkness. The farm lane he'd pulled into was partially grass-covered. It stopped at the edge of the field as if absorbed. Cole decided there had once been a farmhouse here.

Must've been torn down and plowed over to expand the field.

A light came on inside the Hull house and caused the closed curtains of the front picture window to glow. Cole engaged the backlight feature of his watch, cupping his right hand over the inside of his left wrist to contain the glow. It was 5:04. He straightened and brought the binoculars to his eyes but there was not enough ambient light to allow him to see anything other than a dull, grainy, luminescence.

Eight minutes later the overhead garage door began to rise. Cole strained to hear it but succeeded in detecting only the chirping of nearby crickets. The binoculars, though, came into play. The interior garage light came on and, as the door rose, Cole could see a set of legs moving behind the two SUVs. They paused, as if waiting for the door to reach a certain height.

Cole realized it was Hull he saw, not the man's wife. Something hung at his side. Once the door was two thirds of the way up, Hull opened the liftgate on the grey SUV and swung the object into the cargo bay.

It was a suitcase.

An hour and a half later Cole coasted up the exit ramp at County Road 25A outside Sidney. The sun was up and Cole was pumped. He'd known things had come together for him when a second set of legs—these in running shorts—joined Hull in the garage. When the door had risen to its full height, both Paul and Lauren Hull were visible. Cole saw them speak for a few seconds before leaning in toward each other and kissing. Hull got into the grey SUV—a Ford—and his wife the second vehicle, a white Jeep. Hull led the way out of the drive followed by the Jeep. Both vehicles turned left and drove away from Cole's position. He hustled to the Traverse and followed, waiting until he was on Polecat to turn on his headlights.

Both Hull vehicles stopped at the next intersection. Cole trailed slowly, a quarter-mile back. The Ford turned left. The Jeep, after waiting for a few seconds, turned right. Cole smiled.

He followed the Jeep for ten minutes, eventually reaching the town of Piqua. After negotiating a series of turns, the Jeep pulled to a stop outside of a YWCA on Wayne Street.

Didn't know they still existed.

Cole drove past the Jeep to an intersection—Greene Street—pulled into a driveway a half block later, and reversed course back toward the Y. He eased to the curb and picked up the binoculars.

Hull's wife—Lauren—stood on the sidewalk, stretching.

Hmmm, pretty lady. Too bad she picked the wrong man to marry.

Two minutes later a second runner came around the corner on Greene from the right. Cole saw Lauren's face brighten as she approached. The women embraced for a quick second and the newcomer joined Lauren in stretching. This was a younger woman. Cole's powers of perception were triggered.

They act like sisters...maybe an aunt and a niece? Hmmm.

Presently the pair stopped stretching and each brought a hand toward her face. Cole saw the glowing screens of smartphones, saw the women peck at them, and watched as they began their run. They took off around the corner, heading west, and Cole laid the binoculars on the passenger seat. As he eased around the corner to follow the runners, Cole couldn't help remembering the last time he saw multiple digital devices start simultaneously. It was the moment he and Tanner left Dom in the stolen Sonata outside of the bank in Toledo, all three of them starting their stopwatches. He set his jaw and narrowed his eyes.

Cole followed the women as best he could. They both wore reflective vests, which was helpful. When they disappeared into a large cemetery he pulled to the curb again and switched off the ignition. They emerged several minutes later and he continued to follow at a distance. The pair finished the run with a sprint on Greene and stopped when they reached Wayne. They chatted for a minute or two—breathing hard— then Hull's wife entered the YWCA. Her running partner jogged slowly back west on Greene. As far as Cole could tell they never stopped talking the entire run. This he took as a good sign. They seemed to be preoccupied with their conversation. Cole knew runners were creatures of habit and tended to run the same routes over and over.

He drove back to Sidney, pondering options. Now coming to a stop at the end of the ramp Cole could see the Motel LaBelle to the left, a tired relic from another era. He looked right and saw a Marathon gas station a half-mile in that direction. He went right.

Inside the station Cole bought a large coffee and several more protein bars. He glanced at a rack holding newspapers. Walking over, he picked up the paper on top, the *Dayton Daily News*. It was thick, consisting of several folded sections. He smiled and grabbed a handful off the top of the stack.

"Them's yesterday's." The woman was in her fifties. She had bleached white hair and a severe expression.

Cole turned to the counter, holding his food and the newspapers. Before he could say anything she continued.

"Them papers...them's Sun-dee's."

Cole nodded, slightly mimicking her speech. "Yep. I always like gettin' the Sundee papers. Lotsa coupons."

Then, "Y'all got any rubber bands back there?"

386

CHAPTER FORTY-TWO

Lauren woke up the following morning at 4:45. She checked the weather and saw it was 71 degrees outside with an expected high of 83. She opened a can of cat food for Chappy and was thanked in return when the feline performed a long, languid stretch and reached his front paws halfway up her leg. She smiled and scratched under his chin, then left him to his meal as she returned to the bedroom to dress for her run.

Lauren selected running socks and shorts. She pulled a short-sleeved shirt made with a wicking material over a sports bra, then sat on the bed and slipped on her shoes. They were Hokas. She owned several pairs. Most were worn to the lab—some workdays required her to spend hours on her feet—but this pair was reserved for running. Lauren found them extremely comfortable. She grabbed her keys and phone, gave Chappy another scratch, and was out the door.

Her reflective vest hung on a hook in the garage. She slipped it on and hit the button to the garage door. She started the Jeep, backed out of the garage, and angled the vehicle toward Paul's 1989 Ford Lariat parked outside on a concrete extension to the driveway. She was careful not to hit the pickup—it had served them well in the past. Stopping short of it, she turned the wheel and headed toward the road, pushing the button on the garage door opener as she went. She left the concrete and heard the crackle of her tires on the gravel portion of the drive. Reaching Polecat Road she stopped, checked both ways for headlights, and eased the Jeep to the left.

She did not notice the silver Chevy Traverse pull out of the farm lane several hundred yards back.

Cole had considered taking the woman at the house. He could wait outside the garage in the shadows and spring inside the moment the garage door went up. But he wasn't one hundred percent sure that Hull wasn't home. He had no way of knowing how prepared a former Combat Controller might be for an intruder. Would the house be bristling with weapons? He thought of the interior of the house owned by the gun dealer in Arkansas—Donny Ritler—that he and Tanner robbed before moving to Ohio. It looked like the inside of an ordnance depot. He didn't figure Hull for an extremist but respected his abilities and thought it best to avoid a confrontation at the house.

When the door rose to reveal just one vehicle inside the garage he knew he'd missed an opportunity. Hull was gone. Cole could've taken the woman at the house. The fact that Hull was unaccounted for complicated the situation. He had a bead on Lauren, but the ultimate goal was Hull himself.

I'll work it out.

The Jeep started and began to back out almost immediately. Cole, from his position near the farm lane, had no chance to reach the house before the Jeep pulled out. No matter, he'd planned on taking care of business in Piqua.

Lauren made the drive to Piqua automatically. A half-mile from the house she stopped at Piqua-Troy Road. She'd followed Paul here yesterday morning, pausing a few seconds to watch him drive toward Troy and the highway beyond. He wanted to get an early start to Pittsburgh and got up with her. He hoped to finish with his meetings in time to return to Troy sometime Wednesday.

Lauren turned right and then, a quarter-mile later, took a left on Eldean Road. This leg, too, was short. She passed an old covered bridge, crossed the Great Miami River, and caught a red light at North County Road 25A. She engaged her right turn signal and waited as a lone car approached from the left. Her thoughts wandered to her phone conversation with Paul the night before.

He'd made it to Pittsburgh in time for his first appointment at 10 a.m. It was, he said, at a bar named Hemingway's Café on Forbes Avenue near the University of Pittsburgh.

"I gotta say, I was pretty excited when I saw that name."

Lauren was confused. Paul was a reader but had never shown much of an interest in the author of *The Old Man and the Sea*.

She queried, "Hemingway?"

"No, Forbes. The bar is right down the street from the site of the Pirates' old ballpark, Forbes Field. It's not there anymore—well, most of it—they tore it down years ago but left up the section of the left field wall that Bill Mazeroski's home run went over in Game 7 of the 1960 World Series." Then, apparently realizing he was rambling, asked in a more subdued voice, "Uh, you know about that, right?"

"No idea."

Paul laughed. "I'll tell you about it sometime. Anyway, the section of the wall is on the University of Pittsburgh campus. My hotel's less than a mile away. I think I'll get up early tomorrow and go for a run...go check out the wall, get a few pictures."

Lauren rolled her eyes. *Get up early to go take pictures of a wall?* Then she remembered who she was talking to—a man that had no selfies on his phone but dozens of pictures of gravestones and historical markers.

"Sounds like that's right up your alley, Paul."

The car passed through the intersection just as the light changed. Lauren made the right turn and headed north into Piqua, remembering the rest of the conversation. She'd asked Paul what he had planned for Monday night.

"I think I'll go downtown and check out Primanti Bros. It's a restaurant that's been there forever...famous for their sandwiches."

Lauren smiled, "Now *that* I've heard of. Sounds fun... enjoy."

Lauren negotiated the streets of Piqua and reached the YWCA a few minutes before 5:30. She exited the Jeep, locked it, and tucked the key fob into a pocket sewn into the waistband of her shorts. She had her house key attached to a ring on the fob, making it a tight fit in the small pocket. She was adjusting the strap that held her phone to her left hand and walking to the corner when Lacey appeared.

Lauren's face brightened. "Hey Little Sis, you're a couple minutes early today."

Lacey's smile mirrored Lauren's. "Couldn't wait...my wedding dress is ready...*finally!* They finished the alterations. I picked it up last night. I was so afraid it wouldn't be ready for this weekend!"

"Oh wow, only five days before the wedding. Talk about cutting it close. How did it come out?"

Lacey beamed, "Let me tell you." She started the running app on her smartphone and began to jog to the corner. "This might take a while."

Cole watched from a block south of the YWCA. When the women disappeared from his view he put the SUV in gear and swung through an intersection. He pointed the Traverse west on Ash Street, which ran parallel to Greene. He drove for ten blocks through a neighborhood that consisted of several dozen wood-framed two-story houses and a sprinkling of churches. Despite having to pause at several stop signs, he pulled steadily away from the runners. Ash T'd into Lincoln and Cole took a right, then another right on Greene. He pulled to the curb, letting the engine run and not switching off the headlights.

He waited and watched for movement. He knew his headlights would illuminate the reflective vests the women wore. Cole checked his surroundings and saw little evidence of activity. A light showed through a window three houses down on the left, another on the second floor of a house further down on the right. Cars were parked randomly along the curb on both sides of the street. Cole's front driver's side window was down. He could smell the fragrance of lilacs coming from a source nearby. Somewhere a dog barked.

A minute later he detected movement. He saw two vests in the distance. They bobbed up and down like apparitions, seeming to float slowly in his direction. From this distance—four blocks—Cole could see only the vests. Thirty seconds passed and the women took form. They were in the street, side-by-side, running into the non-existent traffic. The younger woman, who was slightly shorter than Hull's wife, was closest to the curb. Lauren was running on the woman's right side, closer to the center of the street. He watched as the pair swung wide around parked cars and eased back toward the curb.

Cole pulled on the floppy hat he'd taken from Dal Harrelson's garage in Toledo and checked the Ron and Nita's shopping bags in the passenger seat. He made a slight adjustment to the pistol tucked into his belt near his navel. *All good.*

He turned on the Traverse's flashers and pulled away from the curb, reaching into a shopping bag as he did so.

Cole set his jaw.

Game time.

Lacey and Matt were from Edon, Ohio, a village of fewer than a thousand people tucked into the northwest corner of the state. The closest Ohio city was Toledo, 70 miles east. Fort Wayne, across the Indiana border, was 20 miles closer. Lacey had picked out a dress from a bridal boutique shop in Fort Wayne months earlier. Alterations were necessary and she was told the dress would be ready well before the wedding. Despite several increasingly frantic calls to the shop, the alterations weren't complete until yesterday. Lacey drove from the hospital in Troy to Fort Wayne immediately after her workday ended to pick it up.

"But the fit is *perfect* now! This is such a load off my mind."

They were making their way along Greene Street. Lacey, excited as she related details about the dress, was a half step ahead of Lauren. As they approached parked cars Lacey eased to her right. Lauren followed, unconsciously dropping back a step so as not to be running in the middle of the street. There was little traffic in the morning but Lauren knew that the few cars they encountered were sometimes operated by drivers with morning eyes that weren't as sharp as they would be later in the day. Then there was the newspaper deliveryman who seemed to think that traffic regulations didn't apply to him as long as his flashers were on.

The women had seen the man pilot his battered pickup truck through the early morning streets now for months. He would pull to a stop at the curb, toss a rolled-up Dayton Daily News out of a window to a driveway or sidewalk in front of a customer's house, and speed to the next address on his list. Sometimes, when the intended target area was the sidewalk a few feet away, the man would flip the paper through the passenger side of the truck. When his desired landing spot was more distant—up a driveway—he would lob the newspaper out of the driver's side window like a hand grenade.

"I didn't know the difference between a portrait and a sweetheart neckline...so many choices!" Lacey veered around a parked station wagon. Lauren followed.

Lauren was interested. "So which did you pick?" She saw a vehicle a block ahead with flashers moving in their direction.

Lacey giggled. "Neither. I just went with a V-neck. I asked Matt what he thought...but you know men."

Lauren smiled as she regulated her breathing between comments. Lacey was running a bit faster than normal this morning. The subject matter seemed to have injected added energy to her pace. "Let me guess, he had no opinion." The delivery driver was now half a block away.

Lacey nodded as she ran. "You got that right. It was hard enough to get him fitted for his tux. There was no way he was going to get involved in dress details." Then, "Hey, looks like our newspaper delivery guy got a new vehicle."

Lauren watched as they closed the distance. There seemed to be other differences as well. The man was lobbing papers out the driver's side at each stop, none through the passenger side. He also seemed to be stopping at each house.

"Not sure that's our same guy. Looks like he's tossing papers at every house... Maybe some kind of advertising thingy?" Lauren turned her attention back to Lacey and the dress. "So does it have a train?"

The vehicle with flashers—it was a large SUV—paused two houses ahead as the driver pitched a tube-shaped roll into the front yard. It pulled back into the street and leapfrogged around a parked motorcycle before dipping back, halting behind a small red sedan.

Lacey's focus went back to the dress as well. "Well, a short one...not too, uh, *princessy*...certainly not long enough that I'll need attendants." She angled to her right to pass the red sedan, her eyes on the flashers of the SUV to its rear. It appeared that the driver had seen them and was waiting for them to pass.

Lauren fell in behind Lacey as they cleared the sedan. The flashers inhibited her vision slightly but she saw the driver's arm loft a newspaper over the roof of the SUV. The paper caught in the branches of an ornamental tree still three quarters full of pinkish springtime blossoms. Lauren frowned as she watched.

The rest happened too fast for her to follow.

Cole moved steadily toward the runners. He'd rolled up sections of the Sunday newspapers and slipped on rubber bands, filling up the shopping bags. He tossed one out the window in front of each house. As he pulled back to the street he looked for a likely spot to make his move and saw a hundred foot gap between a motorcycle and a small red car up ahead.

That's my spot.

He flung a paper over the roof of the Traverse and pulled around the motorcycle before easing to within ten feet of the red car. He put the Traverse in park. His senses heightened, Cole collected and processed information at an increased rate. He saw his flashers rhythmically lighting the approaching reflective vests on the runners and even noted a University of

393

Dayton sticker on the rear window of the red car. He again detected a lilac fragrance, stronger now, and subconsciously knew it was coming from the tree to his right. He had another paper in his hand now and chucked it out the window, unconcerned with its path.

Cole had planned to the smallest detail. He made sure all of the doors on the Traverse were unlocked. He had several large zip ties in his right rear pocket, their ends within easy reach. He also had an eight-inch strip of duct tape hanging from the bottom of his door mirror. It flapped in the air stream as he drove between houses. Cole had allowed himself a smile when he'd place it there. He'd bent the leading edge of the roll back over itself before stowing it in the glove box.

Thank you Dal Harrelson.

As the last rolled newspaper settled into the tree, Cole drew the pistol with his right hand and threw open the door with his left. The younger woman in the lead was barely a step from him. He could see in her eyes that she'd detected his movement but it hadn't yet registered in her brain. In the split second before it did, Cole swung his left fist in an arc and connected with the right side of her jaw. Her forward momentum contributed to the kinetic energy of the blow and her head snapped back and bounced off her left shoulder. Her upper body limboed back as her feet rose, her legs reaching a near-horizontal position at the same height as Cole's waist before following her upper body backward toward the red car.

Cole heard, but did not see, her head strike the rear bumper of the car and her body crumple to the ground. He was already moving to Hull's wife with the pistol up. He saw to her credit that she'd instantly realized the danger and was already beginning to turn to escape while opening her mouth to scream.

"Not a fucking sound."

He hissed the command. The pistol was inches from Lauren's face.

As she flinched, wide-eyed, Cole barked, "You run and I shoot you. Then I shoot her." He swung the pistol to Lacey's still form behind the red car.

As Lauren struggled to process the situation, Cole grabbed her by the front of her shirt and jerked her toward the Traverse. The reflective vest came loose and hung on one shoulder as Lauren was spun to the front left fender and pinned against it. Cole snatched the strip of duct tape from the outer mirror and roughly pressed it over Lauren's face, trapping strands of her hair underneath on both sides.

Lauren had no time to react to the attack. She saw Lacey go down and instinctively turned to flee. She began to scream but the man—it had to be Jelcik—was on her. He threatened her, and more importantly Lacey, before she felt herself being propelled against the SUV and the tape covering her mouth. It had taken less than three seconds for these events to occur and Lauren knew it might already be too late for her to survive the incident. Her training, though, kicked in.

Lauren had attended a number of self-defense classes in the military. These had served as the foundation for additional techniques Paul had stressed. He emphasized a quick reaction, saying it was important to use any weapon available and to overcome the natural human tendency to avoid harming another person. *If it comes to it, it'll be you or the attacker, Lauren...don't let it be you.*

She fumbled for the key fob in her waistband with her dominant right hand, tearing the pocket completely from her shorts. Her back was to the attacker. She gripped the key fob so her house key protruded from her fist and thrust it backwards over her right shoulder in hopes of catching him in the eye.

Cole pushed the pistol back inside his belt and reached for a zip tie. He grabbed Lauren's left forearm with his left hand and wrenched it back. At the same time his right hand, with the zip tie, was coming up to do the same to her other wrist. If his hand hadn't already been moving he may have lost an eye. He saw the flashers from the Traverse reflect off the key in Lauren's hand as it drove back toward his face. His hand caught Lauren's wrist with the key two inches from the polar blue contact lens of his right eye.

Cole pulled down violently on Lauren's wrist, hearing a popping sound in her shoulder followed by a muffled cry of pain. The key fob dropped to the road and Cole quickly pressed her wrists together. He realized her iPhone was attached to her left hand, impairing his ability to get the tie on properly. He tore it away, snapping the elastic strap and causing another expression of pain from Lauren. He stuffed the phone into the pocket of his sweatshirt. Now able to attach the makeshift wrist cuffs, he frog-marched her to the rear door of the SUV, threw it open, and pushed her inside face first. He quickly zip-tied her ankles together and covered her with a blanket he'd taken from his motel room.

Cole slammed the door—harder than he'd planned, he wanted to keep sound to a minimum—jumped behind the wheel, and pulled away from the curb. He eased past the still form of the bride-to-be and pulled out onto Greene Street. Turning off the flashers, he accelerated to the speed limit, his eyes darting from one mirror to the next looking for threats.

It had taken 19 seconds.

CHAPTER FORTY-THREE

Paul sat on his hotel room floor and bent his left knee. He gently tugged on his foot and felt resistance in the muscles of his thigh. He was always hesitant to put too much strain on the leg. He'd broken it in a devastating parachute accident, an event that eventually ended his military career. His therapists told him the broken femur was now good as new but the surrounding muscles, built up by countless hours of rehabilitation and exercise, needed to be properly stretched before strenuous workouts. Paul did this—most of the time.

He found his way to the lobby and stepped through the automatic door to discover a sunny morning. A light breeze pushed puffy white clouds to the east. Paul took a deep breath and set off. The Mazeroski wall was a mile away, tucked into what is now Schenley Plaza on the University of Pittsburgh main campus. The Plaza—a one-acre green space shoehorned between several campus buildings—occupied part of the former site of Forbes Field, the one-time home of the Pittsburgh Pirates. Paul made his way to the Plaza, telling himself he had two reasons to run.

The first was the wall. Paul had seen the replay of the home run dozens of times. "Maz," the Pirates' slick-fielding second baseman, sent New York Yankees pitcher Ralph Terry's one-ball, no-strike offering over the left field wall in the bottom of the ninth inning of the seventh and deciding game of the 1960 World Series. The black and white video showed Mazeroski, a future member of Baseball's Hall of Fame, rounding the bases while windmilling his batting helmet in his right hand. The 10-9 Pirates victory set off an epic celebration.

Paul's second reason was more mundane. He wanted to burn some calories. The night before he'd driven to Primanti Bros. Much like his visit to Tony Packo's in Toledo, Paul preferred the original location, not one of the spin-offs. He found the brick building at 46 18ᵗʰ Street and proceeded to down one of their famous sandwiches along with a couple Iron City beers. He'd gone full-bore Pittsburgh.

The sandwich—Italian bread, choice of meat, vinegar coleslaw, tomato, melted provolone, topped with French fries —must've had an astronomical calorie count. Paul ordered his with roast beef and enjoyed every bite, figuring he would, as they say in the military, "pay the man" in the morning. He was now doing just that.

Paul arrived at his destination and found there were actually two sections of wall remaining. Both were brick and appeared to be roughly 15 feet tall. One was a lengthy portion that had run from left-center to straightaway center field. This section was in its original location. Another smaller section was the portion that had been cleared by the home run. Its distance from home plate was painted on it in white—406 FT. Paul was disappointed to see that it had been moved slightly from its original location. A bronze plaque in a nearby sidewalk marked the original spot.

Still, he thought it was cool. He walked up to the wall and touched the bricks. Turning, he tried to imagine the scene in 1960. He pulled his phone from his pocket and brought up the video, feeling a bit of a chill run up his spine when Mazeroski connected. After taking a few pictures, Paul set off. He wondered vaguely if the wall had its own website, then laughed at the thought.

There's something Lauren would roll her eyes to.

The thought of his wife brought Paul back to the present. He felt relieved knowing Cole Jelcik was not a threat to her. Granted, he had not yet been apprehended, but Paul had made another call to the FBI Sunday night to check for developments. This time he was patched through to Tyson Foxx, who said he was home, watching the San Francisco Giants game on ESPN.

"Sorry to bother you Agent Foxx, I didn't know they were putting me through to you."

Foxx sighed in exasperation, "No problem Paul, don't worry about it. My Giants just blew the lead in Atlanta. Their catcher, Murphy, hit a bases loaded triple. Their *catcher.*"

Paul laughed. "Ouch."

Foxx changed the subject. "I assume you're calling for an update on Jelcik?"

"Yeah, I'm supposed to go out of town in the morning and just wanted—"

"A sitrep, right?"

Paul confirmed Foxx's guess. "You got it."

Foxx related several facts. Jelcik, or someone that looked very similar to him, had been sighted in a number of locations in Buffalo, including a Bar-B-Que restaurant on more than one occasion. There were still some discrepancies in the reports of his physical description and—somewhat worrisome—there was as yet no concrete information on where he might be staying. Still, the leads that pointed the FBI to Buffalo in the first place were solid.

"One other thing, Paul. It will be announced tomorrow that Jelcik has been added to our Ten Most Wanted List. That can only help when it comes to tightening the net."

In the end Paul decided to make the trip. Lauren encouraged him to go.

After returning to the hotel Paul showered and dressed. He wore khaki pants with a Tutor's golf shirt. He had a number of stops to make in the area around the university and then planned to work his way east, closer to the establishments that surrounded the private college in the city, Duquesne University. Further east of this—near the confluence of the Monongahela, Allegheny, and Ohio Rivers, would be a large cluster of bars and restaurants that catered to the fans of the city's professional sports franchises.

Obie didn't say he wanted to go after Pirate, Steeler, and Penguin fans, but I'll bet he won't turn down any business I can drum up.

Paul intended to see as many people as he could that day and finish up with the remainder on Wednesday before heading home.

Cole was taking Lauren to Columbus. The quickest way there was to jump on I-75 on the west side of Piqua and take it south to I-70, then head east. Cole didn't do this. He passed over the highway and continued due east on a two-lane road, State Route 36. His reasoning was sound. If there had been witnesses to the abduction the authorities could soon be looking for his vehicle. Rather than drive on the highway, which for long stretches had no exits, he would be on a road with crossroads every mile or so. This could give him a fighting chance of eluding a pursuing cruiser. The second reason was the reputation of the Ohio State Patrol, who was responsible for law enforcement on Ohio's major highways. Cole knew them to be professional and effective. He would take his chances with the small town cops if it became necessary.

He was surprised and somewhat amused when he noticed the Piqua Post of the Patrol as he passed beyond the city limits.

Didn't know that was there...see ya later boys.

He watched the building grow smaller in his mirror.

A few miles later he turned into a small grocery store parking lot in the village of St. Paris. It was not yet 6:15 so the lot was empty. He put the SUV in park, turned in his seat, and pulled the blanket off of Lauren's head. She was still on her stomach. Her eyes bore into him showing a combination of rage and fear.

"I'm gonna pull the tape off your mouth. No one is close enough to hear you scream...so don't. If you do, you'll regret it." His eyes were cold.

Cole ripped off the tape, removing several strands of hair.

"Where is your husband?"

Lauren hesitated for the briefest of moments then snarled, "Go to hell."

Cole nodded, a slight smile on his lips. He knew he could make her talk but this wasn't the time or the place. He pushed the tape back over her mouth as she struggled to prevent it.

"Okay, let's see what your phone might tell me." He pulled it from his sweatshirt before twisting completely to face the back seat. Reaching back with the phone he found Lauren's right thumb and pressed it to the Touch ID button.

"Got it on the first try."

The screen brightened, showing rows of app icons. Cole scrolled through and saw what he was hoping to find.

"Well, well, well. Find My iPhone...Excellent!"

He touched the icon and was rewarded when a map appeared on the screen. At the bottom he read "Paul's iPhone." He couldn't tell from the scale where Hull's phone was located so pinched at the screen to expand the view.

He turned to Lauren.

"Pittsburgh? Hunh...When's he coming home?" He realized as he asked the question that Lauren couldn't answer, even if she was so inclined. He began to reach for the tape again but caught himself.

"I guess *I* control that now."

He grinned.

Larry Wilberding stepped onto his front porch and squinted through the darkness. The sun's rays were beginning to brighten the sky but his front yard was still shrouded in darkness. He thought he'd heard the newspaper delivery vehicle in front of his house a half hour earlier as he lounged in bed, half awake. He was retired, though, and would get to the paper in due time. He rolled back over to catch an extra two minutes of sleep. Two turned into 30 and Larry was awakened for good when he heard his wife Donna banging around in the kitchen downstairs.

Larry yawned, slipped into a worn pair of moccasins, and made his way downstairs. He peeked into the kitchen and drew the attention of his wife.

"Morning Larr, coffee'll be ready in a jiff."

Larry gave a grunt of acknowledgement and shuffled to the front door. He wore a pair of boxers, an old Dayton Flyers t-shirt, and a hopeful expression as he stepped onto the porch. In this digital age he still preferred a physical newspaper.

He scanned the front yard without success and was about to turn back to the house when he caught site of a tube-shaped object in the flowering redbud tree near the street.

"What in the world?"

He stepped to the concrete walk that led to the street, eyeing the object the entire way.

It IS a Dayton Paper, what—

Larry paused, seeing the body of a young woman splayed below the bumper of his Toyota.

"DONNA, CALL 9-1-1!!!"

The responding emergency squad crew made the decision within moments of arriving that Lacey needed to be transported to the nearest Level One Trauma Center, Miami Valley Hospital in Dayton, bypassing several other facilities on the way. In their efforts to get her safely on board their vehicle, the paramedics missed her phone. During the attack it had come loose from the strap on her hand and slid under the Toyota, wedging between the right front tire and the curb.

There being no witnesses to the incident and Lacey's identity being unknown, there was nothing to point to the absence of a second runner. When neither woman showed up for work at 7 a.m., calls were eventually made to their cell phones from their respective departments at Kettering Health. Lacey's was set to vibrate. From its tucked away position this noise went undetected and the calls went to voicemail. Matt had left for work minutes after Lacey started her run so had no idea what had happened. It was only after Larry Wilberding took a broom handle to his front yard in the early afternoon to dislodge the newspaper from the tree that the phone was recovered and, eventually, Lacey's identity discovered.

When the calls from the lab began they also went unanswered. But they were also greeted by a smirk. Cole Jelcik

402

glanced at the phone's screen as he continued the drive to Columbus.

Paul arrived early for his meeting with one of the owners of Shale's Bar, a brick building with a heavy wooden door. There were dozens of hockey jerseys hanging on the walls. The lunch rush was wrapping up. Paul decided to order a burger while he waited. A waiter took his order and left to get it started. Paul pulled out his phone and checked for messages. There was one from Marge McClary checking on his progress, one from a restaurant owner in West Lafayette asking about rescheduling their canceled meeting from the previous week, and one from Charlie Hunter. Her message told him the release date for the first of the Tutor's Bourbon from barrels in the Sawyer rickhouse was moved up to the Fourth of July weekend.

There was nothing from Lauren. Paul tried her number and it went directly to voicemail. This didn't raise concern since she would be at work in the lab and theoretically should only be able to answer if she were on break. But he assumed she would keep her phone close in case a development in the Jelcik case led to a call from Paul or the police. He swiped the screen to the Find My iPhone app and saw the icon that represented his wife's phone on the map east of Piqua.

What the hell?

A hint of concern tugged at his consciousness. He was about to call the desk phone at the lab when the bar owner sat in the chair across from him, a bar towel draped on one shoulder.

"You're the Tutor's guy, huh?" He held out a hand.

Paul discussed the bourbon with the man, distractedly at first. But he soon settled into the narrative. The food came and the conversation grew informal. The owner offered Paul a ticket to that night's Pirates game and Paul begged off saying he thought it might be unprofessional to accept a gift from a potential customer.

"Gift, Schmift...they're playing the goddammed Marlins. There won't be 10,000 people there. You got the MLB Ballpark app on your phone? I'll transfer the ticket now."

403

Paul left a bottle of Tutor's and walked out of Shale's with the ticket on his phone.

A free baseball game. Nice way to spend my last night in Pittsburgh...

Still, he felt just the least bit of unease about Lauren. Stepping to his SUV he felt his phone vibrate in his pocket. He saw his wife's photo on the screen and smiled.

It would be his last smile for some time.

CHAPTER FORTY-FOUR

The last thing Cole did before calling Hull on his wife's phone was to summon the image of Tanner at the cemetery in Toledo. Cole sat at a red light in downtown Columbus watching pedestrians move through the crosswalk. Many wore sunglasses to combat the early afternoon sun.

A vision of Tanner on his knees, helpless, absorbing the blow from Hull, drew him in. It was infuriating, captivating. It was the perfect prelude to the discussion Cole was about to have. A reminder of what was necessary: vengeance.

Cole had just come from Huntington Bank on South High Street where he'd retrieved the cash in the safety deposit box—over $180,000. Before entering the bank he'd changed to a new pair of the polar blue contacts. He was concerned—probably irrationally—that some of the blue may have faded in his old pair. He wanted to appear as close to the Cormier Gullickson persona as possible. He was already going in wearing the floppy hat to—hopefully—hide his shaved head. The picture on the driver's license did show a bald man but Cole had always appeared in the Huntington Bank with hair.

As it turned out, Cole's concern was unwarranted. The young Ohio State graduate, Blair, signed him in to the deposit box area with little more than a "Hello Mr. Gullickson." Cole entered the room with two empty backpacks. He'd dumped both Dom's and Tanner's on the floor of the storage unit, forming a pile of cash, prepaid debit cards, and gift cards, just feet from the wide eyes of Hull's wife.

A horn sounded behind him and Cole eased through the intersection, the vision of Tanner dissolving. He reached for Lauren's iPhone.

He had spent some time searching through the pictures while inside the storage unit with the woman. He saw several of an orange cat, a picture of her at a race with a young woman

405

Cole recognized as the early morning partner he'd laid out in Piqua, and several of her husband. These angered him and he'd moved on, finding little else of interest. The most important interaction he'd had with the phone was in the grocery store parking lot in St. Paris earlier this morning. Once he'd found the Find My iPhone app and verified Hull's location in Pittsburgh, Cole immediately switched the phone to Airplane Mode, disabling all wireless communication functions, including GPS and cellular data services.

In this mode the phone could not be tracked, at least not by Hull.

He'd driven from Piqua directly to the storage unit, again angling his vehicle to block prying human or electronic eyes, and easily hefted the blanketed woman, moving her inside before pulling down the door. The movement activated the overhead lights.

Next Cole used the woman's phone to take several pictures of her. She looked up at him with hatred in her eyes as Cole moved the phone, creating different angles.

"Say cheese."

After checking the photos to make sure they were of sufficient quality, he spread out the large floor mat and rolled the woman on top. He then rechecked the ties and added a few for good measure. He put a couple of additional strips of tape across her mouth to ensure she couldn't call out. Finally he rolled her, blanket and all, in the floor mat and cinched it tight with sections of cord he'd known was in the hodgepodge of items in the unit.

Cole stood over her, hands on hips, trying to imagine what might go wrong while he was gone. Could the woman somehow roll to one side or the other and bang into something, causing a noise that drew the attention of another storage unit renter that just happened by at the worst possible time? He worked his way back to the drum that had held the bolt bags and removed several bricks from its interior. Returning to the prone woman he wedged several bricks along both sides of the rolled mat. He stood back and crossed his arms. She wouldn't be going anywhere.

"Darlin', you look like a burrito."

Cole went to settings on the phone and turned off Airplane Mode. He found Hull's name in favorites and touched the screen.

"Heyyy Lauren, I was starting to worry about you, are you —"

"Shut the fuck up, Hull." Cole allowed a few seconds of silence, imagining the confusion and foreboding Hull must be experiencing. He continued.

"Okay hero, here's the deal. I have your wife. I'm gonna send you a few pictures to prove it in a minute. You have one chance to save her. You follow my instructions, she walks away. Get it?"

The line was silent. Cole expected to hear an illogical question like *Who is this?*

"Jelcik...if you hurt her..."

"What? If I hurt her, *what*? You'll crack me over the head with a rifle butt?"

Cole was shouting. He was on Spring Street now, coming up on Front Street in the Arena District. He signaled a right turn and gained control.

Hull snapped back, "What the hell was I supposed to do? Your brother was going to shoot an innocent man." Then, "Leave Lauren out of this. I'll meet you. She doesn't need to be —"

"*SHUT UP!*" Cole was enraged by Hull's insinuation that Tanner had caused his own demise. "Now you listen to me. I know you're in Pittsburgh. When we hang up, you're going to drive back to your house. Don't speed. Don't get pulled over. You should be there by 7:00...7:15. Top off your tank before you leave Pittsburgh. You'll need it. I'll call you again from a

407

different phone and give you the meeting place. You see a call come in from a strange number...you better answer it."

"Wait—"

"I said... Shut. The. Fuck. Up."

Hull went silent.

"No cops. No FBI. I get a sniff of them and I'm gone... somebody will find your wife's body in a month or two. No weapons. You just show up the way you're told and your little runner girl gets to go free." He let this sink in for a second.

"You come and take your medicine tonight."

Cole disconnected the call as he turned left on Marconi Boulevard. He followed it west for a short distance until it curved to the south. He pulled to the curb near the Marconi Parking Garage and checked his surroundings. Seeing no one nearby he quickly scrolled to the photos he'd taken and selected three before texting them to Hull. He did not add a comment. He then put the phone back in Airplane mode, again checked the area, and pulled away.

The Traverse traveled three blocks south on Marconi, passing Battelle Riverfront Park on the right, before turning right at Broad Street. Cole got in the right lane and rolled down the front passenger window. He was on the Discovery Bridge now. He checked his mirrors, noted the sparse traffic, and chucked Lauren Hull's phone out the window and into the Scioto River below.

He had one more errand to run.

Paul heard Jelcik's final word, then...silence. His phone was next to his ear, his thoughts elsewhere. He looked at the screen as if hoping there would be some information there that would help him make sense of the situation, help him see a way out.

He saw only icons of apps. Jelcik was gone.

My God, he has Lauren.

His phone dinged and he saw a text with photos attached from Lauren's phone. He opened them with dread. He saw three different images of his wife, taken from slightly different angles. She had duct tape across her mouth and appeared to be rolled up in a piece of carpet. Paul fought back a surge of rage, then noticed the look in Lauren's eyes as she viewed the camera echoed his feelings.

Paul moved distractedly to his SUV, mechanically opening the door and falling inside.

What do I do?

He started the Escape and his eyes went to the fuel gauge— half full.

Okay, gas...THINK!

He drove three frustrating blocks looking for fuel and finally ducked into a Shell station. He fumbled with the credit card, finally getting the pump to accept it, and got the pump handle into the opening behind his fuel door. The gas flowed for two seconds and shut down.

"DAMMIT!" He shouted at the pump and started the flow again, this time moving the nozzle back an inch. He looked to the next pump and saw a young woman, barely more than a girl, dispensing gas into a subcompact car. The look on her face as she gawked at him helped him to center his thoughts. He flashed her a quick smile and turned back to the pump.

Paul took a few seconds to select "Home" on the navigation screen of the Escape and set off. The system showed he had a drive of 4 hours and 17 minutes. That would put him back at the house at 7:12.

It was a long time to think. Paul was determined to make it productive.

He started with the time frame. If he made it home by 7:15, that left less than two hours of daylight. Paul seized on something Jelcik said—*You come and take your medicine tonight*—that whatever he was planning would take place after dark. Mentally he drew a 120-mile circle around Troy.

Everything in that circle is within two hours of Troy.

Paul was forced to make a number of assumptions. He didn't feel confident doing this, but had no choice.

If he wants me to show up somewhere after dark it might be somewhere near the edge of that circle. That area is huge. No way I guess it in advance.

409

He pondered possibilities before giving up, realizing it was at least as likely that Jelcik was holding Lauren somewhere close to Troy. Paul was on I-70 now, west of Pittsburgh. He set the cruise at five miles over the speed limit to eliminate the temptation to go faster. The vision of Lauren, bound and restrained, came to him. He felt the fury building from within and fought to control it.

Gotta think! He said no cops, no FBI...

Paul weighed the risks associated with bringing law enforcement into the situation. He had no doubt that Jelcik would carry out his threat if he sensed Paul had alerted the authorities. The man made it clear he wanted to settle the score with Paul and claimed he would let Lauren go. He actually thought there was a chance Jelcik would abide by the claim.

Then again, there was a better than even chance than he would kill Lauren even if Paul followed the directions to the letter. Could his friend Gatewood be of assistance? Woody had come up huge for him in difficult situations in the past—not all of them in the military—but what could he offer in this situation? Miles crawled by as Paul debated.

He reached for his phone. He really had no choice. He had to bring in the FBI. They were the only entity that had the resources for this sort of thing.

This time he dialed Tyson Foxx's cell number directly.

"Paul? What can I do for you?"

Paul sighed and began to tell the story.

CHAPTER FORTY-FIVE

The FBI Hostage Rescue Team is based inside the sprawling FBI Academy property at Quantico, Virginia. It is the federal government's only full-time counterterrorism unit. Its 100-plus operators consist of skilled assault and sniper teams and have specialized training in a variety of disciplines. They train with the most elite units in the U.S. military as well as international units such as the British SAS and Germany's GSG 9. Technically under the command of the FBI's Critical Incident Response Group, HRT is a fully functional stand-alone unit that even has its own aircraft.

HRT is, for lack of a better term, America's SWAT Team.

When Tyson Foxx's call came in to the Operations Center at Quantico it generated a frenzy of activity. To the outsider it perhaps would look disjointed. But to the practiced eye of a warrior it all made sense. The shooters and assaulters loaded carefully arranged gear and weapons cases into vans that would take them to their waiting plane.

"Listen up people. We have some new details." Bengie Brenner stepped to the center of the room and gestured for the agents to gather round. Brenner was the senior man of Blue Team, one of three such units that composed HRT, the others being Red and Gold.

"This tasking comes from our Violent Crimes Task Force based in Chicago. A fugitive is suspected to have kidnapped a woman in Ohio. He's holding her—location unknown—and using her as bait to lure in her husband."

The dozen agents gave Brenner their full attention. He continued. "The suspect was a member of a bank robbery team that was involved in a shootout in Toledo, Ohio. They killed a police officer and at least one civilian. Two members of the team were killed. The third member escaped and, apparently, has kidnapped the wife of a witness. The witness was involved

411

in assisting the Toledo Police during the chase that followed the shooting at the bank. Sounds like our boy is out for revenge...one of the deceased gang members was his brother."

"Is this that Fireteam thing?" The question came from Tom Clark, a former Army Ranger who led one of the assault elements in Blue Team.

"Yep, these are the guys that hit banks all across the Midwest...used World War Two weapons. An M1 carbine and .45 pistol were recovered from one of the gang members... another .45 from a second member. This last guy is believed to have carried a Thompson during the robberies. We're not sure if it's fully automatic. Best guess, it is not—the carbine was a reproduction—we think the Thompson is too, but..."

"But assume it's a working machine gun, right?" This from Destino "Dez" Bravo, Blue Team's lead sniper.

Brenner nodded, "Copy that, Dez. Like the Boy Scouts... always be prepared." He glanced at a printout then continued. "The Task Force commander reports we have no current electronic tracking of the suspect. He's believed to be in Ohio. The commander, Tyson Foxx, says his people believe the most likely site for the meet is in the kidnap victim's hometown, Troy. Second choice is Columbus. This guy, Cole Jelcik, lived there and operated a cover business for his bank robbery operation. He knows Columbus. It's his home base."

"Is this the cat that just got added to the Ten Most Wanted list?" It was Clark.

Brenner touched his nose and pointed at Clark. "The same." He looked again at the printout. "Cole Thomas Jelcik, 31. Six feet, five inches, 250 pounds. No record. Suspected to have been involved in over 20 bank robberies, home invasion, felony murder. A real bad actor."

Jeff "Lobo" Lobianca, Dez's spotter, whistled, "All that and *no record*? Must be a cagey one. What's the plan?"

"We'll ride in style today. We get one of the Gulfstreams."

"Oh baby!" Tom Clark grinned and pumped a fist.

Brenner allowed himself a small smile. "We're gonna be packed in there like sardines. We're taking two 6-man cells.

412

We fly from here to Columbus, that's a one-hour flight time, drop off Bravo Cell"—he looked at Clark who led Bravo's assaulters and at Dez and Lobo, the sniper team—"the Gulfstream hops over to Dayton to deliver Alpha Cell. From Dayton it's a short drive to Troy. I'll be with Alpha."

Brenner looked around the room. "We'll get more info on the plane. Local police units will meet us on the ground and provide support. There are weight limits on the jet so take your gear to the loadmaster before stowing it on board. You might have to leave some things behind." He looked again at the printout, nodded as if everything that could be covered had been covered, and added a final note.

"Let's make this guy's stay on the Ten Most Wanted List a short one. Saddle up."

Lauren Hull had never been this uncomfortable. She knew her wrenched right shoulder was damaged. She also thought some of the bones or tendons of her left wrist might be broken or torn. She'd tried to defend herself with the key and Jelcik had made her pay. The zip ties were so tight that she feared the lack of proper blood flow to her feet and hands might lead to further damage. The heat of the day caused stifling conditions in the interior storage unit. After the exertion of her morning run, the attack by Jelcik, and the drive to Columbus, Lauren's thirst was becoming unbearable. But at this instant, lying on the floor of the dark storage unit, the overriding factor in her discomfort was something altogether different.

She had to pee.

Lauren clung to the natural urge to hold it in. She thought back to the attack. Could she have done something to stop it, to at least have recognized the danger and warned Lacey?

Oh, poor Lacey.

She saw the attack again in fragments. The flashers, the newspapers, the quick movement from the vehicle...the devastating blow that sent Lacey backward and had frozen Lauren—it had all happened so fast.

Even though she was in mortal danger and Paul almost certainly would be soon, Lauren felt anguish for her friend. *Lacey was supposed to be married in a few days and now she might be...*

Lauren tried not to dwell on Lacey's fate. She forced herself to think again of a way to escape. She'd strained for 20 minutes trying to generate movement in the cocoon formed by the blanket and the mat. She hadn't even succeeded in activating the overhead lights. The pile of cash—there must be tens of thousands of dollars—was three feet from her face but barely visible in the darkness.

And she had to pee!

She thought of the ride to the storage facility. Was there anything she could glean from the trip that might help her escape? Jelcik had said nothing to her after going through her phone when they had stopped somewhere outside of Piqua. He turned up the radio and listened to country music stations, occasionally singing along. She could see the back of his head from her position on the seat, saw him raise a cup to his face every minute or two, and heard him spit. She'd frowned, thinking *disgusting habit*. After an hour or so she began to see green overhead highway signs flash past the top of the windshield. She'd recognized some of the street names. They were in Columbus.

Having relived the drive now for what must've been the fifth time Lauren thought again of Lacey—*my friend!* The younger woman had come to be a special person in her life. Lauren felt tears roll down her cheek. They were tears of sadness. They were also tears of rage. Jelcik, she realized, was motivated by a desire to harm her husband for what he'd done to his brother. Lauren was beginning to feel the same dark motivation.

She wanted to get even.

Her bladder was insistent. Lauren vaguely remembered the humiliation of peeing her pants on one occasion as a little girl. It was a memory she hadn't experienced for decades. She closed her eyes tightly, trying to eke out a few more minutes.

Then she had a thought. She didn't know what Jelcik's plans were for her. How depraved was he? She could only guess. But if he intended to molest her at some point in the hours ahead, she would make it unpleasant for him.

She unclenched her bladder.

Paul noted the lowering sun as it moved across his windshield. He was leaving I-70, merging north on I-75. He'd been driving now for four interminable hours.

As a Combat Controller, Paul had a high degree of control. He had the capability to lay waste to enemy targets by communicating with the planes overhead. The combat power he controlled and employed gave him a God-like feeling.

But now, following the instructions of the man who held his wife, he felt powerless. The one step he'd taken to try to wrest back control—calling in the FBI—was causing him angst. Had he done the right thing?

He'd had a series of conversations with Foxx as he crossed Pennsylvania and Ohio. The plan, so far as Paul could tell, was to rush a couple HRT Assault/Sniper elements to Ohio. One would be dropped at Rickenbacker Air National Guard Base southeast of Columbus. They would be staged there ready to deploy to any area Jelcik might indicate during the call Paul expected to get in the next half hour. The second team would fly to Dayton International Airport and motor to Troy. Paul glanced at the clock and saw that it was 6:54. He realized that the two FBI teams were almost certainly already in Ohio, having streaked overhead as he drove.

Paul was starved for information. In between calls with Foxx he dialed up Rita Kekich. She was able to fill in some of the gaps in the day's events. Lauren and Lacey had apparently been running for less than a mile when they were accosted by Jelcik. Piqua Police believed he was masquerading as a newspaper delivery driver and this allowed him to get close without drawing suspicion. He attacked Lacey, breaking her jaw, several ribs, and her left clavicle. Lacey also sustained a serious Traumatic Brain Injury—TBI—and was in critical condition in Miami Valley Hospital.

The broken jaw...he must've punched her...the son of a bitch.

Jelcik is believed to have turned his attention to Lauren, overpowering her and leaving with her phone. Lacey's phone and Lauren's keys were found at the scene. Both women were expected at work. Calls from the lab to Lauren's cell and from radiology to Lacey's went to voicemail. Matt, Paul learned, knew nothing of the incident until contacted by Piqua Police later in the day. He was now at Miami Valley. Kekich understood that Lacey's parents were on their way to Dayton from their home in northwest Ohio.

About the time Paul was passing through Columbus on his way to Troy, Foxx called back. The FBI had focused their technological capabilities on the case. Jelcik's phone had been seized when the FBI raided his house after the robbery. To their knowledge he had no phone other than Lauren's, though logic suggested he would be contacting Paul with another—probably a burner—shortly. There was no sign of his wife's phone. Jelcik, it was assumed, had destroyed it after calling Paul so it couldn't be used to track him. Foxx said the FBI was set up to trace any incoming call to Paul's cell.

"We're trying to close in around him once we have a location...trying to build a box around him."

Paul, silent, thought, *Yeah, put him in a box...let's put him in a box...where he belongs. When I get home, I'm getting Gatewood's Sig Sauer. It goes with me to wherever I meet Jelcik.*

Foxx, juggling the operation from the conference room in Chicago and suppressing his regret over the failure to catch Jelcik in Buffalo, tried to offer consolation.

"Hang in there, Paul."

CHAPTER FORTY-SIX

The call came at 7:08, just as Paul passed Tipp City. He was ten minutes from the first Troy exit. It was, as expected, from an unfamiliar number. He answered.

"This is Paul."

"Where are you...*exactly*?"

Paul looked through the windshield. "I just passed Tipp City...I don't know what mile marker."

Jelcik was silent for a few seconds, then commanded, "Okay. Get off at the next exit. That's State Route 55 at Troy, exit 73. Go over the highway and get back on I-75. You're coming back to Columbus."

Paul nodded. There it was. The FBI believed Jelcik's familiarity with Columbus might lead him to return there with Lauren. If he was setting up some kind of trap it made sense he would take advantage of this familiarity. Paul assumed Jelcik would let him know of the final destination once he got closer to Columbus. He was surprised by the man's next words.

"You and me are gonna meet at a place you're familiar with, that big ol' round Veterans Memorial building off Broad. I saw a picture posted online of you giving a talk there last year. By the way, what was the subject? How to beat up defenseless people?"

Paul scoffed, "*Defenseless*? He was trying to shoot an unarmed man!"

Jelcik ignored the comment. "Let me remind you, no cops. I smell a cop, I do your wife and I'm gone. You'll spend the rest of your life wishing you played this my way."

Paul was wondering, *Why the hell would he tell me now where we're meeting? It gives me too much time to try to set a trap for HIM.* Jelcik's reference to Lauren snapped him back to the call.

417

"I want to talk to her...how do I know she's alive? Have you hurt her?"

"You'll just have to take my word that she's alive and well, partner. Listen up, there's more. Just in case you get tempted to call in the cops, I'm gonna have you drive around the 270 beltway for awhile. Gonna see if you're being followed...look for helicopters in the air. If I sniff them—and I'm pretty damn good at sniffin'—say bye-bye to Miss Lauren. Got it?"

"Yeah, I get on 270." Paul was trying to figure Jelcik's play.

"Northbound. You get on 270 northbound and start driving that big circle around the city. When you've gone almost full circle, get off on 23, due south of the city. That's Obetz, you know it?"

Paul had a general idea. "I'll find it."

"Good boy. You should have just enough gas to get to where you're goin'. Now make that U-turn at Troy and get your ass back here." Jelcik paused before adding a final comment.

"Watch out for deer, they move this time of day. Wouldn't want you hittin' one and spoiling our party."

He was gone.

Foxx called ten minutes later, just as Paul was going down the southbound ramp of I-75, returning to the highway.

Paul answered. He'd desperately wanted to talk to the FBI Agent but knew Foxx must have been busy after the call with Jelcik ended. "Yeah, Foxx, what's the plan?"

Foxx got right to the facts with no preamble.

"It was a cellphone. We had a bead on it but it was moving. He was on the 270 beltway up near the Easton Mall. During the call he passed from one cell tower to another further west. He turned off the phone as soon as he hung up."

Foxx shifted gears. "HRT's Alpha Cell is already in Troy. We're working to get them turned around and bring them to Columbus but they might not get there before this thing goes down. We've scrambled the team from Rickenbacker, getting them headed toward the Veterans Memorial building. We have a contact with the owner of a German restaurant in Columbus who has agreed to let us use one of their Sprinter vans to insert the team. The restaurant caters to events at the building and their logo is plastered on the outside of the van...we're hoping it doesn't throw up any flags for a watcher."

Paul interjected, "Call my sister, Patrice. She works there. She can give you specific directions of how to offload your team out of sight." He scrolled to her number on his phone and recited it to Foxx.

Foxx continued, "We have unmarked Columbus PD vehicles and a helicopter—"

"NO! No cops, no helo. We can't take a chance of spooking him. He'll disappear again and Lauren..." Paul let the thought hang.

Foxx sighed. "I expected you to say that...hoped you wouldn't, but expected it. This guy has something else up his sleeve. You know that, right?"

Paul was nodding. He now knew he would be facing Jelcik without the borrowed Sig Sauer pistol. "Yeah...but we have to play it his way...hope to get lucky."

Cole ended the call and turned off the burner phone. He reached the Worthington exit at the northern point of the beltway and got off. Twenty seconds later he was back on 270, now heading east. He would work his way back to the storage unit.

Cole had used the iPhone he'd acquired in Buffalo to work out the logistics. He found the fuel capacity and expected range of a full tank of gas for a Ford Escape and was pleased to see he could keep Hull driving for hours before arriving at the final destination nearly empty. He'd pulled up a map of the exits near Troy on the phone and was able to quickly consult it while he was driving and tell Hull where to turn around.

Cole had left the storage unit at 6:45 p.m. After picking up the money from the safe deposit box and completing his other tasks, he'd spent a good portion of the afternoon readying his gear for his escape from Columbus later that night. The money on the floor went into a large trash bag. The backpacks were

419

now lined up inside the unit. He wouldn't risk leaving them in the Traverse that he'd stashed in the apartment parking lot. The Tommy Gun leaned on the wall beside them.

Having completed his call with Hull, Cole continued on his way back to the storage unit. He stopped first at a Panera Bread drive-thru and ordered a chicken sandwich and a Diet Pepsi. He parked at the apartment complex across the road and walked back to the unit. Inside, Cole sat on one of the folding chairs and ate the sandwich, scrolling on his iPhone. He barely looked at Lauren, spending a few seconds to confirm the bricks had kept her from moving, and didn't say a word to her. As he bent over her he sniffed.

She must've pissed herself.

After finishing the sandwich and the drink he pulled out his can of Copenhagen, packed the tobacco with the familiar motion and resulting thwacking sound, and inserted a large pinch. He scrolled on the phone for 20 minutes, searching for stories on the manhunt.

Well, the FBI might know I'm in Columbus, but the media still thinks I'm in Buffalo.

Cole spit into the cup periodically as he reviewed the plan. He had assumed Hull would call in the FBI. Cole thought it was better to bring them near and put them in a location he could work around than to have them focusing all of their technological and manpower assets on locating him. Once he made the call to Hull, he believed the Bureau would rush their people—probably their Hostage Rescue Team—to the Veterans building. They would want to blanket Columbus to locate him before the final stage played out. Hull would resist, not wanting to increase the risk to his wife.

Cole spit the entire pinch of tobacco into the cup and fished the residual flecks out of his mouth with his tongue. He set the alarm on his iPhone for 8:10 p.m., stretched out his legs, and closed his eyes. The lights blinked out a few seconds later.

Soon he was snoring, the woman at his feet.

420

HRT's Bravo Cell was driven from the Rickenbacker National Guard Base in two vans to a car dealership parking lot on the outskirts of Columbus. There they were met by a Sprinter van bearing the logo of a popular restaurant in the German Village section of the city. It had been cleaned out and had no seats in the rear compartment so the team sat on the floor with their gear. A Columbus Police Officer wearing a hastily acquired uniform from the restaurant drove.

Dez Bravo, the sniper, was the smallest member of the team and had little trouble getting comfortable—snipers were accustomed to putting their bodies in odd positions and making the best of it. Dez had short black hair that stood at attention when it wasn't covered by a helmet or another piece of tactical gear. By virtue of the last name Bravo, Dez was assigned to the Blue Team cell with the same name. It would've been unnecessarily confusing to have a team member named Bravo in Alpha Cell.

"Where did you dial in the range, Dez?" It was the spotter, Lobo, asking what distance Dez had selected for the scope on top of the sniper rifle in the case at their feet.

"A hundred yards. I'll have to adjust for any shot I might have to take at a shorter or longer range. I figure Jelcik is having the husband come to the building to do him in. Everything will happen close to the building. Any luck, we see Jelcik sneaking around before the husband even gets there and do the takedown."

Lobo nodded. Dez was the most talented shooter in HRT, having done the unit proud in shooting competitions with elite military units. In addition, the diminutive sniper had exhibited prowess in real-world situations, making kill shots on two separate occasions. Lobo respected Dez's judgement.

"Right. Looks like my spotter scope might come in just as handy as your rifle today. The priority is finding this guy."

The van negotiated the streets of Columbus, finding Broad Street. As it passed over the Scioto River on the Discovery Bridge the driver spoke up.

"There's the building...comin' up on the right." The team jostled for position in the back of the van, straining to catch a quick look at their destination. They had seen numerous photos on the tablets they'd brought along but there was no substitute for getting eyes on it for real.

It was a large structure, 53,000 square feet, and more or less round in shape. It was nearly 60 feet tall and 300 feet in diameter. Full-length windows faced Broad. The team knew the windows were located on the mezzanine level. The building had a roof that was mostly covered by grass. This provided visitors with a view of the Columbus skyline across the river to the east. It was designed as a place for visitors to come and reflect.

On this day it would serve as an excellent observation post for the FBI team.

The Sprinter van pulled into the drive leading to the parking lot on the building's west side. The occupants saw an overhead door on the ground level of the west side of the building go up and the police officer driving skillfully backed inside. A Museum staffer—looking scared out of her mind—immediately hit a button to lower the door.

The team piled out and got started at once unloading their equipment. Tom Clark, the Team Leader of Bravo, spoke as the members continued to work.

"Alright, the remaining staff are exiting the building in the Sprinter." He gestured to the van where a half dozen people were climbing aboard, searching for a place to sit. "Once they leave, this place will be empty, except for us. All doors will be locked. That said we don't know what Jelcik has in mind. He may still try to get in...so I'm leaving two assaulters, Groves and Ratlaw, downstairs."

Two men, both armed with H&K 416 carbines, nodded.

"I'll be on the roof with Knasel. Dez and Lobo, you have overwatch with the spotter scope and the rifle."

All members of the team wore earpieces and throat microphones. They did a comms check on these as they finished gearing up. Clark finished.

"It would be nice to have more sets of eyes covering this place and the surrounding area, but Alpha can't be here for at least 30 minutes and showing up then will likely spook our boy. So...we have what we have." He looked at five sets of eyes. "Positions, everyone."

Paul reached the I-270 outerbelt at 8:15. He was feeling the effects of the drive. He'd been on the go for over five hours. The worry over Lauren's circumstances weighed heavily on his mind. Add the spikes of adrenaline during phone calls with Jelcik and the FBI and he was beginning to feel fried. He looked to the sky as he signaled to move to the ramp. He saw no sign of helicopters. He believed Foxx would keep his word and limit the manpower involved in the hunt for Jelcik. They were not only listening in on Paul's phone, they were tracking its movement. Paul knew that where he went, Jelcik would soon follow. The FBI would have to deal with him then.

Paul rotated his head in an attempt to loosen a stiff neck.

How the hell do the truck drivers do this every day?

Paul's SUV rolled down the ramp, heading north. He checked his mirrors when merging then shot a glance at the fuel gauge.

Less than a quarter tank.

He tried to envision the outerbelt. He wondered about the loop's circumference.

Gotta be fifty miles or more. I have to drive over three fourths of that to get to the Obetz exit.

He wasn't sure he had enough gas remaining to do that. He dreaded what Jelcik might do if Paul didn't show up at the right place and time.

Paul drove on. The fuel gauge and the setting sun sank at the same rate.

CHAPTER FORTY-SEVEN

Cole woke to the sound of the alarm on his phone. He stretched, unintentionally activating the lights. His eyes snapped open. Momentarily confused by his surroundings he looked about and noticed Lauren on the floor. She was glaring up at him, heat in her eyes.

"Mornin' darlin'."

Cole had a comedic vision of a comic book thought bubble appearing above her head. He tried to imagine what might be written inside.

"Don't be so pissed. You get to see your knight in shining armor in—" he rotated his forearm to check the watch face on the underside of his wrist, "just about an hour."

Cole opened the door a few inches to confirm there was no one nearby. He knew he couldn't come and go from the unit indefinitely as he had that day without someone getting suspicious. Fortunately when he left after loading his SUV tonight he would be departing Columbus for good. He snapped the lock shut when he left.

He took two of the backpacks and walked to the gate. After punching in the code and waiting for the gate to roll open he walked to the sidewalk and waited for a gap in the traffic. He crossed at a trot and unlocked the Traverse. He put the backpacks inside the rear cargo area—the rest would follow in a few minutes—and started the engine.

Cole, careful of the traffic, guided the SUV back to the storage unit gate. He punched in the code, thinking *one last time* as he waited for the opening to grow wide enough to enter. Back at the unit he began to pack the Traverse. All of the money went into the rear compartment, as did the Tommy Gun. A few items, such as the M1911 .45 caliber pistol and the phones, went on the front passenger seat. Now that it was coming down to game time he wanted the pistol within reach, not under the seat where he might have to fumble for it. He was wearing the mechanic shirt from the restaurant in Buffalo. The two extra magazines for the pistol were tucked into the left breast pocket.

Last to go into the Traverse was the rolled up floor mat that restrained Lauren Hull. Cole lifted it by the two tied loops of cord and swung it into the back seat. Lauren went in headfirst and thumped against the armrest on the far side.

Cole was tucking the other end of the mat inside the vehicle so the door would close. Without thought he uttered "Sorry." He paused, realizing the absurdity of the comment. Bumping her head against the door was far down the list of things that might warrant an apology.

He slammed the door and got behind the wheel. He checked his watch.

Time to call Hull.

Paul had driven a half circle around Columbus. He was now on the east side of the city, traveling south. He was passing the Gahanna exit near John Glenn International Airport when his phone rang. He recognized the number and picked up.

"Jelcik." Paul spoke the word as a statement, not a question.

"Hey hero. Where are you?"

"I just passed the Gahanna exit. I should be at the Obetz exit in—"

"Change of plans." Cole interrupted him. "You're getting off now at..."

Paul listened as Jelcik seemed to be consulting something. "I-70 West."

Paul fought the feelings of anger and exasperation that had been building all day. "Got it, I-70 West." There was silence for a few seconds as Paul strained to see a highway sign in the distance. "Looks like I'm two miles away. What—"

Cole snapped, "Shut the hell up and listen. Drive the speed limit. I'll call you back in ten."

When the line went silent Paul took a deep breath. He had to stay focused—for Lauren's sake. He'd been in any number of high-stress situations in his life. This was different, but he would force himself to think and act, as much as possible, with a measured approach. He knew the FBI was listening in. He hoped this call—the second one from the same burner phone—could provide the FBI an edge that would result in Lauren's recovery.

At the Violent Crimes Task Force Center conference room in Chicago a dozen agents were grouped around the conference table. Most were standing. A few sat with their shirtsleeves rolled up. Half-empty coffee cups were scattered across the table.

When Jelcik said *Change of plans* the collective hearts of the group sank. Hull's phone was tapped and its location was visible on the video monitors that were mounted on the wall, but all present knew that they had little else to go on when it came to monitoring the situation in Columbus. If Hull was directed to any location other than the Veterans Memorial Building where HRT lie in wait, the FBI would have virtually no way to intervene.

Foxx looked up quickly from the round set of speakers that had been mounted at the center of the table. He'd been alternating his gaze between them and the screens on the wall.

"Do we have a fix on Jelcik's phone?"

Scott Remick stood at one corner of the table, a cellphone to his ear. His tie was loosened, the top button of his shirt undone. Lines of concentration formed on his forehead. He held up a finger as if buying time.

"Tech has it...coming up on the screens now."

All eyes turned to the video screens. They saw a second dot appear on the map of Columbus. It was on the east side of town as well, not far from the icon representing Hull.

There was a murmur of comments in the room as the grouping of agents spoke random thoughts, all the while adhering to the policy of keeping speech to a minimum while listening to the live audio feed. Jelcik finished his instructions and hung up. The agents watched as Hull's icon merged onto

I-70. The second dot, now on East Main Street, headed east. It intersected with I-270, hovered for a second, then began to move north.

Rita Kekich broke the silence. "Columbus PD has units spaced all over the city waiting for tasking from us. Do we vector them toward Jelcik?"

Foxx pondered. He could feel all heads turn to him. *We don't know what he's driving...we flood the area...Jelcik bails. Hull's wife won't survive.*

"No. We keep monitoring."

Cole drove north on 270 until he reached the next exit. He got off and jumped back on southbound. He was almost certain that the FBI now had his phone. He needed to keep moving to prevent them from pinning down his vehicle. He checked his watch and dialed Hull again.

Paul was nearing the downtown area when his phone rang in his hand.

"Yeah?"

"Exit 101B. Mound Street. Tell me when you see it."

The line was silent for 30 seconds then Paul spoke. "Comin' up on it."

Jelcik ordered, "Get off there. Straight at the light at the bottom of the ramp. Stay on Mound for seven blocks. I'll stay on the line. You read off each street as you come to it."

Paul took the exit, got a green light at the end of the ramp, and continued west. He began to call out street signs.

In Chicago Foxx was increasingly anxious. As Hull called out street names the FBI personnel could see the video screen icon match the narrative exactly. Some saw the second dot, after having traveled south for two miles, get off the highway and execute a series of seemingly random turns.

Hull called out, "Fourth Street."

Jelcik immediately said, "Take the next left, Third Street. Turn on your flashers. Go two blocks—corner of Third and

Fulton. You'll see a man holding a green sign with your name on it. Pull over and follow his directions."

There were audible groans in the conference room as the agents realized Jelcik had an unknown accomplice.

Paul was shaken. *What?!? Is there another member of the gang that the FBI doesn't know about?*

He took the left and depressed the button activating the Ford Escape's flashers. He crossed Engler Street and just made out a figure a block ahead on the right. Paul drew closer and saw a disheveled man craning his neck in his direction. Apparently recognizing Paul's flashers, the man reached for something at his feet and held it up.

Paul's headlights illuminated a lime green poster displaying handwritten letters. It read:

PAUL HULL
PULL OVER HERE

What the hell?

Paul complied and rolled down the passenger window. As he edged to the curb the smiling man stepped forward.

"You must be Mister Cole's friend. He said we make a trade."

Paul was confused. He was about to ask for clarification when Jelcik's voice came back on the phone. Paul had nearly forgotten the call was still active.

"Hand your phone to him. I want to talk to him."

Paul frowned, "What?"

"HAND THE GODDAMMED PHONE TO RUFUS...NOW!"

Paul reached his phone toward the open window where it was accepted by a grimy hand. He listened as the man spoke into it.

"It's me Mister Cole." The man listened for a few seconds then smiled and nodded. He reached under his shirt and produced a walkie-talkie, then handed it to Paul. "He says turn it on."

As soon as Paul switched on the unit, the disheveled man turned and walked away. He took the phone.

CHAPTER FORTY-EIGHT

Cole drove randomly on the city's east side directing Hull to Rufus. He'd had some doubt that this part of the plan would work. It had been difficult to find the man earlier in the afternoon. After cleaning out the safe deposit box, Cole had driven through the downtown area, killing two birds with one stone.

He was speaking to Hull, having called the man on his wife's phone. At the same time he was looking for Rufus. He'd cruised the Marconi Garage area with no luck. After tossing Lauren's phone into the Scioto he began to pass by homeless shelters and finally spotted him outside the shelter near the Fourth and Elm Parking Garage where the three Fireteam members had originally encountered him. That night he'd been pissing in an area of the garage they'd just cleaned. Cole smiled and honked his horn.

He explained to Rufus that a friend needed to return a phone to Cole that night and needed a walkie-talkie in return.

"Any chance I can have him drop it off to you up at your panhandlin' spot? I'll make it worth your while?"

Cole explained how it would work then made a suggestion. "It'll be later than you're normally out. Why don't you spend the night at the shelter after you make the trade with my buddy?"

Rufus agreed and accepted the Midland X-Talker and a hundred dollar bill.

Cole smiled. "Thanks partner. There'll be another hundred waiting for you when I get the phone back from you. I'll stop at the shelter tomorrow morning...we'll get breakfast."

Rufus had come through for him. Cole heard the static from the second walkie-talkie on his passenger seat. He ended the call on the burner phone without a word to Rufus on the other end and picked up the X-Talker.

"You there, Hull?"

After a second an answer came back. "I'm here."

"Punch this into your navigation system: Gravity Parking Garage. It's on Broad, east of the National Veterans Museum. Tell me when it comes up."

After a short wait Hull spoke. "I see it. Six minutes away."

"Go there and park. Call me when you get there. No funny business when you pass the museum. I'll be watching. I figure you didn't follow directions earlier and there just might be some people waiting inside that I don't wanna meet. We'll talk about that later."

Cole stopped transmitting on the X-Talker. He spotted a McDonald's ahead and pulled in. The lights of the parking lot were on as darkness fell over Columbus. At the rear of the building Cole put the Traverse in park then got out and flung the burner phone onto the roof of the restaurant.

Ducking back into the SUV he thought, *Okay, time to go get set up for the big finish.*

In Chicago the conference room had gone silent. The icon for Hull's phone was barely moving, seeming to float away from the intersection. The line stayed active for a few seconds, long enough for the agents to hear an unfamiliar voice say, "Mister Cole?" Then it went dead.

Foxx looked at the video feed and saw they were still tracking that phone. His eyes clicked to the right and he saw the second dot pull off the street and stop at a building.

"What's at that location?" Foxx put both fists on the table and leaned toward the screen.

Someone said. "It's a McDonald's."

They continued to stare for a full minute. The dot didn't move. Kekich, next to Foxx, breathed, "Christ, is Jelcik inside getting food?"

"Well, the drive-thru might be really slow...sometimes that happens." It was Remick. All eyes turned to him, incredulous that he'd made the comment.

He held out his hands, "What?"

Foxx shook his head. "Get me a line to Columbus PD. Time to bring them in...fast! Where the hell is Alpha Cell? What's their ETA for getting back to Columbus?"

In a corner of the room a female agent leaned toward a male colleague and whispered, "Who the fuck is Rufus?"

Cole was passing through downtown, moving toward the Arena District, when he heard Hull's voice on the walkie-talkie.

"Okay, I'm at the garage. Over?"

Cole smiled. *I guess some habits die hard. Mr. Hero is talking like he's back in the military.* Cole decided to get in on the act.

"Roger, Hero. Wait one." He grinned as he turned onto Marconi Boulevard and followed it around to the entrance to the parking garage that bore the same name. Steel poles wrapped in blue plastic formed a wicket to the opening. Cole pulled in, took a ticket, and watched the arm rise. He pulled through. He drew the X-Talker to his face as he searched for a spot.

"Okay Hull, you got me?"

"Yeah."

Cole nodded. The X-Talkers had an advertised range of 20 miles. He knew Hull was less than a mile away, across the Scioto to the west, yet he was impressed that the walkie-talkies performed so well when both users were in parking garages. He spotted a space not far from the entrance and swung in before checking his watch. It was 9:12.

"Wait three minutes in your vehicle then walk to the back of the property. You'll see a path that goes down a hill to a railroad track. When you get there call me back."

"Got it."

433

Cole did a walk-through of the Gravity Garage a few months earlier for Klean Sooner. He remembered standing on the top floor and watching a train pass to the structure's rear. It trundled over a railroad bridge to the east before disappearing into the city on the other side. Here, in the Marconi Garage, Cole was at almost exactly the same spot the train vanished from sight.

He got out of the Traverse and tucked the pistol into his belt. He wore jeans under the mechanic shirt and the New Balance cross-trainers he'd purchased in Sidney. He searched the interior of the garage and saw just one other person—a man in a suit and tie—entering a car a hundred feet away. While he waited for the man to drive off, Cole stepped to the entrance and checked the surrounding area. It was a maze of narrow streets and walkways, one of which crossed the railroad tracks a short distance away. He noted that the 20-foot tall art deco parking sign was lit up, its red and blue neon lending an artsy cast to the train tracks that lie beyond it.

There was no foot traffic in the area. Hockey season was over so there was no activity at the nearby arena used by the Bluejackets. Cole walked back to the garage and verified the man had gone.

He opened the driver's side rear door and pulled on the floor mat. It slid toward him until it reached a tipping point. The end that covered Lauren's feet swung down to the ground, putting her body in a diagonal position.

Lauren felt herself being pulled across the seat. Her upper body was elevated somewhat and she could see the garage ceiling through the open door. Jelcik's hands grasped the sides of the mat at her shoulders and roughly pulled her upright. She winced and offered a muffled cry as pain from her injured right shoulder shot through her body. When she opened her eyes she realized her face was buried in Jelcik's chest. He pushed her back slightly and stared down.

His eyes were ice blue. There was not a trace of mercy. Lauren had heard Jelcik's phone conversations with Paul. She had no doubt that the fugitive intended to kill her husband. She hadn't been sure if the man's claim that he would release her was true.

Looking into his eyes now, she felt she knew the answer.

She felt herself being slung over Jelcik's shoulder. The door to the SUV closed and the locks chirped. Lauren's head bounced slightly as she was carried out of the garage.

Tom Clark stood on the roof of the National Veterans Museum listening intently. He let his rifle hang from the sling on his shoulder and held his hands over his ears, hoping to catch every syllable of the message being relayed. When the transmission ended he turned to Dez, Lobo, and Knasel. He'd gathered them into a tight circle and they all listened to the report through their own earpieces. It was a recap of developments, mentioning an accomplice and the fact that both Hull and Jelcik were probably no longer being tracked. There was a possibility that Jelcik—and theoretically the hostage—were inside a McDonald's on the east side of the city but virtually no one with the Task Force believed it.

Clark said simply, "Roger," into his throat mike and spoke to the threesome. "I don't know if this takes us out of the game or not. Let's proceed as if it still goes down here. If it doesn't, we go home...but we have to be ready." He got nods all around.

"I'm calling Groves and Ratlaw up here to get more sets of eyes. I'll put them on the southeast and southwest corners." He indicated the side of the building facing Broad Street. The shape of the building didn't occur to any of the other HRT members at that moment, but for the rest of his career, Clark would receive friendly razzing from every operator in the unit that he had deployed shooters to the "corners" of a round building.

Clark continued, "Dan, you take the west side." Knasel, a sandy-haired man who spoke softly, if at all, simply nodded and trotted off. Clark turned to his sniper team. "I'll keep you two together. Set up to cover the east side—that entire river plain. I'll be over here to your left watching the rear after I get

435

Groves and Ratlaw situated." He hesitated before hurrying off, "Look sharp."

A concrete ramp ran from ground level around the east side of the building, wide enough for golf carts to carry ageing Veterans to the roof level. A concrete wall formed the inner border to the ramp. Dez and Lobo set up behind the wall. Due to their height differences Lobo set up on the right where the wall was higher. His spotting scope had infrared capability and would pick up body heat at great distances. The scope's tripod fit nicely on top of the wall.

Dez was ten feet to his left with the rifle, an H&K PSG-1, an exotic black rifle that appeared to be futuristic but had actually been developed after the Munich Massacre during the 1972 Olympics to assist in countering terrorism. Though too heavy —nearly 18 pounds—to be carried by military units, it was a favorite of elite police marksmen who often found themselves in situations exactly like this one. The rifle was semi-automatic and—in the hands of the right shooter—could put a 7.62 millimeter-round through a bullseye at a thousand meters.

Dez was the right shooter.

CHAPTER FORTY-NINE

Paul found his way down the trail behind the parking garage. The footing was somewhat treacherous but the glow from the city across the river to the east provided enough illumination to light his way. He reached the railroad tracks—there were two sets—and lifted the walkie-talkie.

"I'm at the tracks."

Jelcik responded immediately. "Start walkin' toward the river. There's a railroad bridge less than a quarter-mile from you. You can't see it yet because of the trees but when the tracks take a little bend to your left it'll be right there." Jelcik paused as if catching his breath from exertion. Paul climbed up between the rails. Jelcik came back.

"You get to the bridge, you keep walking. Your bride is waiting for you on the other side."

Paul set off without hesitation.

Cole stepped out of the parking garage to the sidewalk. There was no traffic on Marconi Boulevard—a bit of a presumptuous descriptive for a street that at this location was a narrow two-lane asphalt strip that ran past a parking garage on one side and a railroad track on the other. To an observer, a man walking with a tubular object on his left shoulder could've been carrying one of two things: a rolled up piece of old carpet or—just what it was—a body being transported covertly.

Fortunately there were no witnesses in the proximity. If there had been Cole thought it was better than even money that a witness would guess he simply had the piece of carpet. When he'd walked these tracks with Rufus Hendershot weeks earlier he'd seen a good bit of evidence that the homeless were more than a little familiar with the area. Cole followed the sidewalk for a short distance. He passed the neon sign and stepped through an opening in a decorative wrought iron fence that followed the tracks on the parking garage side. Before stepping on the tracks he had a thought.

It'd be a damn shame to get this far and get hit by a train.

He turned to the left and in the low light was just able to make out the spot where the tracks vanished under the parking garage beyond. Or, as Rufus had described it, *where the trains disappear.*

Cole turned toward the bridge and set off. He figured the walk to the bridge to be about 800 feet. He'd made it almost halfway, building up a rhythm, when Hull called on the walkie-talkie to say he'd made it to the track behind the Gravity Garage. The X-Talker was attached to Cole's belt. He stopped, slightly out of breath, and had the conversation with his adversary, directing him to the bridge. That done, Cole slipped the unit back on his belt and trudged on.

Paul reached the bend in the track and saw the framework of the bridge in the distance. It was visible through a tunnel of trees that framed the tracks. Paul felt a touch of wonder at the existence of a stretch like this in what amounted to the heart of a modern city.

How the hell did Jelcik find this spot?

He heard crickets, saw stars overhead. Had his reason for being here not been so desperate, he might've enjoyed the serenity. As it was, it reminded him more of the missions he conducted in Afghanistan and Iraq, where he and his customer units often found themselves in darkness, facing a capable foe in that foe's own back yard.

He continued on to the bridge.

There are three railroad bridges over the Scioto River in the Columbus area. They all have five words in their title, the first four of which are the same: Columbus Scioto Railroad Bridge. The fifth word is one of the following: North, Middle, or South. Paul was approaching the Middle Bridge. It was a steel truss structure, 676-feet long. CSX trains rumbled across it several times a day.

Paul drew nearer to the bridge, barely noting the presence of the National Veterans Museum and Memorial building visible through the few gaps in the trees on his right. It glowed from exterior floodlights in the distance. He reached the edge of the bridge. At this point the CSX line ran southwest to northeast. Paul stared at the great length of rusted steel, knowing a gunman waited. He also knew Lauren was there, and he was her only chance.

The walkie-talkie crackled. "I see you over there, Hero. We're waaiiiting." The last word was drawn out.

Cole reached the eastern edge of the bridge and let the bundle he'd hefted drop to the ground. He heard a mewing sound come from inside and disregarded it. It was a warm night and he wiped sweat from his brow. He hadn't taken into consideration the amount of perspiration that used to be trapped by his hair. A fair amount of it made its way to his eyebrows now, much of that finding its way to his eyes.

Cole peered across the bridge for a long minute, searching for movement that would confirm that Hull had appeared. As he concentrated on the far side he detected a different movement. It was from the rolled up form on the ground to his left. He turned to see that it was beginning to rock back and forth. He had placed it to the left of the tracks near the gap under a bridge support that Rufus called home. It was near the top of a slope. If it started to roll...

"Goddammit!" Cole leapt down from the tracks and grabbed the roll. He dragged it back to the spot where he'd been standing. He pulled the wire cutters from one back pocket and went to work on the cords, finally freeing them. He then unrolled the mat and tossed it down near Hendershot's hide.

There ya go, Rufus...you're welcome.

He bent down and tore away the urine soaked blanket, wrinkling his nose. Cole then grabbed Lauren roughly under her arms and pulled her up, seeing her wince again.

"Nice try there trying to roll away. I didn't have any bricks to keep you still. Better luck next time." He smiled at her and turned back to the other side of the bridge.

There was Hull.

Cole made the singsong *We're waaiiiting* call over the X-Talker and saw the figure move. He turned Lauren to face the other side of the bridge. He watched as tears rolled down her face, her eyes on her husband.

Cole reached for Lauren's wrists. He knew he could control her with one arm, leaving the other to hold the pistol. When he pulled his right hand from under her arm he felt her begin to fall. Looking down he saw the reason. The extra zip ties he'd used to restrain her had caused her ankles to enlarge. The running shoes on her feet seemed to be bulging. She couldn't support herself.

Sonofabitch.

He used the wire cutters to cut all of the ties on her ankles. He needed her to stand on her own.

"Try to move your legs up and down...get some goddammed circulation going." He turned back to the bridge to see that Hull was now halfway across. Glancing back to the woman he noticed her hands were swollen as well, maybe more than her feet and ankles. He decided to remove all but one of the ties and began to cut. He watched out of the corner of his eye as Hull approached.

His brother's killer was less than 100 feet away.

Groves and Ratlaw manned the roof at the front of the building, watching as desultory weeknight traffic drove past. Knasel, on the west side, had seen nothing. Tom Clark walked from his position at the rear of the building to check in with the sniper team.

Dez saw him coming and answered before the question was asked. "Nothing, boss. You?"

Clark shook his head. "Not a damn thing. Nothing back there but a line of trees a couple hundred yards away. There's a clear field of fire between here and the trees. Nothing'll get to the building from that direction without being seen. And if it comes to a gunfight, this 416," he patted his carbine, "will be enough gun. Won't need the big dog back there." He indicated the PSG-1 sniper rifle whose tripod Dez had resting on the concrete.

The sniper smiled and went back to scanning the west side of the river.

CHAPTER FIFTY

Cole pulled Lauren roughly toward the first sloping girder on the bridge's east side. There was a No Trespassing sign mounted on it as well as another that read *WALKWAY OUT OF SERVICE*. Cole noticed that Hull's wife seemed to be supporting herself a bit better already. Hull had stopped. He stood in the center of the bridge, hands at his side.

Cole forced Lauren further. They were now 30 feet beyond the edge of the bridge but not yet over the water. The running path that traced its way along the river and cut through Battelle Riverfront Park was below them.

Still, Hull waited.

"You gonna come face the music, Hero?" Cole grinned. The pistol was in his hand, hanging at his side. He gripped Lauren's wrists with his left hand.

Paul heard Jelcik's mocking question and ignored it, concentrating on his wife. "Lauren, are you—"

"Maybe you didn't hear me Hull. Come closer, I'll make sure it's fast."

Paul shook his head. "The deal was, I show up, she goes free." He pointed at his wife.

Jelcik frowned. "You killed my brother, you son of a bitch. You're in no position to be telling *me* what the deal is."

A word that Paul's buddy Gatewood often used popped into his head, *nevertheless*. He almost said it to Jelcik, but stopped himself.

"Look, I come over there, you shoot me and then kill my wife. Why the hell would I set that in motion? You let her go, you get me."

"*No, Paul!*" It was Lauren.

Paul took two steps back as if starting toward the western side of the river. "You only get one of us tonight Jelcik."

Paul watched as the man considered his options. He noticed for the first time that Jelcik was bald. There was something else...something about his eyes. It was difficult to tell from this distance with the fugitive and Lauren partially backlit by the lights of downtown Columbus.

Cole spoke, "Okay, tough guy. We split the distance. You walk this way. I walk toward you. When the distance is right, I let her go...then you go bye-bye."

Cole saw Hull nod and take a tentative step toward him. Cole smiled. He adjusted his grip on Lauren, slipping two fingers over the remaining zip tie and between her hands. This allowed him to shift slightly to the right, opening up a wider field of fire.

The three silhouettes on the bridge continued to close on each other.

Paul's mind was in overdrive. He searched desperately for a way to save Lauren. He didn't believe she would survive this night even if he sacrificed himself. If she somehow managed to get away, Paul believed Jelcik would come for her in a month, a year...

Gotta find a way.

He flicked his eyes to the water flowing nearly 40 feet below. Air Force Combat Controllers had extensive training in the maritime environment. If Paul got to the water, in the dark, he didn't think Jelcik could touch him.

But I need Lauren!

Was there a way to reach her and dive for the water? He knew the chances were almost nonexistent. He was now just 40 feet from Jelcik and Lauren.

444

Cole's polar blue eyes bore into Hull. This was the man who brought down Tanner in a cowardly manner. The scene flashed through his head again.

Cole's eyebrows lowered and one corner of his mouth pulled back. He thought of his daddy—Turk—and imagined what he would tell Cole now as he had a chance to avenge his younger brother.

Kill that sumbitch!

Cole took another step and hesitated. Hull's wife had stopped, as if knowing one more step would be the last for her husband.

Cole thought, *and herself.*

He took a half step back to gather her.

Lauren felt Jelcik's grip on the zip tie between her fingers loosen slightly as he stepped back. Using a technique she learned in the Air Force she raised her swollen right foot and stomped her heel down on Jelcik's left instep. He reacted to the blow, raising his affected foot and contracting both arms slightly.

Feeling his grip loosen even more, Lauren ripped her bound hands free of his grip then drove her right elbow into his midsection. Because her wrists were zip-tied behind her she couldn't deliver a full arching blow.

But it was enough.

Lauren was free and she hobbled across the railroad ties toward the eastern bank.

Cole absorbed the blows. They didn't do real damage. But the shock value had allowed the woman to escape.

Goddammit!

He recovered quickly and swung the pistol toward her.

She was an easy target.

Paul saw Lauren's actions. He was momentarily stunned.

Had that just happened?

He suddenly had hope that her life would go on.

Then he saw Jelcik recover and turn, bringing the big .45 up to point at his wife's back.

Paul was still nearly 30 feet from the fugitive.

No way I can get there in time! THINK!

He screamed *"JELCIK! I hit Tanner, she didn't!"*

Cole brought the M1911 up and put the front sight on the wife's back. He began to squeeze the trigger when he heard Hull scream his name. *JELCIK! I hit Tanner, she didn't!*

He hesitated and turned to Hull. Both the husband and wife were in easy range. He had to choose.

In the movies, the man with the gun would kill his enemy's family member, forcing them to live the rest of their life without their loved one.

Cole had a millisecond to decide.

This wasn't a movie.

Cole swung the pistol toward Hull and began to squeeze off shots.

Paul saw his gambit work. A smile of joy appeared on his face as he saw Lauren stumble toward the edge of the bridge. The smile was short-lived when Jelcik brought the .45 around and began to fire. Paul vaguely registered one of the rounds hitting the rusted steel bridge span 80 feet to his rear.

SPANGE

On top of the National Veterans Museum across the river the HRT Agents instantly picked up on the sound of gunfire.

Clark, who was on the master channel that sent his voice back to Chicago, screamed, *"GUN!"*

In Chicago, every agent turned his head to the speaker. They had been monitoring two separate scenarios in other parts of Columbus. In one, a Columbus Police tactical team raided a homeless shelter and located Paul Hull's phone. It was in the possession of a bewildered homeless man. In the other, a joint Columbus PD-HRT Alpha Cell takedown of a McDonald's on the east side of the city had resulted in little more than an offer of free hamburgers for the shooters. Bengie Brenner, the Blue Team commander, had climbed up on the roof himself and found Jelcik's burner phone. He nearly sent it flying in frustration.

Now the Agents in the conference room were confused.

Scott Remick muttered *"What the fuck?"*

On the roof, Dez and Lobo swung their scopes to the left, trying to pick up the shooter. Lobo saw it first—flashes from Jelcik's pistol that showed up clearly in the infrared mode he was using on the spotter scope. He called out to Dez, who was ten feet to his left.

"On your ten o'clock! Far side of the bridge!"

Dez pointed the sniper rifle in that direction, flipping off the safety.

Paul rolled to his left as Jelcik continued to fire. He scrambled for one of the vertical girders even as one of the .45 rounds crashed into it.

SPANGE

He found cover behind it and had a quick thought. *Would Lauren have stopped running and come back to try to help?*

His heart sank, imagining her doing just that. He screamed, *"RUN, LAUREN!"*

Cole fired until the pistol was empty. He quickly released the empty magazine and inserted a full one from the breast pocket of his shirt. He had an idea. He retrieved the empty magazine from where it landed on the track and crept toward the beam that Hull hid behind. He edged to the right, near a knee-high steel cable that ran the length of the bridge. When he was within ten feet, he tossed the empty mag with his left hand onto the stones between the track and the steel beam.

447

Paul heard a metallic noise to his right and instinctively moved left to the outside of the beam. He instantly saw his mistake. Jelcik was ten feet away, squeezing the trigger of the .45.

Lobo got the range to the shooter. "Three-eighteen." He kept his voice calm but his pulse rate was spiking.
Ten feet away Dez registered the information...*318 yards*.
Dez knew that the rifle's scope was dialed in at 100 yards. There was no time to change settings. Any successful shot would have to be accomplished by talent.
Clark came up and instantly interpreted the situation. "Take the shot, Dez."

Jelcik fired.

Paul felt the impact on the right side of his chest. He was thrown backward, his legs catching on a cable.
He fell into blackness.

Dez inhaled then slowly let out a breath. The crosshairs of the scope were above the target and slightly to the right, accounting for—Dez hoped—the vagaries of distance and windage.
The sniper rifle bucked.

The 7.62-millimeter match-grade boat tail bullet streaked across the floodplain and struck Cole Jelcik in the sternum. The kinetic energy of the round transferred itself to the kidnapper and drove him off the side of Columbus Scioto Railroad Bridge Middle.

Paul fell. He made an attempt to adjust his body position in the air but still struck at an awkward angle. He landed in five feet of water and his body drove to the bottom. He was in shock before he hit the water. He tried to right himself but his right arm wasn't responding. Paul felt himself being pulled under the bridge by the north to south current. Despite his training he found it difficult to keep his head above water.

He tried to swim, performing a few half-conscious strokes with his left arm, but his right wasn't responding properly.

He was fading.

But Lauren would be fine.

And then she was there.

EPILOGUE

Paul stood at the edge of the bridge. It was shrouded in a thin mist. He squinted and just made out dark towers that stood on the far bank on either side of the structure.

The towers hadn't been there before...the last time Paul made the crossing. Was this the same bridge? He looked above the towers and saw the Columbus skyline, glowing through the mist.

Why was he here? He struggled to recall and it came to him. It was Lauren. She was on the other side and she needed him.

A voice.

"Who's coming with me? I'm going across."

Paul turned to his left and saw a lanky man in Army fatigues. He wore a helmet and carried a rifle. But it was not the equipment usually carried into battle by Paul's customer units. The helmet was green metal, the style commonly referred to as a steel pot. It was covered in netting. The rifle was an old M1 Garand, not the modern M4 often carried by Delta or SEAL Team Six.

Paul blinked at the man, uncomprehending. The look in the man's eyes conveyed purpose. He had a job to do. Wordlessly the soldier turned toward the towers and began to run along the left side of the bridge. Somehow Paul knew he had to follow.

He ran.

Sound began to manifest itself. Paul recognized it as the rattle of combat. Bullets began to ricochet off the steel girders that framed their path.

SPANGE, SPANGE

Paul caught up to the soldier and watched as his helmet fell from his head and tumbled to the surface of the bridge. The man continued to run without hesitation. Nearer now to the towers, the ripping sound of one machine gun drowned out all

451

others. Paul ducked behind a steel support and peered up at the tower on the left. The gunner depressed his weapon and fired a burst. Gunsmoke obscured the top of the tower. Gradually, a breeze carried it away. The face of the gunner came into view.

He had cold blue eyes.

Paul recognized him...tried to recall the name.

Jelcik!

Paul watched as Jelcik rose and stepped to the side. There, behind him, stood Lauren. Her hands were bound. She looked down to the surface of the bridge as if waiting for rescue.

Paul looked back to the soldier. He was rushing ahead.

Have to get there.

Paul began to run again, trailing after the soldier.

The gunner resumed his fire.

SPANGE, SPANGE

The soldier ran on with intent.

Follow him!

The bullets continued to impact near him, but the sound began to change...

SPANGE, SPANGE, BEEP, SPANGE, BEEP, BEEP, BEEP...

Paul opened his eyes. He heard the beeping of a monitor. He was in a hospital room.

Paul and Lauren were rushed to Grant Level One Trauma Center some 20 blocks from the bridge. Tom Clark of HRT called Columbus Police and Rescue units immediately after Dez fired. Six minutes later the first four responding police officers led rescue personnel to the scene. It was a difficult spot to access by vehicle so the cruisers and ER vehicle had to drive down a grassy slope off of Marconi Boulevard and access the running path.

The flashing emergency lights bathed the bridge and the entire river basin in light. The officers crept to the base of the bridge and discovered three bodies. They first encountered the Hulls, who were lying intertwined on the shore, just south of

452

the bridge. Lauren's wrists were still zip-tied behind her back. Paul's left arm was hooked into the loop formed by her arms. He had unintentionally become ensnared with his last stroke before losing consciousness.

After freeing herself from Jelcik, Lauren had struggled to get off the bridge. She knew that if she could reach safety, Paul, in turn, could disengage from the killer. Her hope was that he could use the cover of the bridge support beams to make it back to the west side of the Scioto.

Then she heard the gunshots. She lurched off the south side of the bridge to a support slightly below, struggled several feet down a slope toward a running path, and hesitated, frantic for Paul's well-being. She couldn't see either man from this angle but had no doubt what was happening. She watched as the girders on the east side of the bridge briefly illuminated each time Jelcik fired.

And then, to her horror, she saw a figure fall off the north side of the bridge and drop, twisting, to the shallow water near the bank. Her scream was drowned out by a sharp crack that originated across the river and echoed off the downtown buildings.

Lauren barely registered a second form plummeting from the structure. This one made no effort to adjust its body position in the air. It fell with the aerodynamic simplicity of a marble statue being toppled headfirst from a building.

Lauren drove herself down, toward the flowing water. Her feet and hands were numb from the zip ties. Her wrist, injured during the struggle in Piqua with Jelcik, ached. But it was her right shoulder that delivered to her brain a particular torment. Jelcik had damaged it badly.

Paul seemed to be thrashing with one arm, irrational since he was just a few feet from the bank. She approached the river as the current carried him toward her. His movement became weaker.

Why doesn't he stand?

But he didn't.

As he neared, Lauren made a decision. She didn't hesitate, jumping into the Scioto feet first. She struggled to intercept her husband. She saw his eyes closing and his left arm coming downward, completing one last, weak stroke.

She turned her back to him and tried to push her bound hands out, forming a loop. Just as she thought she'd acted too late Paul's arm hooked between hers, then went motionless. Lauren drew her hands toward her back, trapping Paul's arm. She struggled to the bank, slipping once. Her head went under the water but she was able to right herself and drag Paul with her. The strain on her shoulder was agonizing.

Lauren reached the slick bank and crawled, still dragging Paul. She turned to make sure his face was above water then collapsed. She was still conscious when rescue personnel reached them, but wished she wasn't.

She'd not hurt this much in her entire life.

The body of Cole Jelcik was found on the river's edge on the north side of the bridge. He had fallen headfirst into a collection of stones that had been smoothed by the flowing waters of the Scioto for centuries. The results were predictable. Rescue personnel determined that Jelcik's head injuries were fatal—or would have been—had he not already been dead before hitting the ground.

Dez Bravo's bullet had drilled a neat hole through Jelcik's lower sternum before blowing out his aorta and exiting his back. He was propelled backwards off the edge of the bridge. The bulk of Jelcik's torso contributed to the position of his body as it fell. It was a killshot that solidified Dez's reputation as the top sniper in HRT. The shot would be talked about for years to come and cited as a prime example of improvisation in the field by law enforcement marksmanship instructors.

Paul and Lauren arrived at Grant Trauma and were rushed to two of the facility's state-of-the-art trauma bays. Paul had been lucky. The .45 caliber bullet struck him below the right collarbone. It missed hitting any organs but delivered a significant shock to his system. It also affected his ability to use the right side of his body during the fall. He was only able to partially twist his body to a position that might limit further damage upon impact. He struck the water in a mostly horizontal position that caused him a slight concussion just before hitting the muddy bottom.

His wound was cleaned and packed. The river water made it necessary to sponge down his entire body. He was wheeled to a recovery room an hour after arriving at Grant and had IV and antibiotic drip lines attached. Doctors expected him to be awake the next day and—based on his level of fitness—to recover quickly.

Lauren was conscious when she arrived. She showed signs of dehydration so a saline fluid drip was started immediately. The first responders had cut away the zip tie but she showed obvious signs of circulation issues in her outer extremities. She, too, was given a sponge bath—had Jelcik still been alive she would have strangled him for putting her through the indignity—and her right shoulder and left wrist examined and stabilized.

It was later determined that three of the eight carpel bones that formed her left wrist were broken. There was some concern that she wouldn't recover full motion. It would require significant rehab. There were multiple tears of the soft tissue at the front of her shoulder. Her glenohumeral ligaments and labrum sustained the most damage. Doctors decided to wait at least a week to do surgery, allowing the swelling to subside. Pneumatic boots were slipped over her feet and her legs elevated for the first night of her hospital stay. This all increased circulation and relieved the doctors' worries.

When Paul woke at 10:15 Wednesday morning he was initially confused. After getting his bearings he looked at a nurse and rasped, "Lauren?"

"She's here, Mr. Hull, in another room. She was in to see you last night—wouldn't take no for an answer. We brought her down in a wheelchair for a few minutes then Dr. Gutman insisted she return to her bed. She agreed but demanded we bring her back the minute you wake up."

Paul smiled, "Sounds about right."

They wheeled Lauren back to Paul's room a few minutes later. She'd been up on her feet and showered and felt much better. She struggled to shampoo her hair with her injuries but was beginning to feel more like her former self already.

Their kiss and embrace could not have been accomplished without the assistance of two nurses. Paul later compared it to a complicated docking maneuver by two space vessels.

Lauren smiled as tears glistened in her eyes. "You owe me a new pair of running shoes."

"I owe you a lot more than that."

Doctor Richard Gutman—a man with a blonde beard who wore scrubs with the Ohio State logo on the left breast—came into the room. "Well, this is convenient. I can review two cases at once."

He did just that, bringing both spouses up to date on their respective conditions. After finishing, he asked if they felt up to receiving visitors. "A man is waiting down the hall. I'm told the FBI will be in to see you soon as well."

Paul got a nod from Lauren and answered, "Sure, doc. Send him in. Go Bucks."

Gutman flashed a smile and gave a thumbs-up before exiting with the nurse.

While they waited for the visitor a flower delivery arrived. It was a spectacular display that must've cost well over a hundred dollars. Lauren accepted and opened the card as the orderly found a spot on a side table for the flowers.

She read, *From your friends and family at Tutor's.*

The orderly remarked, "There's another one just like it in your room Mrs. Hull."

Lauren's face softened, "Awwww."

Gatewood Dowdell knocked at the doorframe and strode into the room.

"Damn, Sticks...*this* is your idea of retirement?"

456

Gatewood asked for details of the ordeal and heard both versions from Paul and Lauren. He whistled.

"Sure do wish you could've made it to your house to pick up the Sig before returning to Columbus. You're pretty damn good with handguns...would've put Jelcik down in nothing flat."

Gatewood switched subjects. "Before I forget, one of you needs to call Patrice. She's out of her mind with worry. She got part of the story from other employees at the museum. She called me, both McClarys—they're picking up clothes from your house and bringing them here, by the way—and Lord knows who else."

A nurse knocked. "The FBI's here." She ducked out.

Tyson Foxx walked through the door. He'd flown in earlier in the morning on an FBI plane to debrief the Hulls. He wore a suit and appeared tired but relieved. He was followed by a petite woman with short dark hair. She wore black pants with cargo pockets and a short-sleeved shirt that revealed toned arms.

Foxx introduced himself to Lauren and Gatewood then turned. "I believe both you, Paul, and Gatewood are familiar with my colleague."

Gatewood's eyes widened in recognition. Paul had an odd smile on his face.

Gatewood boomed, "Dez! Damn, girl, did *you* make that shot?"

Lauren, baffled, looked from the woman to Gatewood, then to Paul.

"Wait...Dez is a woman?"

Gatewood turned his attention to both Hulls. "She sure is. Best damn shot in the FBI. Better than a lot of our guys, right Sticks?" Then, grasping the situation, demanded, "Wait, you never told your wife you were outshot in Mississippi by a woman?"

Paul's grin turned sheepish.

Gatewood's laugh was long and loud.

457

Lauren simply shook her head.

"Oh Paul."

Lacey Billingham became Mrs. Matt Wells on the 21st of October. The ceremony was rescheduled from June due to her injuries. Matt didn't want to wait, asking her in her room at Miami Valley South if she would like to be married right there in the hospital.

"I'll go get a minister, a Justice of the Peace. Hell, there's a guy at work that got ordained on the internet, he'll do it."

He did not want to take a chance of losing her ever again.

Lacey, who regained consciousness three days after the attack, shook her head no and picked up the note pad on the overbed table she was using to communicate.

She wrote, *Nice try, but I want to wear my dress.*

Lacey sustained a broken right lower jaw in the attack. She also lost one molar and part of another. The lost tooth would be replaced by a dental implant, the damaged one would receive a crown. Her broken ribs and collarbone would heal in two months.

It was the head injury that had the longest recovery time. She had vision and balance issues for weeks, requiring vestibular therapy. She wasn't able to return to work until September and that was on a limited basis. Throughout her therapy she was driven by the desire to walk down the aisle "without looking like I just came from a kegger."

Paul and Lauren attended the wedding. Lauren was still rehabbing her right shoulder. The surgeon was able to make the necessary repairs arthroscopically, reducing scarring. She'd resumed normal activities but was told it would be six months before everything felt normal again. The cast on her left wrist came off after eight weeks so she was able to enjoy Lacey's big day. It was a crisp fall day in northern Ohio. The betrothed couple lucked out with the weather as the ceremony was held at an indoor-outdoor facility that had a beautiful backdrop of changing fall leaves. They were able to utilize the outdoor portion when saying their vows. A number of attendees commented to the couple that they had been fortunate with the weather.

Matt, holding tightly to Lauren's hand, gave the same answer each time.

"I think the man upstairs owed us one."

Paul and Lauren extended their stay in northern Ohio. They made a trip the next day to Toledo. Paul had promised to take her to Tony Packo's. He also had some unfinished business.

Paul drove Lauren's Jeep through the gate of Resurrection Cemetery. Memories of his altercation with Tanner Jelcik returned when he passed the spot where it had occurred. He pulled up behind a red Jeep in Section 6. The Jeep was parked exactly where it had been back in June when he'd first seen it.

Paul and Lauren got out of their Jeep. Ahead of them Jim Harvey did the same. The passenger door opened and a smiling woman emerged. The two couples approached each other. Harvey held out a hand to Lauren.

"I'm Jim Harvey, and this," he gestured to his left, "is my wife Judy."

Lauren shook his hand and then both she and Paul shook Judy's.

After some small talk the foursome walked to the Drabik marker. They stood there silent for several seconds.

Harvey spoke, "Well Paul, you said you'd come back and visit and you kept your promise."

Paul nodded, thinking of everything that had happened since he stood on this same spot in June. "Yeah, well I wanted to get back up here to take Lauren to Packo's." He smiled wanly.

After another minute Judy turned to Lauren. "After your, uh...incident, I made you a present. It's a bathrobe. I'm afraid it took me a lot longer than I anticipated." She smiled. "My seamstress skills are a little rusty."

Lauren appreciated the gesture. "That's so sweet."

459

Judy looked to the men and motioned to her Jeep with her eyes. "It's over here in the Jeep."

Lauren caught on and walked with Judy away from their husbands.

Lauren leaned over and whispered conspiratorially, "*I guess you have one of those husbands too...a man who visits old soldiers in cemeteries.*"

Judy cast a glance over her shoulder and nodded. "*If I know my Jim, they'll be there for a while.*"

As the wives retreated, Harvey turned to Paul. "So you wanted to come back and visit Alex? Your last visit was sure cut short. If you hadn't been here that day I'd be keeping him company right now."

Paul nodded and looked at the marker. "Yeah...let's just say I've gained a new appreciation for what he did on that bridge at Remagen."

Harvey nodded knowingly.

Paul continued. "Let me ask you a question, Jim. The books agree that Alex was the first to cross the bridge, but there seem to be two versions of what happened next."

Jim nodded. "Yep, you're talking about the German soldier he ran into on the other side, right?"

Paul turned to him. "Did you ever ask Alex? One version says he fired on the Germans as soon as he crossed. Another says he took a soldier prisoner and had him dig foxholes for Alex and his men."

Jim crossed his arms. "Let me answer your question this way. Sergeant Drabik made several return trips to Remagen over the years. One was for the fortieth anniversary of the battle in 1985. While he was near the towers—they're still standing, by the way—an elderly German man walked up to him and asked to shake his hand. Alex said he was confused but held out his hand. The man shook it with both of his and said, 'I'm the soldier whose life you saved that day in 1945.'"

Paul's eyes opened wide. "So what happened?"

460

Harvey chuckled, "Alex thought the man surrendered fair and square. He was afraid if he sent him across the bridge to the American side he might get shot trying to cross...by the Americans *or* by the Germans. He thought it would be better if the soldier spent that first night in a foxhole next to him."

Paul stared at Harvey, finally uttering "Wow."

The pair turned back to the headstone. Leaves blew lazily across their feet. In time Paul let out a sigh.

Harvey asked, "What's bothering you, Paul?"

Paul turned. "I can't get over how the whole thing went down in Columbus. I was trying to save Lauren...If it hadn't been for her actions, and for the sniper—Dez—Lauren and I would both be gone...I feel like I failed her."

Harvey smiled and slowly shook his head.

"You had a bridge to cross to face down evil..."

He turned to look back at Alex Drabik's grave.

"You went."

ACKNOWLEDGEMENTS

This book simply does not happen without the efforts of my daughter Suzanne Lang. She not only proofread the manuscript, she performed the edit—catching a number of errors—and formatted the book for publishing. She suggested several changes in phrasing that, I believe, makes the story flow easier for the reader. Fortunately I took her advice on nearly every one of them. If you found any passages in the book less than polished, you can be certain they are there in spite of her best efforts.

Suzanne's husband, Kevin, and my four-year-old grandson Leo drove me around downtown Columbus one day checking sites that made their way into the book. The ultimate destination that day was Schmidt's Sausage Haus in German Village. Leo was promised his first ever cream puff at the end of the drive. Thanks Kevin for bending a few traffic laws during the drive. Leo, your patience was appreciated. I hope the cream puff met your expectations.

Many thanks to Lauren Reneau for, once again, creating a cover that draws the eye while conveying just the right amount of the story. Had the mechanics of generating the cover been left to me, you would now be holding a book whose front, back, and spine resemble a black and white instruction manual.

Brad Beams, a newly minted grandpa, did a final proofread that was extremely helpful. He lent the project a detailed eye and offered helpful suggestions. He might say he put his "nitpicking superpower" to work. Thanks Brad.

My son Jack Van Horn, a physical therapist, gave thoughtful answers to obscure questions about subclavian arteries, soft tissue injuries, and the ability of the body to perform certain tasks when damaged. All were incorporated into the story. Jack also, in a way, lent another important part of himself to the book—his middle name, Alexander.

I met Alex Drabik in the early 1980s while attending the University of Toledo. Exactly like the character Jim Harvey in this story, I came across a mention of his name in a book about World War Two. The title of the book is long forgotten but the lasting impression made by the man lives on.

Alex was a perfect blend of two characteristics more associated with his generation than ours. He was quietly proud of the accomplishments he and his colleagues performed to better our world, while at the same time being thoroughly unimpressed with himself.

He and his wife Margaret welcomed my wife, Ann, and I into their home on several occasions. His actions on March 7, 1945 were the stuff of legend. Unfortunately his name is virtually unknown today. Hopefully, in a small way, this book helps bring his actions more of the attention he avoided, but certainly deserves.

Every year on March 7 my son Jack Alexander receives a call or text from me stating "Happy Alex Drabik Day." I'll always think of the date in this way.

Thanks for reading!

Also by Mike Van Horn

CONTROLLED FLIGHT

Paul Hull, a medically retired Air Force Combat Controller, and his wife Lauren pay an impromptu visit to an obscure historical site. It is associated with the Wright Brothers, the ingenious Dayton, Ohio pair that developed the theories and hardware that culminated in the first heavier-than-air powered flight. An occurrence at this location puts the Hulls in the crosshairs of a criminal who has no peer in the realm of cyber crime. He is evolving, becoming more like a character in the first-person shooter video games that he enjoys. Paul must pit his skills developed in the Global War on Terror against a foe that is several steps ahead of him. Events play out across a number of sites connected to Wilbur and Orville Wright.

An Eric Hoffer Book Award Grand Prize Finalist and a Chanticleer International Book Awards Finalist in the CLUE category for Suspense & Thrillers.

www.ingramcontent.com/pod-product-compliance
Lightning Source LLC
Chambersburg PA
CBHW051939020726
47501CB00001B/185